RUN
■ WITH THE ■
WOLVES

Volume I
'THE PACK'

T c Tombs

iUniverse, Inc.
Bloomington

Run with the Wolves
Volume I 'The Pack'

Copyright © 2011 T c Tombs

This is a work of fiction. All of the characters, names, incidents, organizations, and dialogue in this novel are either the products of the author's imagination or are used fictitiously.

iUniverse books may be ordered through booksellers or by contacting:

iUniverse
1663 Liberty Drive
Bloomington, IN 47403
www.iuniverse.com
1-800-Authors (1-800-288-4677)

ISBN: 978-1-4620-1133-9 (sc)
ISBN: 978-1-4620-1093-6 (hc)
ISBN: 978-1-4620-1092-9 (e)

Printed in the United States of America

iUniverse rev. date: 11/4/2011

The Mesa-of-the-Moon

Out across the coastal moor, a forbidding mesa stands alone
It's home to an ancient castle, with walls of blood-stained stone
Though lightning flashes and thunder crashes, it stands impervious to the storm
Out at the Mesa-of-the-Moon, a monstrous evil is being born

So heed my advice
You best think twice
For many a man has met his doom
In the dark and forbidding castle
At the Mesa-of-the-Moon

From high up in the courtyard tower
Windswept voices can be heard
If you listen very carefully
You can just make out the words

"We're whipping up a potent spell
Calling upon the hounds of hell
Lucifer, Beelzebub, Apollyon
Belial, oh Prince of Darkness, mighty Venus
We're calling to you ... strengthen us!
From Hades, Gehenna, Tartarus
From Sheol ... the great Abyss
We're calling to you, welcome us!"

Out across the coastal moor, a forbidding mesa stands alone
It's home to an ancient castle, with walls of blood-stained stone
Though lightning flashes and thunder crashes, it stands impervious to the storm
Out at the Mesa-of-the-Moon, a monstrous evil is being born

Preface

Run with the Wolves is a fantasy/adventure epic set in the turbulent historical period of the fifteenth century. The trilogy consists of three volumes: *The Pack, The Oracle,* and *The Beast.*

This continuing saga was inspired by a number of musical works, including Pink Floyd's *The Dark Side of the Moon* and *The Division Bell*; as well as songs by Elton John and Bernie Taupin (my all time favourite lyricist); Don Henley and the Eagles; The Moody Blues, Supertramp, Chris De Burgh; James Blunt; Chris Rea; and by many other gifted songwriters. Music is the soul of inspiration.

I would like to express my thanks to family and friends who helped guide the telling of this tale and who lent me their eyes and ears from the beginning, as well as the use of their names for the many fictional characters found within the story.

Thanks to Lynn Walks for the lead. One doorway led to another.

A very special thank you goes out to Robert J. Lewis for his creative illustrations. The storyboards helped bring the project to life at the Universal Studios pitch fest in L.A.

I dedicate these volumes to my wife, partner, and best friend, Sandra. Thanks for your attention to detail and for your unconditional support and understanding of the many long hours I spent with my keyboard over the past decade writing these three volumes. You have my love and gratitude always.

I'd like to thank S & S; and especially everyone at iUniverse for pulling this all together. I would also like to thank Val Gee and David Bernardi for their editorial assistance and guidance. Any writing errors that remain are entirely my own.

Cycles of the Moon

The full moon for each month is given a name that represents the season or agricultural events of that month. These are some of the most common in use. The highlighted names are used through the three volumes of *Run with the Wolves.*

January	**Old Moon**; Storm Moon; Moon after Yule; Cold Moon
February	**Hunger Moon**; Wolf Moon; Ice Moon; Chaste Moon
March	**Seed Moon**; Sap Moon; Raven/Crow Moon; Plough Moon
April	**Grass Moon**; Hare Moon; Budding Trees Moon; Egg Moon
May	**Planter's Moon**; Milk Moon; Goddess Moon; Dyad Moon
June	**Honey Moon**; Flower Moon; Strawberry Moon; Mead Moon
July	**Thunder Moon**; Hay Moon; Ripe Corn Moon; Storm Moon
August	**Barley Moon**; Fruit Moon; Grain Moon; Blackberry Moon
September	**Harvest Moon**; Blood Moon; Wine Moon; Cherry Moon
October	**Hunter's Moon**; Falling Leaf Moon; Shedding Moon
November	**Frosty Moon**; Beaver Moon; Mourning Moon; Snow Moon
December	**Yule Moon**; Long Nights Moon; Winter Moon

The Lunar Phases

New Moon Waxing   First   Waxing   Full Moon Waning   Last   Waning
          Crescent Quarter Gibbous   Gibbous Quarter Crescent

For the purposes of this story:

The *Full Moon Phase* is considered to occur over a three-night period and includes the night prior to the full moon apex, the night of the full moon apex, and the night following the full moon apex.

Calendar for year 1461

January 1461

Mo	Tu	We	Th	Fr	Sa	Su
			1	2	3	4
5	6	7	8	9	10	11
12	13	14	15	16	17	18
19	20	21	22	23	24	25
26	27	28	29	30	31	

3:◑ 11:● 19:◐ 26:○

February 1461

Mo	Tu	We	Th	Fr	Sa	Su
						1
2	3	4	5	6	7	8
9	10	11	12	13	14	15
16	17	18	19	20	21	22
23	24	25	26	27	28	

2:◑ 10:● 18:◐ 24:○

March 1461

Mo	Tu	We	Th	Fr	Sa	Su
						1
2	3	4	5	6	7	8
9	10	11	12	13	14	15
16	17	18	19	20	21	22
23	24	25	26	27	28	29
30	31					

4:◑ 12:● 19:◐ 26:○

April 1461

Mo	Tu	We	Th	Fr	Sa	Su
			1	2	3	4	5
6	7	8	9	10	11	12
13	14	15	16	17	18	19
20	21	22	23	24	25	26
27	28	29	30			

2:◑ 10:● 17:◐ 24:○

May 1461

Mo	Tu	We	Th	Fr	Sa	Su
				1	2	3
4	5	6	7	8	9	10
11	12	13	14	15	16	17
18	19	20	21	22	23	24
25	26	27	28	29	30	31

2:◑ 10:● 17:◐ 24:○

June 1461

Mo	Tu	We	Th	Fr	Sa	Su
1	2	3	4	5	6	7
8	9	10	11	12	13	14
15	16	17	18	19	20	21
22	23	24	25	26	27	28
29	30					

1:◑ 8:● 15:◐ 22:○

July 1461

Mo	Tu	We	Th	Fr	Sa	Su
			1	2	3	4	5
6	7	8	9	10	11	12
13	14	15	16	17	18	19
20	21	22	23	24	25	26
27	28	29	30	31		

1:◑ 7:● 14:◐ 22:○ 30:◑

August 1461

Mo	Tu	We	Th	Fr	Sa	Su
					1	2
3	4	5	6	7	8	9
10	11	12	13	14	15	16
17	18	19	20	21	22	23
24	25	26	27	28	29	30
31						

6:● 13:◐ 21:○ 28:◑

September 1461

Mo	Tu	We	Th	Fr	Sa	Su
	1	2	3	4	5	6
7	8	9	10	11	12	13
14	15	16	17	18	19	20
21	22	23	24	25	26	27
28	29	30				

4:● 11:◐ 19:○ 27:◑

October 1461

Mo	Tu	We	Th	Fr	Sa	Su
			1	2	3	4
5	6	7	8	9	10	11
12	13	14	15	16	17	18
19	20	21	22	23	24	25
26	27	28	29	30	31	

3:● 11:◐ 19:○ 26:◑

November 1461

Mo	Tu	We	Th	Fr	Sa	Su
						1
2	3	4	5	6	7	8
9	10	11	12	13	14	15
16	17	18	19	20	21	22
23	24	25	26	27	28	29
30						

2:● 10:◐ 18:○ 24:◑

December 1461

Mo	Tu	We	Th	Fr	Sa	Su
			1	2	3	4	5	6
7	8	9	10	11	12	13
14	15	16	17	18	19	20
21	22	23	24	25	26	27
28	29	30	31			

2:● 10:◐ 17:○ 24:◑ 31:●

The Fifteenth Century Events of Interest

1412 Joan of Arc is born in France.

1413 Execution of Jan Hus, Czech religious reformer, for denouncing the sale of indulgencies.

1415 Battle of Agincourt. Part of the Hundred Years War between England and France.

1428 Joan of Arc leads the French forces against the English.

1429 Henry the VI becomes king of England. He is less than a year old.

1431 Joan of Arc is burned at the stake after an ecclesiastical trial.

1445 Plague strikes England.

1450 Johannes Gutenberg prints the Bible. University of Barcelona is founded.

1452 Leonardo da Vinci is born near Florence.

1453 Constantinople falls to the Ottoman Turks, ending the Byzantine Empire.

1454 Wars of the Roses in England last for thirty years, with conflicting claims to the throne between the houses of York (White Rose insignia) and Lancaster (Red Rose insignia).

1456 Vlad the Impaler's rule begins in Wallachia. (Inspires Bram Stoker's Dracula).

1461 Advent of firearms in Europe (approx. date).

1462 Ivan the Great becomes the first Czar of Russia, ruling until 1505.

1473 Copernicus is born in Poland.

1475 Michelangelo is born. The Hundred Years War ends.

1478 Ferdinand and Isabella initiate the Spanish Inquisition to flush out secret Jews from among the (New) Christian population.

1479 Plague strikes England again.

1481 The first Inquisitional tribunal opens in Seville. Confessions sought by torture authorized by the courts under the Inquisitional-General, Thomas Torquemada.

1488 Bartolomeu Dias sails around Africa and names the Cape of Good Hope.

1492 Christopher Columbus sails from Spain in search of the Indies. Muslims and Jews are expelled from Spain.

1493 Columbus sails on his second voyage to the New World.

1495 Leonardo da Vinci designs a parachute and paints the famous *Last Supper*.

1497 John Cabot sails from England to North America. Michelangelo completes the *Bacchus* sculpture. Vasco da Gamo sails around the Cape of Good Hope. Jews are expelled from Portugal.

1498 Columbus sails on his third voyage to the New World.

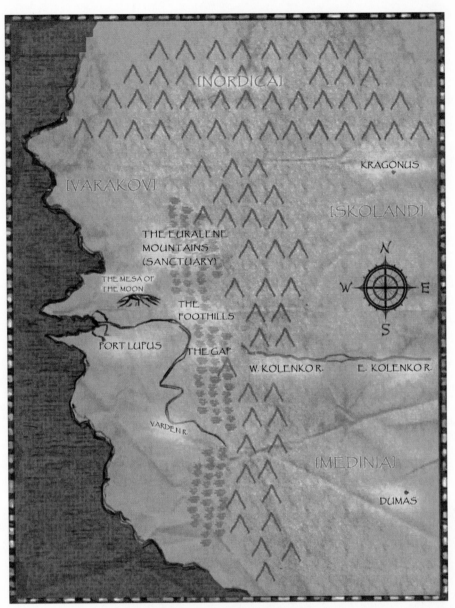

Map drawing courtesy of Robert J. Lewis

Contents

CHAPTER 1

ATTACK OF THE PACK

There's no light quite like moon light
There's no night quite like a full moon night
There's no sight quite like the Pack's plight
And there's no bite quite like a wolf's bite

July 23, 1461
Medinia

"WILLIE, C'MON OUT HERE!"

The barn doors opened and a tousle-haired youth appeared, still holding the pitchfork he'd been using to clean out the horse stalls. Willie was of average height, but strongly built for his age, which he didn't know exactly, although he did know he was at least sixteen and maybe seventeen. The most noticeable thing about his appearance was a pair of sparkling hazel eyes that showed a youthful intelligence. He gave a hopeful grin to the stocky man perched on the heavily laden wagon in front of him.

Jacob Smythe was a middle-aged freeman farmer whose land nestled beneath the Euralene Mountains along the western border of Medinia, and Willie was a serf who worked for the Smythes in return for his room and board and a small wage. He'd been abandoned at the nearby monastery when he was still a young child, and the small order of monks who raised him for a time had placed him with the Smythe family when he was about eleven years old.

The Smythes had taken on the responsibility of his care for an agreed-upon period of indentured service, and Willie had spent the last half dozen years learning the routines of farming and raising livestock. He'd been reared along with their children, and the Smythes treated him almost as one of the family. He was expected to work hard, although no harder than they did themselves.

"Help me tie off the wagon, Willie," the farmer directed.

The youth pulled the tarp tight over the baskets of strawberries and other produce and then carefully secured the ropes Jacob passed down to him.

"Are you sure I can't go with you, Mr. Smythe?" Willie asked, for the third time that morning.

The farmer gave him a rueful smile and another shake of the head. He understood the youth's anxious appeals. The summer market was a huge event in the distant village. There'd be stalls and corrals of prized animals, music and dancing in the evenings, and a host of food and festivities, all of which made it the place a young man dreamed of being after the labour of harvesting the spring and early summer crops.

Perhaps in late September, after the fruit trees were picked, he'd take him along to the Medinian army post for the fall market. Everything occurred in its season, and the fall festival would be an even bigger treat, especially if the caravans came down through the pass again this year. Not that this was a certainty. The fighting still brewed in the lengthy war over the fertile river valley that separated Medinia from Skoland, the neighbouring kingdom to the north.

The Kolenko River flowed down from its source in the Euralene Mountains, cut through the centre of the disputed valley, and then emptied into a long, narrow lake that surrounded a single small island. Some three miles later, the river resumed its course and continued to divide the valley separating the two kingdoms. From there it flowed on into the inhospitable wilderness to a distant inland sea.

Simple geography dictated that each kingdom ought to possess half the rich valley lands, since the Kolenko River and its lake formed a natural border between the two nations. Nevertheless, in Jacob Smythe's view, greed usually prevailed over common sense, and the result of that failing was that both kingdoms claimed ownership and control of the entire valley and its fertile soil. Over the years, some terrible wars had been fought between the two kingdoms, and the river lands had become known to many as the Valley of Blood.

King Renaud of Medinia was a determined ruler, and he'd waged three such wars with the equally intractable King Verdonk of Skoland during their coinciding reigns. The first war had been fought in the early years of their respective rules. It lasted for only a year, but there had been a great loss of lives on both sides, and neither side could claim a conclusive victory. The second war had broken out a few years after that, lasted for more than six terrible years, and was followed by another brief period of troubled peace before hostilities had broken out once more. The current war was now entering its fourth bloody year, with still no decisive victory for either side.

In all, there had been almost a decade of skirmishes, raids, and full-scale battles. Control of the valley had changed hands numerous times, and war had become a way of life, as had the loss of lives on both sides.

At long last, however, there was talk of a peace accord being negotiated, with possibly a royal marriage to seal it. The rumour circulated that the two feuding kings, now older and perhaps a little wiser, had concluded that the endless war was only depleting the treasuries of both kingdoms. Complete harvests were being lost, crops going unplanted or being burned to deny them to the enemy. The losses in manpower and the materials expended to fight the war were more than sole ownership of the river valley lands could compensate for. Gossip had it that the two rulers had begun a dialogue through their ambassadors. Peace was its ultimate goal, and the suggestion of a marriage between the two royal houses had already been broached.

Life on a farm near the mountains went largely untouched by these concerns, however, and Jacob Smythe was more than content to leave it that way. They had enough concerns of their own. The remote frontier farms had to fence in most of the foothill pastures where their livestock grazed and keep a vigilant watch. The farmers were ever leery of the forest and mountains, and with good reason. The mountains were home to numerous predators. Bears, wild boars, mountain lions, and fierce wolf packs were a real concern, more so than the war. There were other strange creatures up there, as well. Or so it was said. Many a child living in the westernmost regions of both Medinia and Skoland had trouble going to sleep at night after hearing tales of mountain ogres and various other demons recounted around the family hearth.

Climbing down from the first wagon, Jacob waited while Willie tied off the second. The farmer thought back to the old stories he'd heard as a child and repeated to his own children in turn. The tales were especially effective on nights the mountain wolf packs serenaded the sky with their eerie and mournful voices.

Like their farming neighbours in Medinia and similar farms in Skoland, the Smythes found it prudent to bring their herds down to the lower pastures, nearer the farmhouses, before nightfall. Even with this precaution, there were still losses in the herds and flocks over the course of a year. That was to be expected. It was wild country, after all.

To be sure, the four-legged predators coming down from the mountains and woods accounted for some of the loss, but two-legged thieves added their share to the total. There were occasional raids by the enemy troops across the river and even some poaching by their own soldiers, although that was difficult to prove. In any event, the farmers in the western frontier of both kingdoms were kept busy just trying to protect their livelihoods.

"Sorry, Willie, but you really can't come this time," Jacob repeated patiently. "I need you to stay behind and keep watch over the place for a few days. Someone's got to take the dogs and bring in the sheep and cattle before dark. There are a lot of chores to do too. The haying is all done, but I still need you to chop up that pile of logs we cut so we'll have firewood for the winter. It needs to dry out through the fall, so it's best to get a head start on it now."

The usual sparkle had left Willie's eyes. The farmer ruffled the youth's sandy hair and gave him another apologetic smile. He climbed into the driver's seat, beside his wife and their young daughter.

"Maybe you can go to the outpost in the fall, Willie," Mrs. Smythe called back as the wagon pulled out.

The second wagon followed a moment later. Their tall and gawky redheaded son, Adam, turned and waved a regretful farewell as he drove away. The two youths were about the same age and were friends despite their difference in station. Earlier, Adam had done his best to convince his father to allow Willie to come along, but Jacob had his mind set. Someone must remain behind and tend to the farmstead.

The disappointed young serf watched the procession until it passed out of sight down the dirt road that led to the closest village, some ten miles away. He took some solace in the hope of going to the fall market at the army post. If the caravan came again this year, he knew there'd be wonders that none of them had seen before.

At his side, as nearly always, his two faithful friends, Sirius and Rigel, also watched the departing wagons. He'd raised the two large herd dogs since they were pups. One, he'd named after the brightest star in the heavens, Sirius, in the Canis Major constellation. It was known as the Dog Star, which he'd found appropriate. The fearless Rigel was named after another star of the first magnitude, located nearby in the Astron constellation, which was also home to mighty Orion the hunter, who, legend had it, had been placed in the night sky upon his death.

Willie had little formal education, but he was fascinated by the stars of the night sky and had learned their names and positions from the scholarly monks. Before placing him with the Smythes, the monks had done their best to raise and educate the child who'd been left in their care and they passed on what knowledge they could to the growing boy.

The monks regretted the abbot's ruling when it had been decided that the boy was old enough to earn his own keep and to learn a vocation. He had an inquiring mind, and several of the monks were sure it could have been developed further, perhaps even leading to service in the Church. Unfortunately, the monastery hadn't the means to fund such a vocation, and their charity went only so far.

So now, while Willie slept in the loft of the barn and worked the Smythe farm from dawn until dusk, he would still often venture out after dark to look into the night sky. He'd usually lie on his back on the crest of one of the foothills, with his two four-legged companions resting beside him.

On cloudless nights, the stars put on a spectacular show as they hung over the mountain peaks with brilliant clarity. It was truly wondrous to see a shooting star or follow a rare comet as it streaked across the heavens. It made Willie feel small and insignificant whenever he looked up at the looming mountain range, and he felt smaller still when he considered the immensity of the universe, with its uncountable star clusters, yet he felt connected to it all somehow, as if a part of some grand scheme.

If truth be told, despite the gratitude Willie felt towards the monks for taking care of him and for what they'd taught him, he did not truly aspire to become one of their order. His dreams ventured more towards the excitement and chivalry of Medinian knighthood, even though he knew full well that was impossible goal for someone of his lowly position.

"All right, you two," he said to the dogs, "I've got chores to do. Maybe they'll let me go to the post in the fall. If the caravan comes again, it'll be way more fun anyway."

Willie set about chopping and stacking the wood alongside the barn. As the afternoon wore on, he worked up a good sweat. Despite hands well callused from his daily labours, he had a sizable blister on his left hand to show for his efforts. It didn't slow his work pace, however.

Rigel heard them first, and a warning growl sounded deep in his throat. Sirius pricked up his ears and then he too growled. Willie took a last swing with the axe and left it imbedded in a log, and then he turned and watched as a growing cloud of dust signalled the approach of riders from the south. Moments later, he could hear the distant but definite sound of horse's hooves pounding over the ground.

Some five minutes later, a troop of Medinian knights crested the hill below the farmhouse. They rode up the dirt lane, scattering the chickens and geese milling about. The knights reined their steeds to a halt where young Willie and his two herd dogs waited outside the barn.

"Where's the master of the house, lad?" the captain of the troop demanded from the back of his snorting destrier.

Willie stood, frozen in awe of both the knights and their giant steeds. The war-horses bore almost as much protective mail and armour as their masters did. The knights wore pure white cloaks over their habergeon coats of mail with the royal blue heraldic chevrons of Medinia embroidered on the back. They carried every kind of weapon, including long lances, sheathed broadswords, and boot knives. Some carried longbows across their backs. A few had deadly looking crossbows strapped to their saddles.

Willie managed to stammer out an answer. "The Smythes left this morning … for the market in the village, sire."

"I'm not your sire, son. I'm just a hardworking knight of the realm. We've been on the ride for two days and nights now. My men need food and drink, and our steeds need oats and water. They could use a good brushing down, too." The captain swung down from his horse and ordered his knights to round up what they needed to care for their mounts.

"We're on our way back to the river post," he explained. "Tell your master when he gets back that there's been a pack of wolves attacking the herds and flocks to the south of here, all along the foothills. Judging by the remains they left behind, I'd say they were a large pack, too, but I'll be damned if we could find them. We tracked them into what looked like a blind canyon near here, but we lost their trail in the damned rocks."

The knight stretched hugely to loosen the kinks in his neck and back. "Give me a good battle with enemy troops anytime," he said, sighing.

"Is there any beer or cider, lad?" the captain suggested. "And maybe you could provide a meal for us, too. Your master will be recompensed of course … in due time."

"There's food and drink in the house, Sir Knight, and more down in the cellar below the barn. Can I fetch some for you?"

"I'll find it, lad. This nose may be packed with trail dust, but it can still smell out good strong ale. You go to the cellar in the barn and tend to my men." The captain strode off, somewhat stiffly, towards the farmhouse.

It was common practice for the frontier farms to supply passing knights with food and drink when requested. Still, Willie was reluctant to let the captain have the run of the Smythe home in their absence. He suspected that Mrs. Smythe would be aghast when she returned.

Willie was in charge of the farm during the Smythes' absence, but what could he do? He lacked any real authority. He was a peasant serf. The Medinian knights were the brave defenders of the realm. Who was he to challenge their captain?

Then, too, the knights represented all that a lad his age could aspire to. They were the stuff of legends. They were valiant and fearless heroes who were trained in swordsmanship and carried an array of other weaponry. They rode large and fierce war-horses that cost more than he could ever possibly afford. To achieve a knighthood was as far beyond his reach as the stars in the night sky. Still, a young man could dream, couldn't he?

Willie put the dogs in the barn to keep them away from the warhorses, which he and the knights led into the farm animals' enclosure to feed and water. It was best that the dogs were kept out from underfoot; if they got in the way, they were apt to get kicked by either a temperamental mount or by a dusty, surly knight.

The Medinian troop kept Willie busy for the next few hours while he helped care for their horses and their personal needs. They quickly consumed the food and drink that he brought them from the cold storage cellar beneath the barn, and then looked for a place to rest before the last segment of their patrol took them back to the outpost.

The knights were content to laze away part of the hot afternoon lying in the shade by the barn while they watched Willie do the hard work. After all, tending to such trivial details was the work of grooms and serfs; their job was to defend the realm. Their only concern seemed to be that their swords and crossbows were kept close at hand even when they rested. It was said of the king's knights that they even slept with one eye open so as not to be taken by surprise.

Willie's shoulders and arms had begun to ache even more now. The combined efforts of chopping wood for hours and then hauling up baskets of fruit and bread, plus kegs of cider and ale for the knights, was labour enough. Added to that, they'd then put him to work brushing and cleaning their horses' coats.

Fortunately, the knights had removed the armour fittings and mail from their mounts themselves; he would never have finished if he'd had to undo the complicated buckles on his own. He wasn't sure that he could even have figured them out.

Some two and a half hours later, the captain of the guard finally emerged from the house, stretched his arms in a wide arc as he stepped out onto the porch, and let loose a loud belch. It was obvious that the man had indeed smelled out the ale, likely together with anything and everything edible in the kitchen. The captain's unkempt hair suggested that he'd made use of a bed to catch up on some sleep, as well.

"Prepare your mounts, men," the knight captain called out as he crossed the yard. "I want to sleep in my own bed tonight." He turned to Willie with a satisfied smile. "And thank your mistress for her hospitality."

The captain roughed up the youth's hair as he passed by and undoubtedly had forgotten him by the time he rousted his troop from their afternoon lethargy. His men reluctantly tossed aside the remains of their repast and went to fetch their steeds. They set about refitting and saddling the freshly scrubbed backs of their destriers. More than one of them commented on the farm lad's good efforts, aware that their grooms would work a little easier that night.

Willie watched the troop set off. This time, their rising cloud of dust was heading north towards the river, where they would then turn eastward and head to the Medinian frontier post.

Once the troop had disappeared from sight, Willie decided he'd best check up on the house. His head was full of wishful thoughts of one day becoming a knight himself, even though he well knew it was only a fantasy. Horses, weapons, not to mention grooms and their upkeep, all cost a fortune.

"Fat bloody chance," Willie muttered aloud.

He knew full well that only wealthy aristocrats and landowners could afford to sponsor a son to become a knight of the kingdom. There was no chance he'd ever have that kind of wealth, nor was it likely he'd be accepted even if he did.

As the sun prepared to set over the mountain peaks, he entered the house, only to be faced by a small disaster. Mrs. Smythe's kitchen was in complete disarray. Remains of the captain's food and drink were strewn all over the pantry. He'd even used her best Sunday dishes!

Willie ran to the main bedchamber and discovered that the captain had also found a place to lie down. Mrs. Smythe's intricately handcrafted quilt was now covered in dust and grime. His heart sank. He spent the better part of the next half hour feverishly trying to get it clean again and then putting the kitchen back in order.

He hadn't half finished that job when he heard the insistent barking of the dogs coming from the barn. It took another moment for the message to sink in. The animals! He'd completely forgotten about the animals. The sheep and cattle were still up in the foothill pastures and the sun was already setting.

Willie raced out the front door and ran for his horse and the dogs. He had far bigger problems than a messy house.

*   *   *

"The Thunder Moon"
One night after the apex of the full moon

July 23, 1461
Medinia

Willie's eyes hadn't been the only ones watching the knight troop's dust trail disappear into the distance. The others were the watchful eyes of predators. They shone with intelligence, seeing everything clearly. Their owners could also both smell and hear the cattle and sheep in the paddocks below.

The pack in question was returning to the mountain pass after two nights of raids on herds and flocks of farms farther south and had settled into the woods near these last pastures about an hour earlier. They were anxious to return home, but the task they'd been assigned was not yet finished. Hidden well inside the edge of the woods, they rested and waited with practiced patience for the cover of night and the arrival of the moon.

This was no ordinary pack of wolves. It was a large pack, numbering twenty-four in all. Still, the least ordinary thing about this particular wolf pack was that only half were of the four-legged variety. There were twelve others that walked upright. They were humans, of a sort. They were referred to as the Pack. Theirs was a unique situation. It was unheard of, in fact.

For the most part, the Pack members had gathered in small groups, well inside the tree line and downwind of the fenced-in pastures. The exception was a tall, solidly built man, whose name was Woodrow. His once ebony black hair now showed the grey streaks of a man about fifty years of age, as did his closely cropped goatee. His dark eyes looked weary, as if they'd seen a hard half century of life. This might not have been exceptional, except for the fact that he was older than fifty—a great deal older, in fact.

His clothes, like those of his two-legged comrades, were mostly in tatters. His skin and hair, and the rags he wore were covered in filth, grime, and dried blood. He was one of them, but he chose to sit apart from the others, perched on a mound of rocks and forest debris, brooding about the circumstances that had brought them here.

Woodrow was a solitary man by nature. For many years he had preferred his privacy and solitude away from the rest of mankind. He had hunted and lived with his lone friend, the wolf he'd known ever since the animal had been an orphaned pup. Yet, for some time now, he had served as the Pack's leader. In that role, he was the person most responsible for the Pack's well-being. The irony was not lost on him.

Off to his side, as if not to intrude on the man's thoughts, lay the largest of the wolves. Golden eyes shone out from his intelligent face. His fur was black, with a touch of silver on his chest and flanks, as if mimicking his human companion. His name was Brutus.

They were the Pack's alpha males. Woodrow was the Pack's leader; Brutus, the Pack's enforcer. They were an inseparable team. They had been together since that first fateful day so long ago. Despite being two different species, they were like brothers. They shared the same scent.

The Pack would hunt again soon, but not in the remote mountain range back home in Varakov and far from mankind, where they preferred to be.

This was the dilemma that weighed heavily on Woodrow's mind. However, he'd been given his orders and he was honour bound to obey them, despite his great reluctance.

Twelve travois leaned against the trees. Some were already fully loaded; others would be used to haul away this night's kill. There was one travois for each human member of the Pack. Attempting to harness one of them to any of the wolves would be to invite getting bitten. The wolves were allied to these humans, but they were far from being domesticated dogs.

The travois were simple in design and had been constructed well beforehand. Each was framed with four sturdy poles. Two long poles were crossed at the one end and strapped together. The poles then extended out in a narrow V-shape. Some two feet down from where the main poles crossed, a shorter pole was lashed across them. Similarly, the fourth pole was lashed into place near the widest end to complete the frame. A hide platform stretched between the two long poles and was laced in place to bear the tied-off load. The final piece of the travois was a leather harness that allowed each human member of the Pack to drag carcasses taken in earlier raids, as well as those soon to be added. The wolves would provide flanking protection on the journey home.

The Pack waited stoically, not for a signal from their leader, which would come in due time, but for the moon. It would be the third and final night of the full-moon cycle of late July. This particular full moon was known as the Thunder Moon in this part of the world. With a familiar feeling of pins and needles coursing through their bodies, the Pack waited to greet Diana, the Goddess of the Moon. They were her children, after all.

*   *   *

Willie grabbed a saddle and threw it on Pegasus. The old gelding he'd bought the year before with his meagre savings shook its head and then looked at the youth as if questioning the need for an evening ride.

The youth prayed that he was wrong, but something in his gut told him the animals up in the pasture were in trouble. *If only the horse could fly, like his namesake tonight!* Willie thought. He grabbed his fire-hardened herding staff, climbed onto the confused horse's back, and dug his heels in.

The boy and his mount bolted from the barn, already trailing a good distance behind the dogs. They half galloped past the fields of crops and up through the orchards, as Willie urged the horse onward. Pegasus was giving his best, as if he could sense the urgency of their mission. Nevertheless, they steadily fell farther behind the two herd dogs. Sirius and Rigel knew their job. The herds and flocks were their responsibility too.

The radiant glow of the full moon lit Willie's way through the growing darkness and seemed to ignite the ground mist that steamed up from the earth. Horse and rider moved through the mist, leaving swirling eddies in their wake. They finally passed the orchard and climbed into the gorse-covered pastures of the foothills. The youth strained to hear something above the pounding hooves of his horse. When he finally did, it was what he dreaded most. He could hear the bellows and screams of terrified farm animals in the upper pastures.

The farm animals' calls of distress were followed by a series of howls that chilled Willie's blood. The frantic barking of Sirius and Rigel rose above the din, and the youth urged the old horse on.

*　　　　　*　　　　　*

At about the same time that an anxious Willie raced out of his master's house, those who waited in the trees at the edge of the mountain forest were going through their own distress, but for quite another reason; theirs was the shared distress that marked them as members of the Pack.

Tonight was the third and final night of the full-moon phase of the lunar cycle, as the Pack measured it, the night after the apex of the Thunder Moon. Both the wolves and their human counterparts stiffened as the near-full moon broke into view. It was a magnificent, large moon, hanging low on the horizon. As the moon began its slow climb into the early night sky, it shone with a luminous light.

The Pack began to stir, not in preparation to launch their attack but in an unconditional surrender to the full moon and the sway it held over them. It was in recognition of the power of Diana, the Goddess of the Moon, their protectress.

Men and wolves were natural enemies under normal circumstances, but these were anything but normal circumstances. Tonight, the Pack had begun its third and final act of madness for this lunar month. It was the transformation of man and wolf into wolf-man and warg-wolf. It sent each of them writhing to the ground in contortions of agony, but it was borne in stoic silence.

As it did with each of the humans, dreadful changes rippled through the face of the Pack leader. His facial bones extended and distended. His jaws and nose doubled in size to form a carnivorous mouth and a protruding snout. New teeth, large and sharply pointed, grew into the gaps created in the mandible and maxilla parts of his jawbones. His ears grew to peaks and laid back against hair that filled out into a flowing mane. His eyes shone with a flaming redness that flared from an inner agony and a growing rage. The muscle mass of his chest, legs, and arms expanded dramatically and made him all the more savage looking.

Each of the wolves went through a similar change, until the twelve were half again their normal size. The Pack enforcer, Brutus, had become a massive animal. His already superior body was now a snarling mass of fury and potential destruction.

Man and wolf were transformed into deadly combatants. And battle they'd had, more times than either the Pack leader or the alpha wolf could remember. The two unlikely comrades had hunted together for many years, and they had fought side by side when confronted by other predators.

There were no worthy adversaries here tonight, however, only helpless farm animals. Brutus, the fierce Pack enforcer, looked up into the blood-red eyes of his long-time companion. The warg-wolf sensed that these series of raids were weighing heavily on the transformed human.

Regardless, it was time. As much as it displeased Woodrow that the Pack was here, they had an obligation to fulfill. Reluctantly, he nodded his head and gave the signal to move out from the trees.

Brutus led his Pack brothers off first. In short order, they split into two separate files of six, into a flanking pattern that would encircle the prey before they became aware of the danger. The second column of warg-wolves was led by the beta male wolf, known as One-Eye, for one eye was indeed missing from his heavily scarred face, the result of an epic battle with Brutus years before. It had been a savagely contested fight over which of them would become the Pack's alpha male, following the death of its previous leader. But that was an event of the past. The order of subordination was now well established and accepted. They were all working members of the same pack family now; that was all that mattered.

The twelve warg-wolves moved in silence. They were quite different from the departed Medinian knights, who had ridden out earlier. The cloaked knights on their mighty warhorses had kicked up a dust cloud that any wolf, or deer for that matter, would have spotted from several miles away. In the eyes of the disciplined hunters of the Pack, this was a contemptible behaviour.

They kept downwind of the farm animals so that there was little chance of the prey picking up their scent. This was a well-practiced manoeuvre; there had been many lunar months in which they'd hunted together, and they had honed their skills. Brutus, One-Eye, and their kind, would be in position when the signal came to launch the attack.

The Pack leader and the other wolf-men waited inside the tree line for their four-legged comrades to reach their attack positions. He looked over his fellow men, his fellow wolf-men. His brain was pounding inside his skull. He could feel the blood surging through his veins. His eyes were on fire and every sense-receptor surged with extraordinary clarity. He felt he was going to explode. He needed release; he felt sure that otherwise he would die. A savage howl welled from deep within him.

The other wolf-men took up the Pack leader's howl. Together, they then burst from the tree line like demons from hell. With long, loping strides they covered the distance across the hill to the fenced-in pasture in a matter of moments.

At the first howl, the animals inside the pasture panicked and stampeded away from the northwest tree line. Cattle and sheep desperately tried to distance themselves from the howling apparitions leaping the fence and descending upon them.

At the lower end of the pasture, the livestock found themselves trapped by the railing fence. The herd and flocks milled about the fence, bawling, bleating, and colliding into one another. In the ensuing chaos, the terrified cattle trampled several of the panicking sheep.

The Smythes' prize breeding bull was kept in a central paddock in the upper pasture. Diablo was known for his ugly disposition, and he was normally kept separated from the other livestock until breeding season called for his services. More than once, Willie or Adam had been chased from the paddock or almost gored by the unruly herd king's dangerous horns. They'd taken to leaving the gates open at night and letting the animal follow the herds down at its own stately pace.

The fierce bull was by far the most expensive purchase the Smythes had ever made for their frontier farm. They'd scrimped and gone without any luxuries for nearly three years to bid for an animal of his worth at auction. Thankfully, the fruit of the prize animal's prodigious loins had compensated them with enough sturdy calves these past two years to have finally paid off the cost.

Now the bull's herd was being attacked, and Diablo went into a rage. The great beast snorted and swung his massive head to and fro. He pawed at the ground as his formidable horns gleamed in the pale moonlight.

The maddened bull charged the paddock fence. His pounding hooves shook the ground as he charged. He crashed into the wooden fencing, thrusting his head high as he made contact. The ferocity of this goring swing tore the heavy railings from their posts.

Free of the paddock now, Diablo surveyed the pasture. The animal's body quivered with anticipation of the fight ahead, and his eyes blazed with anger at the intrusion into his private domain. The bull shook his head, snorting jets of steamy breath and snot from his flaring nostrils as he sought a target to vent his anger.

By the ample light of the full moon, he saw them moving towards the herd. They were two-legged intruders. The bull bounded forward to take his stand beside the pile of rocks and boulders that had been cleared from the fields. He now stood between the intruders and his herd. He bellowed his challenge to the creatures that had dared invade his turf and stomped on the ground as he prepared to do battle.

The wolf-men slowed their approach. At the Pack leader's signal, they spread out in a half-circle and faced their adversary's challenge. Diablo pivoted back and forth on his hind legs, selecting his first target. As the bull prepared to attack these interlopers, the rear and flank attacks that were launched by Brutus, One-Eye, and the other warg-wolves cut into and through the milling animals like ploughshares through soil. The Pack leaped the fences in snarling fury, and it took them only moments to cut down a dozen or more animals.

The balance of the herd stampeded to the southeast, instinctively seeking the protection of the farmhouse and barn. Behind them, the agitated bull twisted this way and that, bewildered by the number of attacks coming from all sides.

To his right, he spotted a warg-wolf taking down a cow. The bull rocked on his hind legs and finally charged. He caught the exposed creature with one horn, goring the invader through the rib cage. With a toss of his head, Diablo flung the dying warg-wolf through the air.

His first opponent vanquished, the bull turned and searched for a new enemy. This time his attention focused on a two-legged creature. Diablo lowered his head, pawed the ground once more, and prepared to charge.

The Pack leader stood alone over the body of a cow. He had just ended its life by breaking its neck with a twist of his powerful arms. Now he stared defiantly at the bull with fiery eyes and stood his ground.

The truth was, he was tired, not physically but spiritually. He was still enmeshed in a bloodlust but at the same time overwhelmed with shame. At this moment, the Pack leader didn't care if he was to die on the horns of this valiant adversary. Let the bull put an end to it all right now. It would be more dignified than what the Pack members were doing here.

Diablo launched his attack. Defiantly, the Pack leader stood his ground.

Then Brutus intervened. The Pack enforcer launched himself off the top of the rock pile in a flying fury. He hit the ground and in two bounding strides leaped onto the bull's back. His teeth sank deep into the bull's neck and refused to be dislodged by the huge, bucking animal beneath him. If Diablo succeeded in dislodging him, his horns would make short work of Brutus. This was no attack on helpless livestock or elusive prey.

Time and again, the bull bellowed in rage. It twisted violently in its efforts to dislodge the warg-wolf. Finally, its neck muscles tearing more in each twisting turn, the bull could no longer raise its head. His energy spent, Diablo slowed to a trembling halt, but still snorting in defiance.

The Pack enforcer's death grip never slackened for a moment, as his opponent wore down and then finally stopped thrashing and bucking. The bull's eyes seemed to focus on the Pack leader, who stood silently, watching the death throes of the valiant animal. More savage mouths lunged forward in a coordinated attack upon the legs, the exposed flanks, and the throat of the herd's protector. The bull was ripped apart until it was unrecognizable.

*   *   *

The two herd dogs arrived at the corner of the fenced pasture at the same time the stampeding animals were going in the opposite direction. Sirius and Rigel were forced to give way to a wave of about forty cows that crashed into and through the fences in their panic. It was all the pair could do to avoid being trampled, and in the ensuing chaos they were separated.

By the time what was left of the herd and the flocks passed by, both dogs had resumed their quest. Leaping broken sections of fence some hundred yards apart, they ignored injured stragglers still attempting to flee the carnage.

Sirius reached the Pack first. Streaking up from behind, he tore into the hindquarters of one warg-wolf, while the Pack's concentration was still focused on the fallen bull. The dog's teeth ravaged the warg-wolf's hamstrings before it could turn and defend itself. The creature howled out in pain and surprise as it collapsed.

Running past the fallen creature, Sirius saw that he was outnumbered by a host of similar creatures, but he didn't stop to try to make sense of these strange two- and four-legged beasts; they were the enemy attacking the herd. Sirius would fight, but he would try to do it on his own terms. He bolted for the high ground.

In this instance, the nearest high ground was the same pile of rocks that Brutus had used to launch his attack on the bull. Sirius signalled Rigel with frantic barking that was answered in kind by his partner as he raced to catch up. He was still a good thirty yards away, and there were several intruders between them.

The sudden intrusion momentarily threw the Pack into disorder. One second they were exulting in their kill of the bull; the next, there was a new threat from another quarter. Many wild animals would have run off at the insistent barking, growling and bared teeth of the two dogs, but not the Pack. They turned to face the new foe, and their red eyes glowed as they appraised the situation.

The Pack leader gestured, and warg-wolves and wolf-men alike moved on his command. The Pack divided as they had before. One group surrounded the rock pile and began to circle it slowly, isolating Sirius on his rock-pile island. The others turned and faced Rigel.

The herd dog was forced to stop and search in vain for an opening he could break through to reach his partner. His every path blocked, Rigel watched helplessly as the second group now fanned out to encircle him.

Together, the two dogs could have delayed the inevitable. They might even have taken more of these strange creatures down with them. At the least, they could have made a valiant fight of it. Separated, and steadily being surrounded, they stood no chance. There were too many of the enemy and far too many approaches for any one dog to defend alone.

*   *   *

Willie and Pegasus met with good fortune and bad fortune. The old horse and his young rider had cut across the hills towards the northwest end of the fields, where the commotion had originated, but the howling wolf-men had already driven the herd and flock down from the upper pasture, into the trap set by the four-legged warg-wolves.

Their good fortune was that the stampeding animals breaking out of the pasture below hadn't trampled them, but luck was with them only in that one regard. Their bad fortune was everything else. There, under the glow of the full moon, was a scene that Willie's brain couldn't process.

In the moonlight he could make out downed animals scattered across the ground, either already dead or dying. He heard pitiful cries from those in their death throes. His eyes moved over the slaughtered animals to the more distant apparitions. Some looked like giant deformed wolves, while others appeared to be large, terribly misshapen creatures that walked upright, but the resemblance to humans ended with that. Nothing that Willie's eyes saw made any sense to him.

He reined in Pegasus and scrambled down. He grabbed his staff and climbed over the fence railing, leaving his horse to recover from the hard ride. With his heart pounding, unsure what to do when he got there, Willie ran until he got to the pasture. The closer he got, the more clearly he saw that his companions, Sirius and Rigel, were surrounded, hopelessly outnumbered by creatures that became more terrifying with each closer step. Willie slowed his pace, barely daring to breathe lest they turn and discover him. He was still a couple of hundred yards away when the two sections of the Pack began to manoeuvre for their attack.

*   *   *

Brutus and the Pack leader were in the group that had Sirius pinned on top of the mound of rocks. The warg-wolf creatures took turns darting up at the dog. As Sirius turned to face each new attacker, another would spring at his flank. The dog had to spin into a new defensive position with each assault.

Although Sirius held the high-ground, either he would exhaust himself to the point where his reflexes couldn't match the next strike or he would be forced into battle with one attacker while the others moved in for an easy kill. On open ground, Rigel's fate would be decided even faster. Separated, the two dogs were finished. If they could somehow get back together they might have a better chance of survival, working in tandem as they always had.

Without even realizing it, Willie had begun to scream. He screamed out of fear and anger, out of frustration, but most of all out of impotence.

The sensitive ears of the dogs, warg-wolves, and wolf-men alike were assailed by these raw and savage cries. Glowing eyes turned in Willie's direction, nostrils flared and ears pricked up as the Pack stopped to assess the latest arrival. The Pack leader and Brutus were both caught on the far side of the rock pile when the fresh interruption happened. They were unable to see whose screams had caused the Pack to stop circling and therefore unable to react.

Herd dogs seem to work with one mind, much as the Pack did, and in this instance, their instincts reacted faster. Both dogs bolted simultaneously. Each headed for the closest point separating them.

Sirius, from his higher vantage point on the rock pile, gathered himself and leaped through the air. The warg-wolf in whose direction the dog flew had exposed its flank when its attention was diverted by Willie's screams. At the last moment, it caught sight of the attacking dog, but was too late to oppose it. Instead of following through with the attack, however, Sirius landed at the base of the rock pile and sprang forward. He had ample manoeuvres of his own. The dog made one feint to the left and then cut sharply right and burst past the startled warg-wolf.

Rigel made his move at the same moment. His tactics were less refined; he simply ran over the top of the nearest warg-wolf in his path. He crossed over its back in a flash, just as he'd done countless times with sheep flocks, when he had to change their direction in a hurry.

Side by side now, the two dogs bolted into the clear and raced towards their master. Willie saw them coming, stopped, and turned back the way he'd come. Still sobbing, he ran back towards Pegasus as fast as his stumbling legs could carry him. For a moment, the Pack didn't react.

The Pack leader and Brutus stood motionless and silent, assessing the situation. There was no immediate threat to the Pack. They could load their clean kill and leave for home. They'd likely get there safely, before an alarm was sounded or any knight troop could be dispatched. They would, however, be fully loaded down and moving slowly and that would leave them vulnerable to any attack.

The Pack leader snorted in exasperation. He met his comrade's eyes and then signalled new commands. Brutus and the first group of warg-wolves would cut off any chance of escape towards the farm and then turn north and head for the river. One-Eye and the second group would give chase immediately. The prey would be forced to run the tree line to try to reach the river and any hope of help.

The fact that these weren't really prey gnawed at the Pack leader's conscience, but the Pack's safety had to come first. He raised a hand to his four-legged brethren and made the sign to take them down.

CHAPTER 2

Captives of Varakov

The fates decreed that you're cursed for life
They've left you dancing on the sharp edge of the knife

"The Thunder Moon"
One night past the apex of the full moon

July 23, 1461
Medinia

WILLIE REACHED THE FENCE and dragged himself over near Pegasus. The old horse was wide-eyed with fright, its senses reeling from the sights and sounds of panic and distress emanating from the farm animals and the smell of blood in the air. There was no time for consoling the poor animal. Willie clumsily undid the reins from the post and with some difficulty hauled his body up onto the saddle.

Sirius and Rigel reached the fence and leaped over it in near perfect unison. The two herd dogs landed and in a few short strides braked to a halt. They came back to their master barking loudly in an effort to urge him onwards.

As Willie turned the old steed's head, he saw the first part of the Pack break away from the rocks and race away toward the boundary of the lower pasture. His brain processed the information slowly, but he finally realized that the danger was far from over.

The farm!

It began to sink in. The wolf-creatures were cutting off his escape route. They were moving fast and had the better angle across the hills. The youth saw that there would be no going back the way they had come.

The second part of the pursuit set out a moment later. He saw this group was dispatched straight for them. The choice was made for him. They had to head for the river. It was their only chance. Maybe they could reach the waterfalls and hide. Maybe they could go on to the fort, but it had to be the river first. It was their only hope, yet he knew that it was a long way off.

Willie dug his heels into horse's flanks. Pegasus stumbled at first, but then set his hooves and responded as best he could to the urgency of their departure. There was a steady stream of froth coming from his mouth as he galloped across the slope of the foothill. Horse and rider disappeared briefly into a shallow ravine, before re-emerging to view as they climbed the next slope.

The Pack leader watched the two platoons of his warg-wolf comrades as they streaked off in hot but silent pursuit. It would be a race for the distant Kolenko River. He knew the speed and endurance of the four-legged Pack members. The race would be over long before then.

The Pack leader turned his attention to other matters. He signalled to the wolf-man known as Simon, the Pack's beta-male human. His long-time lieutenant nodded his understanding and then led the other wolf-men off to gather up the clean kill. Their orders were to leave the kill brought down by the mouths of the warg-wolves, and possibly diseased in the process. This was why the wolf-men of the Pack had sought only necks to break among their kills. Now they hauled those carcasses to the woods to load the remaining empty travois. It was time to head for home. Their task here was done.

While his aide and the other wolf-men moved off to prepare the kill for transport, the Pack leader waited with a stoic patience. He watched until he was satisfied that they had inner rage under control and were following Simon's directives. Another grim task still remained to be performed, but it fell to him alone to do it.

Woodrow knew the others were in a state of agitation, as he himself was. They were still afflicted with the lunar transformation, but the raging madness was ebbing. The intensity of the third night of the full moon was waning now. The hunger in their bellies and the burning in their brains had been like a fire. By now, the fire had all but consumed its available fuel. The three-nights of the hunt were almost over. It was time to make their way homeward, back to their Sanctuary.

Only two of the Pack's warg-wolves had remained behind after their brethren had split up again and set out after the boy and his dogs. One of them was dead, having fallen victim to the goring of the bull's horns. The other was the unfortunate warg-wolf, which the one herd dog had crippled when it first arrived on the scene and attacked. The Pack leader walked over to where the distressed animal lay licking its still-bleeding wounds.

The injured warg-wolf snapped a warning at his approach, baring its savage teeth. The creature then issued a deep-throated growl and its hackles rose. Undeterred, the Pack leader bared his formidable teeth and issued a threatening growl of his own. The animal's hackles dropped immediately and it lowered its head in a contrite act of submission to the alpha male human.

The Pack leader continued his approach with steady steps, yet cautiously, knowing that the wounded animal might still strike out at him. He knelt at the distorted creature's side and roughly kneaded its neck with one of his distended clawed hands, as he carefully examined the warg-wolf's hind legs with the other.

The damage was too severe. The tendons and muscle were torn away clear through to the bone. The animal was crippled and would not walk properly again, let alone ever run with the Pack.

The wolf-man growled in an almost soft whisper now, as he rocked the animal like a parent would an injured child. They were two kindred spirits who shared the same affliction. They submitted to the same Goddess. They shared the intimacy of the hunt.

The Pack leader continued stroking the animal's powerful neck, feeling each vertebra with practiced fingers. Then, in one quick motion, and with a sickening snap, he broke the creature's neck. He watched as the red glow in the warg-wolf's eyes faded away, until they were dull and lifeless.

The Pack leader slowly stood upright again, and then he howled into the night-sky at the loss of a valued comrade. Simon and the other wolf-men ceased their work for the moment to join in.

The Pack said its good-byes, together, but the Pack leader still stood, very much alone. As his dying howl echoed off the mountains and into the dark distance, the Pack leader set off. With long, loping strides, the wolf-man ran in the direction of the river. At full speed, if he chose to, he could match a normal dog's fastest gait over a moderate distance. Perhaps, he could even keep up with some of the Pack's warg-wolves, for a time.

Tonight's run would require a more measured pace. The Pack leader kept to a steady lope, yet he still covered considerable ground with each passing stride as he crossed the summer meadows of green grass and purple clover under the light of the moon.

*   *   *

They had barely covered a full mile of the foothills that rose and fell away again beneath the pounding hooves of Pegasus. It was a hard mile of hills and gullies, each of which claimed a bit more of the old horse's stamina. The animal was running on fear alone now, and at the continued urging of the two dogs and the youth on its back.

Sirius and Rigel were holding in place at Pegasus' heels, barking and imploring him to give more, and then still more. It was in a losing effort, however. The horse was literally running itself to death, yet the warg-wolves were steadily closing the gap between them.

Willie stole a glance back over his shoulder. At first, he didn't see them, but then the Pack crested the hill immediately behind them. He could see their hot breath as it spewed forth like blasts of fog into the moonlit night. He could even see their demonic red eyes glowing as they came on in their relentless pursuit. The Medinian youth's heart sank. The river was still some two or three miles away. It might as well have been a hundred.

The two herd dogs must have also sensed that the end was fast approaching. After they came up out of the next shallow, gorse-covered gully and passed over the rise, Rigel came to a sudden halt. Sirius slowed and then stopped and looked back to his partner.

The two dogs stared at each other, as if to convey some silent message. Rigel barked loudly, pranced a few steps in the other dog's direction, and then turned back. Sirius hesitated, but then, with a final bark, turned away and raced after their master.

The lone herd dog timed it perfectly. Just as the warg-wolves were about to breach the hilltop, Rigel burst back over the crest of the hill and tore down into their ranks. The momentum of this unexpected action bowled over three of the pursuing creatures, causing the other two warg-wolves in their ranks to crash to a halt. The loyal herd dog had completely stopped one of the pursuing Pack groups. In the melee that ensued, however, he was hopelessly outnumbered.

Rigel kept to the offensive, turning and lashing out in a fury at the nearest of the wolf-creatures. Fangs were bared and furious growls were issued from the throats of each adversary. As they came together, fur and blood flew from both animals.

Hearing the savage commotion rising up behind them, Willie reined Pegasus in and stopped as he reached the peak of the next ridge. The old horse stood exhausted and trembling. The poor animal's breath came in ragged gasps, and its eyes shone with terror.

The youth was looking back just as Sirius came bounding up to his side. He couldn't see the battle taking place, but he could hear the snarling mass of fighting animals. He saw Sirius look back, too, as the dog stepped back and forth in its agitation. Willie began to weep when he realized what was happening. Rigel had sacrificed himself. He was trying to buy them some time, with his life.

Then, at the insistent urging of the lone remaining herd dog, Willie again dug his heels in and urged his mount onwards. The youth was sobbing openly as he rode away.

Behind them, Rigel's noble efforts were soon brought to an end. With his teeth clamped onto one warg-wolf's throat, the other predators tore into his exposed flanks. The herd dog died, never releasing his death grip, taking one of the enemy creatures with him.

Willie and Pegasus rode onwards, galloping past the trees of the forest that extended up from the foothills and onto the mountainsides. Sirius ran by their side. The snow-capped peaks loomed high above them but offered no escape there. The river was closer now but still so far away. For another quarter mile they were alone, never letting up in their determination to reach it, but their gait was still slowing as the horse grew evermore tired.

As they reached the next rise, Willie's heart sank again. The youth saw the streaking four-legged figures that were coming across the fields. They were the ones who had cut off any escape towards the farm.

Even from a distance, the youth could see that the lead wolf creature was huge. It was a dozen yards ahead of the others as they crossed the slope on an intercept course. He could see that they would cut off his escape route once again. This time permanently.

Sirius saw the threat, too, and he sprang forward to meet it. Willie's sobbing protest was ignored, as the lone herd dog raced ahead to engage their new foes.

*　　　　　*　　　　　*

Brutus had taken his flank of the Pack far enough to force the youth on the horse and his two dogs to seek the distant river and abandon any idea of reaching the farmhouse below. He had then led them northwest in a steady, ground-eating lope. They were the second arm of a scissor attack, designed to cut off the slower prey if they somehow managed to stay ahead of their other pursuers.

The Pack enforcer's sensitive ears had picked up the sounds of the fight involving the other half of the Pack, but they also heard the horse still running north along the tree line. He sensed that the prey had split. One or possibly both of the herd dogs were engaged with the other warg-wolves. Brutus didn't vary his stride or his direction. They would catch up and take the horse and its rider.

The remaining herd dog and the warg-wolf saw each other in the same instance, as they approached the opposing sides of a shallow dip between two rises. Brutus slowed and snarled at the others of the Pack, sending them onward after the horse and rider. The Pack enforcer then bounded towards Sirius, leaving the dog no choice but to fight him alone.

Sirius took one last look back up at his master and then turned to accept the challenge of single combat. There was nothing that he could do about the rest of the Pack now. Its leader had forced the issue. The herd dog raced to meet the attack of its much larger opponent.

Like two jousting knights, the animals carried their initial charge past the other. They each sought a sweeping slash of the legs, or the flank of its opponent. Neither delivered a decisive wound, but they both drew blood.

Turning on the slopes of the opposite hillside, they charged a second time, meeting in a furious clash of bared teeth. The dog looked for any opening where it could deliver a quick and hopefully crippling wound. The alpha warg-wolf attempted to use its size and weight advantage to force the dog back onto its heels.

Rising up on their hind legs, the two combatants briefly resembled two boxers sparring in a clutch and fighting chest to chest. They snapped fiercely at each other with mouths agape and fangs bared. Once again, the advantage went to the warg-wolf's superior size and brute strength.

*   *   *

Meanwhile, Willie was having troubles of his own. Pegasus was faltering and the four remaining warg-wolves were now only a scant twenty yards away, on an intercept course. In a few moments, their two paths would converge, and it would be over. The youth clutched the reins in one hand and his staff in the other, for all the good it would do him against these determined creatures.

The Pack cut the distance in half. Wild eyed, Pegasus was frothing at the mouth, dying a little more with each stride. When Willie saw the new pursuers closing in, he reined the faltering horse closer to the tree line and a few more feet away from their advance.

There was precious little else that he could do.

*   *   *

The Pack leader stood over the herd dog and the warg-wolf, where they lay side-by-side in death. He could see that it had been death with honour, if there really was such a thing. He could only hope that his own death would come as a result of combat with an enemy that was as noble as this loyal dog had been.

The Pack leader stood alongside the warg-wolves gathered at their dead comrade's side. He joined in their death howls. It was a bitter tribute to yet another fallen friend. His heart ached, and then an angry fire began growing in his belly. His ire wasn't directed towards the dog or its young master. They were only attempting to survive this nightmare, and they could not be faulted for fighting back. His anger was with himself alone. He was ultimately responsible for this nightmare, regardless of who had given the order for them to be here. He should never have agreed to it.

The Pack leader signalled for his four-legged comrades to rejoin the wolf-men at the pasture, where they made preparations for the Pack's departure. The warg-wolves departed quickly. They would take up their defensive positions guarding the humans and the heavily laden travois on the trek home.

The Pack leader stood watching them as they loped away. Despite their deformity, they moved with long and graceful strides. When they were out of sight, he turned back and said a final private good-bye to his fallen comrade, in the only way he could.

As his howl died off, the Pack leader gave the brave dog at his feet a solemn nod in salute. He felt a kinship to the noble dog, similar to the one he felt for the four-legged Pack members. He recognized and valued the sacrifice the brave animal had made in devotion to its master.

*　　　　*　　　　*

Sirius would have stood a better-than-even chance against any ordinary wolf, but Brutus was far from ordinary and in his current state, the Pack's enforcer's additional size and ferocity could not be denied. In a final, desperate gambit, the herd dog dropped his head down in an attempt to slash the warg-wolf's belly, or possibly a leg.

In the split second that the nape of the dog's neck was exposed, Brutus lunged downwards and seized it in his powerful jaws. He whipped his head first to the left and then hard back to the right, causing the neck to snap like the crack of a branch breaking. It proved fatal for his adversary. Sirius hung limply from the warg-wolf's fierce mouth. His body was lifeless now. His valiant battle was over.

The Pack enforcer slowly, almost gently, lowered the herd dog down to the ground and released his death hold on him. Standing over his vanquished foe, he saluted him as only a wolf of the Pack can. The howls that pierced the night had an air of mourning to them, as if Brutus had suffered the loss of a family member. His victory felt hollow, but in the heat of the battle, it made very little difference.

One of them had to die.

*　　　　*　　　　*

As they edged ever closer to the tree line, Willie suddenly found himself airborne. The youth did not know if Pegasus had stepped in a hole or been bitten on the leg, or if the steed's noble heart had simply given up and it had fallen down dead. Whatever the cause, just as they rode down into a shallow swale, the young serf was tossed over the horse's left shoulder as it collapsed beneath him. He landed hard, bounced twice, and then slid down the slope. His head narrowly missed a boulder, which would have splattered his brains all over the landscape. Somehow, he managed to retain his grip on his shepherd's staff.

Willie got up off the ground as the four warg-wolves came over the lip of the depression and set upon the old steed. Helpless to prevent it, he turned towards the woods and ran blindly. Twice, his sturdy staff was the only thing that saved him from falling as he stumbled into the tree line.

As Willie was disappearing into the darkness of the trees, one of the warg-wolves spotted his movements and broke away from the assault on the fallen horse to give chase. The lone wolf-creature set off towards the woods before the others, perhaps sensing that the chase was still on, turned to follow. They left behind the gruesome remains of the valiant old steed.

Pegasus, too, had made the ultimate sacrifice for his master.

Willie crashed through the darker woods in a wild panic, not knowing where he was going but only that he had to get as far away as quickly as possible. His heart was pounding so hard that he felt it was going to explode in his chest. His legs were cramping and his lungs burned. As yet another branch whipped across his face, the youth seemed to sense the danger rising up behind him.

Without turning to look, he stopped short, spun about, and swung his staff around and down as hard as he could, all in one desperate motion. The lone warg-wolf advancing behind him was just about to make its leap and pull down the fleeing prey. The fierce predator was already committed to its attack and could not avoid the fire-hardened head of the staff that crashed into its skull. The creature went down in a heap at the youth's feet.

Dropping the bloody staff, Willie stood gasping for breath as he eyed the motionless creature, which could only have come from the gates of hell itself. Not caring if the creature was truly dead or merely knocked out, he turned and ran on.

The other three warg-wolves were coming through the woods in hot pursuit now. The fleeing youth could hear their snarls as they came across the one he'd struck down. He didn't think it would slow them for long.

Moments later, Willie dodged past a pair of trees and ran out into a small moon-lit clearing. It was the momentary absence of trees that finally forced him to momentarily halt his panicked flight and consider his options. *There would be safety in the treetops!* Out in the middle of the clearing, an old, gnarled oak tree stood by itself, as if shunned by the woods around it. The promise of a safe haven was about ten yards away. The youth ran for it.

Willie barely got to the base of the tree before his snarling pursuers burst out into the clearing. He flung himself at the lowest branch, caught hold of it, and started to haul himself up. The warg-wolf at the front lunged forward after him. Its savage mouth searched for a taste of the elusive prey.

Willie was almost up onto the branch when the warg-wolf's teeth sank into his thigh and locked there. He screamed out and was nearly dragged from the branch. Somehow, his aching arms retained their clamp on the limb and he clung to it with all his remaining strength.

For a moment, the warg-wolf swung in the air, suspended a few feet above the ground by the grip it held on the prey's leg with its teeth. Just seconds before the youth's strength gave out; the weight of the deformed animal tore it away, taking part of Willie's pant leg, and a piece of his thigh with it.

The warg-wolf fell away to the ground and into the midst of its brethren. The youth screamed anew from the slicing agony and fire in his leg, but he managed to hang on and pulled himself the rest of the way up on top of the branch. Before another of the creatures could gather itself to make a leap at him, he dragged himself a little higher up into the branches and father away from the danger below. He finally collapsed into a sheltered nook, formed where two larger branches diverged from the trunk.

Willie's last thoughts, before he mercifully passed out, were of the three loyal friends he'd just lost. His heart ached for those who had given their lives for him. As he lost consciousness, he was murmuring a delirious prayer that the souls of Rigel, Sirius, and Pegasus be sent on their way to join their namesakes in the heavens.

Down below, the three warg-wolves circled the old oak, sniffing and licking at Willie's blood as it fell from his body and landed in splatters on the ground. They would wait. Their prey was wounded and wasn't going anywhere.

*　　　　*　　　　*

The Pack leader and its four-legged enforcer arrived almost together to see what appeared, at first, to be the finale of the chase. They found the remains of the destroyed horse lying sprawled in a shallow depression at the edge of the woods. Viewed like this at night, the animal's blood soaked the ground in what looked like a dark, black pool. The absence of the other warg-wolves told them that the hunt had continued past here, however.

Even in the darkness of the trees, the two skilled hunters had no problem following the trail. They had only to sniff at the air and follow their noses. Within a few minutes, they came across the body of the warg-wolf that the youth had felled with his shepherd's staff. The Pack leader picked up the staff that had done the fatal damage in his clawed hands. In a flash of hot anger, he snapped it effortlessly over his knee.

The three living warg-wolves ceased their circling as their two leaders approached. It was clear to the Pack leader that the farm youth was treed, and judging from the amount of blood that dripped down from the branches, he was severely wounded, perhaps, even fatally so.

With a brief snarl, the Pack leader leaped upwards, easily reaching the tree limb. His claw-like fingernails dug deeply into the rough bark as he pulled himself into the lower canopy. He followed the blood trail to the injured youth. There was a kill for him to finish.

Yet, as the Pack leader looked down at the unconscious, ashen-faced youth, his rage deserted him. The sight left him drained and strangely empty, even ashamed. His body began to shake from the strain to control his primal urges. He smashed a fist into the nearest branch, scraping his knuckles raw. There would be no more killing tonight. The hunt was over.

Picking the youth up, he cradled him in his arms as he dropped to the ground, instinctively flexing his knees to absorb the shock. He knelt and lay the youth on the ground, resting his head on an exposed root of the old oak tree. He looked up at Brutus and the other warg-wolves, his deformed face now devoid of its fierce expression, save for the fading glow of his red eyes.

He made signs then to Brutus. The Pack enforcer was to take the others and rejoin the rest of the Pack. He would tend to the injured youth and wait for them at the tree line until they returned with the loaded travois. It was time that they were finished with this foul business and made the journey home, back to their Sanctuary.

The Pack enforcer never questioned his leader; they had been together far too long. The warg-wolf's eyes glowed red with the same moon madness as did those of his two-legged comrade, but they were fading as well. The animal seemed to sense his companion's conflicted state. He too understood that Diana's power over them was ebbing. The hunt was indeed over.

Brutus approached the Pack leader and nuzzled his neck briefly. As savage as they appeared, there was no denying that there was a deep bond between the two. His long-time comrade uttered a low, throaty growl in response.

The warg-wolf turned away then and led the others off, setting a strong pace. There was still considerable ground to be covered before the dawn broke and the Pack enforcer wanted to be long gone from this place by then.

*   *   *

July 24, 1461
The Euralene Gap

Over the next few hours leading up to the dawn, two separate raiding parties would approach the turbulent river that flowed forth out from the base of the lower waterfalls. Both groups would be returning home to Varakov by way of the Euralene Gap. The first was returning from their three nights of raiding farms in Medinia. The second raiding party would be coming back from their mission into its neighbour to the north, Skoland.

It was the first of these groups that the Pack leader led, his back bent under the strain of the load he pulled behind him. His travois was secured to him by the leather harness strapped to his broad shoulders and back. The load of carcasses had been redistributed among the other two-legged members of the Pack. The wolf-men struggled up the grade with the weight of their overloaded travois harnessed behind them. They slowly climbed the trail, past the height of the lower waterfalls, and then beyond.

Young Willie of Medinia was now strapped to the Pack leader's travois, where he remained unconscious. His wound was roughly bound with strips of the shirting that the wolf-man had torn from his back. They were well soaked with his blood by now. The youth's sweat-stained shirt had been the only means that the wolf-man had to stanch the bleeding. His own clothes were little more than tattered rags. The Pack leader had fashioned a crude tourniquet to stop most of the bleeding. It was the best that he could do given the circumstances and his current state of affliction. He had made several stops along the way to ease off the tourniquet pressure, so he would not do further damage to the leg.

It occurred to him that the youth would likely die anyways. He'd lost a lot of blood. Even if he did live, it might not be for the best. The Pack leader pushed this notion from his clouded mind as they pressed onwards up the trail towards the pass and home to Sanctuary. Dawn was approaching. He could feel it coming now. The telltale prickles had begun coursing through his body once again. If the injured youth was to have a chance, they had to reach their first destination and then suffer the dawn's transformation.

After that, he would travel a little further still, to a place where he could properly treat the youth's injuries, hopefully before the remaining life drained out of him.

*   *   *

Skoland

The second raiding party was some two hours behind the Pack leader's group. However, these raiders approached the river from the northeast, where they'd carried out their own forays into the kingdom of Skoland.

Unlike the Medinian raiders, this party contained no mix of man and wolf. Nor were they affected by the full moon overhead. This was a band of well-armed, olive-skinned mercenaries, whose long, dark hair was tied off in back of their covered heads. They were clad in dark robes, and they'd ridden on horseback while making their raids into Skolish territory.

These raiders hadn't been out hunting farm animals. They had an entirely different focus to their raids, and a different prey in mind. Like the Pack, they'd traveled down from the mountains and quietly moved through the woods, but along a different trail, until they were securely into Skolish territory. They had then begun a series of attacks on a half dozen isolated farms in the region. The raiding party had commenced these attacks starting in the northern reaches of Skoland, working their way in a wide, snaking arc eastward before heading back southwest towards the river and home. Up to this point, they'd been careful not to leave any trail sign that would give their pursuers any obvious direction to follow. They knew that there'd likely be Skolish troops out investigating the raids—and hunting for them.

Laying low during the daylight hours, wherever they could find appropriate shelter, they had watched several columns of Skolish knights wearing their distinctive crimson red and white striped cloaks ride by. The closest patrol had passed by about noon that day, and only a scant fifty yards from where they were holed up in a copse of trees and bushes by a small streambed. They had muzzled their horses and remained silently watchful. Their captives had remained silently, bound and gagged.

This last night's raid had added three more prisoners to their captive total, a woman and her two daughters, captured from an isolated farm a few miles from the river. They'd been taken in the attack just a few hours earlier. The woman's husband, two sons, and a number of field hands had been killed in the ensuing fight.

The darkly robed warriors were driving along a total of twenty-two prisoners, flanking them from their horses. None of the captives who were living this waking nightmare even thought of trying to escape. They'd been driven hard through the night, forced along by the unrelenting horsemen who cared little if they were tired, terrified, or in a state of shock.

It was only as they approached the river, that the raiders took less care in sweeping away their tracks. When one of the older captives stumbled and fell, he pleaded to be left behind and that he couldn't go on. His wish had been granted. One of the mounted warriors had disposed of him on the spot by letting fly a crossbow bolt that pierced the man's chest, sending him spinning to the ground. The other prisoners needed no further incentive to keep up. The bolt that protruded from the dead man's chest was fletched with three swan feathers, which had aided in its flight. Two of the feathers were dyed blue, while the third remained white. Like all the arrows left behind them on this Skolish raid, as well as a pair of broken lances, and a long sword still imbedded in its victim, they were of Medinian design. Yet, no one in the raiding party came from that kingdom.

The scouts from the raiding party reported back that the river crossing ahead was clear. Unlike the Pack, this band intended to ford the river and cross to the other side. To do this, they'd selected a place a few miles downstream from the falls, below the portion of the river known as the cataracts. They would cross the swift-moving shallows and into Medinia before turning west and climbing up the same trail past the waterfalls, as the Pack leader's group had.

The trail on the northern side of the falls was serviceable, but their orders called for them to ford the river into Medinia before turning for home. That had to be done further down river, for in the cascading cataracts, a myriad of underground mountain streams came together to join the waters that tumbled down from the double waterfalls overhead.

These were the alpine waters that sourced the Kolenko River, sending it eastward in a turbulent state. Where the river broadened it was shallow enough to cross in safety this time of year. Still, they would have to be very careful.

The greatest danger came not from the turbulent river but from the proximity of the crossing to the two frontier posts. These army posts lay on either side of the river, about a half-mile further to the east of where they intended to cross. Patrols in the area were frequent, even at night, but the raiding party knew that both frontier posts had most of their respective patrols out searching the farmlands in response to their local troubles.

As they approached the crossing, the raiding party left behind a barely readable trail, but it was there. It was uncharacteristic of these mercenaries to leave any sign of their passing, if they had chosen not to. Even so, it would still take a skilled tracker to discover the signs. They didn't want it to appear too obvious, after all. The scant trail would end at the river crossing and lead to the conclusion the raiders wanted the Skolish troops to reach.

They forded the Kolenko River without mishap. The horses and the roped-together captives waded into the waist-deep water at the urging of their captors. Only the dark robed warriors on their mounts remained dry. Fed by the mountain snows, the water was clear and pure. It was also icy cold, even in the heat of summer, and the coldness only added to the misery that the captive prisoners already felt.

*   *   *

Varakov

The Pack leader's motley band entered the Euralene Gap and climbed the pass towards the gates that stood atop the divide. As they trudged up through the narrow confines of the pass, they ignored the feeling of being watched by a pair of unseen eyes. The warg-wolves of the Pack were wary and moved along cautiously. The wolf-men were just tired. Their loads were heavy, and they were hard pressed to keep up with the Pack leader's pace. He was well out in front of them, pulling his lightened load with a single-minded purpose.

Unbidden, the eastern gate, the largest of the two fortress gates, swung open as he approached. The Pack leader didn't even have to break his stride in order to gain entry to the kingdom of Varakov. Only the garrison commander stood on duty, and that was done from the shadows of the gatehouse. He alone saw who and what approached and passed through. The smaller western gates were already open. The Pack leader sensed him as he passed by, but ignored him. They were almost home. Soon they would reach Sanctuary.

Sanctuary was the Pack's refuge in the dense forests on the western slopes of the Euralene Mountains, in the kingdom of Varakov. Little or nothing was known of this land by either one of the two kingdoms to the east. The soaring mountain peaks all but cut off any contact with their western neighbour. Over the years, in which Medinia and Skoland had contested the valley lands that separated them, only sporadic contact had occurred between either of the kingdoms and Varakov. The only trading done was by the yearly caravan groups, which were allowed to route through the Euralene Gap to sell their wares to the two kingdoms on the eastern side of the mountain range.

The Varakovans controlled the passage through the mountains. They maintained a large, impregnable fortress in what was known as the Euralene Gap. The fortress had been constructed several centuries before, and very few Medinians or Skolish had been permitted entry since. Only a few dozen refugees had ever been granted access, and then only by special leave of the Varakovan king.

On occasion, in the distant past, armies from one or the other of the eastern kingdoms had tried to gain entry to Varakov through force, but they had been severely rebuffed by the entrenched defenders. The Varakovan defenders were well-trained and seasoned soldiers in their own right, and they were quite capable of handling any invader. The fortress force numbered only about four hundred in all, but they were well provisioned and positioned to repel any army twenty times their size, which might attempt to take the pass by force.

The Varakovans' greatest advantage lay in the narrow width of the passage itself and in their vantage point high overhead. Any approaching enemy would have to climb to meet them, and the Varakovans were waiting behind well fortified walls. They had long known the strategic importance of the pass through the Euralenes and had carefully planned their fortification in the best defensible position.

Two decades of dedicated labour had been required to cut away sections of the rock face and to barricade the gap with thick stone walls that extended into the opposing mountains of the great divide. They had then constructed their fortress, with its protected parapets, on the rock outcropping that protruded over the passage.

This impregnable fortification allowed them to rain down a furious barrage of rocks, logs, and arrows on any intruding force. Any invaders would find themselves bunched together, struggling uphill, and strung out in an unprotected column. Even if they somehow survived that deluge, their troops would still have to overcome the massive gates that were erected at the top of the divide. There was precious little space from which to lay siege with the large instruments of war that were required to assault the gated walls.

So futile was it to challenge the Euralene Gap that no assault had even been attempted in the last few generations, by either kingdom from the east. They just gladly accepted the yearly caravans that came down from the pass, and the much-sought-after goods that they brought.

As for the Varakovan garrison, they didn't allow the fact that the fortress walls had never been breached to decrease their vigilance. Their troops were kept well trained by a series of dedicated commanders. Although it was a remote mountain location, the defenders were watchful and always prepared for the worse. Their king was known to punish those who failed in their duties—and punish them severely.

Since the Varakovans controlled the gap, the Skolish and the Medinian kingdoms settled for maintaining armed posts on their respective sides of the river, not far from their western borders. Both frontier posts were constructed near the section of river that was fordable in the drier months of the year. The two fortified posts served to guard against any incursion from their immediate neighbour, as well as any intrusion that might arise from the west. They'd found no such threat arising from that quarter, however. The Varakovans seemed content to remain on their side of the mountain range. They didn't see a need to meddle in the affairs of the kingdoms east of the divide; at least they hadn't up to the present.

The main duties of the knight patrols of the two kingdoms on their respective western frontiers were to guard the river crossing and warn against any invasion force coming from the other side. The only contact with Varakov came when their mysterious neighbour to the west allowed trade ambassadors to pass through the gated fortress and come down to arrange for foreign caravans to visit the two kingdoms for a specified trading period.

The precious wares that these traders from afar carried with them were a welcome sight in the markets of war-torn Skoland and Medinia. So much so that the two kingdoms readily agreed to a period of truce and cessation of their mutual hostilities for the duration of the caravan's visit.

The crops, livestock, and other commodities that the Skolish and Medinians wished to trade were then brought to their respective markets set up at the frontier posts, as was any recognized coinage, like the much preferred ducat. The rare goods they sought were well worth the coin they cost. Thus two separate but equally laden caravans would then come down through the gap from Varakov and set up at each of the posts. There was never any preferential treatment given. It could be said that Varakov kept both her neighbours evenly supplied with this foreign trade and equally at arm's length.

The wagons and carts of the caravans emerged from their respective forest trails at the point where the lower of the two falls spilled its contents into the raging cataracts below, forming the Kolenko River, which separated the two kingdoms. The caravans would then enter the western end of each kingdom and be met by a delegation. They would, after inspection, proceed to the frontier post with an armed guard escort.

The heavily ladened caravans were remarkable. They brought fine silks and a variety of sturdy, colourful cloths, as well as much-desired barrels of salt, rich spices, and even exotic fruits. They also brought new tools and occasionally a limited supply of much-prized sturdy swords, or well-crafted lances or bows.

It was believed that the caravans and their merchants came to Varakov by way of great ships that plied the vast ocean beyond. No one from the east knew this for a certainty, as none had seen the fabled sea, and the caravan traders kept this information closely guarded. Wherever they came from, the quality and uniqueness of the goods they brought were ample reason for the Skolish and the Medinians to continue to leave the mighty fortress in the Euralene alone and not jeopardize their best outlet for these valued commodities.

After the last two-legged wolf-creature had dragged his travois through the open gates under the watchful eyes of his four-legged escort, the garrison commander turned the mechanism that swung the gates shut again. A few hours later, the process would be repeated as the raiding party into Skoland returned through the gap. In the meantime, the commander would have the guard turned out again in case some enemy force followed the Pack up into the pass. He thought this was highly unlikely, judging from the ferocious looking creatures he'd seen tonight, but it was better to take the precaution in any event.

Like others, the garrison commander had heard the rumours of the existence of these afflicted men and wolves that lived in the mountains of Varakov. He'd heard the tales of how they hunted together beneath the full moon. Until tonight, he'd considered those stories as only superstitious nonsense. He no longer did.

The commander had been given his explicit instructions regarding tonight's actions from Lord Victor himself. That in itself was a rarity. He'd been instructed that he alone was to witness the coming and going of the Pack members. He'd been further told that he was to say nothing of it afterwards.

The commander was experienced enough to know better than to question Lord Victor's orders, much less disobey them. He doubted that anyone would believe him anyways, as a shudder passed along his spine.

CHAPTER 3

WOODROW'S RETREAT

July 24, 1461
The Euralene Mountains, Varakov

THE DAWN WAS APPROACHING, and with it would come the final tortuous and exhausting reversion of the lunar month. The members of the Pack returning from the raids into Medinia were reunited with their mates and other brethren who had remained behind for a more traditional hunt in the mountain forests of Varakov. For those comrades that did not return from the raid, there would be a mourning period, a profound sadness felt by all. The Pack was diminished by the loss of four of its own.

The remaining Pack members were gathered inside one of the largest of the caves found on the western slopes of the Euralene mountain range. Many such caverns could be found in the heavily forested slopes on the Varakovan side of the mountain divide. This particular cave lay a few miles north of the pass and was often used as a communal meeting place, before and after, the three nights of their monthly hunts together.

After the agony that the dawn would bring upon them and the cleansing ritual was completed, the members of the Pack would split up and go their separate ways. The wolves would return to their dens established among the many smaller caves and grottos nearby. Some of the humans would return to their homes and loved ones who lived in Sanctuary. Others would wander off to more reclusive homes hidden away in their forested enclave.

The tree growth was much larger in Varakov and the forest was far denser than that on the eastern slopes of the Euralene mountain range. It was the alpine watershed divide that accounted for this fact. Heavy clouds, laden with the moisture gathered from the ocean, crossed over the coastal plains of Varakov. Moving inland, the clouds were forced upwards by the towering peaks of the mountain range they then encountered. As they struggled to gain altitude, the clouds were forced to lighten their loads before continuing their voyage across the continent. The majority of the rain fell on the western slopes.

A considerable yearly rainfall resulted in a lush, abundantly treed forest that extended well up into the towering mountains. A wide variety of hardwood trees grew tall and proud on the lower slopes. The largest of these were so thick in their girth that it took several men joining hands to circle their circumference.

As one climbed further up the mountain heights, the forest growth gave way to pine trees that stood like tall sentinels spreading across the middle slopes. The woods eventually gave way to a variety of scrub bush and a few stunted pines in the higher altitudes, and then finally to mere rock face and the year-round snow of the peaks.

In the thick of the forest, however, excepting for an occasional expanse of meadow, it was difficult to find a place where you could even see the sky above. The dense forest was perpetually shadowed and it was an eerie and disorienting place to be in. A person could easily lose their way among the giant trees, and a shrouded mist often rose from the ground to hang in the air, hovering and pulsating, like a living thing.

The forest was also home to an abundant wildlife population. There were a countless variety of birds, grazing deer and elk, and dozens of other gentle creatures that shared their habitat with a wide variety of not-so-gentle animals. There were mountain lions, bears, wild boars, foxes, and wolves that made their home here and found their sustenance. The forest provided a prime example of Mother Nature's food chain of grazers and predators.

These animals also shared their forests with those of the human race, or rather, refugees and recluses who were trying to escape from it. In the lush forests of the Euralene Mountains of Varakov, there lived those who sought a safe haven away from the cruelties of the outside world of mankind, a Sanctuary.

*   *   *

As they passed through, the Pack had left a large portion of their clean kill with the garrison at the gap fortress. The garrison commander would see to it that the meat was carefully packed with blocks of ice taken from the glacier field in the upper reaches of the neighbouring mountain in preparation for this cargo and then covered over with straw as it was loaded onto carts and wagons. He would also see to the transport down the mountain to the king's castle located at the Mesa-of-the-Moon on the coastal plains. The ice and straw would ensure that the shipment of meat was kept fresh on its journey to the castle.

After exiting the gap fortress through the western gates, the Pack members had slipped away in the pre-morning darkness, on the way to their communal cave with the remainder of their haul of carcasses in tow.

The black-robed raiders from the Skolish incursion who followed behind them, however, remained overnight with the garrison until the sun rose skyward. The hired mercenaries maintained a silent watch over their captives in a corner of the fortress compound. They didn't mingle with the Varakovan soldiers, who'd been ordered back to their duty stations. In fact, they regarded these conventional troops in an almost disdainful manner.

For their part, the garrison troops went about their assignments with nervous efficiency. They were seasoned soldiers in their own right, yet these foreign mercenaries who stood guard over their helpless prisoners created a degree of anxiety. They would be more than glad to see them go.

The garrison commander stood alone at the window of his barracks looking out over another section of the compound, where a squad of his men was preparing the wagons for shipment. Like the troops under his command, he too felt ill at ease. The olive-skinned mercenaries were only part of the reason, however.

The commander had followed Lord Victor's orders to the letter, but the sight of the deformed Pack members as they'd passed through the gates dragging their loads of carcasses had sent shivers of dread running through him. He knew it was best that his men went about the business of packing the meat into the wagons, not knowing of its origins. They were better off not knowing what he did.

The commander had found the glowing red eyes of the creatures the most haunting detail of all. Despite having been forewarned by the Varakovan king as to what he should expect to see, he had been unsettled by the sight. It had been truly unnerving to see those wolf-men as they strode past wearing only bloodstained rags over their savagely transformed bodies, guarded by those fierce looking four-legged warg-wolves on their flanks. It was a haunting vision, one which would likely visit his dreams for several nights to come.

The commander could only be thankful that they weren't his enemies and that they all served the same master, Lord Victor.

*   *   *

The breaking of the dawn brought the Pack members to their knees, as if in a final tribute to the Goddess Diana's passing. The intense agony they suffered so stoically during their transition back to a "normal" state seemed overly cruel, however.

The Pack leader's concern for the injured youth was forgotten for a time, as the all-consuming transformation set in for him and his similarly afflicted comrades. The Pack endured bone-aching chills, coupled with burning fevers, profuse sweating, and crippling nausea. Their bodies convulsed horribly as bone and muscle groups reverted in painful spasms. The members of the Pack felt the pressures building uncontrollably within them. The racing of blood streams threatened to burst their arteries and veins apart, if not their hearts. Their eardrums pounded. They bled from their noses and mouths, and the excess hair shed from their bodies, as if they were moulting.

When at last the tortuous event was over, they lay where they'd dropped for quite some time. They were soaked in their own sweat and blood, and in the filth and dried blood of their respective hunts. They were slow to recover, but finally, one by one, they got themselves to the back of the cave, where an underground mountain stream surfaced to form a small pool of running water.

Showing little or no modesty, the humans among them stripped off their rags and stepped into the fresh mountain water to bathe and refresh their selves. The water in the cavern pool was frigid, but it was also invigorating. It helped in reviving them from their stupors.

As they regained their strength and wits, the Pack members climbed out of the pool and dried themselves off. They then went about a communal group grooming, where hair and nails were clipped, and those with beards had them cut back to more modest lengths. Other extraneous body hair brought on during the transformation tended to shed off on its own accord. The hair would be swept up along with the other gore while those who had suffered wounds were attended to. There were well-stocked supplies of salves, bandages, and splints that were kept on hand for just that purpose.

These physical traumas were seldom overly severe. They usually paled in comparison to the mental and emotional strain that each of the humans and wolves alike had to endure. The rage, the madness, and the hunger were all but gone now. In their place, numbness, fatigue, and disorientation usually set in. The living nightmare that was brought on by three nights of full-moon affliction was over, at least for another lunar month.

Once stripped of their rags, bathed, and groomed, the humans looked pretty much like any other group of naked men and women. Except, perhaps, that as a group they bore more than their fair share of scars and healed-over wounds. Many of these past injuries were evident as the members of the group went about retrieving their clean clothes that had been previously hung on the pegs imbedded in the cave walls.

They dressed slowly and mechanically. Each of them seemed distant from the others and lost in their own thoughts, as if they were still awakening from a trance. It was always this way following the reversion.

The Pack leader moved with slightly more purpose. Stripping off his rags with a disgusted grunt, he had hurriedly washed and dressed before moving off to attend to the injured youth. The last item that he put on after he'd changed into his clean clothes was a chain of gold that he carefully fastened about his neck. There was a finely detailed emerald-green amulet suspended from it.

Woodrow stared at the intricately carved wolf-head image for a long moment. As it had when he'd first received the amulet, it occurred to the Pack leader again that the type of gem was not one he was familiar with. He was almost convinced that it was not of this world, if that were possible, for the jewel had properties unlike any other known gem. He only knew for sure that it was Lord Victor who had found it, arranged for its carving, and had presented it to him to wear. What Woodrow didn't know was that the amulet design was the work of a skilled artisan who had done an admirable job of capturing a wolf's essence in his work. Nor did he know that the gifted craftsman had been discreetly employed by Lord Victor to make several individually crafted amulets out of what appeared to be broken shards of some foreign gemstone.

Although the artisan too had been unfamiliar with the emerald-green, opaque pieces he'd been given to work with, he'd completed his task in just over a month. The craftsman had been especially proud of the wolf-head piece, and Lord Victor had praised his workmanship highly, just before having the man quietly put to death in the dungeons beneath the ominous castle tower.

The Pack leader tucked the amulet into his shirt and moved silently to where the still unconscious youth lay. He struggled to keep his focus on the task at hand as he sought to regain his full senses. He untied and then stripped the youth. He then carried him over and roughly washed his sweat-soaked and blood-stained body by the communal pool. With somewhat greater care, he then carefully removed the filthy shirting covering the injured limb and cleansed the leg wound, before drying the youth off and treating the injury with a salve. When he was finished he tied a large strip of clean cloth bandaging around it to stanch the fresh bleeding. It would have to do, at least until they reached the mountain retreat and the supply of more serious medicines kept there.

Brutus was standing beside his mate, but he was keeping a close eye on the Pack leader as he bundled the youth up, and then strapped him back into the travois. Sensing that Woodrow was preparing to leave, the large alpha wolf moved in closer and looked at him with a steady, reproachful gaze. There was no questioning the animal's intent. If the Pack leader was going off into the mountains, the Pack's enforcer was fully prepared to tag along.

The Pack leader stared back at his four-legged comrade for a moment and then knelt down and roughly rubbed the animal's head and neck.

"Yes, Brutus, my old friend," he said with a weary but indulgent smile, "you can go with me to the cabin, but then you've got to return to your mate and help care for those offspring of yours. They need you, too."

It wasn't necessary for the Pack leader to give instructions for the remaining kill to be distributed throughout the Pack. The remaining carcasses would be divided up equitably amongst them and then dragged off in pieces to dens by the wolves or carted off by the humans to their respective homes. The Pack shared equally in all prey that was taken down.

If food was ever scarce, first the young would be fed, and then the healthiest adults would eat next. The weak and the old would be fed last, or in the worst of conditions, not at all. This was an instinctive response of all wolf packs that helped ensure their long-term survival.

"Be sure to arrange to have a few sheep dropped off to the Old Man and his people," Woodrow reminded his aide, as he strapped himself back into the travois harness.

Simon nodded his head, indicating that he would see to it. The Pack lieutenant's chiselled jaws were clean shaven. His freshly scrubbed auburn hair hung damply down to his shoulders with a healthy sheen, but he looked as weary as the Pack leader felt.

"And make sure he's told to have the meat well cooked. We don't want anybody getting sick from it," the Pack leader added, with a touch of irony.

He signalled for his lieutenant to accompany him. With Brutus at his side, Woodrow lifted the wooden handles on the sturdy travois and began dragging his unconscious passenger out of the cavern. The three Pack comrades emerged together into a crisp dawn in the Euralenes. The trio took a few moments to breathe the fresh mountain air deeply into their lungs, knowing instinctively that it would help to clear their minds.

"There's more, Simon," the Pack leader prompted quietly.

Woodrow's lieutenant, and his long-time comrade, stepped forward and acknowledged their leader with a bow of his head. It was the beta male's way of showing his submission to the Pack leader's authority. Despite their long friendship, Simon was always properly respectful. He waited patiently for his further instructions.

"Have someone else take the meat to the Old Man. I want you to accompany Barozzi's men and the wagons to the castle in my stead," Woodrow said. "You're to report to Lord Victor and extend to him my sincere apologies. Tell him that I am detained further on a personal matter, but that I shall return to my duties as soon as I am able to."

"He won't be pleased, Woodrow," his long-time aide warned.

"I know it, but it can't be helped." He clasped the man's arm in a gesture of brotherhood.

"I need to tend to the youth while there still might be time. He's lost a lot of blood. The Mesa-of-the-Moon is a full day and a half's journey. He wouldn't make it," the Pack leader stated. "Keep your eyes and ears open, Simon. These raids still don't make any sense to me. I'm still not clear as to why Lord Victor ordered us to make these raids into Medinia, or why he would send Barozzi and his men to attack farms in Skoland in the guise of being Medinians. He's never meddled in their affairs before. He's up to something and this is only the beginning of it. I can feel it."

"I sense it, too," Simon agreed, with an insightful shake of his head. The king's actions of late were a cause for concern for all of them.

The Pack lieutenant stretched out his arms and yawned mightily. Like the others, he found that the morning-afters were hard to bounce back from.

"We can be sure that Barozzi and his raiders acted out their roles as Medinian troops for reasons other than mere deception," he added. "The evidence that they were ordered to leave behind them may well cause the Skolish to believe that Medinia is behind the raids. If the Skolish fall for it, they'll likely retaliate and the war between them will escalate again."

"The question that puzzles me too is why Lord Victor would want that," he pondered aloud, with a shrug of his shoulders. "What does he have to gain that's worth the risk?"

"You always did have a good nose for trouble, my friend," the Pack leader said. "And, I think there's a shit load of it brewing out there."

"I shall serve as the Pack's eyes and ears for you, Woodrow," Simon promised. "I'll learn what I can."

"Just be careful doing it, and tread softly," Woodrow reminded him. "The castle can be a dangerous place—even for a wolf like you."

The two men paused to take in the majestic view surrounding them. Their breaths seem to hang in the crisp mountain air. Even though it was summer, the morning sun brought little warmth to this altitude. The snow-caps above them on the mountain peaks might retreat somewhat at this time each year, but they still remained perpetually covered, even in the hottest of summers.

The Pack leader and Brutus took their leave then. Simon remained behind watching them off as he stood outside the cave entrance. He understood Woodrow's concern for the injured youth he dragged behind him, but he knew the Pack leader was risking the king's disapproval. The other Pack members would be joining him briefly as they emerged from the cavern in smaller groups. He would pass on Woodrow's instructions to those concerned as they began their own journeys home.

*　　　　　*　　　　　*

As the Pack's two alpha members were working their way along the tree line, the Pack leader turned to his long time four-legged comrade and spoke to him quietly. There was a touch of unease in his voice.

"Brutus, my old friend, I think that our lord and master may have designs outside our borders that go far beyond these raids. Victor has grown more and more remote from me. He's delving into areas that worry me greatly. And that damn coven of his, they're feeding his powers somehow."

"That's more for the worst, I fear," he added. "I suspect that these new experiments he's been conducting have entered the realm of the black arts. Those damn warlocks and their perverse hags he's gathered around him have knowledge of arcane rituals and ancient spells. The Pack will have to be on its guard, lest we get caught up in schemes that are not of our choosing, and which might bring harm to this Sanctuary of ours."

The large alpha wolf gave the man an indulgent look, as if to say that he understood him and shared his concerns. Whether he actually did or not, the Pack's enforcer was certainly used to hearing the Pack leader's thoughts spoken aloud. On occasion, the wolf even put forth a vocal opinion of his own, albeit not necessarily on the subject at hand.

In Varakov proper, Woodrow bore important responsibilities in his role as Lord Victor's castle keeper, but to Brutus, the man was simply the Pack leader. He had always been so, ever since that distant day when tragic events had left just the two of them alive. The wolf had been just a yearling cub, back when it had all begun for them.

Today, the alpha wolf just uttered a low growl in response to the Pack leader's words.

"I know. I know," Woodrow said. "More walk and less talk. Let's get our young friend here to the cabin and see what we can do for him, shall we?"

For a time, they followed a faint mountain trail leading northward and away from the pass, until they found a suitable spot to enter the great forest itself. The Pack members were at home in the dark woodland.

As the two unlikely traveling companions disappeared into the trees, they no longer followed a discernable trail now, but rather they seemed to flow through the forest much like a stream would, bending and winding along the course of least resistance, until it reached its destination.

*   *   *

Simon remained at the cavern entrance long enough to kiss his wife good-bye yet again. Thankfully, she was an understanding woman. Her name was

Tiffany, and she was his lifelong mate. She was a tall, slender woman of high standing within the Pack but whose natural beauty was marred by a large wine-stain birthmark that almost covered the entire one side of her face and neck.

The Pack's beta-male saw past this superficial blemish. He knew the goodness that lay in Tiffany's heart, and in her manner. Most people of the outside world could not do that. They thought she carried the mark of the devil on her face. People were either terribly cruel to her, or else they were deathly afraid of her. It was one of the reasons that they'd sought out this refuge rumoured to be a safe haven.

That was one reason. The other reason, of course, was the undeniable affliction that was brought upon them by the three-night cycle of the full moon. It was, perhaps, the greater reason of the two.

The Pack lieutenant promised her that he would return before the next cycle of the moon arrived. Tiffany smiled indulgently and told him it was okay, that she understood. She then kissed her husband long and passionately. She understood that Simon had to split his time between the duties required by Woodrow and the kingdom and those he devoted to her and the others in Sanctuary. She loved him all the more for the responsibilities he took on without complaint.

With a final hug and another quick kiss, she saw him off down the mountain trail, which would take him back down to the gap fortress. The tears didn't start until he was around the bend and out of sight.

When Simon reached the mountain stronghold, he was passed through the western gates and then escorted to the garrison commander. He found the raider leader waiting there, as well. The olive-skinned mercenary was armed with at least three visible weapons, the most distinctive and deadly being the curved scimitar housed in the ornate scabbard that was strapped to his waist. The head mercenary wore his oiled, jet-black hair tied back in a ponytail and held in place by an ornate barrette. His coal black eyes flashed with annoyance as he paced near the window, impatient to be on his way.

"Where's your master?" Barozzi demanded gruffly, as soon as Simon entered the room. "He's supposed to be riding to the castle with us this morning."

The Pack lieutenant chose not to recognize the raider's implied authority.

He ignored him, opting rather to report to the garrison commander, patiently waiting behind his desk.

"Woodrow extends his apologies, commander," he said politely, "but he is called away to other duties. He has instructed me to accompany the wagons to the castle and to report to Lord Victor in his place."

"Well, I don't think that's appropriate," Barozzi protested. "He has his orders to attend to the king following our missions."

The garrison commander waved off the mercenary's objection as he pushed back his chair and got to his feet. The commander recognized the courtesy being extended to him by the Pack member, Simon. Further, he'd known Woodrow for several years and knew the importance of his position in Varakov.

The commander was also familiar with many of the people who dwelt in the nearby mountain Sanctuary at the king's forbearance. He'd always found them dutiful and honest in their dealings with the fortress. The garrison traded with them fairly regularly. The mercenaries, on the other hand, were another matter. He had no love for them, nor did he intend to bend his knee to their leader.

"My orders," the commander said, looking at the raider sternly, "were to have your wagons loaded and ready to move out today. They are. Your orders, in case I need to remind you, were to wait here until morning came and the castle keeper was ready to report in to Lord Victor. As I recall, it was never specified that he must do so in person. If Woodrow has chosen to send that report in with his second-in-command, then I'm sure that he has sufficient reason to do so. It is also my understanding," he added, "that the members of the Pack have lived in these mountain forests long before you ever came along. They are Lord Victor's friends and they have given loyal service to his highness. I think it is for the king alone to decide what is appropriate, especially when it comes to his long-term associates."

The commander's not-so-subtle reminder to the raider as to his place in the greater scheme of things didn't sit well with him, but there was no further recourse for the mercenary. Barozzi gave both men a sour look as he turned on his heels and left them to go and see to the loading of his prisoners.

The mercenary leader fumed inside. He took some solace in knowing that the Skolish captives would be driven the last leg of their journey in wagons, which were actually little more than large iron cages on wheels. They would get their first view of Varakov from behind sturdy bars, and he and his men would be well compensated for completing a successful mission.

Behind him, the Pack's lieutenant remained long enough to thank the garrison commander for his support in the matter. He also expressed his appreciation for the commander's assistance in handling the Pack's travel out and back through the fortress with due discretion. He knew that the fewer people who saw them in their transformed state, the better off they all were.

"The return of you and your comrades was a sight that my men were best not to have seen," the garrison commander replied. "To be perfectly honest with you, I wish that I hadn't been witness to it either. You and your kind have my sympathies, Simon. Yours must be a terrible burden to bear."

The Pack lieutenant nodded his head slightly.

"It can be that." he agreed.

Once outside again, Simon walked across the compound towards the small train of five wagons and carts, and the troop of mercenaries now sitting on horseback. Preparations for their departure were almost complete.

The last seven captives were being herded aboard the rear-most wagon and locked up inside. The Pack lieutenant made his way past them and then along the side of the other prisoner wagons. He figured to ride up front with one of the drivers of the meat-laden carts. It was more appealing to him than sitting overhead of the unfortunate men and women who were held captive and terrified behind their iron bars.

As he approached the lead wagon of captives, however, the Skolish mother with her two daughters called out to him. She implored him for some water and something to eat for her children. Simon paused for only a moment and then turned about and went back to a nearby out-building. He returned a few minutes later with three large goatskin water-bags and several loaves of freshly baked bread. He passed an equal share of each through the bars to the woman and then moved to the next prisoner wagon to do the same.

After the Pack lieutenant had dropped off bread and a water-bag to the middle wagon, he moved on in turn to the last wagon. He was about to hand in the much welcome repast when the raider leader stepped up and grabbed hold of his arm.

"The prisoners are my responsibility, wolf-man," Barozzi snarled. "I say when, and if, they're to get any food and water."

Simon stood perfectly still. He did not resist. He simply stared at the mercenary's hand where it gripped his arm and then uttered a low growl from deep in the back of his throat.

The raider leader pulled his hand back as if he'd just been scalded.

"I think a little bread and water is appropriate now, don't you?" the Pack lieutenant stated. His eyes flared menacingly.

Not bothering to wait for a reply, Simon finished passing the items through the bars to the eager hands inside.

"And," Simon advised the mercenary then, "I'm sure Lord Victor would want his trophies to arrive in decent condition."

"Perhaps you're right, wolf-man," Barozzi conceded sullenly, glaring at the Pack's lieutenant all the while. "I suppose the condemned should get a last meal."

The raider leader laughed harshly as he strode off towards his horse, where he then quickly mounted.

"Move them out," he hollered abruptly.

The wagon drivers cracked their whips in near unison at his command and Simon was forced to run to catch up to one of the covered meat-carts as it pulled out behind the mounted robed warriors at the head of the column. The remainder of the mercenaries fell in behind the last prisoner wagon to guard the rear of the small convoy.

Simon managed to pull himself up onto the seat and then sat silently in thought alongside the driver. He caught the look of malevolence, however, which the raider leader sent his way as Barozzi rode past to take his position at the head of the column.

The Pack lieutenant realized that he'd likely just made himself an enemy. That fact didn't bother him unduly, however. He had little respect for these men-for-hire anyway.

The small convoy left the confines of the garrison fortress and started down the forest road at a steady pace. They were soon gone from sight, seemingly swallowed up by the immense trees.

*   *   *

The forest closed in on the convoy almost immediately, despite the roadway that had been cut through it. High overhead, the trees on either side of the road almost came together again, as their spreading branches formed a canopy. The little ambient light that filtered down through the leaves only served to make the forest around them appear even darker, more mysterious, and more sinister.

The Skolish captives shared their water and bread rations, but they consumed them in silence. The eerie world of the mighty forest overwhelmed their senses. They'd clearly overheard Barozzi's callous comment concerning their condemned state, and each of them struggled with that dire thought. Their lives, so routine until now, were in the hands of people they barely knew existed prior to their abductions. Those thoughts fed their misery and despair as much as the bread did their empty bellies.

Barozzi gave the outwardly appearance of calm and control as he rode at the head of the convoy. Inwardly, he was anything but calm. The mercenary was anxious and impatient. They were forced to rein in the pace of their horses to accommodate the plodding wagons. It left him feeling naked and exposed on this narrow road. If an enemy were to attack out of the woods, he and his raiders would be decimated before they even knew what was happening.

This dense, dark forest was alien to him. It was a far cry from anything they had known back in their native homeland. The raider leader hated the feeling of helpless fear that had settled in his belly, and he hated the way the forest shadows appeared to move along with them. Even more, he detested the fact that his fears were shared with those of their prisoners.

The hair on the back of his neck bristled and his sixth sense told him that they were being watched. Varakov was the undisputed kingdom of Lord Victor, and their wagons carried the king's banner, so logic told him that no one would dare attack them. His instinct for his own personal survival, however, urged him to be out of this place as quickly as possible. Unfortunately, he knew it would be several hours before they would be clear of the wooded mountainside.

Simon was the only person in the small procession who wasn't the least bit concerned by the dense forest. This was part of Sanctuary. This was his home. The forests and the mountain range were the Pack's domain, and they roamed within it freely. He and his wife and the others of their kind were quite happy here. The wildlife in the forests and meadows was abundant, and the hunting was usually good. Nevertheless, the Pack lieutenant found himself brooding once more as to the king's reasoning for these foul raids across the mountain border.

Simon didn't understand the purpose of taking Skolish prisoners. For that matter, he didn't comprehend the purpose of the farm raids, either. He knew that the meat they brought back wasn't needed. There was plenty of game here in Varakov, not to mention the abundance of domesticated herds and flocks in the foothills and on the farms of the coastal plains below.

There was no answer forthcoming for the moment, however, and as for Barozzi's feeling that the small convoy he led was being watched, it was. Indeed, every bird, every animal, even every insect in the area knew that they were passing through the great forest. The noise of the horses and the wagons, the smell of the fresh kill on ice in the carts, and the smell of the fear of the captives announced their presence for all the forest's inhabitants.

Some of the eyes watching them belonged to another group who resided here in Sanctuary along with the natural wildlife and the members of the Pack. This was the group that was mostly made up of refugees from the outside world. They were the people of the Old Man's clan, the ones that were called the Oddities.

Sanctuary was a retreat where misfits and troubled souls and those persecuted for their religious beliefs could find a refuge to live out their lives in peace. Some had been invited to come here, while others had found the way here on their own.

It was understandable to Simon that armed convoys like theirs passing through the heart of the forest refuge would be watched and their intentions evaluated. He knew these dense woods. He knew the people who lived here, and they in turn knew him. He had no concern for his safety, at least not here in the forest.

Once they reached the Mesa-of-the-Moon and Lord Victor's castle, now that was another matter.

*   *   *

The forest ended abruptly on the next mountain north of the pass and about a third of the way up the slopes of the peak. The Pack leader and his two traveling companions finally broke clear of the trees about five and a half hours after they'd set out. It had been a long and difficult trek following the rigors of the transformation.

The two who were still walking and conscious were each visibly drained, having traveled a great distance without any sleep. The human was the more depleted of the two, due to the harnessed load that he bore. The last bit of rest that the pair had gotten had been a long time back when they'd been holed up during the daylight hours before the last Medinian farm raid.

They emerged out of the darkness of the dense forest and into the light of day. One moment they were encompassed by trees, and then the next few steps brought them out into a broad mountain meadow. The change was dazzling. Bright sunlight bounced off a golden field, ripe with the blooms of wildflowers. To then gaze up at the snow-capped peak was painful to their adjusting pupils. The icy whiteness sparkled with the glittering refraction of the sun's rays.

The man and the wolf paused to rest as they quietly took in their new surroundings. Although they'd experienced this spectacular scene countless times, they never ceased to feel the serenity and harmony of what nature had created here. Each time they stepped from the mighty forest into this enclave, they felt a primal stirring, akin to that of a rebirth. It was a sensation of both innocence and wonder.

For the Pack leader, this was his home away from home. It was his private piece of Sanctuary. It was a place where he came to rest or to study and experiment with his many medicinal remedies. It was a retreat away from the demands of his duties at the castle, and those to the Pack. Understandably, considering those weighty responsibilities, he didn't get up here nearly as often as he would have liked.

In accordance with his role as the keeper of the castle, Woodrow resided in a splendid manor home, sited just east of the Mesa, where the Varakovan castle stood. It was ideally situated, he often mused. He was close enough to be at Lord Victor's beck and call, and he was well located for his monthly lunar departures when his Pack duties were called for. Both roles he played were demanding of his time and energy.

Up here in the mountains, however, he was at peace. When the royal court of Varakov wasn't sitting, and he had time off from his official duties, he invariably came to this mountain retreat. It was only in this hideaway that he was able to put aside the demands of his dual duties.

Brutus led the way as Woodrow wearily dragged the travois up through the shale-based meadow. The mountain lea grew upon an ancient rockslide that in its time had pushed the forest lower down the slopes. As the unlikely duo of man and wolf crested the ridge at the top of the meadow with their injured cargo in tow, they found themselves overlooking a huge gorge, where a spectacular waterfall cascaded down the cliff of the mountain on the far side.

From where they stood, it appeared as if a huge slice of the mountain had simply fallen off and been sent tumbling down the far slope into an abyss. In fact, that was very nearly what had occurred in the region. In the distant past, these mountains had risen up in a vast shifting of the earth's plates. During the ensuing centuries, several dozen earthquakes and aftershocks had rocked the land. One such quake had caused an entire face of the opposing peak to fall away.

The melting snows of summer fed myriad streams whose waters collected for a time in a large mountain tarn. The thawing lake then emptied itself at the distant breach, and like a funnel, sent its overflow cascading over the cliff that was formed by the quake. This undeniable force of nature eroded away the rock below where the tumbling waters struck. The result of this continual barrage over the centuries was the deep gorge they looked down upon now.

The Pack leader had constructed his retreat here, but he had chosen not to build it facing to the west. If he had, he would have overlooked the beautiful meadow and the mighty forest. He would have also looked down over Varakov. His view would have encompassed the foothills below and then out across the farmlands that spread across the coastal plains. It would have even given him a view of the distant coastline and the endless ocean beyond.

Woodrow had chosen not to do that. He didn't want to look down upon the distant bustling harbour town of Port Lupus, which thrived upon the trade from the shipping lanes and from its fishing fleets and ship building. Nor did he wish a view of the solitary mount commonly known as the Mesa-of-the-Moon, which rose some two miles to the north and east of the town. He was well aware that Lord Victor's castle loomed there, casting its authority across the land.

Rather, the solitary man by nature had chosen to build his cabin just over the ridge, where a rock shelf jutted out high above the gorge. He'd discovered this hidden enclave while exploring the mountain many years before, and he'd fallen in love with the isolated view. With the help of a few trusted companions, he'd constructed his hidden retreat to be a part of the mountain ridge, where it could withstand the seasons, nature's storms, and time itself.

They'd hauled eight solid oak beams cut two feet by two feet square and twenty-five feet long. They'd then dug out and embedded the beams into the upper ridge to an equal depth, at intervals of four feet. The beams protruded some ten feet above the rock shelf and were notched into the top of support posts that were firmly set into the rock ledge. From that basic framework, they'd constructed walls, the cabin floor, windows, and the doorway. When they planked the roof across the beams, they'd created a slope for drainage and covered it all with a base of rock and gravel. They'd then added enough soil for the meadow grasses to take root. In less than a year, the roof had become a simple extension of the ridge overhang, and virtually indistinguishable from it. Even the chimney they'd constructed escaped into a mound of rocks and shrubs that camouflaged the outlet and diffused the smoke whenever the fireplace was in use.

The front of the concealed cabin faced due east. When he sat outside on the porch, Woodrow's gaze crossed the remaining rock shelf that protruded beyond the cabin and then out over the gorge towards the opposing breach in the mountain, where the tarn that sourced the falls sent its waters tumbling to the rocks and river far below.

If he were to get up from his perch on the porch and walk down to the edge of the shelf, Woodrow could see where the waterfall crashed into the gorge and where perpetual mists rose on the rocks far below. Looking straight out from the porch, the Pack leader was simply in awe of the majestic view of the Euralene Mountain range. His retreat was surrounded by steep rock faces rising high above the tree lines, which in turn gave way to the perpetually snow-bound caps where the mighty peaks met the sky.

Woodrow felt small and unimportant here. It was a perspective that brought him great peace of mind. This valued retreat was seldom shared with anyone, except perhaps with Brutus, as it should be. Their two lives were entwined, and they had been for over a century now.

The two companions made their way carefully down a faint trail, which brought them around the ridge to the front of the cabin. The Pack leader unhitched the travois and gratefully eased his load to the ground. He was exhausted but strangely refreshed at the same time. It felt good to be back, whatever the circumstances.

He undid the straps that held the youth in place and then lifted him up and carried him onto the porch, where he carefully balanced him in his arms as he lifted the simple latch and pushed the cabin door open with his foot. There was no need for locked doors up here.

Still, the Pack enforcer passed him by and entered first, looking around the cabin carefully and sniffing at the stale air. Satisfied that things were as they had left them, Brutus came back and settled into the doorway as Woodrow lay the injured youth onto one of the beds and then opened the windows to let in some fresh air.

The alpha wolf took up a position that was half in and half out of the cabin. His head rested upon his front paws outside on the porch. It spoke something about the wolf's nature. He was a wild and feral predator, yet he was totally devoted to the human that he acknowledged as his Pack leader.

*   *   *

At about that same time, Barozzi and the raider's convoy had finally cleared the great forest as well, albeit in another direction entirely. The road they travelled led into a series of open foothills, orchards and grazing lands. As the convoy of prisoners broke free of the trees, they felt as if they were awakening from a deep, troubled dream. They still had a lengthy trip ahead of them, and a stopover for the night along the way, but at least the warmth of the summer sun felt inviting on their faces after the eerie, dark, and dankness of the forbidding forest.

From the upper foothills, the convoy was afforded a dazzling clear view over the coastal plains of Varakov. The Skolish prisoners strained to see what they could of their captor's domain. Through the bars of the wagons, they could see the road that lay ahead as it wound down through foothill pastures and orchards. In the plains farther below, the road followed a river that slowly wound its way through the farmlands for a lengthy distance. The captives had no way of knowing that this was the Varden River, one of the main commercial arteries through the kingdom of Varakov.

There were a series of arched bridges that spanned the river at various intervals, but the main road continued to follow the river's course until it wound back towards the distant bay on the coast of the vast ocean. Although it was still many leagues distant, from this elevation they were afforded their first glimpse of a distant ship's sails as it was putting into the natural harbour formed on the jagged coastline.

Several of the prisoners commented in hushed voices that the landmass surrounding the distant harbour bore a strong resemblance to a wolf's head, with the harbour entrance serving as its gaping mouth. Their observations were, in fact, quite accurate. It was why the thriving harbour town bore the name of Port Lupus.

Not yet in view, one of the last bridges that spanned the Varden River in the distance led to another roadway. This road approached the solitary mesa that stood alone and towered over the coastal plains. It was the road the captive's convoy would be taking on the last leg of their journey, on the morrow.

From this elevation, the mesa didn't look like much. It had once been a coastal mountain, which time and the elements had reduced to the level-top mount it was now. Despite this weathering over eons, the mesa still stood high enough to dominate the coastal plains and was afforded its own view to the coast and the harbour town below. Only the relatively younger chain of Euralene Mountain peaks towered over it to the east.

At this distance, the prisoners were also unaware of the ancient castle that was built against one face of the Mesa-of-the-Moon, as the solitary mount was better known. It was there that the captives were being taken, and it was there that their fates would be decided. Perhaps it was just as well that they didn't know about their destination for the time being. They would be finding that out soon enough.

For now, the long trip down into the plains was uneventful. The convoy joined the river road, where the carts and prisoner wagons rolled past pastures of grazing livestock and through a variety of farm fields with their abundant summer crops. The fields appeared much the same as those they'd come from back in Skoland. The farmsteads were of varying size, from large landowner estates down to the smaller yeoman, or free farmer holdings. Even the least of these had homes and barns that were well kept and prosperous looking.

Seeing this abundance, Simon was again reminded that the raid for Medinian livestock made no sense. It still bothered him. He supposed that he'd just have to wait until he met with Lord Victor to discover the answer to that puzzle.

The wagons rolled through the countryside without mishap. They passed by several sturdy, stone country churches whose spires rose towards the heavens. They rolled past farms and people moving their commerce by way of the river road, or out on the river itself, in barges laden with produce. They rolled on through small towns and villages where the inhabitants were going about their everyday business.

The Varakovans that the prisoners saw came from all walks of life, just like back home. There were farm serfs, landowners and their families, bargemen, and monks and friars going about their pious duties. The one attribute that all these foreigners seemed to share was a devout aversion to looking at the prison wagons as they were passing by. It was as if they were afraid that they would be inviting trouble upon themselves if they showed any interest in the heavily guarded convoy.

It was late into the evening when they finally stopped at the outskirts of one of the pleasant country villages. They would spend a comfortable night in an inn there before continuing their journey in the morning. At least Barozzi and most of his men would. The prisoners were left huddled in the barred wagons stored in the stable and under the guard of two of raiders who had lost the coin toss to determine who drew the boring duty.

It was only because they had no authority over him that Simon wasn't prevented from bringing the captives additional food and water. It was only his personal threat directed at the two guards, which allowed the captives out of the wagons in supervised turns to relieve themselves in some form of privacy.

It had been a long day and prior night. When he had done what he could for the Skolish captives, the Pack lieutenant gladly retired for the night. He slept soundly on the straw in the stable loft.

Had he known the ultimate fate that was in store for these hapless prisoners, it would have been a different matter entirely.

*   *   *

July 25, 1461
Varakov

It was mid-afternoon before the convoy of Skolish captives and the load of Medinian meat arrived at the last bridge spanning the Varden River, before it reached the coastal harbour of Port Lupus. It was here that they would take the new road on the far side of the river. The wagons and their mounted mercenary escort were forced to wait for a time on the river road, until a troop of Varakovan knights finished crossing over the long, seven-arched stone bridge that echoed with the clattering of their steed's iron-soled hooves. The knights wore their light armour and chain mail beneath cloaks of a deep indigo blue with an embroidered rising sun over snow-capped mountain peaks crested on the back.

The Varakovan knights paid the prisoner convoy no more attention than they would have wagons filled with produce, although Simon did notice several less-than-friendly looks that were exchanged between a number of the knights and the mounted mercenaries. Barozzi and his men had that effect on most people.

When the troop of Varakovan knights had finally trotted past them, a surly Barozzi gave the signal to move on past the cloud of dust they left in their wake. The wagons followed dutifully behind them as the raider leader and his men crossed the bridge and took the right fork in the road that led towards the solitary mesa.

For a short time, only the heights of the Mesa-of-the-Moon were visible up ahead, but as they grew closer, the captives could make out the high walls and begin to see the distinctive features of the distant castle. Even from afar, the central tower of the castle appeared to climb up the entire mesa cliff face itself.

The ancient, fortified castle grew in stature the nearer the convoy approached. When the wagons finally rolled to a stop at the outer gates, a pair of massive walls with scores of arrow loops, parapets, and battlements loomed high overhead. The town and the castle that were secured behind them rose up further still, in ominous, gothic grandeur. To all the Skolish captives, the formidable Mesa-of-the-Moon castle fortress appeared utterly impregnable to assault.

The roadway brought the convoy to a heavy drawbridge in its lowered position, spanning an engineered moat lined along its bottom with heavy iron spikes. Beyond this, a pair of heavy, ironbound gates were set into massive stonewalls some twelve feet thick. The fortified gatehouse was well-manned and diligent guards dutifully inspected all who came and went.

The well-defended outer wall was in the shape of a large arc that bowed out from the southern face of the Mesa-of-the-Moon. The gates of these stern outer defences opened upon a bustling castle-town with inns, taverns, and a variety of open markets with booths and stalls for tradesmen and artisans.

Well inside that outer ring, an even taller second wall rose up with its own massively encased gateway that led into the castle proper. There was no direct approach that led from the outer gates to the gates of the inner wall. It was necessary to pass through the maze of winding, crookback streets and the labyrinth of lanes and alleys of the town first.

This purposefully staggered construction was intended to slow down any enemy that somehow managed to breach the well-defended outer walls. It was designed to bring any invaders under fire from the inner wall's parapets, while they fought their way through the streets and lanes below. If an enemy force somehow managed to overcome the outer wall defences, or to breach its gates, they would find themselves confined in the streets beneath the main garrison and thus exposed to a murderous deluge of further defensive measures.

The knights of the Varakovan army were as efficient and capable as their counterparts in either Skoland or Medinia. In Varakov, however, they were assigned to the defence and safeguarding of the countryside, the fortified coastline, and the castle's outer walls. They were only permitted inside the castle's inner gates on rare occasion, and then only upon invitation by the Varakovan king. Lord Victor preferred to use another breed of men of arms to man the defensive positions of his inner sanctum.

To say the least, these men were a little rougher around the edges than the Varakovan knights. For the most part, they were a variety of hired mercenaries. For some years now, Lord Victor had been recruiting men of their ilk to his coastal kingdom. Many came from great distances, often by way of a lengthy sea voyage to provide their services. They came with battlefield experiences and with proficiency in all forms of weaponry. Some offered a variety of other skills as well—skills that the Varakovan king greatly valued and found ways to put to use.

As soldiers of fortune go, they were amply compensated. Equally important to the mercenaries were the diverse range of vices those generous wages could be spent on. It was often said that armed service in Varakov was a fighting man's dream. Wine, women, gambling, and virtually any other craving could be sated in their off-hours, especially in Port Lupus.

Between the Euralene Mountains and the great ocean, Lord Victor's rule was absolute, and absolutely unique. The harbour town of Port Lupus was a wide-open, sea-faring stopover, and the king allowed almost anyone to ply their trade there. The ship captains could sell their cargoes, and their passengers could sell their various services and wares. Everyone was welcome to partake in whatever legal or questionable commerce they chose to, for a price of course. All such commerce took place under Lord Victor's umbrella of protection. The king's enforcers saw to it that any activity, legal or otherwise, was protected, provided that a fair share was paid out. In this manner, a portion of all Port Lupus transactions found their timely way into the kingdom's royal coffers.

These king's enforcers were a large, well organized gang known as the Multinationals. The gang had their hand in every enterprise in Port Lupus and in the castle town's markets. Even out in the countryside, there were river and road usage fees. The higher-ranking members of the gang were known collectively as the Ohs and the gang's leaders were diligent in seeing that Lord Victor's interests were well accounted for.

The cash influx easily paid for the services of the mercenaries and the wages of the soldiers, most of who then spent freely in their off-duty periods. It was a give and take arrangement that worked well. Lord Victor paid generously for their services, but the Varakovan king didn't tolerate getting less than he paid for.

The raider's convoy was carefully inspected by the guards on duty, therefore, before being admitted through the outer gates. The convoy's passing drew a few curious glances from the town merchants and tradesmen, but as in the countryside, it was not done overtly. Any speculations were either discussed quietly, or not at all, as the prisoner and meat wagons wound their way through the maze of streets to the inner gates.

Under the towering inner wall and its fortifications, the convoy was made to wait again while they underwent a fresh inspection at the second pair of massive gates. By this point, the captives were showing signs of increased anxiety. Their homes, and the lives they'd known, were now far away and out of reach. Any last hope they'd held of a rescue had disappeared as they entered through the gates of the inner walls. When the wagons were rolled into the courtyard and the massive gates were closed up again, the Skolish captives couldn't help but feel that they would never see their homeland again.

CHAPTER 4

LORD VICTOR

Always was and will always be
The future's right there in our history

July 25, 1461
Skoland and Medinia

A TROOP OF SOME thirty knights, led by Prince Paulo of Skoland, approached the river crossing near the cataracts. Unlike the red and white striped cloaks worn by the regular regiments of Skolish knights who were out scouring the kingdom, this particular troop wore the solid crimson red cloaks that designated them as the king's Royal Order of knights. Under the command of the king's son, these select knights were following the scant tracks of the raiding party, which led from the last decimated farm they'd investigated. There was no doubt in their minds as to who the culprits were that they were looking for. The faint trail was leading them to the river, and Medinia, on the other side. It was a clear violation of the recently agreed upon truce.

The Skolish knights were in a grim mood. They'd been on the trail of the raiding party for days now and so far all that they'd accomplished was to bury the dead at each farm they investigated. The last burial was for the old man found on the side of the trail they followed. Apparently, being this close to home, those responsible had abandoned their caution and left an unmistakable sign of their passing. An arrow bolt from a crossbow protruded from the old man's chest. The feather configuration was in the distinct blue and white colours of Medinia.

Sir Geoffrey Gaullé of the Royal Order of knights rode alongside the angry, brooding prince. His outrage at the raids on the civilian farmers was muted by the distracting ache in his backside, which came from subjecting his forty-year-old body for far, too many days in a hard saddle.

The barrel-chested knight commander sighed through his greying blond beard but never gave voice to the complaint. It wasn't in his nature. After all, his place was properly here, beside the young prince and heir to the throne, just as it had been his duty to serve in the king's personal guard when he was a young knight. Twenty-five years later, he was now their seasoned commander, second only in military position to the prince. As such, it was his sworn responsibility to advise and to protect Prince Paulo at all costs. His men were handpicked and they were trained under his watchful eye. The knights had to meet his rigid standards, for the Royal Order of knight's most sacred duty was to ensure the prince's safety and they were pledged to a man to lay down their lives for him, if need be.

"Sir Geoffrey!"

The call came from one of the riders on the flank about fifty yards out from the main body of knights.

The young prince joined up with the commander as he turned his steed's head and trotted towards the young knight who had summoned him. They reined their horses in where the knight had dismounted to better examine the ground.

"What have we got here, Francis?" the elder knight questioned as he got down stiffly from his mount.

The Skolish commander took a moment to stretch out his legs and arms, before walking over to see what the keen pair of youthful eyes had spotted. He could feel the pins and needles in his limbs as some of the feeling began to return to them.

"More tracks, sir," the young knight said. "The trail's been carefully swept away, but they missed a few more tracks here. They're still heading to the southwest."

As the Skolish commander started to bend down to take a closer look for himself, the king's only remaining heir interrupted him.

"Come on, Gaullé, it's obvious by now where they're heading," Prince Paulo called out impatiently.

The prince's normally clear blue eyes were hooded with barely suppressed ire and his horse pranced beneath him as if the war steed was more than ready to settle this matter now too.

"We have all the proof we need as to who's behind these damnable attacks on our frontier farm lands," Paulo swore bitterly.

The tall, blond-haired Skolish prince was impatient to be on their way to the river. The prince was half the commander's age and not the least bit saddle weary. He also had a seething anger fuelling his heated blood. He wanted to confirm that the Medinian raiding party had indeed crossed back into their own territory with their Skolish captives. They could then decide what form of reprisal action they would take in light of this violation of the truce.

It was perfectly clear to the Skolish prince that the enemy's stated desire to pursue a true peace between their two nations was a sham. His father would have to see that now and forget his idiotic notion of negotiating a peace accord. It was an old man's pipe dream. Good God, there was even talk of a marriage union between the two kingdoms!

"Get mounted," Paulo directed. "I want to get to the river crossing and see for certain that they've returned to Medinia."

The young Skolish prince turned his steed's head and galloped off to catch up to the main body of knights.

"Well done anyways, Francis," Sir Geoffrey said, before returning to his steed. "Something about this just doesn't feel right though. Stay on the flank and keep your eyes open for any other signs."

The junior knight fairly beamed at this recognition before he sprang back into his own saddle. If it were at all possible, he would make his already keen eyesight a hundred percent keener.

Sir Geoffrey watched the young outrider gallop off. He remembered a time when he could still leap onto his own horse. These days, it sometimes seemed that it was all he could do to just haul his stiff limbs over the broad-backed charger he rode.

The Skolish commander managed the feat, but not without a bit of a struggle. Thankfully, there was no one watching. Digging his heels into his mount, he broke out of his self-indulgent muse and set off to rejoin his troop.

It was just as he was approaching the rear of the knight column that the first warning shouts from the river crossing could be heard.

*   *   *

The dozen knights of the Medinian patrol approaching the river had been dispatched from their outpost to aid in the investigations of the strange series of wolf pack attacks among the farms that bordered the Euralene Mountain range. The patrol was riding west along the Kolenko River towards the cataracts, where they planned to turn south and work their way back through the frontier farms. They would continue working south until they met up with the other patrols, which had been dispatched from the castle in Dumas.

Coming up to the river crossing, the Medinian knights were startled to find a Skolish force riding up on the opposite side of the cataracts. In light of the peace talks that were underway there hadn't been any armed posturing or confrontations for several weeks now.

The knight patrol reined in their mounts at the river's edge and then waited to see what would develop next. If they were trying to ascertain the Skolish force's intentions, they didn't have to wait long to find out.

The first Skolish knights who reached the river spotted the enemy patrol across the cataracts. Yelling curses and personal challenges, they plunged their steeds into the shallows as they fitted arrows into long bows and crossbows. Moments later, the first ragged volley was let loose in the direction of the Medinian knights.

Although no one was actually hit, several of the deadly shafts passed close enough to be heard splitting the air and then the foliage nearby. The angry Medinians responded by drawing their own bows and returning an equally undisciplined and ineffective volley of arrows.

A second volley by both sides was issued but proved equally ineffective. The only casualty at this point of the confrontation was to one of the horses at the water's edge. The poor animal took an arrow in its hindquarters, just where its protective leather covering ended. The war steed promptly reared, screaming its fury and pain, and deposited its unprepared rider into the icy-cold water.

Sir Geoffrey reached the water's edge just as Prince Paulo was about to plunge his warhorse into the fray. The commander reached out and collared the reins of the prince's horse in his left hand. The young knight, Francis, upon seeing his commander's actions, galloped up, placing himself between them and the cataracts. He got there just as another volley descended through the air.

One arrow found a target and struck hard, cutting deeply into the young knight's right side. With a grunt, Francis fell to his left, causing his horse to dance skittishly sideways. Gaullé managed to turn his mount's head again and block the destrier before it pranced back and trampled the knight. He then quickly dropped from his steed and passed the reins to Prince Paulo. His aches and pains were forgotten for the moment.

"Call those men back," the commander ordered the prince, forgetting his place for the moment. He knelt by the fallen young knight, clutched him firmly under the arms, and then dragged him well away from the river bank.

Prince Paulo signalled for the recall to be sounded. Judging from where the arrow had impacted the brave knight, he realized that had not Sir Geoffrey reined him in and young Francis interceded, it would probably have split his own chest. He moved quickly now to get the knights reassembled and to form up in a defensive position out of range of the Medinians' weapons.

"You and Francis may have just saved me from that giant splinter, my old friend," the prince said with a tight smile when he'd dismounted and rejoined Gaullé.

"I didn't think the king would appreciate it if I brought his only living son back on a miniature spit," the knight commander replied.

As gently as he could, the commander turned the young knight onto his side. The swan feathers at the end of the arrow's shaft, he noted, were a distinctive blue and white. It was just like all the others they'd gathered these past few days.

Gaullé inspected the deeply embedded wound. He did so with dispassionate eyes. He didn't need to state that it didn't look good for the young knight. He'd seen more than his share of battlefield wounds, as had Prince Paulo. They were experienced enough to know that this one would likely prove fatal.

While their two commanders were inspecting young Francis, the other Skolish knights did as they'd been trained to do. They formed up in two lines, the inner standing and outer kneeling, weapons at the ready. They would face down any enemy that may appear, at any cost. It was their kingdom's prince they protected.

Across the river, the Medinian patrol took the opportunity to regroup as well. They sent two of their number riding hard back to the outpost, to summon reinforcements to help guard the river crossing. Eight of them dismounted with their weapons at hand to keep watch on the Skolish and await the arrival of reinforcements.

The final pair of knights galloped off on the southern trail to find and bring the news to their own commander.

*　　　　　*　　　　　*

Medinia

At the marketplace, the Smythes had heard the reports of wolf attacks on herds that were said to have occurred not overly far from their own farm. The news had spread throughout the market town. When the report of the most recent raid arrived and the troops pulled out in the direction of their homestead, they were soon following behind them in their wagons. Their thoughts were no longer on the harvest festivities they'd been enjoying.

The Smythe family had stayed in an inn in town last night. This morning, suffering an aching head from imbibing in several jars of mead the prior night, the farmer and his family had set out, eating the troop of knights' dust. Their worst fears came to pass. As they neared their farm, they could see sheep and cattle roaming aimlessly across the countryside. Several of the animals appeared to be injured. When they reached the farmhouse, it was evident from the wide-open barn doors that Willie, his old horse, Pegasus, and the two herd dogs, were all unaccounted for. The farmer spotted the knight commander where he stood looking into the empty barn and he approached him there.

The commander of the Medinian forces was well known in these parts, even though they were a long way from the king's distant castle city of Dumas. Sir Reginald Toutant was a fit and vigorous, veteran knight commander. He wore no white cloak with its crested insignia upon his back, preferring a well-worn, unadorned padded leather surcoat. It was his prerogative as commander of the Medinian forces to dress as he pleased. His well used broadsword was sheathed in a like-wise unadorned leather scabbard across his back. The leather covered hilt protruded up over his left shoulder within easy reach. His clean-shaven face and head belied his age of some forty-two years. His face sported an old, jagged scar, which ran from just below his left eye down his cheek to the jaw line. It gave him a rather fierce countenance.

"The animals roaming around must have escaped from the upper pastures and paddocks. All the gates down here are still locked up," the farmer reported nervously.

Sir Reginald nodded his agreement. "Get a horse unhooked from your wagon and show us the way," he ordered.

Jacob set Adam to work rounding up the stray animals and getting them into the stables and corrals. His wife would lend the boy a hand once she put their young daughter to bed. Minutes later, the farmer was mounted bareback and leading the contingent of knights up through the orchards to the lower foothills. He fairly bounced along on top of the horse, quite unlike the knights, who seemed bred to the motion of their saddles. Fear of what they would discover had set into his belly like indigestion from some bad meat, and his thick head continued its merciless pounding.

It only got worse. When they arrived, the pasture and its paddocks were a scene out of hell itself. The farmer vomited shortly after they arrived, upon seeing a rat scurry off what remained of his prize bull. The vermin had been feeding through the night. Hundreds of birds and countless thousands of flies filled the air and covered the rancid remains of the carcasses spread across the pasture. Pools of drying blood and gore were made even darker and more gruesome by the multitude of insects feeding on them.

The knight commander breathed shallowly in a vain effort to keep out the stench. He took his time, however, when he was examining the remains of the two dead wolves. He could see that one of them had been gored clean through. Doubtlessly, the bull had fought bravely. The second wolf's rear legs were a savagely torn. He surmised that its neck was broken, judging from the unnatural tilted angle of the head.

Toutant had no way of knowing that the two dead animals had died bearing the size and misshapen features of warg-wolves the night before. The full moon was long over and death had released them from Diana's grasp. Their bodies lay stiffening in the late afternoon sun in their natural wolf state.

"It must have been a hell of a fight," the Medinian commander muttered aloud, "one hell of a fight, indeed."

Yet, it made no sense to Toutant as he looked around the paddock. He'd never heard of a pack of wolves attacking a maddened bull before, let alone being able to rip it apart like this.

The Medinian commander had his men spread out across the pasture and hunt for tracks that led away from the slaughter. They soon found them. Two sets of tracks were discovered, and then a third. Now, the puzzle grew more complex. The tracks at the end of the paddock where the animals had stampeded showed wolf-like prints leading out across the foothills. Yet, the prints were too large and widely spaced for any normal wolf-tracks, as would have been made by these two dead animals. These prints indicated much larger animals.

The tracks that were discovered leading up towards the tree lines were stranger still. Here, it was evident that humans had somehow been involved in all of this, or at least something resembling the tracks of barefooted men. Although these tracks appeared to be made by men, they were larger than normal in size, as well. The fore edge of the impressions dug deeper into the ground than the rest of the print, as if the feet were clawed.

The third set of tracks they found were more of the large wolf-tracks again, but mixed in with them were the strange prints that seemed to come from claw-toed humans. These tracks were discovered at the upper end of the pasture. Nearby, they found a set of boot prints and then the tracks of a horse. The boot tracks were of an average size and they ended at the horse's hoof prints, so it was thought that these were made by the young farm hand, and that he'd mounted and ridden way. Mixed in with these prints were two sets of paw prints, most likely made by the herd dogs that farmer Smythe had spoken of.

The knight commander dispatched his troops into three separate groups to follow each of the trails leading away from the paddock. He rode out leading the faction that followed the third set of tracks. In due course, the group he'd dispensed towards the tree line rejoined them. The trail they followed had re-emerged from the trees, to then head in the same direction as Toutant and his men moved.

The puzzle took another curious turn, as now drag marks appeared on the ground leading from the tree line until the two trails converged. The signs indicated some heavily laden travois had been pulled through here. Bits of wool and tell-tale blood spots led the trackers to surmise that they bore carcasses taken from the raid.

It wasn't long before the trackers found the dead herd dog that the farmer mournfully identified as Rigel. Beside him was the body of the wolf that the loyal dog had taken into death with him.

Farther along the way, they discovered the gruesome remains of the youth's old horse, Pegasus, and then after entering the light forest on foot, one last dead wolf with its skull clearly fractured. The knight commander bent down and picked up the broken pieces of the fire-hardened staff. He guessed correctly that this was the instrument of the last wolf's demise.

When Toutant and his men came out from the forest into the clearing, the knight commander gazed up at the lone, gnarly old oak. Around the base of the tree were the distinctive prints of the larger wolf-like creatures, and those of the booted youth that the farmer had said was named Willie. There were also the solitary prints of one of the large human-like barefooted creatures.

"There's blood up here, too, sir," one of the knight trackers called down from the branches, a few minutes later.

Sir Reginald turned to the farmer.

"It doesn't look very good for this lad of yours, I'm afraid. The young man is either dead or he's been carried off," he stated frankly. "Judging from the look of these tracks, I'd say it would be a whole lot better for him if he were already dead." He shuddered at the thought of anything to the contrary.

"These damnable creatures must have been sent here by the devil himself," farmer Smythe swore. He crossed himself quickly and looked to the heavens as if for confirmation.

"As preposterous as that sounds, I can't say that you're wrong," the knight commander said with a slow shake of his head. "Nothing else here makes any more sense."

The knights assigned to follow the lower pasture set of tracks converged on them as they were coming out of the woods. They'd barely finished reporting their discovery of another dead herd dog and wolf to their commander when the sound of riders approaching could be heard. The commander turned to see two hard-riding Medinian knights galloping towards them across the foothills.

When the knights had reined in their chargers and given their report of the river crossing confrontation, Toutant's eyes flashed with anger. The frustration that had been slowly building up in the veteran knight commander all day long was finally given a focus to vent itself upon. In his many years of service, he'd never seen anything like these farm slaughters, or the strange tracks they'd found. The forces that were gathered at the river were something more within his experience. He climbed onto the back of his warhorse and then ordered his men to mount up as well. He led them off at a determined gallop in the direction of the Kolenko River.

*   *   *

Jacob stood there dumbly for a time, watching the knights as they rode off. He knew without seeing it that the other dead dog they'd found was Sirius. It only added to his despair. The frontier farmer bent over and retched out what remained in his stomach alongside the remains of poor old Pegasus.

When he was able to catch his breath again, Jacob pulled himself back up onto his horse and followed the dust trail of the disappearing troop of knights. He was determined to see this through to the end.

*   *   *

The Mesa-of-the-Moon, Varakov

Simon walked alongside the mercenary leader as they navigated the castle's initial hallway. The captives were herded ahead of them to the flight of stone stairs that he knew led to the dungeons below. As they were passed through the doors of the central checkpoint, Simon could see part way down the curving stone stairway that the prisoners took to the dungeon levels. It was still daylight, but there were heavy iron lanterns set into recesses in the walls of the stairs that would be lit when the sun went down. They'd cast ample light for the guards who worked the night shifts. There were guards on duty around the clock.

Simon's last view of the prisoners took in the face of the fearful Skolish mother, clutching her two daughters protectively, as they were prodded down the steps by the guards. He was powerless to prevent it.

That sight disturbed the Pack lieutenant a great deal, perhaps as much as the upcoming meeting with Lord Victor did. This would be his first visit into the castle's inner chambers, and the Pack's lieutenant found the notion more than a little intimidating. In none of his many prior visits to the castle with Woodrow had he ever been permitted entry to the king's inner sanctum. A sense of foreboding coursed through him that caused the hairs on the nape of his neck to bristle.

At the hallway's end, the castle's large reception area was stationed with more senior guards who controlled all access to the outer chambers of the castle proper. He was familiar with this area, but he was always impressed by the gothic grandeur of it. The walls were draped in the various banners and pennants of the realm, but the main impression one received was of massive blocks of stone and soaring heights. They bespoke of the strength and impregnable fortitude of the castle's construction.

The highly arched hallway they passed into next was unfamiliar to the Pack lieutenant. It was ornately lined with rich tapestries illustrating several great battle scenes from the annals of history. One lengthy piece depicted two immense armies encamped on opposing hilltops and engaging in battle in the valley between them. There were countless thousands of figures, from regiments of mounted knights to legions of archers and pikers on foot. Each figure was captured in a precise moment of battle. Simon could have spent a full day studying it. In fact, he would have preferred that to what lay ahead.

Four armed guards were posted by the doors at the end of this hallway. They stood silently observing the movements of the two approaching visitors for any sign of trouble. Their captain rose up from his nearby desk to inspect them. Without apology, he submitted each of them to a thorough search.

The raider leader had an assortment of weaponry on his person in addition to his scimitar in its ornately etched leather scabbard. Foot-long knives were removed from sheaths on each of his legs. More weapons were discovered strapped to his back, concealed beneath his flowing garbs. The captain grunted, but made no comment, as each piece was removed from the mercenary's person and laid out on a desk to be reclaimed when their audience was over. Barozzi seemed amused each time another one was discovered hidden away. It was like a game for him. Only when the captain was satisfied that nothing had been overlooked did the other armed guards step aside and allow them entry to Lord Victor's inner sanctum.

With a slight look of disdain directed at the captain of the guard detail, Barozzi led Simon through the short foyer, and then pushed open the embossed brass doors at the end of it. They came into the enormous great hall as the richly wrought doors swung closed behind them.

Simon was quite unprepared for the lavish wonders his eyes beheld. There was sitting capacity for hundreds with room to spare. There were also numerous secluded nooks. At regular intervals, granite columns with finely chiselled figurines rose upwards to meet the vaulted ceiling, which was raised at least eight stories high and supported by beams that were secured with iron tie-rods. Muted light passed its way inside through beautifully crafted stained-glass windows. They were more intricately detailed than those of any church he'd ever visited.

Alongside the ornate windows, rich tapestries of silk were hung. They gleamed with vibrantly coloured threads that had been woven by the hands of many skilled artisans. These works of medieval art covered three of the walls of the great hall, draping down between the Romanesque arched windows. Each of the intricate patterns depicted some momentous occasion in history. Captured were the likes of Hannibal and his elephants crossing the mountains, Genghis Khan and his Mongols sweeping across the steppes, and Roman legions, both on the march and in the act of putting down barbarian uprisings.

It was the incredible works of marble statuary and mosaic tiled flooring and that really took Simon's breath away. The flooring throughout the cavernous hall consisted of levelled granite slabs for the most part. The exception was a central walkway that ran the length of the great hall from the outer doors to the raised throne. This broad path consisted of intricately laid pavement tiling in mosaics of red, white, and black marble. The long pavement walkway was interrupted in the exact centre of the great hall, where a circle of tiling in a twenty-four-foot diameter was constructed. This artisan's masterpiece was known as the Roundel, or Wheel of Fortune.

The wondrous centrepiece depicted four of the great philosophers of antiquity: Aristotle, Euripides, Seneca, and Epictetus. Each of these figures held an unrolled scroll that was inscribed with sayings about one's fortune, all ornately chiselled in Gothic lettering. At the base of the circle was inscribed a motto that bespoke of the constant changing nature of fate: "Regno, Regnabo, Regnavi, Sum sine regno."

The marble pavements were decidedly Sienese in nature and construction, having been constructed by skilled craftsmen brought in from distant Siena in 1372. Many of the mosaic depictions they'd created were scenes that one might expect if this were a grandiose cathedral. Their subject matter, for the most part, pertained to crucifixions, beheadings, slayings, and sacrifices. One harsh biblical story known as the Slaughter of the Innocents, took up a six foot section.

There were additional tiled sections that captured great battle scenes from throughout history. There were mountaintop castles under siege, great armies encamped on plains, armies on the march, armies in pitched battle in what otherwise would have been idyllic landscaped settings. In all, there were thousands of figures depicted along the length of the walkway, the majority of them in the actions of fighting, killing, or dying.

Simon found that the scenes exquisitely represented but more than a little gruesome at the same time. The Pack lieutenant realized it would take him weeks to properly examine them all. He could only imagine how long it must have taken the artisans to create the intricate paving.

It was the marble statuary, however, that captured his immediate attention. In one corner of the great hall there was a life-sized elephant being ridden by the great strategist Hannibal. It towered high overhead, rising up from a rough, unfinished marble block base, as if it were breaking free from its stone imprisonment. In the same manner, in one of the far corners, the mighty Khan straddled a rearing snow-white mount. In the opposing corner, Alexander the Great drove his chariot behind two charging black Arabian steeds.

Each marble setting was perfectly crafted in every detail: from a straining leg muscle to the tip of a deadly javelin. Each sculpture was inlayed with ivory and gemstones, which sparkled iridescently as they moved farther into the hall. The Pack lieutenant could only gape in awe and wonderment. He could almost envision the dedicated sculptors working, delicately chipping away at these enormous slabs of richly coloured marble to release the form held within. It must have taken them a lifetime of labour and love.

Only the inner wall was devoid of any tapestries or marble pieces. Instead, it was lined with displays of armour and weaponry along its entire length and reaching far overhead. Simon walked slowly along it, taking note of each display as they passed it by. He deduced that a good portion of the weapons were foreign-made pieces, which Lord Victor must have collected from distant lands or from the ships putting into port. The usage of many of them was beyond his personal expertise. It occurred to the Pack lieutenant, however, that the silent mercenary walking alongside him probably knew what they were for and how to use them effectively. He was aware that Barozzi was decidedly more knowledgeable when it came to implements of death and vastly more experienced in their uses.

The display of weaponry was crass and vulgar. To Simon, they represented nothing more than brutality and indifferent slaughter. He felt that they demeaned the elaborate tapestries, the intricate flooring, and the exquisite sculptures in the rest of the great hall.

At the end of weapons display, an enormous stone fireplace rose up in the fourth corner of the great hall, to disappear through the vaulted ceiling beams high above. Above the mantle of the giant fireplace, three large portraits were hung. The two men paused to examine them.

In the raised centre portrait, Lord Victor was captured in his caped finery. The Varakovan king was depicted standing on one of the castle's battlements and overlooking his realm. His piercing blue eyes appeared as if they missed nothing that was out there. The portrait to the lower right depicted a beautiful but somewhat sad-looking young woman on a settee. On either side of the woman were two serious-looking young boys of about eight and ten years of age. They had their mother's blue eyes.

It was the third portrait, the one to the lower left, which then captured Simon's interest. In it, a king sat upon his throne. It was the same throne that rested on the dais near the middle of the inner wall with the weapons display. On the steps, at the king's feet, sat three young men. There were four wicked looking daggers embedded in the canvas and whose hilts protruded from the artwork. The king and the three young men were each precisely impaled through their hearts.

As the two men stood gazing up at the portraits, Simon's ears picked up a faint slithering sound, something his senses would have picked up sooner had he still been in his wolf-man state. In the heartbeat between awareness and action, as he was poised to turn, their host spoke up from a few scant steps behind them.

"Good day, gentlemen."

Simon had just enough warning to allow him to control his reflex actions. That was not so with Barozzi. The mercenary instinctively spun away into a low crouch, his hands flying to the nape of his neck, where his dark ponytail was knotted through an ornamental barrette and held in place with a wooden peg. When he realized that it was his master standing behind them, the raider leader slowly lowered his hands and stood back up with a look of chagrin on his face.

"My Lord Victor, you surprised us," the mercenary said, lowering his eyes and bowing from the waist.

"Barozzi, captain of my raiders, welcome home," Lord Victor replied with a warming smile.

The Varakovan ruler stood some six feet tall. He was dressed formally, in his ubiquitous shimmering black cape over a white silken shirt. His shoulder-length black hair was touched with a trace of silver-grey at the temples. It gave an indication of middle-aged years, but the king still appeared as fit and robust as a much younger man. His body was muscular, broad across the chest and shoulders yet tapered and lean at the waist beneath his loose-fitting silken garments. His skin tone was pale, but at the same time, it would be said that he was handsome with a strong, masculine jaw line. It was his icy blue eyes, however, that dominated his facial features. They were penetrating and undeniable when they held you in their focus.

The Varakovan king extended his arm in greeting and the raider leader eagerly stepped forward to accept the handshake.

What followed next occurred in a blur of motion. Lord Victor grasped Barozzi's forearm instead of his hand. Using the mercenary's forward momentum, the king propelled him over his hip and tossed him through the air. The raider landed hard and awkwardly on his back, bounced twice and slid nearly ten feet away.

The wind was knocked out of Barozzi when he landed. He grunted, more from the suddenness of it than from any injury. Simon stood there staring as in a second burst of speed, and with his cape flaring out behind him, Lord Victor was on the mercenary before he'd even come to a complete halt. The king dropped his one knee onto Barozzi's chest, seized the mercenary's windpipe with one hand, and then calmly reached behind the raider's head with the other. He deftly removed the wooden peg that held the ornate hair-clip in place. As Victor drew it forth, the peg separated into two pieces. A short wooden handle with an evil looking needle-sharp blade some three inches long was unsheathed from the casing that housed it.

"What do we have here, my captain?" the king enquired, with a look of feigned puzzlement. "My guess is that you simply forgot about this hidden toy of yours. I'm quite certain you know that weapons are forbidden in my home, unless of course they're my own. You do know that you're supposed to surrender them to my guards? Of course you do. It was just a slight oversight, I'm sure. Wasn't it?"

While Lord Victor's tone of voice was friendly enough, there was no mistaking the cold look in his gaze. They bore into the raider's eyes as the king straddled him and retained his tight grip on the man's throat.

Barozzi remained still and expressionless; even as Victor fingered the blade a scant inches from his face. The mercenary didn't beg forgiveness, nor did he cry out when his employer lowered the needlepoint of the small knife to his cheekbone and then, starting just below his left eye, etched a line down to his jaw. As the tip of the blade crossed over his skin, a thin rivulet of blood followed. The wound itself was not deep, but it would most assuredly leave a razor thin scar to serve as a future reminder.

Victor got up off the man, now. He snapped the blade from its wooden handle and tossed the two pieces towards the door from which they'd entered.

"When you leave, please turn those into the captain of the guards and let him know that I'll be speaking to him later," the Varakovan king instructed the raider leader. His tone left little doubt that further punishment would be meted out.

Lord Victor ignored the raider leader then, leaving him to press his sleeve against his face to stanch the bleeding as he got to his feet. He turned his attention to his other guest.

"While I may not have shown it just now, I want you to know that I value my talented friend, Barozzi. He's exceptional at what he does."

Victor spoke as if the mercenary was not standing right there. He was focused entirely on the Pack lieutenant now, clearly appraising him.

"Make no mistake, there's no humiliation on his part," the Varakovan king added. "He has simply learned an object lesson today. In fact, he'll be even better now, because Barozzi is highly adaptable. He's a man who learns from his errors in judgment. If I didn't believe so, his eyeballs would be on that little blade now, and then I'd turn him loose in the woods for the wildlife to feed upon."

"You may go now, Barozzi. Have your face attended to. We will meet later to review your mission."

Victor's eyes never left Simon's as he spoke to his well-compensated hireling. His back remained turned indifferently to the raider leader. Regardless, the head mercenary took a moment to bow again before he withdrew, to show his obedience. Without the ornate barrette in place, his hair tumbled forth on either side of his head as he did so.

As he was leaving the great hall, Barozzi stopped long enough to pick up the pieces of the knife that had brought about his physical reprimand. Moments later he closed the embossed doors behind him.

"You understand the need for this lesson, don't you, wolf-man?" Victor asked. As he spoke, the king began to walk in a wide, slow circle around Simon. He appeared to be studying the lean, clean cut Pack lieutenant from all angles, as if taking his full measure.

"I believe I do, milord," Simon replied, remaining where he was. "To be a leader, one must be obeyed unconditionally. A leader cannot allow his followers to transgress or become lax and inattentive. It would undermine his necessary authority."

"Exactly so," Victor agreed.

"But then, a leader must also assume the responsibility of leading his followers for their collective good," the Pack lieutenant added. "His leadership should inspire their loyalty and desire to serve."

"I'm not certain that applies when you're paying for that loyalty and desire to serve, does it?" Lord Victor asked. "Mercenaries can be a tricky bunch to rely on, but they have fighting in their blood and usually the skills worth paying for. I'm far less concerned with their collective welfare than I am with their obedience to my orders. That's what they're paid for. In any event, I've come to appreciate the men-for-hires' honest lifestyle," the king added. "It's brutally simple and straight forward. If your employer has the coin to pay you, then your sword arm is his to command without question."

"As long as there's a war and fighting to be done, then I suppose there'll always be a need for those who are good at it," the Pack lieutenant observed, a little cynically. "Otherwise, I've found the mercenaries to be more of a social menace, and not overly pleasant. They tend to hang out in Port Lupus and stir up trouble. They get bored, I suppose, from not having any battles to fight, or anyone to slay."

"Theirs is not exactly the life of a farmer, is it?" Lord Victor mused, from behind him. "Though, I'd say they both serve a purpose in my kingdom. Somewhat like Woodrow and yourself, perhaps?" Victor's head tilted slightly to the side and the eyebrow over his left eye rose in an arch.

Simon didn't rise to the bait, nor turn his head. He kept his tongue and waited for the king to continue

"I've been observing you since your arrival in the castle today," the Varakovan king added then. "I was impressed by your careful study of the hall's exhibits. There are several more fine pieces in other parts of my inner sanctum, but unfortunately visitors aren't permitted access there." Lord Victor was letting it be known that the Pack's lieutenant was being granted a courtesy that extended only so far.

"I value loyalty, and I know the importance of observation and awareness of one's surroundings. That's why I identify closely with the Pack and its structure and character. I believe loyalty and awareness are the key reasons for the continued survival of you and your kind. It must be instinctive. So it is with me. So must it be for these mercenaries. Warriors, hunters, predators: we all must live by our collective wits and intelligence, and if necessary by our ruthlessness."

"The Pack hunts its prey for our survival, not for power or reward," the Pack lieutenant said. "We do not covet gold and silver, or our neighbour's land."

He wondered if Lord Victor caught this veiled reference to the recent raids into Skoland and Medinia. If he did, the king chose not to acknowledge it.

"A king hunts. I hunt, for many reasons," Victor replied. "I've also been the hunted in my time, much as you've been, I suspect. Being the hunted tends to hones one's skills for survival too. Don't you agree?"

The Pack lieutenant was aware of the Varakovan king's penchant for hunting. He had also been made aware long ago by Woodrow of Lord Victor's special hunts. He knew the king had an affliction of his own. While he wasn't affected by the full moon as the Pack was, Victor had appetites that were beyond his control and just as undeniable.

Lord Victor had completed his circling now and he was once again standing in front of his guest. He was impressed that the man hadn't flinched or turned while he was being inspected. It confirmed the castle keeper's ability to choose qualified men for important positions.

"Simon, isn't it? You're the Pack's beta male? My friend Woodrow has spoken well of you on numerous occasions." The Pack lieutenant lowered his eyes and then bowed from the waist in acknowledgment to his king. Lord Victor appeared to accept the act of subservience without any special regard or thought. It was simply his due as the man's liege. "Well, Simon, now that you've had an opportunity to enter this part of the castle, what are your impressions?"

Woodrow had spoken about the reclusive Lord Victor, as well. In meeting with the king in person, the Pack lieutenant was now getting a better inkling of the man himself. He found that Victor dominated the room, despite its enormity. His icy blue eyes were penetrating and captivating. His commanding presence exceeded even those of the life-sized sculpted exhibits. Simon found that the caped Varakovan ruler emanated an almost tangible aura of power and control. He stood with a strong, confident ease, yet his hungry eyes seemed to devour whatever they laid their view upon. All this, and more, had Simon observed here today. As he considered his response to Lord Victor's query, he remembered Woodrow's advice to tread carefully. He made sure that he kept his reply neutrally toned and softly spoken.

"You obviously have a great appreciation for the arts," the Pack lieutenant responded, gesturing towards the tapestries and marble statuary with one arm. "At least in so far as they relate to your true passion—the study of warfare. You are a student of history, at least within that context. You have a fascination with all aspects of warfare and with the implements needed to conduct it successfully, and you especially admire those great generals of the past who excelled at expansionism and conquest."

Victor nodded his head slowly in agreement with Simon's observations.

"To be a student of history is to be a student of warfare and conquest," the Varakovan king said. "There's always been war of some kind. Wars fought for the spoils of the enemy, for slaves, for their women. Wars fought over more fertile lands, for better water, over mountains mined for their precious ore and metals, or perhaps simply between two princes laying claim to a vacated throne. There's never a shortage of reasons to start a war."

Victor paused for a moment, but Simon made no comment, waiting to see where his liege was headed with these thoughts.

"Nor, is there ever a shortage of men to do the fighting," Victor added then. "In every land there are men who are bred and trained in the ways of battle, just as their sons will be, and in time, their sons' sons. There will always be generation after generation of fighting men, preparing to conquer, or preparing to defend against being conquered. There's never a truly harmonious relationship between kingdoms. There is never a time of true peace. There are only lulls between the storms of war."

Simon noted the growing intensity in Victor's tone and the way his eyes flashed as if in indignation that anyone could hold another viewpoint.

"And let's not forget the almighty Gods." the king added fervently. "Deities are always a great cause to take up arms for. My God is mightier than your God, and all that. Look at the history of religion and the endless wars waged in its name. It's been that way all over Europe and all over Asia—endless crusades and endless jihads. There have been centuries of holy wars and persecutions carried out in the name of their gods."

The Varakovan king paused for a moment, as if to collect his thoughts. He gazed steadily at the Pack lieutenant, perhaps to see if his points were being received and understood. Simon still made no comment, however. He sensed it wasn't really required of him.

"I have little use for religious hypocrisy," the king stated. "One bunch of them swears by Allah and Muhammad. Another bunch worships Brahma and Buddha and claims to be all the more enlightened for it. And, let's not forget about good old Jeremiah and Jesus. They're worth killing and dying for, too. Don't you think? Trust me Simon. It doesn't matter which religion you believe in, there'll always be someone who says you're wrong to believe it—and then be willing to go to war with you over it."

"Does that offend you, as much as it does me?" Lord Victor asked then.

Once again, the Varakovan king appeared not to expect a response from the Pack lieutenant, only his attention.

"All their so-called religious beliefs are based on tenets of peace and worship and harmony," the king added disdainfully. "Yet their actions lead to nothing but strife, intolerance, and war. They cloak themselves in piety and preach of the afterlife, but their naked avarice clearly demonstrates their ambition and hunger for worldly power. That's why you won't find any priests inside these walls. They can preach their nonsense to the peasants of the countryside, but not to me."

The Varakovan king took pause to look about the great hall at the statuary and artworks for a few more moments, before shaking his head and letting out a deep sigh.

"Yes, Simon," Lord Victor stated then. "To be a student of history is to be a student of war. War is the one constant throughout time. I've collected tapestries and I've commissioned works of marble paving and carved statues. Inadequate as they are, they manage to convey some of the more momentous events in history. They depict the occasions when a few great leaders of men made their mark on the world, for however brief a time. The waging of war and the fighting of great battles gives kings and generals the taste of immortality. To be able to dispense death to others before they do the same to you. Only then, can you feel really alive. Only then can you truly appreciate what it is to have life."

It occurred to Simon that Lord Victor's focus was solely on the tyrants and conquerors throughout history. No one remembers the peasants or common soldiers who fought and gave their lives for the ambitions of these kings and generals.

"Great kingdoms must forever reach out for more, Simon," the Varakovan king said then. "Look at the world around us now. Ships are traveling farther and farther to trade. There are even voyages of pure discovery now to find new sea routes and fresh lands over the horizon. One distant day, I believe mankind will even discover how to conquer the skies. They'll build ships that can sail into the air on the winds and then the whole known world—and that which is not yet known—will all be within their grasp, and all there to make war over. Who knows, perhaps men will even learn how to sail out to the distant stars, and then do battle with the gods themselves. What a rich tapestry that would weave, Simon. Can you envision it?"

Without waiting for a response, Victor walked over to the giant fireplace where he silently scanned the portraits that hung over the fire hearth. He stood lost in thought for a time. Simon remained where he was and waited patiently on his liege, wondering if he'd been forgotten. At last, the Varakovan king turned away from the portraits and shook his head as if he were dismissing some dark notion. He brought his attention back to the Pack lieutenant.

"Don't mind me, wolf-man," he called out. "Sometimes my thoughts wander." The king returned and stood before the Pack lieutenant. His deeply penetrating eyes were refocused now upon him. "So, tell me, Simon, do you think the two missions I dispatched were a success?"

That's the key to this man, Simon realized then in a revelation. *It's the king's vision of things. This is a man who thinks he is fated by the hand of destiny. He's a man in touch with the fabric of history and quite capable of weaving his own grand design.*

It was a moment of great clarity for the Pack lieutenant. It was a moment of serious foreboding also, for it indicated to him that there were dangerous times to come. Great upheavals had occurred throughout history around just such men of "vision." He was struck by how alike Lord Victor's bearing was to those of the historic figures captured here in marble. His pale, intense features and the powerful aura he emanated were undeniable and troublesome. The Pack lieutenant chose his answer carefully, knowing he was being both tested and judged. He was also aware that the Varakovan king had not yet even asked where Woodrow was, or why the Pack leader wasn't in attendance.

"I suppose the missions were a success, sire," he reported. "The two raiding parties were able to achieve the goals you set out for them. As I understand it, Barozzi and his men left behind a number of Medinian weaponry during their raids into Skoland. They crossed over the river and into Medinia without mishap, before moving west into the pass. That should reinforce the desired subterfuge. They also brought back a number of Skolish captives."

Victor flicked his hand impatiently, indicating he'd get these details later from Barozzi himself.

Trying to keep his tone neutral, Simon continued his report. "Sadly, we lost several Pack members during our last raid on a Medinian farm, but we brought back the carcasses of meat that you required of us." Despite his attempt to remain stoic and passive throughout his report, a touch of bitterness crept into the Pack lieutenant's voice.

"And you have questions," Victor surmised. "Questions that surely all begin with why? Why this? And why that? Life is just full of the big question 'why'. Isn't it, Simon?"

Lord Victor walked over to the dais and climbed the steps to his throne, swirled his cape to one side and sat down.

"Questions come easily, wolf-man. It's the damn answers that are always the hardest part to come by," Victor mused as he looked down upon Simon. "Answers sometimes come with time. Though sometimes, whether we like it, or not, there simply are no answers, at least, none that we can discover or hope to understand."

Lord Victor locked eyes with the Pack lieutenant while seeming to ponder whether it was worthwhile trying to enlighten him.

"You are my guest here today, Simon, so I will try to give you some answers to your unspoken questions," he said. "Why were the raids necessary?

Why would I want you to drag off livestock kill? Why bring back prisoners? Why try to make the Skolish think the Medinians were responsible for the raids into their land?"

Victor supplied the questions and then the answers. At least the answers that he chose to reveal. "As we have determined, Simon, there will always be war of some kind over any issue of importance. Mankind seems to follow a fairly predictable cycle of making war and then pausing for a period of respite, or a time of peace, if you'd prefer to call it that. Right now, our two neighbours to the east are tiring of a lengthy period of warfare, and now they're talking of alternatives. Not just a cessation in the fighting, mind you, but a peace brought through an arranged marriage. This solution would unite their two kingdoms like never before. Then when the cycle turns again, they would have to look elsewhere for a place to make war. That elsewhere could very well be Varakov. United, their armies would pose a serious threat to Varakov, and to me," the king intoned solemnly.

Simon nodded his head briefly to indicate that he understood the king's concern.

"Then you can understand why I'd prefer that they remain in armed conflict and preoccupied with each other," Lord Victor added. "Barozzi's raid into Skoland and the appearance that it was the Medinians who were responsible for taking the Skolish captives may sow enough distrust to upset, or at least delay, their peace talks. It may also gain us the time that I need."

The king didn't explain what he meant by this, but the Pack lieutenant made note of the remark to discuss it later with Woodrow.

"On another level is the use of fear," Lord Victor added then. "Fear is a very real weapon, Simon. The raids into Skoland and the farms that Barozzi and his men burned and the captives who were taken away will cause fear and insecurity. And then there's the further mystery brought on by your Pack's raids into Medinia. "The animals slaughtered on their frontier farms and carried off will cause fear and insecurity of the unknown there, as well."

"There were no witnesses," Simon responded, with a nod of his head to show his understanding, "just dark and unexplainable events. Any signs they discover will point to the unnatural. People will be afraid of what they can't understand, and rumours will spread that even troops of armed knights can't protect them from the demons in the mountains."

The Varakovan king smiled slightly. "I would suspect that we'll soon see an exodus of people from the frontier farmlands in the western part of both kingdoms. Wouldn't you agree?" Victor stated with some satisfaction. "We can only hope that there'll be less inclination for their armies to venture in our direction now, too. Fear, Simon. Fear can be as great a barrier between their kingdoms and Varakov, as the mighty Euralene Mountains are."

"And what will become of the Skolish captives, my lord?" the Pack lieutenant asked.

"The captives are not your concern, Simon," the king responded bluntly. The history lesson was over. Lord Victor straightened his posture, sitting upright on his throne. "So tell me, Simon of the Pack, not that I haven't enjoyed your company, but where is my good friend Woodrow? I was expecting him to be here to resume his duties."

The Pack lieutenant had learned a lot today, both from Lord Victor's lectures and from his own observations. The most important thing he'd learned, however, was just how little he knew of the king's plans—and what his future actions held in store for them.

"My Lord Victor," he replied formally, "the Pack leader sends his apologies, but he is detained on an urgent personal matter."

Shortly after Simon finished his report on Woodrow's behalf, he was dismissed by the Varakovan king and left the castle's inner sanctum. When the Pack lieutenant had gone, Lord Victor made his way back down the dais steps. Once again, he paused for a few moments in front of the huge stone fireplace, staring up at the portraits that hung above.

The Varakovan king's attention focused on the sad-looking but beautiful lady and her two young sons. His facial features remained largely devoid of expression, except perhaps for a slight tightening around his intense blue eyes. When he took his leave of the great hall, his passing went unnoticed by any of the castle guards.

Lord Victor's destination was the castle's inner tower. He would climb the many stairs and meet with his coven council there. Together, they would send out a summons to Woodrow. The castle keeper's place was here at the Mesa-of-the-Moon, not still up in the mountains. The cycle of the full moon was over.

*   *   *

They awaited him in the largest chamber in the upper reaches of the mesa tower. The tower was in the very heart of Lord Victor's castle inner sanctum, and neither guests nor guards were ever admitted here. Not even the castle keeper had access to the tower, only Victor and, of late, his council of dark souls.

The coven members were clad in dark robes with drawn hoods. They were seated in a circle on the floor when Victor entered. They numbered twelve in all. Six were male and six were female. They were equally perverse, these sorcerers of the black arts, whichever their gender.

"You saw? You heard?"

"Yes, master." They responded in unison.

The Varakovan king made his way across the tower chamber to a short pedestal, which sat below a stained glass window of unusual design. He carefully removed the draping that covered the object that was perched on the stand. Returning to the coven circle, he stood in its centre. With the assistance of his warlocks and their hags, Victor reached out to make contact with Woodrow, the Pack leader. It was time that he returned to his duties as keeper of the castle.

CHAPTER 5

THE RIVER CROSSING

July 25, 1461
Skoland

ON THE SKOLISH SIDE of the river cataracts, Prince Paulo stood by the coals that glowed in the ebbing fire. A long, sharply honed knife was heating in the embers.

The Skolish prince watched with concern as Gaullé tended to the gravely injured young knight. The enemy arrow had sunken too deeply into the side of his chest to be dug back out. Its barbed point had burrowed almost clean through to the other side. Thankfully, it was away from his spine. Still, it was a miracle that the young Skolish knight was even alive. His right lung had been punctured, at the very least. The arrow shaft would have to be forced through the last few inches and then pulled out through his back. It was going to prove painful and quite likely fatal.

His chain mail had been removed and the blood-soaked shirting had been cut away. Several of the knights moved forward to hold Francis in place while Gaullé positioned the wounded young man the way he wanted him. When he was fully secured and his arms held back out of the way, Sir Geoffrey cut the feathered end of the shaft off. He was careful to leave enough of the shaft still protruding for him to work with.

When the knight commander was ready, he nodded to one of the older, experienced knights under his command. The knight prepared himself to grab the head of the arrow and pull the shaft through when he saw it break the skin of the back. The others tightened their grip on the semiconscious Francis.

Picking up a flat-sided rock he'd selected for the task, Gaullé gave the cut-off end of the shaft a single hard smack. The force of the blow drove the tip of the arrow the balance of the way through. The older knight grabbed the head and drew the shaft out, all in the same motion.

The young knight screamed from the fresh injury and then passed out again. This was a mercy, because now the entry and exit wounds had to be cauterized before Francis bled to death. There was nothing they could do about the internal bleeding and damage. That would be in God's hands.

The knight commander walked to the fire, nodding grimly to the prince as he passed. He removed the knife that was heating over the coals. The commander brought it back to the unconscious young knight and set to work on the wounds.

The stink of burning flesh was nauseating, but none of the knights allowed themselves to react to it. They'd seen their share of battlefield wounds, and death, for that matter. It was up to the fates now. Their comrade would either live, or he would die. In the meantime, their concerns returned to the task of providing protection for their prince.

While the knights attended to this task, Prince Paulo brooded. He didn't know exactly why the Medinians would violate the truce when peace talks were about to be held. The only thing he knew for certain was that the Medinians were responsible for the raids. The arrow that had dropped that helpless old Skolish farmer to the ground was one of many Medinian signs that they'd uncovered. The same arrow type had just been pulled from the young knight.

Not letting his concern show, Prince Paulo contemplated their current predicament, as Sir Geoffrey bandaged the young knight's chest and back. The prince knew his force wasn't prepared or large enough for a military expedition into Medinia, especially since the Medinian patrol would have sounded the alarm over half their damn kingdom by now.

The Skolish prince figured that it would take at least until midday tomorrow before any reinforcements of their own could arrive. The young knight was severely, if not, mortally wounded. He surely wouldn't survive the return trip to the castle in Kragonus for better medical attention, even if there was anything more that could be done for him there. It was already late in the day, but the prospect of spending the night camped at the river held no appeal.

Prince Paulo decided that the best course of action would be for them to ride to the Skolish frontier post. They'd have to make up a litter to carry the wounded Francis. He waited until Gaullé was finished tying off the bandages, and then he went and conferred with him. He laid out his thoughts concerning their predicament to the knight commander as he watched him washing the young knight's blood from his hands.

In short order, a small detachment of knights was dispatched to ride overnight to the castle. The Skolish prince gave them orders to bring back a battalion of reinforcements, and one of the Skolish king's best physicians. When the troops arrived, he would decide how best to deal with the Medinians.

The knight commander turned his attention back to his patient, while Prince Paulo then relegated two men to the task of constructing a secure litter. He told the rest of the knights to be ready to leave as soon as it was prepared.

*   *   *

Medinia

On the Medinian side of the river crossing, the knight commander and his detachment rode in from their frontier farm investigation. Sir Reginald Toutant demanded and received a detailed report from the knights who had been left to watch the Skolish force across the river. Once he was satisfied that they had engaged the opposing force only after the Skolish knights had initiated the fight, he set his knights to the task of setting up defensive positions. While his orders were being carried out, the Medinian commander sat on his horse staring across the river crossing at the Skolish force. He deduced that there were too many knights for it to be a normal patrol, yet far too few to be an invasion.

The commander's seasoned eyes then spotted the solid crimson red banner that they carried, which proclaimed them to be the "Knights of the Royal Order." It was yet another puzzling matter to consider. He had no idea why the Skolish king's personal regiment would be out here.

"You there," the commander ordered, indicating one of the newly arrived garrison knights. "Climb up one of those trees and cut me down a straight branch, and then rig up a flag of truce. Let's see if we can't find out what's going on here before we have another confrontation on our hands."

It had been a week of strange occurrences for the seasoned Medinian commander. He was determined to solve the mystery behind this one.

The garrison knight came back with a cut branch that he'd trimmed, to which he had tied his shirt after taking off his breastplate to climb the tree. The shirt was more of a dingy grey than white, but it would serve its purpose. The commander ordered his men to remain behind on guard. He nudged his mount into the river water before they could protest.

*   *   *

Skoland

The sentries alerted the Skolish prince as to the solitary rider's approach under his makeshift flag of truce. Prince Paulo ordered them to allow his safe passage but to remain vigilant lest the other Medinians showed signs of following.

The Medinian knight commander was searched roughly and quickly disarmed once he got down from his steed, after which he was brought before the Skolish prince.

"You would be Prince Paulo, if I'm not mistaken?" the Medinian commander stated upon seeing him up close.

The commander greeted the king's heir with proper deference, giving him a short bow from the waist. Toutant knew the young prince was King Verdonk's only remaining son. It was a well-known fact that his two older brothers had both been killed during the long years of warfare.

Toutant also knew that the peace negotiators were discussing a marriage between this Skolish prince, and Lady Hillary Michelle, the eldest daughter of King Renaud of Medinia. The princess had just reached the age of consent and was considered to be one of the fairest damsels in the kingdom, in both beauty and manner. From such a union as this, peace was thought to be a real possibility.

"Again today, Prince Paulo," the Medinian commander stated, "I am faced with a strange event that raises questions that have no obvious answers. One of my patrols reported that a force from Skoland had engaged them at the river crossing. I've arrived here, only to discover troops under the banner of the Skolish Royal household, and Prince Paulo himself, at their command."

The young prince scowled but made no response as yet. He eyed the Medinian coldly. He noted the lack of mail and white cloak with its royal blue chevron insignia that was usually worn by the knights of Medinia. The man standing before him had more the appearance of a hired swordsman, but he claimed that the opposing patrols reported to him. His face and appearance certainly suggested a man who had seen his fair share of battle.

"May I inquire," Sir Reginald asked then, "what your intentions are? It appears that an error in someone's judgment has started some folly that needs to be rectified before it escalates any further."

"There's been no error in judgment," Prince Paulo thundered, "unless it was by the Medinian swine responsible for looting and burning our frontier farms and kidnapping and killing our people."

"I know nothing of any such attacks into Skoland, Prince Paulo," the knight commander responded, with seemingly genuine surprise.

"Liar!" the angry prince charged. "Show him the evidence."

Several knights brought forth the arrows, lances, and broken blades they'd collected and dropped them at the feet of the Medinian knight, regarding him scornfully as they did so.

"These were cowardly acts, directed at helpless farmers and their families," the Skolish prince raged. "They're not even worthy of being called acts of war!" Prince Paulo's hand went to the hilt of his sword, as he spoke next. "We demand the release of the Skolish citizens you hold captive, or all Medinia shall feel our wrath as never before!"

"I cannot deny that these weapons are Medinian made," the commander admitted calmly, as he fingered the distinctive feathers of an arrow he'd retrieved from the ground. "But I do deny that any Medinian troops were involved in these attacks."

"You're a cowardly liar," the Skolish prince accused him for the second time. "We've been on their trail for three days. The trail leads right here to the river's edge, and then on into Medinia. When we arrived, your men were on the other side. No doubt they were keeping an eye out for any reprisal force, such as ours."

The Medinian commander took his time before replying. He was clearly straining to keep his composure. He straightened his posture and looked the young prince directly in the eye.

"Sir, I have the privilege of being the commander of the king's personal knight regiment. My name is Sir Reginald Toutant. I am neither a liar nor a coward. When I say my knights did not attack your farms, I have spoken the God's honest truth. I—"

"Toutant, is that really you?"

This interruption came from behind the nearby cluster of Skolish knights. The figure of Sir Geoffrey rose up from beside his patient. On hearing their commander's voice, the knights stepped back to clear his view.

"You know this man?" Prince Paulo demanded, as he took the senior Medinian knight by the elbow and led him to Gaullé.

"Yes, milord," the Skolish commander replied, as he got stiffly to his feet and stretched mightily. "That is, I do if it's the same Toutant I met as a young knight back when your father and King Renaud were at peace for a time. As I recall the day, I knocked him on his ass a couple of times when we were jousting at the tournament that was held. He had to buy the round of ales, afterwards."

"As I recollect things, it was you who was doing most of the bouncing off the turf," Toutant responded with a quick laugh. "And that would make you the renowned Sir Geoffrey Gaullé, whose exploits I have followed closely for these many years. You've become an excellent strategist."

"I've had the honour of facing you across the battlefield, good sir," Gaullé responded. "You've managed to come up with a few surprises from time to time yourself."

"I suppose we've both learned a few things about our trade over all these years," Toutant replied. "We're both still alive and breathing, although you're looking a little worse for wear at the moment, I'd have to say."

The Medinian commander spoke with genuine concern. He could now see the gravely wounded knight on the ground, whose blood it was that stained the clothes on his Skolish counterpart. He didn't take the matter lightly. His eyes took on a deadly seriousness to them.

"Sir Geoffrey," he swore. "On my word of honour, we were not responsible for the atrocities your prince speaks of."

Prince Paulo looked sceptical, but he held his tongue and deferred to his commander.

The senior Skolish knight gazed steadily into Toutant's eyes for a long moment. He felt fairly certain that the knight commander had no deceit in him. The man may have fought with them on many a battlefield, but his sworn oath was a matter of honour.

"I heard you say something about another recent event, which you didn't understand," Gaullé said. "What else has occurred that troubles you?"

The Medinian commander grimaced. He then related the series of strange events of the past few nights. He further explained how his knight patrols throughout the western region were taking part in the investigations and that they couldn't possibly have been carrying on raids across the river into Skoland at the same time.

When Toutant came to the part about the most recent pasture slaughter, he related how a young serf from the farm had been dragged off and that his body had not been recovered. They'd found numerous tracks and later several bodies of wolves, but the tracks of much larger creatures had been discovered, both four-footed and two-footed ones, as well.

"I can't account for any of them. None of it makes any sense," Sir Reginald said, shrugging his shoulders. "Whoever, or whatever, made the tracks; they were heading towards the river, too."

This odd connection occurred to both commanders and to Prince Paulo about the same instant. They turned almost as one and looked up towards the mountains and the distant waterfalls there. No one spoke for a time.

"In the off chance that someone, or something, else is involved in all this," Gaullé spoke up finally, "I think we had best delve into this matter further—and before we take up arms against each other again."

"I don't think I need to look that far off to see who's really responsible here," declared Prince Paulo, dismissing the notion with a derisive snort. "None of your tale of wolves and other mysterious creatures explains what happened in Skoland or how your weapons came to be there. Wolves didn't make off with our people!"

"Well, neither did we!" the Medinian commander retorted, equally as fervent. He wasn't about to back down. He'd already given his word on the matter.

"We have a badly injured man to get to our garrison," Paulo replied coldly, clearly unconvinced. I'll give you until midday tomorrow to come up with some proof to the contrary. After that, I assure you, we will be seeking reprisals, and it won't be done sitting around a peace table!"

Paulo called for his men to prepare to move out, and for those selected to man the wounded knight's litter. He was about to mount his own giant charger when Sir Geoffrey clutched him by the arm.

"I think it best that I go with the Medinians and look into this further," the Skolish knight commander suggested. "All the evidence to this point makes it look like they're responsible for the raids, but my head is coming around to the idea that we might have a new enemy out there."

The prince considered this for a moment.

"Very well," he agreed, as he mounted his armoured destrier. "It's probably a good idea to keep an eye on them, anyway. I'll assign a few of the trackers to go with you just in case the Medinians try to invent some more fairytale ogres to blame these events on."

Prince Paulo was looking directly at the Medinian commander when he spoke, and he'd made sure that he was loud enough to be heard by him. He then went about designating a small detail of knights to remain behind and assist Gaullé before he turned his mount's head and returned briefly to where the two commanders now stood together.

"Oh, and Sir Reginald," he added, "I'll be holding you personally accountable for the safe return of my men. Make sure no harm befalls any of them."

Without further words between them, Prince Paulo turned away and signalled for the rest of his troop to move out. They set off at a slow but steady pace to accommodate the litter bearers. The prince did not look back.

One of the more youthful knights in the detail they'd left behind rushed off to round up his commander's horse, hardly able to contain his excitement that he'd been selected to cross the river into Medinia. He'd almost forgotten that it was his good friend Francis who the others were carrying away.

"Were we ever that young?" Sir Reginald asked with a look of amusement, despite their serious circumstances. "These days, I actually look forward to quiet, uneventful days, when I can take some time off for a little fishing or hunting."

"If a peace ever truly comes about, maybe we can do a little hunting together and swap a few tall tales over our ale," Gaullé suggested. "The brew will be my treat—this time."

"I look forward to it," the Medinian commander replied. "For the moment, however, you and I have other tall tales to look into. And I think my men are likely getting a bit antsy at my delay. We'd best be getting back while there's still light for the search."

Toutant strode off to reclaim his steed and then quickly mounted up. While leading the small party across the river, he contemplated how alike his own life was to that of his counterpart, Sir Geoffrey. Both of them were now seasoned commanders, men who trained and passed on their creeds of honour to their youthful charges.

"Do you believe him, sir?" the young knight, who'd fetched his horse, said quietly to his commander as they eased their mounts into the water.

"Yes, I think I do," Gaullé replied evenly. "Whatever is happening around here, it seems to be occurring on both sides of the border. There appears to be unexplained events taking place all along the western frontier."

He looked the young knight in the eye to see that he had his attention. "It may be that somebody is deliberately provoking trouble between us," the Skolish commander ventured. "If so, the answers we seek might be in those mountains, or possibly even from over the pass in Varakov."

"If that's the case, then we may be dealing with a clever new foe—perhaps one who commands devilish creatures of some sort," Sir Geoffrey added, with a quick, mischievous grin. "I want you to be sure you keep your eyes and ears open and your wits about you." He then urged his mount forward through the cold water in an effort to catch up to the other commander, leaving the young knight to ponder the possibilities.

*   *   *

Medinia

Jacob Smythe had reached the river crossing in time to see Sir Reginald return in the company of the Skolish commander and his detail. He listened in as Toutant briefed his men on the occurrences in Skoland, which had led up to their confrontation at the river. The commander also explained how these raids had coincided with the attacks on the Medinian farms and livestock. There was a distinct possibility that the actions were related.

Orders were given to disperse in several search parties and to look for any variety of tracks. They were told that these could belong to the raiding party that attacked Skoland, or they could be those of wolves or larger wolf-like creatures, or those of large two-legged creatures. Nothing, they were told, was to be discounted.

When this was said, the farmer's eyes weren't the only ones that turned to gaze up at the mountains, nor was he the only one who wondered what type of devils might reside up there. Jacob wondered further if it might not be time to take his family and move elsewhere in Medinia and well away from the rugged western frontier. Even if that meant moving to a smaller land holding, at least they wouldn't have to deal with these strange and fearsome unknowns.

The Medinian frontier farmer left the knights then and set off at an unsteady, but determined gait for his farmstead. He left the knights to their investigations. He certainly wasn't about to venture up into the mountains with them.

That evening, about an hour before the summer sun would sink from the sky, a lone rider galloped up to fetch Toutant and Gaullé. The tracking party near the top of the falls had found something above the tree line. A short time later, the two commanders were hunkered down beside a stretch of moss and dirt near the small mountain tarn, where the upper falls emptied into it. The experienced trackers had been careful not to disturb anything. Together, the two senior knights examined the multitude of prints that had been captured there before the rocky terrain above took over the landscape.

"It looks like a lot of traffic has come through here recently," Gaullé observed aloud. He then gazed father up the trail that led to the distant Euralene Gap.

"These are the same tracks that we found this morning," Toutant confirmed, pointing out the human-like prints. "And here's some of a wolf. At least I think it's a wolf. They're too big, though."

"They all are," Sir Geoffrey agreed.

The wolf pads were indeed far larger than any the senior Skolish knight had seen before, but it was the large barefooted human prints that truly amazed him.

"If a person actually made those," the Skolish commander stated flatly, "then he must be one damn big brute."

"And he needs to get his toenails clipped," his Medinian counterpart added in a vain effort to lighten the mood.

"Well, it's possible that whoever they are, they're still around here someplace," Gaullé observed. "I can't say I'd fancy running into this fellow, or any of his four-legged pets, for that matter—at least not while stumbling around out here in the dark of night. I think we'd better make camp and move up the pass at first light."

The search parties were called in, and they then set up a camp near the mountain lake. They posted sentries and made sure to keep several fires well fed throughout the night. Even still, it was mostly a sleepless night for everyone.

*   *   *

July 26, 1461
Skoland

Later the next day, the Skolish detail made its way back across the river once more, still in the company of Sir Reginald Toutant of Medinia. Prince Paulo and his troops soon met up with them as they rode out from the Skolish garrison, where they'd spent the night. When the two knight commanders and the prince had dismounted to confer together, the prince was less than pleased with what they related.

The commanders reported that their search party had been unable to find any further clear signs on the rocky terrain above the waterfall. It was impossible for them to say with any certainty whether the tracks they'd found led farther up the trail or ventured off into some enclave in the mountain forest.

They then told the prince that when their search party had entered the Euralene Gap that morning and approached the fortress gates, they had not been given a warm welcome. No response was given to their repeated enquiries about a group approaching the pass from the east. No response, that is, save for when they'd ventured a little too near the massive gates. Then, suddenly, a cluster of arrows had struck the ground all around them with distinct precision. It was a clear warning, and there was nothing for them to do but return back down the pass.

The two commanders couldn't tell the prince whether the Varakovans had anything to do with the events of the past few days. Their neighbours to the west weren't talking, and they clearly weren't welcoming any visitors. The only thing they knew for certain was that Varakovan arrows were different in make from Medinian arrows. They'd returned with no answers to the mysterious events that led to the river confrontation. There was no resolution to their common losses or any return of captives. There were only shared fears that they had not seen the last of whomever, or whatever, was behind the raids into their two kingdoms.

While this unresolved situation didn't sit well with Prince Paulo, the Skolish prince did listen to his senior knight commander when Gaullé told him that he was convinced the Medinian knights were not responsible for the raids. Sir Geoffrey said he adamantly believed Toutant was being sincere when he'd denied those allegations. He didn't think Medinian knights were the culprits they sought, despite the evidence to the contrary.

Begrudgingly, the Skolish prince accepted that possibility. He resolved that his father's peace initiatives would continue unabated. He suggested, however, that they should report back to their respective kings all that occurred on both sides of the border. They would, in turn, discuss what measures should be taken to safeguard the western Euralene mountain region on both sides of the frontier border.

As Sir Reginald prepared to take his leave and return to Medinia, he inquired as to the condition of the wounded young knight.

"Sir Francis succumbed to his injuries during the night," Prince Paulo replied, curtly. "We buried him this morning."

Toutant saw the stricken look that this bluntly delivered statement brought to Sir Geoffrey's face. The Skolish commander was clearly distressed by this turn of events.

"I'm sorry to hear that," the Medinian commander stated, holding in his temper in check. "It was an unfortunate misunderstanding."

"At least we can say for sure what it was that killed him, Sir Reginald," the Skolish prince responded curtly. "That's more than can be said for the many others."

"Hopefully, those answers will reveal themselves in time, milord," the Medinian knight responded, with great restraint. "I wouldn't be at all surprised if we hear more from whoever's truly responsible for these events."

"Perhaps," Prince Paulo conceded grudgingly. "We'll certainly be better prepared next time if that proves to be the case. You have my word on that."

The three men remounted their war steeds. As they were about to depart on their separate ways, the Skolish prince ventured a last question. This time, his tone of voice was less hostile.

"Tell me, Sir Reginald," the prince asked, appearing a trifle embarrassed as he did so. "Your king's elder daughter, is she … ah … well?"

"The Lady Hillary Michelle, milord?" Toutant queried. "Indeed, the lady is well. Well and good."

From the saddled back of his steed, the knight commander leaned over slightly and winked at the young man. He smiled for the first time while in the prince's presence.

"Prince Paulo of Skoland," he stated kindly, "I can assure you that there isn't a man in all Medinia who wouldn't make peace with the devil himself if it meant taking her as his bride. You are a lucky man, indeed, if a wedding is on your horizon."

The young Skolish prince sat astride his horse, gazing after the Medinian commander as he rode off to ford the river crossing. His mind, however, was pondering future possibilities. While he disagreed with his father's desire to make peace with the Medinians, he conceded that it might happen anyways. If it did, it could well entail an arranged marriage. That marriage would mean that he would one day become the ruler of both these kingdoms and have a beautiful foreign queen at his beck and call.

"It sounds like the princess would make for a lovely bride, milord," the dispirited Gaullé commented, breaking the prince's private musings.

"Well, it isn't really a question of falling in love with her, is it?" the prince responded, with a harsh tone. "It's simply a necessary affair of state. It's a matter of expedience for the sake of peace. Yet … it would be ever more endurable if she weren't a nag, or homely and fat. Wouldn't you say?"

The prince signalled for the troop to move out then. He didn't see the grimace that passed over Sir Geoffrey's face resulting from his callus remark. The Skolish knights set off at a steady gait. In due course they would meet up with the reinforcements that had been dispatched from the castle in Kragonus. They would return with them to meet with the King of Skoland, his father.

*   *   *

Medinia

Across the river, the Medinian troops split up into two groups. While one column of knights departed for their frontier post, Toutant and his detail rode off towards their own king's distant castle, in Dumas. The commander's thoughts dwelt upon the fact that they'd nearly seen an escalation in the war, rather than a peace accord. He was troubled that someone had obviously gone to great lengths to plant evidence to frame the Medinians for the raids into Skoland. He vowed to himself to continue his investigation until he found out who was responsible for those raids, and for their own frontier farm incursions.

Some thirty minutes later, fresh sounds disturbed the stillness that had settled over the river crossing. Two solitary figures used birdcalls to signal to each other from the branches of trees on either side of the river. Dressed alike in black trousers and shirting and sporting their distinctive ponytails, two mercenaries lowered themselves quietly to the ground. After taking a few minutes to stretch and work the kinks out of their bodies, they sped off on foot towards the west. A couple of hours later, they rendezvoused above the double waterfalls, where the two trails up into the mountains converged.

"I damn near took an arrow in the head during that first volley yesterday," the raider, who'd hidden on the Medinian side of the cataracts, complained. "And I could have done without spending the night in the treetops."

"I wouldn't be telling Barozzi that," his fellow mercenary replied with little empathy. "Besides, his plan worked perfectly. I overheard everything that was being said between them."

"You mean Lord Victor's plan, don't you?" the first raider said.

Regardless whose precaution it had been, the spies they'd left behind had garnered some valuable information. The two raiders trotted the remaining distance up into the pass, where they gave the correct signals at the fortress gates and gained admittance to Varakov.

They had a detailed report to deliver when they returned to their masters.

*　　　　*　　　　*

July 27, 1461
The Euralene Mountains, Varakov

Woodrow's mountain retreat was encased into the secluded ridge on three sides, and the roof was covered over and looked like part of the natural environment. Only the rear-most face with its entry and porch were exposed, overlooking the gorge and giving him a clear view of the surrounding mountain range.

The Pack leader had kept the inside construction of the structure simple.

Essentially, it was one large room, some twenty feet deep and thirty-six feet long. The sturdy oak roof beams that protruded out over the porch were usually found with baskets of herbal plants and wild flowers hanging from them.

Inside, there were two bedchambers at one end of the cabin. A short partition wall separated these from each other. The fireplace was located in the centre of the cabin and vented up through the roof. Its hearth was open on two sides. It served the dual function of cooking and heating the entire cabin in the cool evenings and during the long winter months.

The adjacent kitchen area was small but functional, with a good sized cold room that was cut back into the ridge itself and entered through a door in the rear wall. The rest of the cabin was a jumbled mixture of living space, an extensive library, and a laboratory. The cabin's owner was a learned man, or more aptly a man who thirsted for knowledge and a better understanding of the natural world around him.

While the castle keeper's knowledge of warfare, history, and the arcane might not have equalled Lord Victor's, he was more than a match to the Varakovan king in other fields of study. The cabin held an assortment of instruments, research materials, and carefully documented notes of Woodrow's experimentations. His collections and equipment were not as extensive here as those to be found in his manor in Varakov proper, but they were still impressive in the range and scope of the material they covered.

The cold room housed as many herbs and compounds that he used for the making of medicines and for his experiments, as it did foodstuffs. The shelves that lined the walls of the cabin were filled with a portion of his collection of manuscripts, scrolls, and booklets. The writings that they contained originated from many parts of the known world. They ranged in subject matter from religious theology to the making and applications of different medicines to astrology and navigation.

Several of these texts Woodrow had sought and purchased from the shipping vessels that regularly visited Port Lupus. Many of the ship captains who plied the ocean trades were well aware of his preferences. They often sought out and brought their literary finds to Varakov's harbour, knowing that both the castle keeper and Lord Victor were grateful, well-paying customers.

To be sure, a number of the manuscripts found both here and in Woodrow's manor had been gifted to him by the Varakovan king, as well. It was both a generous gesture on Lord Victor's part and a challenging one. Many were the nights that the two men spent in long discussions over some newly found document, at times offering their distinct and fierce interpretations of their contents. Despite any disagreements, the two men treasured this aspect of their relationship greatly. They were equally adept at defending a notion and at playing the devil's advocate. Indeed, they each respected the insightful mind of the other. Their discourse was often a mutual testing of the other's stated position on a matter, whether it was truly believed or not. Their debate was often like a game of chess, with several fronts being waged at the same time in order to keep their opponent off guard.

Other written documents in the mountain retreat had been collected during the years of Woodrow's wanderings. These came from long before he'd discovered the place called Sanctuary, in the kingdom of Varakov. They came from a time when he had traveled in the lone company of his mate, from a time long past.

Finally, there were the writings penned by the castle keeper's own hand. These were the records of his own research and studies, whether successfully completed or not. When it came to scientific study, he had long ago learned the value of making careful observations over an extended period. It was a habit he'd found useful in the study of human behaviour as well.

This late afternoon, Woodrow sat at the rough-hewn table that he used for both dining and working. The lanterns that were hung from the beams overhead provided him enough light by which he could toil over the task at hand. At the moment, he was busy blending new batches of medicines for both the leg and the stomach of his injured young patient.

It was the castle keeper's long-held observation that nutrition played as important a role in the healing process as did any external treatments to a wounded area. He knew that a patient needed proper sustenance if he were to make a full recovery.

The evening they'd arrived, he'd carefully cleansed the youth's leg, stitched his wound, and then applied his concoction of herbal salves. When he'd finished, he had bandaged the leg in clean dressings. Satisfied that he'd done his best to prevent infection, Woodrow had put the boy into the seldom-used sleeping cubicle next to his own. He'd covered him with a coarse woollen blanket and then watched over him through most of that night in case he'd taken a turn for the worse. The wound was severe but treatable. His greatest concern was the loss of blood and shock to the lad's system.

Over the last two days, Woodrow had been force-feeding the youth sips from a brew of herbs and strained vegetable matter whenever possible. He knew that the mixture would give the lad strength and help prevent dehydration. It was already a good sign that the youth's breathing had stabilized into a deep and regular pattern, although he still slipped in and out of consciousness. When the lad stirred into partial awareness, he accepted the home made brew mechanically, but at least some of it got into his belly. It would help.

Now, as Woodrow was working up a new batch of medicines for later use, he felt a bump against his chair. The Pack enforcer had come in from the doorway. The wolf laid his sizeable head across Woodrow's thigh and looked up at him with his golden eyes.

"Ah, Brutus, my friend," the Pack leader said, with a gesture towards his heart. Woodrow was in the habit of using both his voice and a simple sign language to communicate with his companion. He sat back in his chair, stiff from lack of movement.

"Have you come to tell me it's time to take a break?" The Pack leader stroked the powerful animal's head with one hand and stretched out with his other arm. He could feel his back and neck muscles protest as he worked out the knots that had set in while he sat hunched over his work. He nodded his head in the direction of his patient. "Why don't we step outside while our young friend gets his rest?"

While Woodrow put the medicines away into the cold room, the wolf padded noiselessly over to the bed and stood staring at the figure lying there. The Pack enforcer lifted his right foreleg and placed his paw gently on the youth's chest. The gesture implied he was pledged to safeguard their injured patient too. It was as if the alpha wolf clearly understood that the youth was no longer prey to be hunted down. He was now one of their own.

The two Pack members moved outside then and Woodrow closed the door quietly behind them. He took a moment to breathe in the thin mountain air, filling his lungs with its freshness. The sun was slowly setting, giving up its claim to the sky. The shadows it cast were steadily climbing the mountainside, devouring the landscape.

They walked around the end of the cabin and climbed up the short path to the top of the ridge. Standing on the ridge extension above the cabin roof, man and wolf were framed on a canvas of nature's sheerest beauty. Out to the west, beyond Varakov, they watched the large, shimmering orange ball dip its edge into the distant sea and then, inch by inch, be swallowed up.

By the remaining light, Woodrow could faintly make out the harbour town that was sited on the sheltered side of the bay with the wolf-head likeness. The town was aptly named Port Lupus. Even at this great distance, he could imagine the port going into an early evening lull, a brief respite before the nightlife took over.

True, it was a bustling seaport in the daylight hours, but it always seemed to quiet down towards the end of the workday. That was when the shop owners, the tradesmen, and the various dock workers wound up their daily activities. The shipyards would close up for the night, and even the hardworking men who toiled in the salt flats by the river marsh would head homeward for their evening repast.

The quiet would be short lived, however. It was as if the town only paused to rest for the evening meal before it was transformed into a creature of the night. As the street lamps were lit, the activities around town would become more and more boisterous with the passing hours. Often the rowdiness ended only as the dawn approached, for Port Lupus was a wide-open seafaring town. The town welcomed those men whose preferences were for the diverse pleasures that the nightlife offered.

Even after all the years he'd lived in Varakov, Woodrow was still amazed at the depravities that some men sought out and what passed for pleasure for them. The depth that some men could sink to was a puzzle that he never could quite figure out. How a man could toil and slave for his wages, simply to cast away for the momentary fulfillment of his lust or some other manner of vice, was hard to fathom.

Port Lupus offered it all for them. There was prostitution, gambling, drugs, spirits, and violence. If you had the coin, there was always something, or someone, to spend it on.

In the town, gang members known as the Multinationals controlled most of these activities in the name of the king. Almost anyone was allowed to operate an enterprise, but only by cutting the gang into the action. The Multinationals were there to keep order and to collect the king's fair share. The fees they demanded and collected replaced the arbitrary and often heavy-handed tax system more commonly used in other kingdoms. The gang watched over their dominion with due diligence. Anyone foolish enough to skimp on the informal tax was dealt with harshly.

Over the years, Woodrow had many dealings with the gang, and with its leader, a young man named Vinnie. The two of them had a history together, in fact. Woodrow's position as castle keeper under Lord Victor's reign had given him authority to oversee the many facets of the kingdom's business. Port Lupus was run as a business, and a very profitable business at that.

As the last portion of the sun gave up the sky with a glimmering tremble and slipped into the sea, Woodrow turned away from his musings and the fading view over Varakov. He roughly stroked the head of his four-legged companion and then brought his gaze up to look at the moon as it rose over the landscape on its nightly journey.

The moon now had a ragged edge to it. The full moon transformations were over, but the Pack leader still felt Diana's diminishing tug deep in his soul. He knew that Brutus could sense it also. Through his fingertips, he could feel the wolf stiffen, ever so slightly. It was time for them to go inside and check up on their young patient. The youth, too, would be feeling the stirring.

*   *   *

Port Lupus, Varakov

The young gang leader gazed out from the upper loft window of the Multinational headquarters at the darkening streets below. From where he stood, he was afforded an unobstructed view over the harbour and much of the surrounding town. As the sun was setting into the ocean, he knew his men would be taking up their positions in the key locales of Port Lupus. The street gangs he controlled were the unofficial police force, as well as the tithe collectors for Lord Victor.

The king's edict was for the gang to maintain a rowdy and entertaining environment in which men could have a good time, for a price. They were to be treated as welcome customers and allowed to happily squander their wages in any manner they chose. Happy customers would then want to come back for more, preferably, the very next night.

The gang leader was a streetwise, toughened young man known to everyone simply as Vinnie. He was loved by some, hated and feared by others. It was widely understood that Vinnie could bring pleasure, or Vinnie could bring pain.

The Multinationals gang was structured so that their members branched out into each of the vice sectors. At the top of their numerous ranks was the central gang leadership known as the Ohs, who reported directly to him. He, in turn, reported only to Lord Victor or to the castle keeper, who acted on his behalf.

With his curly brown hair and boyish good looks, Vinnie stood out in most crowds. His frequent smile naturally conveyed an amusement at what life brought his way, both the good and the bad. That same smile could be thought to be cruel at times, however, if he felt crossed or took offence at some slight.

Despite his youth, the gang leader was wise to the ways of men. He had learned that they could best be controlled through a combination of reward and a fear of punishment. He rarely interfered in a man's pleasure, as long as it was bought and paid for and was consensual between the parties involved. On the other hand, he never failed to take stern measures against anyone who broke one of his simple rules.

It was nearly time for him to make his own rounds. Each night, he took to the streets with a few of the other Ohs and dropped in on some of the many establishments in Port Lupus. If word of any trouble reached his ears, he would promptly direct the appropriate gang members to deal with it. His men could be rapidly dispersed to any trouble spot in a matter of minutes. By sheer numbers, weapons, and ruthlessness, they could put down a small riot if need be.

Turning away from the window, Vinnie headed downstairs to gather a few of the Ohs and set out on the night's patrol. As they left the Multinational's headquarters and stepped out into the night time streets, he walked along side his second-in-command, Lorenzo. Three of the other Ohs took up positions on their three, six, and nine o'clock. They knew the routine without needing to be told.

The oldest was Sergei, now commonly known as Sergio, and a fugitive from the steppes of Russia. He was a bear of a man and handy with a club or his fists. The second was Edward, who they had renamed Eduardo. He hailed from the isle of Britannia and was equally adept with a sword or a knife. The last, and the youngest of the Ohs, was Filippo. He'd arrived as a stow-away aboard a Portuguese ship the year before.

As they passed by the docks, Vinnie spotted some younger lads who were out and about and likely up to no particular good. He smiled indulgently. Lorenzo caught the look.

"They remind me when you were their age, or a little younger," he said. "I remember when you first arrived in Port Lupus and had to live by your wits on these very same streets."

Vinnie remembered too. He'd been a bold urchin who survived by stealing whatever he could lay his hands on. That had changed the fateful day he'd spotted an obviously well-to-do man and had tried to pick his pocket. That man had turned out to be Woodrow, the king's castle keeper. Woodrow had caught him in the act and calmly knocked him out cold.

"I was lucky they didn't hang me," the gang leader replied. "I still don't know why the castle keeper decided to take me under his wing, instead. I'm just grateful that he did."

Indeed, over the ensuing years, he'd been mentored by the man, and never once had Woodrow looked for some kind of payback. On the contrary, the castle keeper had never ceased to be there for him whenever he needed advice. Vinnie valued that council and he held the man, who gave it freely, in the highest esteem.

All was in order in the first two establishments they dropped in on, but it was still early. At the second tavern, Vinnie saw two gang members having a chat with some sailors from a recently arrived ship, as they were being bought a free round of ale on the house. He was pleased by that. Enter any bar, hall, or a den of iniquity and you'd find members of the Multinational's organization. It was the gang's policy to treat new arrivals to a beverage, and then calmly be told of the many diversions in town that were there to enjoy and partake in.

Just as calmly, and more seriously, the sailors were also being informed of the rules of the house and the consequences of non-compliance. The gang members were clever enough to pre-empt most of the potential for trouble with these talks. Most men who were still sober at the time of these talks realized that the stern young men sitting opposite them were not to be taken lightly.

Vinnie covered his territory like an experienced field marshal, but he wasn't above getting his hands dirty. He had the scars to attest to it. He had helped put down his fair share of brawls. Tonight would prove to be no exception. As he and the Ohs moved on towards the next tavern, they could hear angry voices and curses all the way out on the street. They picked up the pace to investigate the commotion.

Stepping in through the doors, Vinnie would have been brained by a flying chair had it not been for Lorenzo pushing him aside at the last moment. He gave his second-in-command a grateful glance and then straightened back up and assessed the situation.

He could see that an entire crew of one ship had lost control. He had no way of knowing that a few sailors had taken exception to something that was said by a local, or that what had started out as a minor difference of opinion had soon escalated to an all-out brawl. It didn't much matter. What mattered was that the ship's ensemble was literally tearing the place apart.

Vinnie and his hand-picked men never hesitated in the slightest. Picking up a broken table leg, the gang leader walked calmly into the middle of the melee and started laying sailors out. Lorenzo and the three other Ohs worked their way towards him from the outer perimeters using their fists and billie clubs effectively, as well.

The fight was over in a matter of minutes. The final count was a dozen sailors on the floor, either unconscious or writhing in agony. Vinnie had taken out half that number himself, the last of whom was a knife-wielding, drunken deck hand who had tried to gut the gang leader with a vicious slash of his blade.

The sailor in question would be in need of some extensive healing time. Vinnie blocked his knife assault with the chair leg, and then he hit the crewman with a right cross that threatened to take the man's head off. That put a quick end to the brawl.

Order had been restored to the tavern, albeit at a loss of some potential revenue. Several of the sailors would need to be carried back to the docks and deposited in their longboats to be rowed back to their ship. They wouldn't be spending any more of their wages tonight. A suitable compensation was removed from their pockets, however, to cover the damages.

Vinnie left Sergio, Eduardo and Filippo behind to oversee the removal of the injured while he and Lorenzo proceeded with their rounds.

"How's the hand?" his second-in-command asked, as they stepped back outside.

"Sore and starting to swell," he replied, checking his hand for damage, "but nothing compared to what my head would have looked like if that chair had connected. Thanks for the timely shove."

"Better a chair in the head than a knife in the belly, though," Lorenzo said. "You should have let me and the boys handle it."

"I needed the practice," Vinnie replied. "You wouldn't me getting soft, would you?

"I don't think that's going to happen any time soon," Lorenzo said, with a chuckle, "but maybe you've had enough practice for the evening. Why don't we check up on one of the brothels? I don't mind if the ladies are a little soft."

Vinnie laughed. "Okay. A brothel it is, but only if you promise not to disappear with one of the Vamps. We've still got some work to do tonight."

The gang leader knew that Lorenzo was a ladies man through and through, whether he was paying for their company, or chasing after someone's daughter, or their wife. He only hoped it wouldn't get him killed one day.

"Now why would I make a promise like that?" his second-in-command replied with a laugh of his own. "It would break my sworn oath to always put pleasure before work. Besides, the ladies would be disappointed if I didn't try to take advantage of them. They know that you won't."

Lorenzo knew that Vinnie held a place in his heart for the town's Vamps, as the ladies of the evening in Port Lupus were known. The gang leader insisted that they not be preyed upon or abused in any way. They had a job to do, just like everyone else. Vinnie's point of view had become law and the gang members adhered to it, despite the fact that harlots were usually held in the lowest regard. The fate of a prostitute in most cities and port towns was in the hands of uncaring and often violent men. They led precarious lives. It was a rough trade, and an even rougher life.

Lorenzo knew that it could be argued that Vinnie was simply protecting his vested interests, since the Multinationals derived a large portion of their income from prostitution. On the other hand, he knew that Vinnie had personally seen to it that the Vamps were allowed to keep a fair share of their earnings. The tithe they and their madams paid was the same as any other town business.

The gang leader had even sought the castle keeper out and convinced him to hold regular monthly clinics, where Woodrow treated the women for minor ailments and even helped some of them who were with child.

A smile came to his face as Lorenzo reflected on these clinics. They'd become a part of Woodrow's assumed duties. Despite the extra work that it entailed, something the castle keeper regularly cursed Vinnie for. Lorenzo suspected, though, that Woodrow drew a pleasant diversion from it. The Vamps possessed a bawdy sense of humour and a vocabulary that could make even a frontier knight blush. They clearly understood the ways of men. Perhaps, because they'd been with so many of them, they realized that with their pants down, all men were pretty much the same.

CHAPTER 6

THE FEAST

July 27, 1461
The Euralene Mountains, Varakov

WILLIE WAS HAVING A terrible nightmare. He was being relentlessly pursued by nameless terrors. He was running, but it felt like he was in molasses. Each stride was a struggle to complete, and the sound of his pursuers grew in his ears. The voiceless images of his lost friends came to hasten him onwards, but he couldn't seem to gain any ground. He was tired. A part of him just wanted to quit trying.

Another part of his being, however, began growing stronger now. It was fuelled by a sense of outrage, which seemed to be like a piece of coal glowing in his belly that was being fanned into a small fire. It was a rage that had no clear direction to vent itself, yet it seemed to sustain his body and its demand for life.

Woodrow bent over his patient, bathing his sweating forehead and chest with a damp cloth once more. The cool moisture helped settle the youth who'd been calling out names in his delirium. His agitation and thrashing had caused his blankets to fall to the floor, but a careful check of his bandages showed no sign of renewed bleeding. He knew that another twenty-four hours would tell the tale.

Meanwhile, he'd keep watch and try periodically to get some nourishment into him, as he was about to do now. This constant care would mean not returning to his castle duties for another few days and then possibly suffering the wrath of Lord Victor.

If asked why he put the welfare of this unimportant youth ahead of his own, Woodrow probably couldn't have said; he just did. His young patient had become his first priority.

As if to question that decision, the Pack leader felt a vibration against his chest. He straightened up slowly and then undid the toggles from the upper portion of his shirt and reached inside to his chest. He withdrew the carved wolf-head amulet that hung from his neck on a golden chain. Its previously dark-green opaque surface was now alive with a hidden power of its own. A faint light pulsed within, which grew in intensity until the gem carving shone with an iridescent glow.

The stone was warm to the touch and vibrated minutely. Lord Victor was reaching out to him. He was being summoned.

It was a summons that he chose to ignore at his own peril.

*   *   *

July 28, 1461
The Euralene Mountains, Varakov

During the previous evening, the amulet had glowed once more, brighter still, and hot to the touch. So hot, in fact, it had burnt the skin on his chest, forcing him to remove the chain from around his neck and to place the amulet aside on the table. It had not glowed today. That did not bode particularly well, however.

The upside was the marked improvement shown in his patient, whose name he still did not know. The youth had regained consciousness several times that morning and had even managed a few disoriented queries. Woodrow responded with soothing tones and took the opportunity to feed him more of his brewed mixture. He'd included a small portion of herbs, which induced sleep. The herbal brew soon sent the lad back into a slumber, giving his body the necessary time to recoup and to further the healing process.

As the day wore on, the youth had become more lucid for periods, although he'd grown wild eyed in panic at one point, when he'd awakened and seen Brutus standing there. The sight of a wolf, even a relatively normal-sized one, had been too much for his troubled mind to accept. Woodrow had been forced to increase his next sedation dosage to calm him back down and let him return to a fitful sleep.

The Pack leader banished his friend from the cabin at that point. He walked him to the door and then told him with a series of hand signals that he should return home to his mate and waiting family. The wolf gave Woodrow a long stare, as if questioning this command decision, but then he'd abruptly bounded off.

Brutus had a mind of his own, however, and when Woodrow went back into the cabin, he'd doubled back and settled himself into a small wooded copse near the rim of the gorge. The alpha wolf would keep a steady watch from there while the Pack leader remained in the cabin, with perhaps a brief jaunt to find a meal. As long as Woodrow was in the mountains, it was his duty as the Pack's enforcer to see to his safety. His mate and their family would have to wait.

From one of the cabin windows, Woodrow observed the wolf taking up station in the little copse of trees.

"You are the truest of friends, my old comrade," he muttered to himself. "I was both cursed and blest the day you came into my life."

*   *   *

The Mesa-of-the-Moon, Varakov

Lord Victor was in a foul mood. There were matters that he wanted to discuss with the castle keeper. There were things to be done, and the great hall to prepare. Yet, there was still no sign of Woodrow and the Varakovan king was growing impatient.

Victor could excuse a temporary absence. After all, the Pack leader had sent Simon to him, to at least maintain appearances. This continuing delay was bordering on sheer insolence, however. The king could not tolerate insolence, not even from his long-time aide.

The castle guards, and even the members of his coven council, tread softly in his presence. It still wasn't always enough. Several of them had felt his wrath over minor offences.

Lord Victor was planning on throwing a rare banquet in the castle's great hall. Normally quite reclusive, the king seldom invited guests to his inner domain. There were dozens of preparations that still needed attending to. If Woodrow were here, he would be taking charge of the details for the gathering that his liege envisioned.

It was a celebratory feast that Lord Victor wished to hold. It would be a feast marking their successful raids into Skoland and Medinia. True, the reports from the river crossing had not been all good. The talks Barozzi's men had overheard between Toutant, the Medinian commander, and the Skolish Prince Paulo and his commander, Gaullé, had been disappointing. It seemed that the Varakovan king's hope for the renewal of their war had been thwarted.

It had been a long shot, anyways.

The report he'd received had indicated that there was now a decided fear factor firmly instilled throughout their two western frontiers. At least that much had been accomplished.

The surveillance of the two spies had also confirmed the reports that Prince Paulo and the Lady Hillary Michelle were likely candidates for a marriage. If so, their union would serve to seal the peace accords. This news gave Lord Victor pause for reflection. It occurred to him that perhaps there was a better way to control events on the other side of the pass. It was certainly worth further consideration.

In the meantime, Victor summoned his stewards to the hall and gave them his final instructions for the feast. Those instructions would normally have been given to his castle keeper so he wouldn't have had to deal with these minions or the minor details. That continued to irk him. It had fallen to him to see to it that the guest list was complete. Invitations had been sent to Barozzi and his men, to the Ohs' leadership of the Multinationals, and to several key landowners and barons from across the kingdom. He'd even had to discuss the menu with the chefs and put them to work preparing the feast that he envisioned. It was demeaning.

The only saving grace for Lord Victor was that they would dine well on the spoils of the Medinian raid. He might even have the Skolish captives provide the after-dinner entertainment. The thought of how they could be used for his benefit brought a smile to the king's face.

While stewards scurried about preparing the hall, Lord Victor's mood brightened somewhat. He decided that it would do him some good to get drunk and let his hair down. It had been quite some time. He would wallow in the mud with his selected subjects. These were loyal men whom he trusted, as far as he trusted anyone. Trust was a commodity, one which he gave out very sparingly.

Tonight there would be wine, women, and song. A little debauchery would be good for morale and it would help to further bind his employees to him.

Reward and punishment; they were two sides of the same coin of obedience that Lord Victor understood so well. Favour and fear both bought and guaranteed their loyalties. Lord Victor was never shy about spending the coin. Be it heads or tails.

Outside, it was late afternoon. The feast would begin at twelve midnight. The castle at the Mesa-of-the-Moon was now a beehive of activity and earnest preparation. Lord Victor decided it was time he paid a visit to the castle keeper. His particular mode of travel would see him there and back before the festivities began in earnest. If Woodrow wouldn't come to Victor, then Victor would go to Woodrow while he still had some time, to kill.

*   *   *

The Euralene Mountains, Varakov

Ever so slowly, the door of the cabin began to swing open, causing Woodrow to look up from the table where he sat preparing a new batch of his herbal-salve concoction. The door had no lock, but he clearly recalled having latched it after he'd tried sending Brutus home.

The Pack leader wasn't overly surprised, however, to see the ominous presence of Lord Victor striding up onto the porch. Victor had a way with doors, and much more, especially since he'd begun delving into the arcane black arts. By the time his caped caller had reached the doorway, the door stood wide open as if in anticipation of that visitor.

"How went the hunt, my dear Woodrow?" Lord Victor asked quietly as he stepped barefoot over the threshold. "You've been back in Varakov for days now, but I haven't seen you. You didn't forget about me, did you?"

The Varakovan king wasn't exactly a forgettable person. He carried himself with the bearing of a man who was used to wielding his authority. His loose-fitting, rich silken garments and the ever-present cape he wore made for a striking appearance. Even up here in the mountains, far from his castle, Lord Victor had an undeniable aura about him. It was almost as if he charged the air around him with the energy of his being.

Woodrow rose from his chair and gave a bow of his head to his liege, but he didn't respond in any manner. It wasn't really expected of him at this point.

"You haven't been to the castle, or to your manor. So I deduced that you must be here," Victor said. "I came all the way up here to see if you were ill or something."

"You aren't ill, or something, are you, my friend?" the king asked. There was a subtle menacing tone to his voice.

The only response to his query was a silence that weighed heavily in the air. Lord Victor stood silent for a long moment, just looking at his castle keeper. His gaze then moved down to the tabletop. He reached out and picked up the amulet from the table and slowly fingered it. He seemed lost in thought.

"So then," the king said, finally, "did you not get your fill of flesh and blood on the hunt? Did you need some more time off from your duties? Is that it?" Victor set the amulet down in front of the still silent Woodrow. He watched as the castle keeper dutifully picked it up and returned it to its place around his neck. "Good," he said. "It's good that a gift given in friendship is valued by the person who receives it. You wouldn't want to lose it." The implications of his words were not lost on the castle keeper.

Lord Victor surveyed the cabin with a long look. It appeared much the same as it always did. Books, medicines, and herbs were everywhere. Of course, the youth lying on the spare bed—that was something new. Victor made a poor attempt at feigning surprise, which in itself delivered a further message.

"And who, do we have here? Did you bring me back a present?" Victor asked. He crossed the room and then stood near the still form lying unconscious on the bed. "Why, it's a boy! Is he a gift for me, Woodrow? Is he someone for me to sink my teeth into?"

"Leave him, Victor."

Woodrow had risen now.

"He's not for you," the Pack leader said. The tenor of his voice was flat and emotionless.

"I'm too tired to engage in a battle of wits with you at the moment, sire," Woodrow added in a more demure tone. "Besides, you wouldn't care for the taste. The lad's been infected. By now, his blood's as poisoned as my own is."

Woodrow brought the salve and fresh bandages over to the bed and prepared to change the lad's dressings once more. The injured youth moaned and stirred on the bed, almost as if he sensed the battle of wills that was taking place over him, which might well determine his fate.

"Why didn't you just let your four-legged pets have him for their dinner?" Victor asked as he looked down with disdain at the restless youth. Looking up again, he then further taunted the Pack leader. "Perhaps, we should just kill him now and be done with it."

"No," Woodrow stated firmly. "You can see that his wound is healing. If he lives, he'll carry the scar of it forever, both outside and in. He'll be one of us."

For a moment, Woodrow wondered if he had overstepped himself. He had known Lord Victor a long time. They shared a similar affliction. Yet, Victor was the king, and as such, he had no equal.

"We suffered several losses on our raid into Medinia, milord. The Pack needs to be replenished," he added respectfully.

Victor gave no immediate response. He cast his eyes over the Pack leader's face, absorbing its every feature. It was as if he was searching for any sign of a challenge to his authority.

Finally, he slowly nodded his head and replied, "Very well, my old friend. I will allow you his life."

"Thank you, sire," Woodrow said, "I—"

"Don't thank me yet," Victor interrupted, raising his hand. "I will allow you his life on the proviso that you accept full responsibility for him. It will be up to you to teach him his place—if he is to continue to survive."

"But surely, sire, I can't be —"

"Yes, you can, Woodrow," Victor said, cutting short his protests. "You can, and you will. You've already discounted any other option that I was prepared to entertain. You can't have it both ways, my old friend." With that said, Victor turned to leave. He stopped at the doorway and then looked back to add a last command. "As soon as he's strong enough to travel, I'll expect you to return post haste. Your castle duties await you, and I will want his training begun."

He indicated the wounded youth with a slight nod of his head in that direction. "Who knows? With you acting as his mentor, perhaps, come one distant day, he'll be the one who'll end up succeeding you as the keeper of my castle—when you retire, that is."

"Yes, milord," the Pack leader said, submissively.

"Don't fail me, Woodrow," Victor added. "I consider you to be one of my closest and most loyal confidants. It would grieve me greatly if you didn't feel the same."

Woodrow straightened his tired and aching back. He allowed his eyes to meet Victor's for a full three seconds before dropping them in obedience. "I am your faithful servant, sire," he said. "In all ways, I am yours to command."

Victor nodded as if this was a given.

"Get some sleep and nourishment yourself," the king advised, and this time he sounded sincere. "You're looking haggard."

Lord Victor turned then and left the cabin. Behind him, the door slowly swung shut, seemingly of its own accord.

*   *   *

As Victor strode barefoot from the cabin, his shimmering cape billowed out behind him in the evening air. He slowed his pace as he approached the rim of the gorge and stopped at its edge. The rising partial moon cast just ample enough light for him to see down into its depths. He could make out where the waterfall crashed into the rocky basin. The rising spray hung like a low, misty cloud in the base of the gorge itself.

Victor mused over in his mind, the ongoing challenge that the wolf-creatures posed. The four-legged varieties were wild, feral animals that could only be controlled, so it would seem, by their two-legged brethren. The humans were almost as wild, and they could only be controlled by their Pack leader. Woodrow only served him in order to protect them and provide this safe haven in the Varakovan forests. He was loyal, but perhaps not totally so, it would now appear.

The king understood that Woodrow, Simon, and the others were part men, part wolves. They had a foot in two worlds and were therefore unpredictable. Well, less predictable. The key to their continued obedience was Sanctuary, and it was he who provided them with their precious refuge. It was the only safe haven where they were protected from extermination at the hands of the superstitious rabble. In return, they were pledged to do his bidding. They were sworn to it, in fact. Loyalty was important to the Pack, as was their precious honour. To date, they had performed their duties well when called upon to carry out a mission.

Woodrow wasn't the first Pack leader to swear their allegiance to him, Victor recalled. The first had been Andropov, until he had finally succumbed to the ruin of age. At the time, Woodrow was being groomed to take charge of the Pack and become its alpha male human when the elderly wolf-man was no longer able to perform that function, albeit reluctantly. When that fateful day arrived, Andropov had brought Woodrow to the Varakovan castle for the first time. In a ceremony of allegiance, the new Pack leader had pledged his loyalty and services to Lord Victor, as Andropov himself had once done. In return, Victor had promised the Pack a continued welcome in Varakov and a home in this mountain Sanctuary.

Up to now, they'd maintained a workable relationship. He was the king, the Lord of Varakov, and Woodrow, the castle keeper and Pack leader. It could even be said that, he valued the wolf-man's friendship, except that friendship wasn't exactly an accurate description for their relationship. A king could never truly have a friend, for he had no equal in the land.

It could be fairly said, however, that Victor appreciated Woodrow. The man was an excellent court administrator, and he handled the day-to-day affairs of the kingdom, admirably. People trusted and respected him. They abided by his decisions, knowing they were made in the king's name. More importantly, it freed Victor from those mundane drudgeries that he had no inclination for.

Yet, there was still more than that to their relationship. The castle keeper was the closest he had to a peer. Their lives had many parallels. Woodrow's intellect and learning approached that of his own. He was someone whom Victor could debate a myriad of topics with, or with whom he could even share a simple, unguarded laugh.

Woodrow was the sole person whose opinions and advice Victor sought out, if perhaps a little less these past few years. He allowed that this was more his own doing than the castle keeper's. Other matters had preoccupied him of late. They were matters that he and Woodrow didn't see eye to eye on, and Victor didn't feel free to confide in him concerning.

Nevertheless, the Pack leader remained of value to him. He was also one of the few men, who understood the nature of his particular affliction.

He would never think to stand in judgement. He knew that it was as much beyond Victor's control, as his having to answer to Diana's call was to him.

Indeed, Victor suffered with an uncontrollable affliction of his own. One that separated him from other men, even more than being their king did. Woodrow was well aware of its nature, although they seldom spoke of it.

After all their years together, even Brutus seemed to understand that they all shared this common bond. The Varakovan king had spent many hours in their joint company. They had come to know one another rather well. On occasion, Victor would make it a point to meet with Woodrow at his manor while Brutus was present. Over time, he and the Pack enforcer had developed a wary respect for one another. The Varakovan king and the Pack enforcer were two strong-willed individuals, and each was a tormented soul in his own right. They shared a connection to Woodrow, in his dual roles as both castle keeper and Pack leader. It made them three beings bonded by circumstance.

This was why, perhaps, as Victor stood looking down over the gorge, he was well aware of the wolf's eyes boring into his back. The hairs on the nape of his neck bristled. He sensed Brutus watching him silently from his hidden position in the small cluster of trees. There was no denying the animal's loyalty to his Pack leader.

He genuinely hoped the same held true for Woodrow, with regards to his liege. He fervently hoped that the Pack leader's current actions didn't foreshadow a change in their relationship. Nevertheless, he decided that Woodrow would have to be watched more carefully and his future actions evaluated.

Perhaps the injured youth and Woodrow would grow close, the Varakovan king considered. It might prove useful, if they did. An implied threat hanging over the lad's head might be just the thing to keep the castle keeper in line, if it became necessary.

With that decided, Victor turned his head slowly, until he was looking directly at the small wooded copse. Only the large wolf's shining yellow eyes gave away his presence. For a brief moment, their gazes locked, long enough to convey to the feral animal that precious little escaped the attention of Lord Victor.

Turning his attention back to the deep gorge, Victor stared down into its depths. His silken garments fluttered in the night breeze. His hands clutched at the edges of his cape, and then he raised his arms out wide. He paused, just for a brief moment, and then he dove off the ledge.

Downwards he plummeted, in an exhilarating freefall. He plummeted down towards the jagged rocks below. The transformation which then occurred did so in a fluid blur. One moment Victor's shimmering cape was streaming out behind him, and the next moment it billowed up, slowing his descent. The form of the cape altered, becoming ribbed, parchment-like wings, as Victor's entire body mutated dramatically as well.

It was a winged, scaled, reptilian Beast, which then flapped awkwardly to a halt just above the gorge mists. The loose-fitting silk clothing the Varakovan king wore accommodated the startling change in his physique. His bare feet were now scaled, enlarged and fiercely clawed. Slowly, the winged creature he'd become rose upwards into the night air, until it climbed above the rim of the gorge once more.

Twice, the strange, alien Beast circled above the ridge. Its ribbed wings flapped with the same jerking motion as that of a bat, only there, all resemblance ended. The winged Beast then set off over the great mountain forest, flapping and gliding downwards towards the distant mesa on the Varakovan plains below.

Yet, despite the manner of its flying, this was no blind bat flying through the night sky using sound reverberations to locate its prey. This flying Beast had emerald green eyes that shone in the moon light.

And the Beast's eyes could see very well.

*　　　　*　　　　*

"Last Quarter–Half Moon"

July 30, 1461
The Mesa-of-the-Moon, Varakov

The guests had begun arriving two hours prior to midnight, as per the instructions in their invitations. They'd been processed in an orderly fashion through the two gates of the castled town, and then submitted to inspection at the castle guard station, before being shown into the great hall itself. Here, their patience was rewarded. The castle stewards greeted them with tankards of ale, honey mead, or goblets of wine, according to their personal taste.

The guests mingled as they drank heartily. They greeted new arrivals, reminisced with old friends, boasted about their latest deeds, and got caught up with the current events in those various parts of the kingdom not their own. Much of the talk centred on what the night's feast might have in store for them.

Among the guests were a number of mercenaries in Victor's employ, as well as several wealthier landowners and barons from the outlying regions of Varakov. Like the Multinationals of the larger Port Lupus, these men had been placed in charge of smaller towns and villages in the widely spread rural farmland areas. They represented their Lord's interest and they collected a percentage of all economic activity on his behalf, from farming and livestock revenue to the production of flour and cloth at the various Varakovan mills.

Barozzi, the raider leader, and a dozen of his fellow mercenaries had arrived about eleven. He and his men were dressed in dark, loose-fitting clothing, and they wore their hair long tied back in a traditional ponytail. Their distinctive look set them apart from Victor's other hired minions. Each of the raiders had used a simple piece of black silk ribbon to tie back their hair this evening. There were no ornate barrettes with their nasty concealed blades in evidence tonight.

Barozzi seemed to be in fine spirits, despite the thin red line that marked his face. The wound was scabbing over. When healed, it would leave behind a scar as a constant reminder to him of Victor's lesson. Yet, for the mercenary, it was a badge of honour as was any wound received on the field of battle. He had survived the Varakovan king's wrath. That was victory enough.

The raiders drank heartily, and while they didn't mingle much with the other guests, they were grateful for the invitation to the feast. They listened to the troupe of musicians who played for the guests, and they wandered around the outside of the dining tables that had been set up in the great hall. As a group, they marvelled at the richness and intricate detail of the tapestries. They stood in awe at the majesty of the life-sized statuary and in wonder of the intricate mosaic tiled pavement beneath their feet.

The paintings over the fireplace gave them pause. They speculated on the significance behind them, especially the one portraying a king and his three sons with daggers buried in each of their hearts. The variety of weaponry on display on the inner wall gave the raiders much to talk about. They argued over the merits and efficiency of many of the instruments of death, with which they had more than a passing familiarity. The weapons seemed to contradict Lord Victor's edict, but then these were out openly on display, not concealed on anyone's person.

Shortly following Barozzi and his men's arrival, ten members of the Multinational gang's leadership from Port Lupus entered the hall. The young, street-seasoned tough named Vinnie led the Ohs in. He was just under six feet tall, with curly brown hair that was kept neatly trimmed, and his green eyes were flecked with gold. The gang leader moved with an easy confident stride, but those engaging eyes of his swept the room as if they were constantly evaluating their surroundings.

Much like the other guests invited to the great hall this evening, the Ohs were in a boisterous mood. This exceedingly rare visit to Lord Victor's private domain was a momentous occasion. They were both honoured and thrilled to be included on the guest list. Among the ranks of the Ohs, only Vinnie had ever been invited here previously.

The gang leader joined his men in accepting refreshments from the stewards who moved through the crowd. Vinnie drank a little slower than the rest of the Ohs, however, anticipating a long night ahead of them. At one point, he inquired of one of the stewards as to the whereabouts of Woodrow. He was a little disappointed to learn that the castle keeper was absent and not expected to join them at any point.

The eyes of the gang leader roamed over the room yet again, taking in the other guests assembled. He knew most everyone and seemed to check each off a mental list. There were perhaps only a half dozen men here who he did not yet know. Vinnie knew that Lord Victor was continuously recruiting new mercenaries to the kingdom. He would make it a point to come to know who they were, as eventually they all came to Port Lupus to partake in its many diversions.

Of all the other guests, however, Vinnie kept himself most aware of the location of Barozzi and his men. Regardless of who he was in conversation with, he made sure to keep them in his line of sight. Their two groups had crossed paths before, and the gang leader knew that the raiders were unpredictable. Vinnie and Barozzi had some history between them, and a few private issues remained unresolved. If it ever came down to a fight, the gang leader knew that the mercenary and his men would make for deadly adversaries.

Shortly before the midnight hour, the hooded members of Lord Victor's coven council arrived. The entrance of the warlocks and their hags produced a brief lull in the conversations. An involuntary shudder passed through several of the gathered guests. After all, it was said these forbidding practitioners of the black arts possessed powers to conjure up demonic magic that was beyond common experience or understanding. They gave off a decidedly foul and menacing aura. Thankfully, they seemed content to keep to themselves at the periphery of the gathering.

The mood of the room soon brightened again. The musicians played robustly and the spirits flowed freely. Everyone gladly partook of the heady brews and the stewards roamed continuously through the room making sure that no tankard or cup ran dry.

The guests were made to feel welcome and special, for all were here on the personal invitation of their king. The friendship of Lord Victor was the common ground, which they all shared, despite their quite diverse backgrounds and interests.

*   *   *

July 31, 1461
The Mesa-of-the-Moon, Varakov

Precisely at the stroke of midnight, their host made his appearance. There was no announcement heralding his arrival. One moment the king wasn't in the great hall. The next moment, Victor was there, standing upon the dais beside his ornate throne.

When the gathered guests became aware of his presence, they broke off their conversations and ceased their wandering about the hall. The musicians halted their playing and quickly withdrew. As the guests turned to face the dais where the king of Varakov now stood, they bowed deeply in acknowledgement of their lord provider. In return, Lord Victor saluted formally back to them with a flourish of his own. His left hand swept his shimmering cape outwards while his right rested upon the back of his throne chair. A steward scampered forth and climbed the stairs of the dais, bringing his master a tankard of ale. Victor accepted it and raised his drink to his guests.

"Dear friends, both old and new, welcome to my hall," their host said, toasting them with a welcoming taste of locally brewed barley malt. "Let us eat, drink, and be of good cheer tonight. We shall feast until dawn approaches, and then, when the sun threatens to rise, we'll stagger off to sleep the day away in our beds … or someone else's," he added with a warm smile. His subjects laughed appreciatively. "Please, allow the stewards to show you to your seats, and let the festivities commence."

The king watched over them as the stewards ushered his guests to their appropriate seats. Barozzi and Vinnie were given positions of honour on either side of Lord Victor's place at the lengthy head table, which was set up in front of the huge fireplace. Other notable men were seated alongside them.

Victor's coven members were given a table that was set off to the side, but the rest of the guests were randomly placed at the adjacent tables so that everyone faced inward towards the cleared centre. The tables formed a large rectangle, allowing everyone a clear view of Lord Victor and the entertainment that was to follow.

While everyone was settling into their seats, Lord Victor strode down the dais steps and walked up to his elaborately carved chair at the centre of the head table. Once there, he waited patiently until he had their attention once more.

"I've been hearing some troubling reports from the other side of the Euralenes. It seems that our neighbours to the east may be looking westward with an eye to expanding their borders," he said gravely, as he set his tankard down on the table.

"As you can appreciate, that eventuality would be to our—to Varakov's—great detriment," the king added, as he looked back up. His tone clearly conveyed that he wasn't about to let this event to occur.

"I thought they were at war with each other over there," one of the regional barons called out. "At least that was the word from one of the last caravans that passed by our way."

"Aah," Lord Victor replied knowingly, "that was indeed the case last year, but alas, I'm afraid it no longer is. There is to be peace in their lands now. There is a pact in place between these old enemies to forgive and forget old grievances. They now look to unite their two kingdoms and to combine their two armies.

It will give them great strength of arms, and they now have a fresh new villainy in their hearts. And, we Varakovans are to be their next conquest."

The king of Varakov held up his hand for quiet as the rumblings grew around the tables in response to this perceived threat. No one questioned his bold statement of the two foreign kingdom's intent or asked what proof there was. They well knew that Lord Victor had ears and eyes everywhere in Varakov. It was a Varakovan fortress which controlled the passage through the Euralene gap. It only stood to reason that he would have spies on the other side of the mountains as well.

"We have recently been looking into the intentions of our neighbours to the east," Victor informed them soberly. "We did this in a rather discreet fashion. We aren't as yet prepared for them to feel our full wrath and reprisal for their arrogance." He smiled warmly and picked up his tankard in salute again. "Still, I'm pleased to be able to tell you that we have been victorious in our recent incursions into the lands of both Skoland and Medinia!" He paused and took a large draft from his tankard while they cheered this news.

"Tonight, my friends," the king said warmly, when they'd settled down, "we will be dining on the symbolic flesh of those enemies, by eating the livestock they have so thoughtfully provided our raiding party." They cheered Victor anew at this statement. "And," the king added, with another broad smile, "we shall be entertained by some of the captives who were brought back as well. My thanks to Barozzi and his men for that," Victor said graciously. "And, to Woodrow, the keeper of my castle, and his party for the food we are about to receive. Both have done us all a great service. They carried out their secret missions into hostile lands with great fortitude and bravery, and with such discretion that our neighbours have no reason to even suspect us."

This further news, and the fact that Barozzi and many of his fellow mercenaries were present, brought a fresh round of loud cheers of approval and toasts. Even Vinnie and the other Ohs joined in offering their congratulations.

"A day is coming, however," Lord Victor added in a stern warning. The Varakovan king looked around the hall slowly, making sure that he had their undivided attention. "A day is coming," he repeated, "when it will take more than a few raids and making off with some of their livestock. A day approaches when we may well have to face and defeat their formidable armies, a day when they attempt to invade us."

Lord Victor allowed his guests to discuss this possibility among themselves for a few moments. He was pleased when he saw that they were responding with outright indignation at the very notion of an enemy force planning to conquer Varakov.

"In the meantime," Victor added aloud, "you can rest assured that the fortress and our garrison in the mountains are still firmly in control of the Euralene gap, as they always have been. Our homeland remains secure from any threat arising from the east—for the moment, at least."

"So, for your loyalty," the king added, and then in increasing volume, "and for your support in keeping Varakov revered and feared, this night belongs to you all."

"Salute, my friends! Salute, Varakov!"

Victor roared out this last part loudly and then drank heartily from his tankard of ale.

"Salute, Varakov! Salute, Lord Victor!" his guests yelled out in response, rising from their seats and returning his toast with enthusiastic roars of their own.

"Let the feast begin," Victor commanded jovially, as he sat down and gestured for them to join him. "Stewards, bring out the food."

As his guests seated themselves again, a stream of stewards entered from the far serving doors. Mixed aromas wafted through the hall. They carried aloft huge trays amply laden with the barbecued beef from the Medinian raid. There were haunches of boiled mutton and racks of lamb roasted with honey and herbs, as well as steamed fish in onions and lemon, cheese, fruit, and prepared vegetables of all descriptions. The guests roared their approval.

"Let there be drink," the Varakovan king commanded once more.

This time, some two dozen scantily-clad serving wenches entered the hall carrying pitchers of ale and wine. The guests roared even louder as the court concubines took up their assigned positions, making sure that no guest went thirsty or without company.

"Let there be entertainment," he commanded a third time, to more hollers of appreciation. The musicians returned and began to play again. A troupe of jugglers, jesters, and acrobats then paraded into the hall to perform their feats for the gathered company of Victor's underlings. They, too, were greeted enthusiastically.

For the next several hours, Victor's guests ate and drank, and enjoyed themselves immensely. Following the circus performers, several talented bards took turns circling the hall and singing familiar lyrics to entertain and rouse them. A trio of raconteurs then told enticing and somewhat crude tales, which were enhanced by performances of even more blatantly vulgar skits of sexual proclivities. These brought about several further appreciative toasts to both king and kingdom.

The drunken laughter and rowdiness grew as the night passed. Even Lord Victor himself regaled them with a few lurid tales of faraway lands and people with strange and exotic customs. When the bards and raconteurs reclaimed the floor, their songs and tales grew raunchier and more colourful still.

When everyone's appetite was fully sated, the tables were cleared away, with the exception of the ever-filled tankards. The guests were invited to remain in their seats, walk about enjoying the amenities of the great hall, or sink back into the large cushioned nooks situated around the hall. They were free to dance or to partake in their own semi-private acts of debauchery with one of the comely serving wenches.

When two of the barons collided with each other in their drunken attempt at dancing, they started wrestling one another. The other guests urged them on and several bets were made on the outcome. Neither of the men was young, nor in very good shape, physically. Their paunch bellies and sparse grey hair attested to that. Nevertheless, they grunted and fought as best they could to save face. The two barons used their bulk to collide together and toss each other to the paving on floor. Neither truly prevailed, but when the two men had finally exhausted themselves, Victor declared a winner, which drew cheers from his supporters, and elicited good-natured moans from the losers.

The Varakovan king then called for practice targets to be dragged out and positioned at various points in the hall. At their master's behest, several of the stewards brought out bows and quivers of arrows, along with a stack of assorted spears and lances. There was even a collection of throwing knives and axes. As they set up the ranges, Victor ascended to his throne for a clear view, taking a few of the court concubines along to keep him company.

Now the wagering began in earnest as those participants still sober enough, or at least still standing, sought to demonstrate their prowess with the weaponry at hand. While Lord Victor didn't choose to participate, he watched the contests with a clear interest, having made a rare exception to his house rules forbidding the handling of weapons in his presence.

As the contests were hotly waged, Barozzi's raiders proved to be the most proficient. The mercenaries excelled in a variety of weaponry, although several of the Ohs from the Multinational gang demonstrated their own skills, especially with the throwing of knives. Sergio showed his ample strength and skill with hurling a battle axe with sure-handed accuracy.

The raider leader, Barozzi, however, was clearly the most deadly accurate of all the guests. He was well into his ale by this point, but was still more than capable of defeating all challengers. It was only the more sober Vinnie who posed any real competition for him. Several of their contests came down to near draws, but they still favoured the mercenary slightly.

"I see you're pretty handy with both a bow and with a spear, lad," Barozzi observed darkly.

The mercenary swigged back his tankard of ale as the gang leader once again hit the centre of the target, throwing a spear at thirty paces.

"You've surprised me tonight," the raider added, provocatively. "And here I'd been thinking you were only good for gutting someone with a knife in some darkened alley."

"I have a long sword being kept for me by the guards, which wouldn't mind having a piece of you on the end of it," Vinnie replied calmly. "If you'd care to step outside with me, I'd be happy to show you."

The raider leader laughed aloud, yet he made careful note of the fact that his men took up position nearby and kept their eyes on the other Ohs should a fight ensue.

"You sure you're ready for the real thing? It's not so easy when you're facing a real live enemy, I assure you." Barozzi challenged. His tone of voice was more than a little condescending as he continued to bait Vinnie.

The smile that the mercenary directed at the gang leader was more of a sneer, and there was no warmth showing in his eyes. He waited for Vinnie's response as the tension in the hall grew.

"Then, let's have some of the real thing shall we? But not with each other, I'm afraid," Lord Victor said, interrupting them before Vinnie could fashion his reply to the mercenary.

The Varakovan king had come up behind them and laid his hands on each of their shoulders. He did so, in a friendly manner, but at the same time he made it clear he didn't wish to hear any further quarrelling from them. He quietly informed them that they were to avoid each other if they couldn't get along. He said that he had need of each of their services, and woe to the man who deprived him of it. He told them that if anything were to happen to either one of them, the other would feel his wrath.

Then, to ease the tension, Victor clapped each of them heartily on the back and called for a steward to bring fresh drinks. When the servant had brought their beverages, he was then promptly dispatched again to round up a full guard detail and descend to the dungeons below. Once there, the steward was told to "invite" the Skolish gentlemen to join the Varakovan king and his guests in the great hall.

After the steward had departed, the other guests returned to their contests. The king turned back to his two lieutenants for one final comment.

"If there will be fighting to the death tonight," Lord Victor informed his two henchmen, "then let it be done—with some of our real enemies."

*   *   *

In the belly of the Varakovan castle, the Skolish prisoners were huddled together amid the straw and the filth of the dungeon cells. Eight cells lined the length of two sides of the dungeon walls. In the centre chamber, which the cells faced, were assorted devices of torture and persuasion. Included among these instruments was the infamous rack, a spiked coffin, whipping posts, and assorted branding irons.

Despite their gruesome surroundings, to this point, none of the new arrivals had been harmed in any way. In fact, they'd been given water and a little food to sate their thirst and hunger pangs. Still, it was a foul dungeon they were incarcerated in and they had already witnessed a number of horrific torture sessions of two prisoners who had been imprisoned prior to their arrival. It wasn't a pleasant experience.

The crimes of these tortured souls were unknown to the prisoners who hailed from Skoland. They could have been thieves and murderers, and thus deserving of punishment. Nevertheless, their screams and suffering had robbed the newcomers of their appetites. Instead, fear and dread filled their bellies. The captives huddled together for solace and comfort inside two of the cells, which their group had been split into. One cage had been designated for the females, another for the males.

Each night, as darkness fell, the wardens had left the dungeons, locking the outer doors behind them. The Skolish prisoners had taken turns trying to get some sleep and standing a watch in case they came back. Sleep was hard to come by. Shutting out the groans and sobbing that emanated from those tortured and broken bodies was a difficult thing to do. For some of them, exhaustion finally won out. Still, their sleep was a restless and troubled one.

Well before the dawn this night, the sound of a troop of guards could be heard coming down the stone stairway. Their footsteps echoed along the hallway at their approach, and those who were on watch prodded the others awake. The outer dungeon doors were unlocked and swung open. The steward and six castle guards then came through them, advancing on the first cell.

The cell door was unlatched and four of the guards entered the Skolish men's cell and seized the first of the prisoners. Two of the captive men, one a young farmer and the other an elderly retired knight, put up a struggle, but they were quickly subdued when the last two guards entered the cell with their swords drawn.

The half-dozen men and four youths were quickly trussed up with ropes and then taken away by the guards. They left behind their weeping mothers, wives, and daughters. It appeared doubtful that they would ever see their families again.

*   *   *

The male prisoners hobbled along in a single file as they entered the great hall in the wee hours before dawn. They were awed by the opulent surroundings that they found themselves led into. These were simple men who worked the fields for the most part. None had ever been inside a castle before. They were both awed and terrified. It was clear to them from the boisterous and drunken reception they received that they were next in line to supply some form of entertainment for the assembly.

Like sharks picking up the scent of blood in the water, many of the guests circled the room looking for an advantageous position to view the proceedings. They roared out their drunken approval and threw boastful wagers back and forth across the hall, without even knowing what the contests would be.

Only Vinnie seemed less than enthused by what he saw happening. He withdrew himself to the sidelines with his half-empty tankard and sat down in a vacant chair. His expression was one of weariness, but it was not the drink or the late hour that brought it on.

Moments later, one of the lusty court wenches spotted the handsome gang leader sitting alone. She came over and perched herself on his lap and topped up his ale as she whispered sweet entreaties into his ear. Thankful for the diversion, Vinnie absentmindedly stroked her hair and waited to see what direction this feast of Lord Victor's was going to take now.

The castle steward gave his report to Lord Victor. He pointed out the young farmer and the old knight who had given them trouble down in the dungeons. Victor nodded slowly as he assessed this news, and then he gave his instructions to the guards. The two Skolish men indicated by the steward were separated from the others. They were left bound in chairs and set off to the side of the proceedings.

Ropes were then thrown over the rafters at one side of the hall. The other eight prisoners were each tied off at the chest with one end of the ropes and then hoisted up into the air with their hands still bound behind them. They were left dangling about four feet off the floor, pleading for mercy from their drunken captors and getting none. They were already dead men. As far as those assembled were concerned, they were the enemy who threatened Varakov with invasion.

The events which then ensued were cruel in the extreme. While the prisoners were swung about helplessly on their ropes, knife throwing, archery, and spear hurling competitions were hotly contested. The blood from the prisoners' wounds fell to the mosaic tiles of the pavements below, mixing with the blood of the many dying images of combatants captured there.

All the while, Vinnie remained apart from the others, fuming in disgust. He found nothing sporting about this. Although he didn't participate, or condone what was happening, there was nothing he could do to prevent it. This was Lord Victor's feast. These were his prisoners, and this was his domain. One didn't challenge the Varakovan king, not if one wished to continue living themselves.

Whereas the Multinational's leader sat out the bloody sport, several of the Ohs took an active role, as did a number of the other guests. Barozzi and his mercenaries seemed to revel in it. The raider leader was clearly demonstrating his skills with his particular swinging target.

Barozzi's precision and accuracy prolonged that unfortunate Skolish prisoner's life. He would take a swig of his ale, and then call out his intended target area. His weapons would invariably strike accurately into less than lethal locations. The captive's legs and torso were worked up and down. As he swung to and fro on the rope, the man's screams only heightened the pleasure Barozzi derived, until at last, he silenced him forever with a final arrow that thudded into his chest and pierced the man's heart.

Among the other guests, bets were wagered, lost and won, paid or collected. Arrows, knives, and spears flew across the hall with varying degrees of accuracy. Some of the contestants were drunker than others. Some missed their targets entirely. Some hit only glancing blows. The end result was a slow and dreadful death for the male Skolish prisoners.

The young farmer and the old retired knight swore adamantly as they struggled futilely against their bonds. They were forced to watch the tortured deaths of their friends and countrymen. There was nothing they could do to prevent it. Indeed, long after the Skolish victims had succumbed to their various wounds, their flesh was pierced again and again, until their captors tired of the blood sport.

At last, Victor had the guard detail recalled. The guards went about removing the corpses and retrieving the weapons, as the castle stewards laboured to clean up the mess left behind. There were copious amounts of blood and gore that needed to be mopped up. It was clear from the stewards wretched expressions that they found the task gruesome in the extreme, but no complaint was dared uttered.

While his servants worked diligently on this distasteful task, Lord Victor's guests wet their parched throats with a renewed vigour. The Varakovan king left them to slake their thirst. He joined the table where his coven council sat apart from the other guests. The warlocks and hags silently attended to their master's instructions, heeding his every word. They then dutifully filed out of the great hall after receiving their orders.

A few minutes later, they were climbing the circular stone stairway of the central tower, on their way to the secluded chamber high above the great hall. Lord Victor returned to his throne and waited patiently.

*   *   *

Inside the chamber, the coven sat in a circle upon the wooden floor surrounding the object perched on a short pedestal, which one of their numbers had unveiled. They began to chant in a slow, rhythmic cant. The words that issued from their bloodless lips were both ancient and dark. Slowly, they sank into a transcendental state, which merged their thoughts into one cohesive will.

The object of their collective focus in the centre of the circle was an ancient orb. It was a dark, emerald green sphere, but not one that was crafted by any human hand. The mysterious origin of which, only Lord Victor and one other living soul were aware.

Subjected to their collective attention, the gem-like orb began to glow. The sphere grew steadily brighter, until finally it filled the chamber with an emerald green, unearthly light, which then cast its beam out through the beautiful stained-glass window overlooking the courtyard and the great hall below.

CHAPTER 7

ONE LAST GUEST

You are a princess, the queen of the ball
In your dress of snow-white satin, not a peasant girl at all

July 31, 1461
The Mesa-of-the-Moon, Varakov

"BRING FORTH THE YOUNG farmer," Lord Victor commanded.

As the castle guards untied the prisoner from his chair and prodded him forward, Victor could sense the orb's force being generated from high overhead. It seemed to reach down and wash over him as he sat upon his throne. His mind grew brighter and more alive, as if it were connected to the very essence of the space around him. It was a feeling of unbridled power. It was a feeling of being in control of the very elements themselves.

"I'm told that this brave young man fought quite valiantly with my guards down in the dungeon," Victor stated, speaking to the crowd from his throne. "Let's have a closer look at him, shall we?"

The Skolish farmer was led bound and shuffling along by two of the guards into the centre of the great hall. He was left standing over the Roundel, or, as it was better known, the Wheel of Fortune. It was somewhat ironic, for his fate was about to be revealed. All the while, many of the guests hollered their drunken abuse at him. The young farmer ignored them, standing silent and sullen beneath their king as he sat upon his regal throne up on the dais.

The young farmer refused to bow down to Lord Victor or to acknowledge him in any way. He stood erect and glaring defiantly up at the caped monarch of Varakov. For his part, Victor didn't seem the least offended by the lack of courtesy shown him by the Skolish prisoner.

"I am Lord Victor, King of Varakov," he said magnanimously. "You are a guest here in my castle. I bid you welcome."

"You call yourself a king? You're nothing but a goddamn, bloody coward!" the farmer yelled up at him.

He whirled about and screamed out at the others next.

"You're all a bunch of filthy, murderous bastards! Give me a sword and I'll cut your fucking hearts out, one by one," the farmer swore.

The young farmer from the other side of the Euralenes was past the point of fear for his own safety and well-being. He knew he had nothing to lose. His indignation and anger fuelled his desire for revenge. If allowed, he would fight them all to the death.

"You may be right about us being filthy bastards," Victor said, with a mocking laugh. "But, I will not be called a coward, not by the offspring of some slutty sow living in the sty of some Skolish farm. Someone cut his ropes, and Barozzi, fetch the man a sword," the Varakovan king ordered congenially. "Let's see if this foul-mouthed young farmer can fight as well as he threatens us."

The farmer's face turned red at the insult to his mother. Barozzi was laughing as he motioned for one of his men to free the prisoner. He then ambled over to the display wall of weapons, where he took down two swords, each of them with exquisitely crafted hilts. He brought them over and stood before the young farmer.

"Good luck, plough man. I think you're going to need it," the raider leader said with a sneering smile.

He handed one of the blades over and stepped back a few paces from the now armed Skolish farmer. He kept his eyes locked on the farmer's and held the other sword at the ready, lest the man be tempted to make use of it before Lord Victor decreed.

"Shall I teach this fellow some manners now, milord?" Barozzi asked Lord Victor, back over his shoulder.

The raider leader hefted the sword in his hand, testing its weight and feel while he waited for Victor's reply, but his eyes never left those of the defiant young farmer.

"I think not, my dear Barozzi. After all, it was me he called a coward, wasn't it?" Lord Victor observed. "What do you say my dear farmer from yonder Skoland? Wouldn't you like a crack at the cowardly king of Varakov?"

"Only if, after I kill you, I can have a go at this foreign pig next," the man replied, indicating Barozzi with a nod in the mercenary's direction.

The mercenary was the one man that the Skolish farmer held most responsible for the raid, their capture, and for the slow and painful deaths of his friends. He knew his fate was to join them soon. He needed no Wheel of Fortune to know this. The young farmer accepted that fact. He only hoped that he could take their brazen king with him into the darkness of death, and then, maybe, the foul mercenary as well.

"Well spoken, good sir. And so it shall be," Victor declared, laughing again. "Let the contest begin."

Barozzi grinned insolently in the man's face and then slowly backed farther away from the prisoner. He passed the weapon hilt first to Lord Victor as the king descended from the dais. The raider leader then sauntered over and rejoined his men to watch what would come next.

He and the intoxicated guests looked on in amazement at that point, when they saw the king calmly lay the sword down on a nearby table. Victor then began walking towards the Skolish farmer without it. The king held no weapon of any kind in his hand.

The stunned crowd parted before him, as Lord Victor strode out onto the floor of the great hall. At one point, he paused to flip his shimmering cape back from his shoulders. The cape seemed to be a piece of Lord Victor. Barozzi couldn't recall ever seeing him without it. It was a definitive part of the Varakovan king, and like his person, totally inviolate.

Victor then resumed his walk, until he stood some ten feet from where the angry prisoner awaited him. When he stopped, he gave a brief nod of his head towards the young farmer.

"Come, slay me, you son of a Skolish sow. Come kill the King of Varakov and avenge your poor countrymen," Victor taunted.

"You're not armed," the young farmer replied warily.

He glanced about the hall, half expecting to be cut down by a spear or an arrow from some other quarter. Surely they wouldn't allow their precious king to face death in this manner. It had to be a trick of some kind.

"You have nothing to fear," Victor assured him, "at least not from anyone else here. No one will interfere. I promise you."

When he saw the farmer still hesitate, he made a further comment.

"What do you care whether I'm armed, or not? I just had your friends slaughtered for our amusement," he taunted. "Perhaps your woman folk will put up more of a fight."

"Kill the fucking bastard," the old Skolish knight screamed out from where he sat, still bound.

That was all the further encouragement the young farmer needed. He lunged forward and with a mighty swing brought his blade sweeping downwards with the clear intent of cleaving Lord Victor in half. The only thing that the sword managed to cut, however, was the air. The heavy blade rang off the floor in a shower of sparks.

Victor had remained motionless until the man's blow was fully committed to. His sidestep was accomplished in a blur of motion. While the Skolish farmer was bringing the blade back up, Victor stepped in and drove the heel of his foot hard into the young man's chest. The blow lifted the man off the floor and knocked him backward where he landed hard on his ass.

The Lord of Varakov allowed the young farmer time to regain his feet and to lift his deadly weapon once more. His second wild attack ended in much the same manner as his first, with him landing hard on his back this time. Once more, he was allowed time to get up and prepare for another attempt.

The farmer paused as he caught his breath. His unthinking rage had dissipated by the second time he'd hit the floor. He now recognized that he was in a life and death battle with an opponent of far superior skills, one who was playing with him much as a cat might with a mouse.

Well, this mouse has fucking teeth! the farmer swore to himself.

This time, the Skolish prisoner advanced slowly with his blade wavering in front of him, held out at waist level. When he came within striking distance, he lunged quickly, slashing the sword across the king's midriff and then back again. With each slash Lord Victor danced back just enough, it seemed, to avoid the blade's razor-sharp edge.

To the more alert of the guests who were scattered about the hall, it appeared like the farmer's sword would soon find its mark. Even the Ohs' gang leader, Vinnie, had gotten back to his feet, depositing the attractive serving-wench onto the floor in a huff. He ignored her curses as he shouldered his way through the crowd to get a better view.

Barozzi swore under his breath and moved to the table, where he retrieved the second blade. He clenched it at his side. If the farmer landed one of his next slashes, he would personally rush in and slice him into a thousand pieces. He saw that Victor would soon run out of room to manoeuvre, and despite his astonishing speed and agility, the situation didn't look good.

Lord Victor didn't appear panicked, however. With each slash, he'd retreated a bit, giving just enough ground to avoid the blade's arc. In truth, he felt exhilarated. He could feel the adrenaline rush through his system. It had been quite some time since he'd been in any real danger.

But, enough was enough, Victor decided. It was time to put an end to this. It was time to teach a lesson. Not so much to the Skolish farmer—he was inconsequential, after all. This was really more a lesson for all those gathered in the great hall.

The prisoner's next slash came and went, slicing open the fabric of Victor's shirt and drawing a fine line of blood across his midriff. Lord Victor laughed abruptly, almost with delight. He then struck the man back.

Except, the Varakovan king didn't exactly strike him. Victor's blow was delivered with the heel of his hand, but it never got within more than a few feet of the Skolish farmer. Nevertheless, the young man was lifted off his feet and sent flying backwards for a third time.

The stunned man slowly pulled himself to an upright position. He retained his sword, but he was shaking his head in a vain effort to come to grips with what had just occurred. He couldn't fathom how, in one moment, he had held the clear advantage, and yet, in the very next moment, he was somehow picking himself up off the floor again. The Varakovan king's blow hadn't actually landed on him. He was fairly certain of that, yet his body felt like he'd been hit by a small battering ram.

While the farmer collected his wits, Lord Victor unbuttoned his ruined and bloodied shirt and briefly examined the superficial wound. The cut across his muscular torso went largely unnoticed by the surrounding crowd. Their eyes were attracted to the glowing, emerald-green amulet that hung about his neck, suspended from a linked chain of gold.

Like Woodrow's, this amulet was handcrafted specifically for its owner. Where the Pack leader's amulet was carved into the likeness of a wolf's head, Lord Victor's depicted a dreadful looking beast. The creature was either a product of someone's vivid imagination or something from out of this world.

The Beast's body was reptilian, although it was not like any type of snake. Its savage looking head displayed a pair of vicious fangs and a protruding forked tongue. The large upper torso was thickly scaled. Its arms were muscular and its hands were wickedly clawed, and the two powerful legs that hung from the underbelly ended in equally fiercely clawed feet.

The gemstone amulet was glowing brightly, casting its emerald-green light, which illuminated Victor's skin and even the air surrounding him. The light emanated around him like an unearthly aura. It inspired awe in the great hall's assembly. It made their king seem like more than any ordinary man. It made him seem to be more than any mere mortal.

With his middle finger, Victor wiped the rivulet of blood that leaked from his minor wound. He brought the finger to his lips and then slowly licked it clean. He looked scornfully at his Skolish opponent.

"Is that the best you've got? The king still lives. Long live the king! I shall be here long after Skoland and Medinia are swept away and forgotten. Just like your friends were tonight," Victor challenged.

The young farmer took in a deep breath.

"Never!" he screamed. Raising the sword over his head with both hands, he charged the terrible liege of Varakov. He only made it about halfway there.

Lord Victor thrust his hand outward and then jerked it upwards. In mid-stride the Skolish farmer was grabbed up by an unseen force. He was lifted and suspended in the air, unable to move or control any part of his body.

Victor's eyes now glowed with the same emerald-green light as the amulet. It appeared that the amulet's energy was flowing throughout him. Slowly, he then clenched his hand into a fist. The farmer's chest seemed to cave in on him. His lungs and heart were being crushed, as if caught in a powerful vice. His mouth gaped open in a silent scream. His eyes bulged out, and then, finally, they glazed over as death claimed him. The sword dropped from his lifeless fingers to clatter noisily on the floor where it landed.

Victor's gaze lowered to it. As if on command, the sharp-pointed blade lifted up off the tiled floor until the sword stood upright on its hilt in the very centre of the Roundel. The weapon quivered, almost as if in anticipation of what was to come. Victor opened his hand, releasing the young farmer from his psychic grip. The man dropped down heavily, impaling himself with a sickening thud. The sword point burst out the backside of his already dead body.

At first, there was silence in the great hall. A silence inspired by reverence and awe. They were witnesses to a power absolute. Their king, Lord Victor, was the master of death itself.

"Victor, Victor," Barozzi began the chant. Others took it up, until the sound swept through the hall, swelling in volume as the rest of the gathering joined in. "Victor, Victor, Victor!"

Even Vinnie, the usually reserved leader of the Ohs, was caught up in the moment. His voice was added to the others. As a group, the guests of Lord Victor's feast were mesmerized by what they'd seen. They were spellbound by the Varakovan king's display of power.

Only the old Skolish knight didn't call out Lord Victor's name in tribute. Understandably, he could only stare down at the floor as tears flowed freely down his weathered cheeks.

Victor felt their praise wash over him, as he walked up the dais stairs and sat back in his throne chair. It was a palpable energy that he felt from them, but quite dissimilar to that which was created moments earlier with the help of his coven council, and the orb.

The king looked down on his adoring subjects. The story of what transpired here tonight would spread with them when they departed for their homes. The lesson was completed. They were his, now and always. When the time came, they would follow him. They would follow anywhere he chose to lead them.

*   *   *

High up in the inner tower's chamber, the draping was returned with almost reverential care to its place covering the orb. The coven members were well aware of their successful bonding with the orb, and through it, to Lord Victor down below in the great hall. They had felt the Skolish farmer's death as clearly as if they had clutched his heart and lungs in their own hands. It had been a powerful sensation, one that stayed with them as they left the chamber and quietly filed down the stairway to rejoin the festivities.

The coven members were also aware that those bonds were growing stronger as they further mastered the orb's powerful secrets. To be sure, there still remained secrets to be unlocked, but they knew with certainty that their master held the key.

*   *   *

The guards removed the farmer's body after retrieving the imbedded sword. Several castle stewards then bent to the task of mopping up the fresh blood and gore that mixed anew with the intricately detailed paving tiles. Another steward scurried cautiously up the dais to his king. He brought with him a fresh white silk shirt in anticipation of his master's needs, along with a towel and a basin of heated water. He placed them on a side table near the throne, bowing deeply as he did so.

Victor accepted the offering silently, dismissing the steward with a flick of his wrist. As the glow slowly ebbed away from the amulet that hung against his chest, he rose and stepped behind the throne. The Varakovan king removed the ruined shirt from beneath his shimmering cape and proceeded to wash away the sheen of sweat and dried blood from his torso. He then towelled himself dry and slipped the new shirt on beneath the cape. Oddly, perhaps, he never deemed to remove the cape first. When he was finished buttoning the fresh shirting, he then righted the cape about his shoulders with a shrugged flourish and retook his seat.

"More food and fresh drinks for my guests," he commanded.

The party resumed its pace as fresh food, more refreshments, and the ladies of the court made the rounds. The musicians returned and resumed their playing with a renewed gusto. His guests sang or danced or sunk into further acts of debauchery. Many did all three.

Lord Victor didn't partake in the food, drink, or the other pleasures at hand. Sitting alone on his throne chair, the king looked on silently as his guests took to their amusements.

In truth, the Varakovan king was drained. The surge of power that had flowed through him earlier had faded away now, leaving Victor feeling empty inside. Worse than empty, for now he could feel the Beast as it awakened deep within his core. He knew that the Beast was demanding to be fed.

It was time for a change in venue. At a break in the music, Lord Victor wearily pulled himself up from his throne. As he descended the dais steps, he signalled for two of the guards to accompany him. They dutifully fell in and followed their liege over to where the old Skolish knight remained bound and tied to his chair. The last male captive was slumped over and in obvious distress.

Victor reached down and lifted the prisoner's chin so that he could look him in the eye.

"As yet, I haven't decided what I shall do with you, old warrior," Victor said, softly. "Perhaps I'll send you home as a messenger, so you can tell your people what you've witnessed here. Or perhaps we'll just keep you in our dungeon and have you provide us with some future amusement."

Victor smiled faintly at the hatred that flared up in the old knight's eyes. The man's spirit was not yet broken.

"Take him back to his cell, and then bring me the most winsome of our female guests," Lord Victor ordered. "I have need of a fresh diversion."

His smile broadened as the old knight cursed profanely and struggled uselessly against his bonds.

The two guards that Victor dispatched were a study in contrasts. One was young, hard, and lean. The other was much older and obese. They each leapt forward, however, to obey their lord and master. Their heads came together almost comically with a resounding *thunk* as they both moved in to untie the prisoner from the chair at the same time. With his hands still bound, the old Skolish knight was then jostled to his feet and quickly dragged away.

*   *   *

In the dungeon cell below the great hall, the women of Skoland sat and wept with despair. There were small slits built into the stone castle walls that allowed the smoke of the torch lamps to escape and fresh air to enter. An added result was that sounds carried well from one section of the castle to another. The screams of dying men traveled far.

The captive women had clearly heard the tortured cries emanating from up above. The death screams of the Skolish men had echoed eerily through the stone corridors. The females could only imagine with growing dread the cruel fate that their men folk had met.

The screams were finally followed by silence, which was perhaps even crueller for the women to endure. It was almost with a feeling of relief that they heard the sounds of footsteps approaching and then saw the dungeon door pushed open.

The two guards half dragged and half carried the old knight into the dungeon and dropped him back into his vacant cell. The younger one kept his foot pressed against the back of the man's neck, which pinioned his face into the straw and filth. The older, heavy guard retrieved a knife from the torture rack and then returned to cut away the ropes that restrained the prisoner. When he was finished with that, the younger guard gave a final disdainful push downward with his boot. The guards then withdrew from the cell and locked its door.

The old knight got slowly to his feet. It took time for the feeling to return to his limbs as his circulation slowly returned. He made no attempt to wipe the muck from his face as he stood glaring at the two guards. He wouldn't give them the satisfaction. He refused to curse them, or to even speak further, for that matter. To speak would have meant to beg, but he knew these guards were only minions. They wouldn't deviate from their master's instructions. If begging would have stopped what was to follow, he would have gladly sacrificed whatever dignity he had left.

"Which one should we take up?" the older guard asked nervously.

It was clear that the heavyset guard had no taste for this duty. He preferred his normal guard assignments where he wasn't expected to think, just obey orders and collect his pay. This task was beyond him. He had no idea which of these helpless women Victor would prefer.

The younger guard felt none of these same qualms. In fact, he rather relished this moment of decision-making. With a lustful leer, he gazed intently into the women's cell. In his mind, he weighed the physical merits of each, as if he were selecting from meats hanging in the butcher's shop. He even fancied himself a carnal authority of the fairer sex.

"That's the one I want," he said, indicating his choice amongst the females with a lecherous smile. "Open the cell, Garcia, and I'll fetch the young beauty out. She's perfect."

The older guard complied, but with the forced reluctance of a man who had little choice in the matter.

The Skolish women were mostly standing now. They cowered at the younger guard's approach. They backed up to the end bars of the large cell, which prevented them from retreating any further. The leering young guard came to a stop towering over the mother, who remained sitting and huddling two young daughters to her in a corner of the cell. He reached down and grabbed the arm of the eldest daughter. She was a wholesome young woman of about seventeen years of age. He hauled her roughly to her feet.

"No, no, please," her mother cried out, struggling to her feet. "Take me instead," she implored him. She clutched at her daughter's free arm in a vain attempt to keep her at her side.

"Your time will come soon enough, bitch," the young guard swore. He then sent the mother sprawling with a wicked smack across her face.

Garcia winced as the cruel blow was delivered. The younger of the two daughters crawled over to hold and console her mother. In a wretched state of shock, the two females clung to each other, weeping helplessly as the older sister was dragged sobbing from the cell. The other women cried out for mercy, but none was forthcoming.

Outside the cell, the younger guard then slapped the eldest daughter hard as well, silencing her sobs. He bound the young woman's hands tightly behind her back, not because it was necessary but simply because he was savouring each moment of his control over her. The young guard began groping her then, finding his manhood growing stiff in his excitement. He then reached down for the hem of her skirt.

The young guard's enthusiasm was abruptly curtailed when he felt the cold steel blade of the knife that Garcia had picked up from the inquisitor's rack of torture implements pressed to his throat.

"Enough of this," the obese guard said, wheezing with the effort. "The king is waiting, and unless you'd care to explain yourself to him, I'd suggest you keep your pants on while you still have a reason to wear them!"

The reminder of the severity of Lord Victor's wrath had a dampening effect on the younger guard's libido. He slowly released his hold on the young woman, and then, very carefully, he pushed Garcia's knife hand away from his throat.

"You ever pull a blade on me again, fat man, and I'll shove it up your ass," the younger guard blustered, in a weak attempt to save face.

Nevertheless, he gave up the notion of forcing himself on the female. He pushed her towards the open dungeon doorway and then followed her out into the corridor.

With a deep sigh and a heavy shake of his head that caused his jowls to quiver, Garcia relocked the cell door. He tried to avoid the eyes of the old Skolish knight. He felt them anyway, like twin daggers in his back. The older guard replaced the inquisitor's knife among the other cruel implements of torture. As he left the dungeon he swung the heavy door closed, but he couldn't close the one that led to his conscience.

Garcia was trailing the other guard and the young woman down the long hallway when the sound of the Skolish mother's voice reached out to them. She was rendering a song of great loss and sorrow, as only a mother could, for the daughter forcibly taken from her. It was a song that had no lyric, simply expressed with wails of despair. Her keening notes of deep sadness reverberated down the stone corridor and beyond. Her anguish was palatable and the older guard knew it would haunt his soul forever.

*   *   *

The arrival of the two guards and their female prisoner brought with them a new air of anticipation to the proceedings in the great hall. Several of the male guests stopped in the midst of their debauchery to follow their progress across the tiled pavements towards Lord Victor.

The Varakovan king stepped forward to meet them, his shimmering black cape unfurling behind him as he came forward. Lord Victor's brow knitted with anger when he saw she had her hands tied behind her back.

"Why is she bound up like some common criminal? And why is her face marked?" he demanded darkly.

The younger guard lowered his head as he stammered some unintelligible reply. Garcia hung back, in an attempt to distance himself from responsibility.

"Release her immediately!" Victor commanded. "The young lady is my personal guest."

Garcia sprang forward to obey as if he had just been scalded with hot water. He was still fumbling with her ropes when Lord Victor focused his attention on the younger guard.

Victor placed a finger under the man's quaking chin. He slowly raised his head up until their eyes met.

"I'll be dealing with you later," the king said. His eyes narrowed and hardened. His tone left little doubt as to his displeasure. "Go, you're dismissed," he snarled.

The young guard's insides twisted into a knot and his bowels turned to jelly. He actually fouled himself, before he turned and scurried out of the great hall to the laughing taunts of several of Lord Victor's guests.

Garcia finished releasing the young Skolish woman and tossed the ropes aside. He bowed humbly to the king and then quickly departed the great hall himself. The older guard left the castle immediately thereafter, heading for his own quarters.

Later, while drowning his sorrows in a bottle of cheap wine, Garcia would relate the evening's events to his equally stout wife. Together, they seriously considered the possibilities of his taking an earlier retirement and buying the small farmstead they'd been saving for.

*   *   *

When the two guards had departed, Lord Victor approached the young peasant woman. She stood visibly trembling before him, in very real danger of fainting away. Never before in her brief existence had she seen the grandeur of a castle. She'd never even set eyes on a king, let alone been in the company of one.

The young Skolish woman was fair of hair, face, and body, but she was also a product of the lower class. She had no formal education, no learned social graces, and no tutored manners. Even if she had her best clothing from back home, she certainly possessed no finery that would be suitable within the royal court of any kingdom.

Yet, here she was, being approached by this handsome, caped figure, whom she correctly assumed to be the Varakovan king! She was overwhelmed with terror, yet a small part inside of her felt a rush of excitement. Perhaps it was the little girl in her that held secret dreams of a handsome prince riding in on his white stallion and sweeping her off her feet like she was a princess.

"What is your name, my dear?" Lord Victor asked her, as he gently took her two hands in his.

Using his thumbs, he gently massaged her wrists where the ropes had dug in. Her reply was inaudible. The answer stuck in her mouth, refusing to come forth.

The king smiled and touched her cheek with a soft caress, as he gazed deeply into her eyes. The young woman felt a glow of warmth and wellbeing spread through her, easing her racing heartbeat. His ice-blue eyes were magnetic, calming, and compelling. They drew her in.

"What is your name, my dear?" he asked her, again. This time she spoke clearly.

"Mary, milord," she replied, although the voice seemed strangely detached. She felt like she was standing outside of herself. It was an oddly disembodied experience.

He's quite handsome, in a mature kind of way, she thought. *There's a slight greying at his temples, and there's a wrinkling about the eyes.*

There was something about those eyes of his. Lord Victor wasn't a young prince on a white stallion, but neither was he old. Surely not as old as her uncle, the one who was forever pinching her bottom or brushing up against her for a cheap feel.

She was focused on his eyes. They were looking so deeply into hers.

With those last thoughts, whatever free will the young woman still possessed left her. The only will that remained now was Victor's, and his will was supreme.

"Bring basins of warm water and scented soap. Our princess needs a bath," he commanded.

The castle stewards rushed off to obey, returning shortly with two large basins of heated water from the kitchen, plus soap, a washing cloth, and a drying towel.

"We must bathe you, dear Mary, and prepare you for the ball," Victor crooned into her ear. "We'll throw out these old rags of yours and dress you properly, as a lady should be in the company of her king. Let me wash away the sins of being poor, *ma petite fleur*."

Dutifully she raised her arms as Lord Victor drew her peasant dress up and over her head. Her undergarments were little more than cotton sacking. These, too, were removed. There was a collective intake of breath among the guests, as the young Skolish woman stood naked and compliant before them. She was unaware of their presence. Her world was Lord Victor.

"Step into the tub, my dear," he commanded softly.

She obeyed, moving as if in a trance. She stepped into the basin of shin-deep water. Her face, arms, and legs were a coppery nutmeg brown from long hours in the sun working on her family farm. Her young hands were already rough and calloused. Her torso, front and back, was white yet glowing with youthful vitality. The pubic patch between her legs was slightly darker than her sun-bleached hair.

Victor rolled up his sleeves and soaped the washing cloth. He slowly, methodically, began to bathe her. Firmly, yet so very tenderly, he washed away the dust and filth she'd accumulated during her captivity. His guests were enthralled and silent, breathing heavily. A collective sigh was released, as Victor's hands brought cloth to breasts, buttocks, and womanhood.

After he'd washed her hair, Victor led her to the second basin, where he rinsed her off, and then while the basins were being removed, he towelled her dry. Her hair and skin shone in the torch-lit great hall. Except for their ragged breathing, no guest made a sound, lest the distraction break the spell.

"Now bring me gowns to choose from for Princess Mary's proper attire," he ordered in a throaty whisper.

A steward raced away and quickly returned with several gowns taken from one of the dressing closets off Lord Victor's private chambers. From among these, the Varakovan king selected a snow-white satin gown. It was a simple cut, but with a rich and elegantly designed bodice. He slipped the dress over the outstretched arms of the young lady as the steward bowed and took his leave.

The fit was adequate, and in contrast with her browned limbs and face, the snow-white dress worked its magic. Properly attired, young Mary was now more beautiful than she had ever been in her life. Her natural attributes were enhanced by the sensuality of the satin gown. She was a girl in the process of blossoming into womanhood.

"Music," Lord Victor commanded, and the musicians began to play.

It was like watching the two of them making love. They danced, as one. Victor's black shimmering cape flowed in contrast with her snow-white satin gown as they moved about the floor. The gown accented the lithe, naked young form beneath it. The two dancers were moulded together, black and white, and oblivious to the voyeurs surrounding them.

Their swirling steps led the two dancers towards Lord Victor's private bedchamber off the great hall. As they approached the door, it swung open seemingly of its own accord to receive them. After they stepped over the threshold, the door slowly closed behind them, again, as if by its own volition.

There was silence in the great hall for a few moments. The musicians ceased their playing. The guest's faces, perhaps save one, were glazed over as if each had reached some personal sexual climax of their own. They looked drained, yet thoroughly exhilarated.

Then the laughter and gaiety erupted once more as the guests cheered and applauded their liege's accomplishments anew. They rightfully assumed that Lord Victor, the king of all kings, was taking his well-earned pleasure. They just had no idea in what manner. They partied on stalwartly in his absence.

*   *   *

Inside the bedchamber, Lord Victor leaned down, bringing his lips to the young woman's throat. At the last moment, his mouth opened. His eyeteeth were extending now into two piercing-sharp fangs, which sank deeply into her neck. Victor drank his fill. The Beast inside him was fed his due, except for a thin stream of blood, which escaped its hunger. The line of blood coursed down the young woman's throat and blossomed into a vivid red stain on the bodice of her snow-white gown.

A single piercing scream welled up from deep within the young woman and managed to rise from her semiconscious state to escape her lips. It reverberated throughout the castle, eventually reaching the dungeon below, where a mother's song of loss had come to a bitter end.

*   *   *

The vast majority of the guests ignored the scream, thinking that the maiden was protesting the losing of her flower to the king's due. Only Vinnie had averted his eyes from the two dancers. Revulsion and then nausea had swept through him, overwhelming the spell that he'd been under. He had looked over at Barozzi while Victor was manipulating the young woman. He'd seen the look of unadulterated awe on the raider's face.

A further glance about the hall revealed the same look on the other faces gathered there, including those of his fellow gang members. It sickened him even further.

Tears brimmed at the corners of Vinnie's eyes as he walked out of the great hall. He was disgusted with everything he had witnessed this foul night, including himself. He was going back to town. He would leave the other Ohs to find their way back.

*   *   *

Victor finished feeding the Beast and then slowly lifted his head. The sharp fangs receded. There remained only a small smear of blood on his lips and a look of deep contentment on his face.

To the more observant eye, his hair might have seemed a touch less grey at the temples. His complexion was a little less pale, and the tiny wrinkles about his eyes were all but gone.

Victor picked up the inert form of the young Skolish woman in his arms and carried her over to the bed. He gently laid her upon it and gazed down upon her for quite some time, almost with a look of tenderness. He then turned away and returned to his guests.

"Victor, Victor, Victor!" the chant recommenced upon his return to the company assembled in the great hall. His guests proudly expressed again their veneration for their all powerful liege.

Lord Victor picked up his drink and saluted his subjects from his throne. He drank deeply, as if he needed to chase down the previous fluid that had so recently bathed his taste buds.

"Victor, Victor, Victor!"

The Varakovan king rose to acknowledge their praise. He then silenced them with a motion of his hand.

"My bride shall remain in her chambers. She needs time … to rest."

His guests cheered their approval anew.

"Music," Lord Victor commanded, and the musicians played with a renewed gusto.

The festivities gradually wound down, and as the sun crept up to herald the arrival of the new dawn, it was declared over. The normally observant Lord Victor failed to notice the absence of the young gang leader as he bid his guests good day. As a crowd of them moved towards the doors, he retired to his chambers—and to his "bride," several commented, causing others among them to snicker knowingly.

Those guests who could manage to keep to their feet staggered out of the castle to make their way to their own beds. Several required the assistance of their comrades, most of whom were only slightly more functional. Those who had passed out or were too drunk to make the effort to leave were simply carried outdoors by the stewards and deposited on the steps leading from the castle entrance.

As the mercenaries left the castle, they were forced to step around several of these inert and inebriated bodies as they made their way down the stone stairway. Barozzi and his men gave these fools who weren't able to abide their intake of spirits a look of distinct disdain. The mercenary leader then gazed across the courtyard at the band of Ohs as they made their way out of the castle grounds, drunk perhaps, but still on their feet. He noted that Vinnie was not in their midst, and he wondered when and why the gang leader had departed.

Back inside the great hall, the day shift of castle staff diligently toiled to scrub away any residue of the night's debauchery, including the remaining blood and gore. They knew that Lord Victor would expect to find order and cleanliness restored when he chose to greet the day.

CHAPTER 8

MAN AND WOLF

The herd grows stronger, losing the old and the weak
It's the balance of species that Mother Nature seeks
The hunters have a role to play
It's nature's way

July 31, 1461
Dumas, Medinia

THERE WAS ANOTHER INDIVIDUAL who didn't get much sleep that prior night either, albeit for a quite a different reason. When the early morning sun rose in Medinia, it found the Lady Hillary Michelle already up and about. The princess had spent a restless night in her castle chambers, finally giving up on sleep and rising well before the dawn.

She'd sat by the window in her sleeping silks gazing out into the darkness. Her thoughts were on the events occurring near the western border. Reports had reached the castle of the confrontation at the river crossing. Coming on the heels of the reports of marauding wolf attacks on farms in that region, it made for a rather eventful week for such a remote frontier region.

Speculation and gossip went hand in hand in the Medinian court, as it did in most kingdoms. As far as the princess was concerned, some of the stories going around now were simply too farfetched. Rumours were rampant of giant-sized wolves and even stranger men! She was convinced that the farm attacks would turn out to be the work of a large pack of quite ordinary wolves that had come down from the mountains. Game was likely scarce and simple hunger drove them to venture down to the farmlands and raid some pitiful livestock.

Lady Hillary Michelle was much more interested in the events reported from the river crossing. Several times now, riders had come in with dispatches for her father, the king, and his council of knights. The women of the court and their various serving staffs had been banished to unobtrusive regions of the castle at the time so that the men could discuss important matters of state.

The princess fumed at being left out of these discussions. It seemed to her that as soon as a battle came along, or plans for a new battle were made, or the dissection of the last battle needed to be discussed, men invariably began to feel their oats. They blustered, boasted, and bitched, and preferred to have only male companionship.

Personally, she thought it was because they didn't want any female witnesses to their foolish antics.

The Medinian princess had not been on hand when the early reports had come in, and so she'd been locked out of her father's assembly hall along with the rest of the women. She was determined, therefore, to be nearby today. Sir Reginald Toutant was expected to arrive.

Since the untimely passing of her mother, when she herself was just twelve years old, the princess had assumed the duties of the Lady of the Manor. As the years passed, she'd learned a great deal about life in the kingdom's court. She had become especially gifted at discerning the manner and purposes of the constant stream of people who bid for the king's attention.

A timely question or an insightful remark on her "innocent" part often exposed the petitioner's true intent. Her father usually welcomed his raven-haired daughter at his side, and he had come to value her instincts. This, of course, did not always sit well with his council of knights, but neither was it a direct threat to them. Her views usually proved to be ones that had the best interests of the kingdom and its subjects at heart.

The young princess knew that in matters of war and such, it was often better to remain mute. Her father certainly appreciated this concession on her part. Still, there were times when some knight would get wound up and full of himself and go off on some tangent that had nothing to do with the matter at hand. On occasion, she might ask for a clarification in such a way that the orator's wind would be deflated. Her interruptions were usually met with relief by the rest of those forced to listen to their peer's ramblings.

The initial news from the frontier had distressed the princess. It seemed to herald an end to the peace initiatives. The latest report, however, had come directly from Sir Reginald Toutant himself. It seemed that the distinguished knight commander had come upon the confrontation at the river and taken charge of the Medinian forces. He had then successfully put an end to the hostilities with the Skolish forces.

His courier recounted the events that had led up to the skirmish at the river crossing. He reported that the forces of both kingdoms had been on patrol, searching for their respective invaders. Sir Reginald speculated that the responsible groups had either come down from the mountains, or they'd come through the Euralene pass from Varakov.

They lacked proof, she knew, but whoever the villains truly were, they'd gone as far as to implicate Medinia in the atrocities carried out in Skoland. This could only mean that some force of indeterminate strength and purpose was taking an aggressive role in their affairs. That begged the question, if they had gone this far, would they get bolder? What further intrusion could they expect?

These and many other questions would be asked, and her father and his council would heatedly debate the answers. They would also likely discuss what further measures for the security of the border should be taken, and whether or not these measures should be discussed openly with Skoland.

It was possible that the outside threat was a shared concern. If it was, and it proved to be a larger threat than it was at present, it might be good to have an ally. The notion of Skoland as a true ally, however, was still a difficult one for many of the senior knights to accept.

The part of the latest report, which the Medinian princess found most interesting of all, concerned Toutant's meeting across the river. It was reported that he'd held talks with the knight commander of the Royal Order of Skolish knights. There was also a mention of Prince Paulo being involved in the action.

Any news regarding Prince Paulo was naturally of special interest to the king's eldest daughter. Her father had already apprised her that a marriage was being considered as an integral part of the upcoming peace talks. The princess had still not come to terms with this. Her entire future could be determined by such a decision, and that notion was proving to be quite overwhelming.

A marriage to Prince Paulo could well cement a lasting peace, which her people desperately needed. It would also seal the young princess into a union with a man that she had yet to even lay eyes on. What irked her almost as much was the fact that the whole damn court was gossiping about it!

Her younger sister, the Lady Sarah Elizabeth, was making it her duty to spy on the council meetings and court proceedings and keep her well informed. Her dependable and loving sister always was the more adventurous of the two. It was she who reported that most of the ladies of the court held the opinion that the eldest sister should already be married by now, anyways. Lady Hillary Michelle was approaching twenty, after all.

Even their personal handmaiden, Charlene, was all a twitter about the possibilities. Personally, the princess wished they would all just keep still and mind their own business. It was just another distraction. Her head was already a tumble of contradictory notions. She didn't need any more. These were the burning thoughts that had already robbed her of sleep. They were the reasons she'd sat up staring out into the empty night with unseeing eyes.

It wasn't that Lady Hillary Michelle hadn't had her share of suitors. She was a lovely young woman, slim and graceful, and filled with a charming vitality. It was that she lacked interest in any of her suitors to date. She wasn't sure if she was even ready for marriage, let alone marriage to any of the men who had approached her father. Now she might have to be wed some foreign prince for the sake of her people and peace between the two kingdoms.

The only thing the young princess knew for certain was that the sun was starting to come up at last. If she couldn't sleep, then it was bloody well time that Charlene and her younger sister rose to greet the day, too. The princess was determined that she and her sister would be on hand when Sir Toutant arrived, and part of the discussions that would surely follow.

*   *   *

The Euralene Mountains, Varakov

Willie woke with a sudden start. He gasped for breath, sucking in air the way a diver exploding up out of a lake's depths might. Wide eyed, he stared blankly up at the sky above him, but it was dim and out of focus. He couldn't see the stars.

The youth lay perfectly still after that, trying to gather his senses. He willed his faculties to focus on his predicament. It was difficult, though. His one leg was throbbing wildly, his heart was racing, and he was in a state of near panic. He took several long, deep breaths in an attempt to calm down and assess the situation.

As the youth's eyes grew more accustomed to the semi-darkness, he could see that it was, in fact, a ceiling high over his head, not the sky. He was in a cot or a small bed. There was a quilt covering him and there was a pillow under his head. He had no idea how was that possible.

"Welcome back, young man."

The man's calmly spoken words came to him from somewhere across the room. Turning slightly to that side, the youth tried to lift his head up from the pillow. That slightest of motions was enough to set off a wave of nausea in his chest and throat. A small explosion of stars erupted behind his eyes.

The youth closed his eyes again and waited for it to pass, and then he gritted his teeth and tried it again. He raised his head slowly and then his shoulders, until he was able to rest his weight on his bent elbow. He sucked in a few deep breaths and fought against the dizzying fatigue he felt.

Stiff from inactivity and sore from his ordeal, he felt a burning discomfort with each movement. His left leg was the worst of it. It felt as if there were a raging fire inside of it, which then radiated upwards into his hip and buttocks. He tried shifting his weight to compensate for that side of his aching body.

"Try not to move around too much just yet," the same calm voice suggested.

The Medinian youth forced his eyelids to open again and peered out across the room. He could only dimly make out the figure that rose up from a chair over there.

Woodrow stooped briefly at the table and lit a single candle, which provided sufficient light without being blinding to the eye. He picked up the mug of herbal brew that he had prepared and brought it over the bed.

"The sun will be up soon," he quietly informed his guest. "Officially, it's dawn already, but it takes awhile for the sun to climb the mountains and cast its light here."

That was a strange thing to say, it occurred to the youth. The sun rose early at home. It was in the evening that the mountains robbed his part of Medinia of the sun's light, bringing an early dusk each night. Home, it began to sink in. He wasn't at home. It didn't make any sense to him.

"Where ... am ... I?" he croaked, his throat parched and raspy dry from his fever.

"Varakov. In a safe place, which we call Sanctuary," the man replied.

"How—?"

"It's a long story, but before I tell it, you need to drink this. It will quench your throat and make you stronger," his host added firmly.

Woodrow wasn't opening the issue for debate. He sat at the edge of the bed and supported the youth while he tilted the cup to his lips for him to drink. He repeated the procedure until the mug was emptied.

The youth found that the brew tasted a touch bitter, despite the honey that was mixed in with it, but it did soothe his throat and spread a warm glow in his belly. As he was finishing it, he realized that he felt calmer and more relaxed. Even his leg didn't seem to be throbbing as much as it had been.

The Pack leader slowly lowered him back down to his pillow.

"I want you to rest a little more now. When the sun's up, I'll have some real breakfast waiting for you, and then we can talk."

He held his finger to the youth's lips to stop any protest. "You need to rest now."

Wearily the youth sank back and closed his eyes again. He was tired but feeling a little more secure somehow. Perhaps it was the man's calming voice and assured manner. His mind, however, was still a jumble of disjointed thoughts and images.

Varakov? How the hell could I be in Varakov? the young farm serf wondered. He was confused. He wasn't even sure what that meant. Varakov was just a name for a place on the other side of the Euralenes. He knew nothing about it, except that every year his people looked forward to the coming of the caravans through the pass.

How could I have gotten so far from home? he questioned, as his mind drifted off. The young farm serf gradually fell back to sleep, but it was a restless and troubled one.

Woodrow stood looking down at the flickering eyelids of his young guest. He could imagine the memories that were there, attempting to rise to the surface, to be re-lived. The youth would settle down shortly. The potion that he'd added to the herbal brew would ease him back into a deep sleep and allow his body further time to heal.

The body would heal. Woodrow could see that by now. He wasn't so sure about his mind though. The terrible loss of the youth's dogs and horse would be hard for him to accept. His four-legged comrades gave their lives so that the youth might live. He could forever be tormented by the terror of the chase by the Pack, too.

Those terrible traumas would leave scars in the youth's mind as surely as savage teeth had left their indelible marks on his leg. He would have to learn to live with both, for the rest of his days.

The Pack leader would tell him the truth, however, all of it. How the youth would cope with it, he did not know. He would likely hate Woodrow and the Pack. He would likely be terrified knowing that he was far from his home, in a distant land where his attackers dwelt. Yet, like it, or not, there was one truth that remained undeniable. He would be one of them now, and that was all that really mattered.

Woodrow walked over to the door and stepped outside. He sat down and looked out over the gorge at the distant waterfall. His thoughts drifted back to the day when he'd first encountered Brutus. The day his life, and later that of his wife's, were changed forever.

It was the day he'd been infected himself.

*   *   *

Woodrow was still sitting outside, lost in his own troubled thoughts, when the sun finally crested the mountain peaks. The glow of its rays stirred him from his reverie. He got up and went back inside, settling into the cooking galley, where he hooked a large iron pot of water over the hearth. He quietly went about preparing a wholesome meal and waited for his young guest to awaken again.

Not much later, the youth slowly surfaced from his slumber. It was more hunger than pain and confusion that greeted him as he woke this time. The aroma of cooking food wafted over to him, and he realized that he was famished. He was already slowly propping himself up in bed by the time his host was serving up the hearty stew he'd prepared.

Willie reached eagerly for the slab of bread and the bowl on the tray that was offered to him. Dunking the bread in the stew he bit off a large hunk soaked with the thick-gravy broth. He ignored the spoon on the tray, opting to use the bread and his fingers to shovel the meat and vegetables into his mouth.

"Slowly," Woodrow admonished him as he returned to the kitchen galley. "Give your stomach a chance to catch up."

He came back to the bed with another mug of the herbal brew he'd given him just before dawn. The youth eyed the mug suspiciously. He could smell it from a distance, but he was chewing a little slower now.

"Relax. It's not poison, and there's no sleeping potion in it this time, just some honey," Woodrow said with a reassuring smile.

"I was more concerned about the taste," Willie replied with his mouth full. "The honey might help, but it still smells like it's pretty bitter."

"I suppose it is," Woodrow admitted. "Nevertheless, you'll have to drink it down. You've still got some healing to do. So sit up and finish your stew. And try the spoon. It's a wonderful invention."

"I'm ready for that talk now," the youth suggested, picking up the utensil. He looked the spoon over as if he couldn't see the real point of bothering with it, but he complied and put it to use as he looked up at his host.

"I've got about a hundred questions that—"

"I'll talk. You eat," the Pack leader told him. "Then, I want to have another look at your leg. If you still have questions, you can ask them then."

The Medinian youth ate obediently. The man had a quiet authority about him, and the farm serf submitted to it. He was, after all, used to taking orders. He had taken them all his young life, whether at the monastery where the monks had guided his early days, or later, on the farm where he was apprenticed.

That recollection caused him to take pause and set the bowl down heavily in his lap.

"The wolf-creatures … my dogs and horse …" the youth gasped, as if he'd just awakened abruptly from a terrible nightmare. Tears formed in the corners of his eyes and trickled down his face. "It was horrible. It was a horrible nightmare."

"Is any of this real?" he demanded. "It can't be … how could it?"

The Pack leader pressed his hand down firmly on the youth's trembling shoulder.

"Your friends, the two dogs you called Rigel and Sirius, and the old horse you called Pegasus—they're gone. I know that they were true comrades of yours. I mourn for your loss. Friends like that … well, they're special and rare." He sat down wearily on the edge of the bed. "You'll have to accept that their lives were given so that you might live. Those were noble acts of loyalty and friendship. I know that it's easier said than done, but you must try to accept it. Trust me, time will help. It won't happen all at once, but the heartache you're feeling will ease with time, and you'll feel honoured by their actions that day."

"How do you know their names?" the youth demanded.

"You've been talking a lot the last few days and nights. Most of it was the fever. You were pretty delirious. At first I thought you were talking about the stars, but then I realized it was the names of your comrades you were calling out to. The only name I do not yet know is yours," the Pack leader added.

"Willie," the youth responded. He offered his hand. "I'm Willie of the Smythe farmstead on the western frontier of Medinia."

The Pack leader smiled as he accepted the youth's hand.

"Mine's Woodrow. I am the keeper of the castle of Lord Victor, in the kingdom of Varakov. We're in my cabin in the mountains." He paused and looked his young guest directly in the eyes. "I am also Woodrow, the leader of the Pack," he said solemnly. Seeing the look of puzzlement that came over the youth's face, he tried explaining further. "We were the ones who attacked your farm. We are … of the Pack."

When the import of these words sank in, the lad pulled his hand back as if he'd just been scalded.

"You're a lying bastard," the youth screamed at him, reliving that horrific and chaotic scene in the pastures in his mind. "They were huge, fierce creatures. They were wolves … worse than wolves. Wolf-creatures and wolf-men … they were …" Willie stammered, sobbing fiercely now.

Woodrow wrapped his arms tightly around him as the youth thrashed about trying to strike him, trying to strike out at the injustice and unfairness of it all. Finally he tired, until only his muffled sobs could be heard from where his face was buried in Woodrow's chest.

When his pent up emotions were spent, the lad wearily pushed himself away, and the Pack leader released his hold. He picked up and handed the youth the mug of herbal brew. He waited while he listlessly drank it down.

When he was finished it, Willie sank back into the bed. Woodrow got up and cleared away the tray and dishes. He would give the young Medinian some time to recover and to assimilate what he had learned so far. The worst was yet to come.

When he returned to the bedside, the youth was staring vacantly up at the ceiling. He appeared to be going into an almost catatonic shell. Woodrow knew from experience that this was but another step in the emotional turmoil that the youth was going through. He decided not to press him. Instead, Woodrow pulled up a chair and sat where he could attend to the youth's leg. Willie offered no resistance, nor indeed did he show any interest as the Pack leader pulled back the quilt and began to gently remove his bandages.

The wound was healing well. The stitches he'd put in were not infected, and the skin colour around the wounds had improved. The wound itself was still an angry red and purple, but it was showing signs of healing. Still, it would leave behind some vivid scarring.

Despite the youth's apparent disinterest, and despite Woodrow's gentle ministrations, when the last of the bandages were carefully removed, it hurt like hell. Willie couldn't help but look. The leg might have been healing, but it was still raw and tender. The wound was deep, as if there was a piece of meat missing, and the pain was undeniable.

"I can give you something to make you sleep if you wish," Woodrow suggested, without looking up.

"I can stand it," Willie said through clenched teeth. "I want to know the rest of it, now. All of it!"

Anger had replaced the vacant look in his eyes. Woodrow took that as a good sign.

"It was you, wasn't it?" Willie challenged. "I remember now waking up earlier. I thought it was part of the nightmare. It wasn't, was it? You had a wolf in here. Not as big as the ones that were in the paddocks, but still, he was big."

"That was Brutus, the Pack's enforcer and my very good friend," Woodrow replied evenly. "We were both at your master's farm."

For the next hour, the Pack leader told Willie the truth. He explained about the raids in Medinia and Skoland, and about the Pack and of its lunar transformations. This part of the story was met by a look of disbelief.

Woodrow talked about the heroic deaths of Willie's friends. He told Willie of the warg-wolves, as they were properly known. He related how some had died on the mission, as well. He also tried to tell him what each of the transformed wolves had meant to him and to those others of the Pack. He explained how he'd found the youth up in the tree and how he'd wrestled between the urge to finish the kill, and perhaps some inner voice calling for mercy. Quite frankly, he didn't really know.

He then told Willie of their return to Varakov through the pass and of the reversal transformation of the Pack members as the dawn arrived. Once again, he was given a sceptical look from the youth.

Ignoring the lad's disbelief of that, Woodrow finished by telling him of their trip through the mountain forests of Sanctuary to reach his cabin retreat, where he could treat the youth's leg wound and hopefully save his life.

"Well, screw you if you expect my thanks," the youth said. "And if you think that excuses you and your kind for killing my friends, you're fucking crazy. I'll never accept your apology, you bastard!"

Woodrow waited patiently, looking the defiant youth in the eye before replying.

"I said that I mourn the loss of your brave comrades, as I do my own," he said evenly. "I didn't apologize for it. We were on a mission for our king. We are the Pack. We are what and who we are. No more, no less."

"You're filthy predators! Our knights will hunt you down and slaughter every last one of you, and good riddance, you son of a bitch!" the youth swore again at him.

The Pack leader held his temper in check. He was tired from too little sleep while working on his patient. He didn't have the energy to waste on arguing pointlessly. He would save his energy to get them down from the mountain. He let the youth rage on for a time, while he treated his leg with his medicinal concoction. He finally spoke up as he was applying the last of the bandages.

"Enough! I ... we ... have been hunted too, Willie. We've been hunted for more years than you can possibly imagine. We've been hunted by knights and by sportsmen and by mobs. You're right, lad, we are predators. But it's mankind that's the predator of all predators. He kills for food, granted, but also for sport and for trophy. Hell, he even kills his own kind in anger and in lust and for personal gain, or for just about any damn reason he can dream up. Wolves kill only for their food, or in defence of their territory. They don't kill just because they don't like someone, or because they want to possess what they have."

He held up his hand to stifle Willie's protest.

"Granted, my Pack is different, Willie. In this instance we acted outside our normal behaviour. I'm not proud of that, but we had orders that we could not disobey. That's something you cannot understand for the moment. Suffice it to say that we're not a normal wolf pack. The Pack is made up of both humans and wolves. And we share a common curse—that's why we run together."

The Pack leader stood up from the bed. He rolled the sleeve of his shirt up and showed the youth the faint scars that remained from where teeth had sunk into his skin so long ago.

"I'm part wolf," Woodrow said. "And I'm damn proud of it! They're noble animals. Their part of nature's plan. They're hunters with a role to play. They live in harmony with the grazing animals, taking down the old and weak. Predators and prey—it's the natural order of life and the balance of the species."

He sighed heavily. *Could the youth ever understand what I've come to see as the truth?* He felt obligated to try to get through to him.

"Willie, it's mankind that lives outside the natural order of things, not wolves. He raises animals for the butcher's knife. He cuts down the trees to raise more fields of crops. He puts up fences and claims ownership of the land. His cities and mills pollute the streams and rivers. All in all, his greed far exceeds his need."

He carefully pulled the bedding back over the re-bandaged leg and then walked over to the cabin door, where he stood for a time looking outside. He could feel the youth's eyes on him. He knew his words were inadequate. He wasn't sure if he had done the youth any favour by sparing his life, and he didn't know if Willie would be able to make the transition to what his life would now become.

Woodrow knew that it wasn't going to be an easy task to teach this youth anything. Nevertheless, he was honour bound to try.

"You can rest today and tonight and recoup some more of your strength," he stated, turning his attention back to the Medinian youth. "When the sun comes up tomorrow, we must leave for the castle."

With that, the Pack leader turned away again and went out through the doorway. He left Willie to his anger and brooding thoughts.

*   *   *

Dumas, Medinia

Sir Reginald Toutant rode into the courtyard of the Dumas castle on his dusty grey destrier. The warhorse snorted as the knight commander reined him in. The Medinian commander looked across the courtyard where a dozen young knights-in-training were practising their swordsmanship. Steel rang off steel as side slashes were blocked and counter slashes delivered under the watchful eye of Sir Aitken, the grizzled old master-of-arms.

Toutant looked across the courtyard and a scowl crossed his scarred face. A figure wearing the distinctively embroidered surcoat of a knight-in-training stood staring at him and deliberately blocking his approach to the castle entry.

Wearily, the commander climbed down from his charger and passed the reins to one of the grooms who quickly led the destrier away to the stables. As Toutant took a few strides towards the castle, the apprentice knight drew a sword from its scabbard and called out a challenge. The other knights-in-training stopped their exercises to watch what would unfold.

Sir Reginald's response was to reach over his left shoulder and grasp the well worn leather hilt of his two-handed long sword and draw it from the leather scabbard strapped to his back. With the deadly weapon then held above his head he continued his approach undaunted by the mocking taunts of the much smaller opponent blocking his way.

As the two adversaries neared, Toutant took advantage of his superior reach and longer weapon. He swung his blade downward from right to left expecting it to be blocked by the blade of his opponent. He then intended to use the hilt to deliver a crushing blow to the helmed head of his challenger. To his surprise, his slashing blade met only air and the momentum of his blow carried it past the point of no return and left him unbalanced.

Not so, his opponent. The challenger moved with both speed and agility as Toutant's blade was in motion. With a quick dodge to the left and then an astonishing forward tumble that passed by Sir Reginald's side; a wicked backhanded slash was then delivered to the knight commander's right calf. He collapsed to one knee. A brief moment later the same sword was pressed to his throat from behind.

"If my training blade wasn't blunted your leg would be severed and your throat would be next," his opponent whispered into the kneeling knight commander's ear in triumph.

The master-of-arms laughed aloud. He was obviously enjoying seeing Sir Reginald taken by surprise.

Toutant's response was to reach behind him and grasp the collar of his opponent's surcoat and then rolled forward, flipping the trainee over his shoulder. As the challenger landed hard, he pressed his own blade to their throat.

"I'd advise less talk and more action. Finish the kill ... if you want to stay alive that is, milady," he advised as he helped the princess to her feet. "Now then, where did you learn that move? Judging from the old coot's laughter, I suspect the master-of-arm's hand in all this." He turned and gave the old knight a dip of his head in a show of respect.

"Sir Aitken has been showing me a few new moves," Lady Sarah Elizabeth confirmed as she raised the visor on her helm. "He says I shouldn't always try to trade blows, especially with a much bigger opponent. He's showing me how to use my size and agility to my advantage."

Sir Reginald had begun Sarah Elizabeth's training at a young age. Since about the age of four she'd been riding ponies and fighting with the boys of the Dumas court. By the age of eight, she could out run, out climb, and out ride most of them. Ever since then, with her father's somewhat reluctant permission, the princess had been training with the young apprentice knights. Neither he, nor Sir Aitken, had shown her any favouritism. To her credit, she took the knocks and bruises that came with the training regime without complaint.

"Well, I'm going to have a large welt to show that he's made a good point," Toutant observed with a chuckle as he rubbed the back of his leg. "Now I'm going to have to hobble my way inside to make my report to your father."

"Speaking of which," the princess said, "my sister and I have a small favour to ask of you."

"Why do I get the feeling that this 'small' favour is going to get me in trouble with your father again?" Toutant asked with a chuckle. "He's been giving me grief ever since you were little, saying that I should have run you out of the stables and back to the ladies of the court for sewing and dancing lessons."

*   *   *

An hour or so later, the Medinian knight commander entered the ornate great hall of the castle in Dumas in the company of the Ladies Hillary Michelle and

Sarah Elizabeth. The two sisters each held an arm of the knight commander as they strode down the aisle to stand before the Medinian king where he sat upon his throne holding court.

King Renaud broke off his discussions with his advisors when he saw their approach and laughed aloud.

"Toutant, I see my daughters have taken it upon themselves to escort you to me this afternoon," he said. "I suppose they thought you might get lost without their assistance."

"It has been some time since my last visit, milord, but I think I might have found my way. Nevertheless, how could I refuse the company of two such charming ladies after a hard day in the saddle," the commander replied with a smile.

The Medinian commander had taken the time to clean up and change before seeking an audience with the king. He was freshly shaven and had donned a quilted doublet embroidered with the heraldic arms of Medinia crested over his heart. In deference to the formality of the king's court, he also wore the pure white cloak of his knight regiment emblazoned with blue chevrons on the back.

"And I'm quite sure my daughters were positioned so as to be sure you took notice of them," the king said sternly at first, but then laughed again when he saw the look of innocence they each conjured up.

King Renaud regarded them for a moment. His two daughters were quite unalike in appearance and manner. Where Hillary Michelle wore her raven black hair long and was dressed in a simple gown of pale blue velvet, Sarah Elizabeth wore her hair closely cropped and was wearing her usual light tan riding leathers with a laced up bodice and plain tan cloak. The sisters shared their mother's dark brown eyes, however, as well as her determined nature.

King Renaud was certain that the two princesses had conspired to be on hand when Toutant made his appearance. By escorting the knight commander into the great hall they likely hoped to linger and learn first hand what had transpired in the western frontier border. He sighed to show his reluctance, but then with a wave of his hand, indicated that they could seat themselves to the side. He brought a finger to his lips to convey that he expected them to be seen and not heard.

"Welcome home, Sir Reginald," he then said. "I understand we've had some difficulties out by the mountains and then with a Skolish regiment."

"We have, milord."

The Medinian commander apprised the king of the 'wolf-like' attacks on the western farms and the odd tracks they'd discovered. He then spoke of the river confrontation, his subsequent meeting with Prince Paulo and the Skolish commander, Sir Geoffrey Gaullé, and their joint investigation that led them up to the Euralene pass.

It was Toutant's accounting of how the Skolish prince had conducted himself that interested Hillary Michelle the most. According to the Medinian commander, the prince had bravely stood in defence of his wounded comrade. While he'd been reluctant to trust Toutant at first due to the Medinian weaponry they'd found at the sites of the raids, the prince had been willing to review the new evidence that he and the Skolish commander, Gaullé, had uncovered. Prince Paulo had conceded that there may have been subterfuge at work, and that a third force might have conducted the raids into Skoland. In the end, the Skolish prince had been open to the possibility that they might have a mutual enemy.

In that regard, Sir Reginald stated that he was convinced they'd not heard the last from whoever was really responsible for the atrocities.

*   *   *

August 1, 1461
Kragonus, Skoland

Prince Paulo found Gaullé sitting alone in the knight's hall. A tankard of ale sat mostly untouched at his elbow. Doubtlessly, the knight commander was still full of remorse over the lost of young Francis. It was a personal blow that he was taking hard.

"If you're not too far into your cup, there's still work to be done around here," the prince said sternly, to get his mentor's attention. "I have need of your council," he added. "You're the one who believes the Medinians are innocent, after all."

Prince Paulo knew his commander well. It would do him good to focus his attention on other matters.

"My father and I have been discussing the Medinian situation. He feels that we should go forward with the peace accords. He's proposing that we should host one large joint harvest festival when the caravans are due to arrive in the fall. There'd be markets, celebrations, jousts, and contests of skills. He thinks it would help us to get to know each other better."

"And what do you think, my prince?" the commander asked.

Paulo grew thoughtful. Then he nodded his head.

"I concur now—with most of it, at least. We've been at war for far too long. I have serious doubts about a long-term peace with the Medinians, but we could use a time of rest and rebuilding. It'll give the men time to go to church with their wives and then go back to their homes and make some more Skolish babies."

The prince laughed and slapped his companion's shoulder.

"And, I'm looking forward to meeting this Medinian princess whom everyone wants me to marry. If she's half as fine as I've heard, then maybe I'll consider breeding a few royal brats myself, Sir Geoffrey." He laughed. "Not to say that there aren't a few of the wee bastards running around out there already, eh?"

The battle-tested older knight joined his prince in a laugh. The king's son was a handsome devil—there was no denying it. It was a well-known fact that many a fair maiden had succumbed to his charms.

"Now then, Gaullé, let's go over the plans for this upcoming harvest festival. I want to be prepared for all possibilities. If we get Skolish and Medinians together for a full week of markets, celebrations, and drinking, almost anything could happen," the prince declared.

"And let's not forget the Varakovans—or whoever else may be out there," the commander added. "With these recent mysteries we should be prepared for any trouble that may arise from that quarter." Sir Geoffrey's mind was engaged and alert now.

Prince Paulo noted this and was pleased. While he'd been opposed to seeking a peace with the Medinians, initially, he was now more of the mind that it was the right course of action. It would give him time to consolidate his position for the future. With the Lady Hillary Michelle as his bride, it would merge the two kingdoms. It would only be a matter of time until both the current king's reigns would then pass to him. With the combined forces and the resources of Skoland and Medinia, his reign could then look outwards for further growth—perhaps even into Varakov. That would secure them a direct gateway to the ocean trade—and a wealth of new possibilities.

Time would tell. The one thing that the prince knew with certainty was that he was destined for great things. This proposed marriage might just be the key to it all. He still bore a hatred for the Medinians. They had been the cause of his two brother's deaths, after all, but a wedding to their princess might be the first necessary step in his plans for the future.

Hell, even if she turned out to be a hag, Paulo decided, he might still marry her. An annoying wife could always be dealt with later should another more favourable alliance present itself. Once he was firmly ensconced on the throne of both kingdoms, they would fly one united flag, and it would be his flag.

"I agree with you about the possibility of the Varakovans being a threat, Sir Geoffrey," the prince said. "We need to be prepared for them or for whoever else poses a threat to Skoland and the peace accords with Medinia."

For the next few hours Prince Paulo and Gaullé discussed the best means for augmenting the security of the western border of the kingdom.

*　　　　*　　　　*

The Euralene Mountains, Varakov

"I can do it myself."

Willie brushed aside Woodrow's attempt to help him out of bed the next morning. Following their heated discourse, the Pack leader had purposefully left the youth alone in the cabin for the better part of the prior day and night. He'd sat out on the porch and had returned only to administer the youth's medicine and their meals. They ate those apart in an awkward silence.

After their dinner, Woodrow had brought in a pair of crutches that he'd fashioned that afternoon. He'd placed them by the youth's cot and departed, expecting no thanks and receiving none. The Pack leader didn't come back in again until it was time for sleep.

Coming into the cabin after dark, he found that the lamp was lit and a small fire blazed in the fireplace. The young farm serf was back in his cot, but it was clear that he had availed himself of the crutches to test his leg out.

Before they retired to their respective beds that night, Woodrow had changed Willie's bandages one last time. He noted with satisfaction that the stitches were still holding well and the leg was continuing to heal quite nicely.

If there was one definite advantage to being part of the afflicted Pack, it was their innate ability to recover quickly from injuries.

The Pack leader had witnessed this many times in the past. Cuts clotted and scabbed over quickly. They healed and were gone in short order. He'd noted that broken bones mended faster than they did with normal people, too. He'd concluded that there must be stronger healing agents in their feral systems. As a group, they even seemed to be less susceptible to colds, flu, and other illnesses.

When the Medinian youth declined his assistance, Woodrow backed off. He allowed the lad to fend for himself.

"I'll be outside packing the travois. Have yourself some breakfast."

Willie waited until the door was closed, and then awkwardly pulled himself up out of the cot and grabbed up the crutches. He had indeed been testing out his leg the evening before. He'd found that by supporting his weight with them, he was able to peg leg about the room without putting strain on the injured limb.

Last night, he'd grown restless, stiff, and cold. He'd crutched himself over to light the lamp and then on to build a fire to warm up the cabin. At one point, he'd considered lighting the cabin itself ablaze. Common sense had prevailed.

It would have been premature. He was weak and injured. He likely wouldn't have gotten far. Anyway, this Pack leader bastard was doubtlessly just outside and would have rushed in. The youth fully intended to make his escape and get back home, however. He would warn the Medinian knights, and they would find a way to punish those wolf-people.

Sitting alone by the fire that night, Willie's curiosity had gotten the better of him. He'd used the crutches to circle-step the room and checked out the cabin's contents. It had quickly become apparent to him that his jailer was an educated man. There were easily twice the number of scrolls and books than even the monks back home possessed. Despite his own limited reading skills, he knew enough to recognize that they dealt with a wide variety of subjects. Indeed, there were more here than the lad could have surmised. While the priests had taught him a little reading skill while he was with them, Woodrow's collection surpassed his learning. The texts included detailed writings on medicinal care, on different religious philosophies and teachings, as well as several discourses of opposing social and political viewpoints.

The storeroom of herbs and medicines had impressed Willie also. Not that he was about to discuss this or anything else with the wolf-man. He would bide his time. He would wait and watch. He would heal first, and then, when the time was right, he'd flee this foul place.

In the meantime, the Medinian youth did as he had been directed and ate the food the Pack leader had prepared. As a precaution, for what the unknown future may hold, he stuffed a few extra rolls inside his shirt. He considered stealing one of the knives from the kitchen, but he had the feeling that the wolf-man would notice, or perhaps even search him before they left.

When he'd finished eating, Willie stepped out of the cabin. He used the crutches to prop himself with one arm and managed to close the door with the other.

"I guess a guy like you doesn't have to bother locking his door, does he?" the youth said sarcastically, as he turned to face the Pack leader. "Wow," he added, a brief moment later.

Willie had stopped short, in wonder and appreciation of the vista that was there before his eyes. The jagged peaks soared high to kiss the azure-blue sky. Their snow-capped tops glistened as the rising sun's rays reflected off the sparkling ice crystals. The distant waterfall drew his attention to the gorge. The youth pegged his way past the Pack leader as he was bent over the travois and looked over the ledge. The height was dizzying. He felt a sinking sensation in the pit of his stomach. His manhood involuntarily shrank, almost retracting into his groin.

It was more exhilarating than scary, though. Far below them, the cascading water crashed into the gorge basin, creating a perpetual hissing cloud of spray and mist. There was the most perfect little rainbow, which arched over the spray in the confined space. The youth hoped that it was a good omen.

"Time to go, Willie."

When the youth joined him, Woodrow indicated the place that he had left for him in the travois to lie down. When Willie protested, the Pack leader's response was quite specific.

"Get in. We'll make a lot better time. You'd never make it down on crutches."

"What about getting some horses, or a wagon?" the youth questioned.

"Not possible where we're going," Woodrow replied bluntly. There was no room for argument in his tone of voice. The Pack leader knew they had a long trek ahead of them. They weren't capable of shortening the trip in the manner of Lord Victor.

Reluctantly, Willie tossed in his crutches and then settled himself into the travois. The Pack leader waited until the youth was positioned before he bent down and deftly passed his hands over the youth's frame.

"Satisfied?" the youth taunted. "I'm not armed."

"Indulge me. I wouldn't want you doing anything stupid," the Pack leader replied. "Enjoy the rolls."

"Well, don't get too comfortable," the youth said. "When the opportunity presents itself, I'll be only too happy to slip a blade into you. You won't be keeping me prisoner here for very long."

The Pack leader's reply was a dismissive grunt. He took up the two ends of a strap and cinched his passenger in with a quick tug, perhaps a little more tightly than was necessary.

"Wouldn't want you to fall out," he said. "The trail ahead gets a little bumpy."

Woodrow paused just before he took up the load.

"Let's get one thing clear Willie, okay? You're not my prisoner. When the time is right, you'll be free to go if you wish to. But like it, or not, you're part of the Pack now. Your blood is poisoned, just like ours. That means that there's wolf in you, too. You had better start getting used to the idea, because you're going to have to deal with it."

The youth's response was a series of angry expletives. The Pack leader shrugged them off as he hooked himself into the harness. Digging his toes in, he set off, dragging the loaded travois behind him.

Willie's view was to the rear. He got one final glimpse of the distant waterfall cascading down into the gorge as they crested the rise above the cabin. They were already traversing down through the meadow as the sun cleared the mountain peaks.

It was as if the wildflowers were waiting for that precise moment. The face of each was turned to greet the late dawn. Their petals were wide open to drink in the light. The explosion of colour they produced was breathtaking. Once again, the youth thought that despite the dire circumstances he was in, this was truly a magnificent setting.

Where the beauty of the mountains and the meadow had inspired a reverence in him, the startling, sudden passage into the great forest quickly crushed it. The trees were huge, much larger than those back home. Within seconds, the world went into shades of black and grey, as the canopies closed out the sun's rays. The youth found it oppressive and even a little claustrophobic. The air grew danker as they moved deeper into the forest confines, and he found that it was harder even to breathe.

After only about only ten minutes, as the Pack leader twisted and turned following some unseen path through the maze of giant trees, the youth was completely lost. Without a point of reference, the best he could do was guess at their general bearing. They were moving down the mountainside, he knew, and to the northwest, he guessed.

In the same few minutes after the two travelers entered the forest, the ripple of wildflowers and grasses betrayed the four-legged animal that followed after them. The wolf had made itself scarce the evening before, knowing that the Pack leader would have discovered him hiding in the copse of trees when he sat brooding on the porch. There was no questioning Brutus's devotion to duty. He'd stayed through the night in the meadow and would now follow the Pack leader until they were safely within sight of the manor.

Once the Pack enforcer was inside the great forest, the wolf closed the distance and ran a parallel course, keeping his comrade and the youth within his keen hearing range.

While Woodrow didn't possess the acute senses of the wolf, he still felt the animal's presence. Call it years of familiarity. He knew that the Pack's enforcer was somewhere nearby. They'd been bonded soul mates for a long, long time now. He smiled, knowing that despite his orders, the wolf would never allow him to travel in the mountains without his personal protection.

It had taken years, and several nasty confrontations, to convince Brutus that Woodrow must walk alone when it came to Varakov proper. Even so, it was only after safely arriving there that the Pack enforcer would begrudgingly retreat to the mountains and his mate. He would remain there until the days preceding the next full moon, when he would return to accompany Woodrow back to the Pack and back to his place as their leader.

Even though he didn't know the wolf was out there, Willie was ill at ease. The forest of mammoth trees never ended! The trees soared overhead and formed a dense canopy that only the odd beam of sunlight managed to penetrate. Rather than making things clearer to his eyes, the scattering of the few specks of light only served to make the shadows more confusing and oppressive.

More oppressive still was the eerie silence.

The musty smell of decaying leaves and rotting wood from fallen trees and limbs seemed to thicken the air. The rainfall here must be substantial, the youth surmised. This forest was ten times as dense as the one on his side of the mountain divide. It was an alien place to him, and frankly, it scared him. Each confusing trail his captor followed took the youth farther from his home, and each further step took away a little more of his confidence that he could ever find his way back to Medinia.

To make matters worse, Willie had the feeling that they were being watched. Some of the shadows seemed to shift along, as if they were following them.

Woodrow was certain of it.

*   *   *

It was some four hours after they'd departed the cabin confines that the Pack leader's pace slowed. He was feeling the strain of dragging his load. His back ached, and he was reminded again that he wasn't as young as he had once been. In fact, he hadn't been young even then. It was only that his particular affliction defied the years and considerably slowed the aging process.

The trees were beginning to thin out a bit now. Up ahead, he could see the sunlit clearing that he sought. Behind him, Willie must have noticed the difference too. The youth actually expelled an audible sigh of relief as they came out of the woods and into the clearing. It was almost as if he'd been holding his breath the entire journey.

They came to a halt in a meadow glade, which stood like an island in the sea of trees surrounding it. Woodrow unhooked the harness and laid the poles down. He stretched his arms and tried to ease the knot that had settled between his shoulder blades.

"Why are we stopping here?" Willie asked, amazed at the endurance and strength that Woodrow had displayed to this point. He wasn't about to say so, however.

"Need a rest, do you?" he taunted instead.

The Pack leader chose to ignore the jibe and came around to release the youth from his bindings.

"Stretch your legs if you like," he suggested. "We'll wait here while they check us out."

"While who checks us out?" the youth asked, a noticeable tremor in his voice.

"The Oddities," Woodrow replied. "They're friends of mine. They're just a little cautious with strangers. This is a greeting place. We'll wait until they invite us into their part of Sanctuary."

The Pack leader sat down wearily on the ground and tried to get comfortable.

"There's a water bag above where your head was. Have yourself a drink and pass it over when you're done," he suggested.

Willie gathered up his crutches and struggled getting to his feet. He was a little stiff and sore himself. He hadn't had to put out the exertion that the Pack leader had moving through that crushing forest. He had, however, to endure being bounced and jostled along backwards, while being trussed up like a side of beef. It was a bit degrading.

The Medinian youth found the water skin, pulled out the stopper, and drank greedily from it. The cool water and the fresh breeze in the clearing helped him to regain his senses. The thick air in the forest had seemed to close his lungs up, but here in this little clearing he could at least breathe again. He jammed the cork back into the bag.

"Catch," Willie said, tossing the water bag towards Woodrow.

The Pack leader was in repose, lying on his back. In a vain attempt, he tried to get his weight off the ground in time to make the grab. The best he could manage was to block the water bag between his one wrist and elbow. When the bag struck his arm, the pressure of the impact caused the cork to pop out and the water to gush forth. He was showered with half its contents.

Given quite a drenching, he couldn't help but laugh. Actually, it was rather refreshing after the long trek through the woods. His shirting was soaked with clammy sweat, anyway. He tilted his head back and took a long drink from the remaining water, and then he poured the rest over his head. He wasn't concerned about running out. There were dozens of mountain streams on the way down to Varakov proper.

Willie had joined in the laughter at first. It had been funny to see Woodrow scrambling off his back and getting soaked. Then he remembered where he was, and with whom.

"The next time, that could be hot oil," he muttered loud enough to be heard.

The youth turned and crutched a few yards further into the clearing. He purposely kept his back to the Pack leader. He stretched to loosen his muscles and get the kinks out of his joints. He tried not to favour his hurt leg. He had to get it strong again if he was ever to have a chance to escape this madness.

A few minutes later, he called back over his shoulder, "So when can we expect these friends of yours to show themselves?"

Not getting a response, he turned around to see if the man was listening to him. He saw that Woodrow's attention was directed towards the far tree line. Willie followed his gaze, but he couldn't make out anything except trees.

Then, suddenly, there they were, already a good distance into the clearing before he even distinguished them from the foliage. His mouth gaped open. His life and world had already sunk into a kind of insanity. What his eyes now perceived told him that his descent into madness wasn't over yet.

CHAPTER 9

Sanctuary

We've been cursed at and accused
We've been mocked at and abused

August 1, 1461
The Euralene Mountains, Varakov

WILLIE SAW FOUR INDIVIDUALS coming towards them. He hobbled back behind the Pack leader, leaned on his crutch, and kept a wary eye on their approach. They were four of the strangest looking fellows that the youth had ever seen. He recalled that Woodrow had said they were waiting for the Oddities. As far as Willie was concerned these guys certainly lived up to the name.

He found it difficult to focus on any one of them for long. They were of such stark contrast to each other that he found himself glancing from one to another and then back again.

The one to his far left was the palest individual he'd ever seen. A simple robe, with the hood resting on his shoulders, covered most of him. His face and hands were so pale that the closer he came, the more they appeared to be translucent. Willie half expected to see through the skin to the bones below. The man's hair was long, well below his shoulders. He didn't appear to be old, but his hair was pure white, as if bleached, and his eyebrows and eyelashes were the same. His eyes were pink tinged. He was carrying a bright red parasol. To block out the sun, Willie supposed, because it certainly wasn't raining.

Next to him, a dwarf scurried along to keep up with the group; he was an ill-proportioned one at that. From the awkward kilter of his gait, Willie guessed that his one leg must be longer than the other. This deformity seemed to extend up his back as one shoulder was definitely higher than the other. His diminutive body appeared on a tilt as a result.

The next fellow just kept growing larger as he approached.

He's even bigger than the blacksmith who runs the forge in the village back home, Willie thought. *He has to be close to seven feet tall. It's no wonder that the dwarf has to half-run to keep up. I'd have trouble keeping up with him myself, even if I had two good legs.*

The big man's skull looked off balance, however, Willie considered. His forehead seemed to go straight up about eight inches, before meeting an unruly thatch of black hair. Even his ears were huge, sticking out from his head like flaps.

The final member of the foursome was a very black man, who moved along with a natural grace that reminded Willie of a mountain cat. He wore pants, but his chest was bare, as were his feet. It wasn't until they were almost face to face that he noticed the markings covering his face. They were almost the same shade of black as his skin, so it wasn't easy to spot them at first.

The Pack leader rose and greeted the four arrivals as they approached with a hand sign that moved inward towards his body. The men went directly to Woodrow, ignoring the youth on crutches who stood there gaping at them. Woodrow smiled and nodded first to the pale man, who kept himself a little to the rear of the others. He received a brief smile in return, but it was obvious that this was a reserved individual. He didn't speak or come any closer.

Not so, the giant. He was obviously a young man, but he grinned from ear to ear, much as a child might. He stepped up and hugged the Pack leader, literally lifting him off his feet as he did so.

"Hey ya, Woodrow. I got things to show ya, for sure. You've been away a long time, you know that?" He spoke quickly, as an excited youngster would.

"Woodrow, you're all wet. That's pretty funny. It's not raining, you know. You can ask Marvin. Even if he's got that red thingamajig of his, it's for the sun, not the rain."

"You can put me down now, Frederick. I told you I'd be back, didn't I? I'd never forget to come and see my friends, would I?" Woodrow waited patiently to be set back down. It was pointless to struggle; the hug would be over when Freddy was ready to let go.

Freddy finally released him, with the same happy smile still plastered across his face. Woodrow laughed at his innocent exuberance, but the laughter made his ribs ache almost as much as the crushing hug had.

Then Woodrow knelt down on one knee. "And how are you, *mon ami? Comment ça va, Yves?*" He extended his hand to the dwarf.

"*Très bien*, Woodrow. *Et tu?*" The little man touched Woodrow's hand briefly and then quickly pulled his arm back as if he found it prudent not to trust his small fingers to the grasp of a normal hand.

Still, it was apparent that the dwarf had no fear of Woodrow. It was quite to the contrary. They shared a lengthy exchange, but in a language Willie didn't understand. Judging from their smiles and the tone of their voices, however, they were just two old friends catching up.

When their conversation ended, Woodrow rose and turned to the black man. Willie examined him more closely now. The man's face was indeed heavily marked, but by design, not by accident. Across his forehead and over the cheek area at either side of the bridge of his nose, notched scars formed an intricate pattern. Willie had seen a few travelers who bore tattoo markings, but he'd never seen anything or anyone like this.

Woodrow addressed the man as Chakula, but he then talked to him by sign. He used his hands, arms, and body, to convey his meaning. He was answered in the same manner, although the black man's body language seemed more natural. To Willie, it was like watching a living portrait from some faraway land and unknown culture that was both primitive and wildly expressive.

At this point, Freddy seemed to discover Willie, standing off by himself and watching them guardedly. He peered at Woodrow's new travelling companion.

"I saw you in the forest," he said. "You were getting a ride from the Pack leader. What's the matter with your leg?" Did you hurt it? Is that why you were getting a ride? What's your name? Mine's Freddy. It's really Frederick, but everybody calls me Freddy."

The young giant seemed to cover the space between them in two strides, apparently intent on giving a proper greeting to the young stranger, even if none of his rapid-fire questions were being answered.

Willie reacted badly. The fast-approaching Freddy seemed to awaken him from his stupor. He let out a holler and recoiled from the approaching menace. He stumbled and dropped one of the crutches but managed to retain his balance. Hopping on one leg, he raised the other crutch and reared back, preparing to defend himself.

"Get back, Jack, or I'll take your blasted head off," he warned, aiming his makeshift weapon.

Freddy ploughed on towards the stranger, blissfully unaware of the impending blow. "My name's Freddy, not Jack. What's—?"

A solid blow to his upper body followed, one that would have knocked any grown man to the ground, but Freddy simply stood there. His expression grew pained, but less from the smack of the crutch than from hurt feelings. He looked genuinely dismayed that this fellow who was with his friend, Woodrow, could turn out to be so devious.

"Why'd you do that to Freddy? That wasn't a nice thing to do. You're a bad person," he stated slowly, as if he'd suddenly discovered a simple and undeniable truth.

With that decided, Freddy lunged forward and collared Willie by the scruff of his neck with one hand and the seat of his pants with the other. He hoisted the protesting youth high above his head and prepared to toss him through the air. Willie's eyes went wide with helpless fright.

Before the others could react, a blur of black and silver came bursting out of the nearby grasses. In even less time than it had taken Freddy, Brutus covered the distance between them. The wolf blew past the Pack leader and the men from Sanctuary. As Freddy started to turn and the muscles in his arms bunched to initiate the tossing, the wolf leaped up at him.

In the same instant, Brutus came into the view of Willie and Freddy. Both of them saw the wolf leave the ground, but only Willie felt a moment of added terror.

The wolf struck Freddy hard with the pads of his front paws into the chest of the young Oddity. His strength and momentum forced Freddy to reel backwards on his heels, and he became unbalanced by the load he held above him. At the point of no return, Freddy crashed heavily to the ground. Luckily for Willie, his adversary held onto him for most of the way down before he was sent rolling across the grass, lessening the impact of the fall.

Freddy recovered quickly. He rolled over, then half rose, and dove at the wolf. The two locked together in battle. As they vied for position, a fierce din of growls and grunts rose from each.

Willie clambered up onto his good leg and hopped about, trying to gain his balance. He was beset by indecision. He didn't know if he should try to recover one of his crutches and help the young giant or attempt another course of action.

He looked to the others for aid, and that was when he heard their laughter, as they watched the antics of the two combatants rolling around on the ground. Freddy had started to laugh, too, and he was calling out endearments to the wolf as they roughhoused together.

"Okay, both of you," Woodrow called. "Freddy, you know Brutus is getting too old for that. One of these days, someone's going to get hurt. If he bit you at the wrong time of the month, you'd turn into the biggest damned wolf-man anybody's ever seen." His admonishments went largely unheeded.

When the two happy wrestlers finally separated, each bore fresh scratches and bruises. Freddy wore a broad grin. Brutus's tongue hung out as he panted. He was obviously quite pleased with himself. After all, he'd averted an injurious landing for Willie. At the same time, he'd turned Freddy's hurt anger into some rough play. The young giant had clearly forgotten about the whack with the crutch for the moment.

"We really have to be moving along now, my friends." Woodrow turned his attention back to the other three men. "If you will make us welcome, I'd like to visit the village for a brief while and speak with the rabbi. Then we must be on our way to the Mesa-of-the-Moon."

His request was granted with almost comic formality. Each of the Oddities consented in turn and bid him welcome. Even Freddy climbed to his feet and gave his solemn approval.

Willie was hustled back to the travois and bundled aboard. Once again, he was strapped in tightly. If that wasn't enough indignity, the dwarf came up, looked him over suspiciously, and then removed his dirty, sweat-stained neckerchief. He then proceeded to blindfold the protesting youth with it. With a heavy accent, the little man calmly told him not to attempt to remove it.

"It is best you not complain, *mon ami*," he whispered into the youth's ear. "If you were not with the blindfold, you would know where we live, and I have to kill you. I might have to slit your t'roat." The threat seemed entirely plausible, considering the four knives that were secured in sheathes about his tiny personage.

"Well then, you better find yourself a stump to stand on, you sawed-off little runt!" Willie retorted.

"*Mais non, garçon.* I only have to kick you in dose family jew-els of yours. Then, when you fall down to my size … zip!"

The dwarf drew his tiny index finger across the lad's throat to illustrate his point. Willie flinched and cursed. He left the filthy blindfold in place, however, and resigned himself to a dark ride to an unknown destiny.

With that argument resolved, the group set off. Woodrow and the dwarf brought up the rear. The Pack leader dragged the travois once more, while the little Oddity kept watch on an angry and sullen Willie.

Freddy and Brutus led the way. They kept wandering on and off of the barely visible path the others followed but managed mostly to stay in sight.

The young giant was playing a game of tree-dodge with the Pack's enforcer. Aside from the people who resided with him in Sanctuary, Woodrow and Brutus were his favourite friends. He accepted the wolf as close to human and talked to him much as he would to anyone else.

"I wasn't really going to hurt him much, you know," he said. "Just give him a real good tossing is all. Besides, he hit me first … and hard, too. That wasn't nice, was it?" It was obvious that Freddy was now brooding again over Willie's unprovoked attack.

For his part, Brutus seemed content simply to listen as he followed Freddy's winding trail through the forest. When the giant looked back and saw the wolf's lolling tongue, he took it for a grin and felt sure he was forgiven. His conscience at ease, he grinned back and then promptly walked into a tree. Neither seemed the worse for the encounter.

*   *   *

They had traveled for about thirty minutes by Willie's best reckoning. Admittedly, he had sulked most of the way. He'd had to endure an endless stream of nonsense spewing out of the mouth of the dwarf— sometimes talking, sometimes singing. Never did the fellow shut up with his constant drivel. It didn't help, either, that half of it was in that foreign tongue of his.

What was even worse was worrying about that damn wolf! The animal had come out of nowhere, and now all the bad memories flooded back into his thoughts. With his eyes covered, his imagination conjured up the worst, and the worst was horrifying. First it was the wolf-men and the ferocious creatures that Woodrow called warg-wolves. Now it was these Oddities. His life was becoming a never-ending nightmare.

When the procession finally came to a halt, he felt Woodrow slide out of the harness and set the travois poles down. He assumed they had arrived at this Sanctuary place of theirs. Confirmation came when the blindfold was pulled off and his bindings released. Willie blinked and rubbed his eyes as the dwarf retied the filthy handkerchief around his own neck. Woodrow offered his hand to help Willie up. He ignored it. The Pack leader shrugged his shoulders complacently and turned away.

The youth struggled to his feet and recovered his crutches. He propped himself up and looked around, but there wasn't much to see. What there was did not impress him in the least.

The trees in the partial clearing had been thinned out, but those that remained still towered overhead. They were on a section of mountainside strewn with boulders and rocks, likely from some past landslide. At the far end, the clearing dropped off into a rocky ravine. On the other side of that, the nearly impenetrable forest reasserted itself.

There was a small livestock pen and a dozen or so ramshackle mud-and-thatch huts scattered about the clearing. They varied in size, but none were remarkable in any way. A few of these structures were freestanding, while others were propped up against various trees. For the most part, they appeared to be in need of the support. Willie concluded that the huts wouldn't provide much shelter against the elements. He saw nothing else of value.

The Medinian youth had concluded that the immense forest obviously received a lot of precipitation, and that meant that the winters would leave this place snowbound and likely bitterly cold. The few crops established near the back of the clearing looked meagre and scrawny. He didn't see how they could support very many families.

If this is their idea of a Sanctuary, they're welcome to it. But who are they? Willie wondered. Other than for their small party, a few livestock in the pen, and some chickens he saw scratching around in the dirt, the place appeared deserted.

Willie was about to ask Woodrow what the deal was when he saw the black man cup his hands to his mouth. The sound that came forth was a perfect imitation of a wolf's call. It gave him a chill. He noticed that even the Pack enforcer's ears pricked up.

A few moments later, the call was returned by a dozen others from varying distances and different directions. The calls echoed from the mountaintops until Willie couldn't even be sure where they were coming from.

Whether the howls were issued from the throats of other Oddities on guard duty or from a pack of real wolves out there somewhere, Willie couldn't be sure. It became apparent, however, that these unseen sentries were giving an "all-clear" signal, and the aspect of the neighbourhood abruptly changed dramatically.

They were no longer alone in the clearing—far from it. People began pouring in from numerous directions. A steady stream of them came down from the mountainside, where they seemed to step out from behind the jumble of rocks and boulders. Others trailed up from the ravine, following indiscernible pathways; still others dropped out of the air. More precisely, they lowered themselves from the tree canopies. Some came down on single ropes, while others were cranked down in basket-like conveyances from high overhead. It was an astonishing sight.

As for the people themselves, it was the largest collection of unusual-looking men, women, and children that Willie had ever seen. There were a few more wee folk like the dwarf, Yves, and a number of cripples and hunchbacks. There were scarred, maimed, and deformed people of all sorts. There were people who were obviously blind, or branded, or missing limbs. There were far too many deformities to take in all at once, and it was made even more disconcerting by the sheer number of Oddities.

Of the entire throng, it seemed to Willie that the most normal in appearance were the children. True, a few of them suffered some form of disfigurement, but most looked like any other child. It seemed that whatever had caused the abnormalities in the adults had not necessarily been passed on to their offspring.

In time, Willie's eyes were able to focus on those few adults interspersed among the crowd who seemed normal in appearance, as well. Yet, even these folks seemed odd, either because of the myriad of strange languages they spoke, their strange mannerisms, or their choices of clothing.

He understood vaguely that some of these differences derived from varying religious and ethnic backgrounds—there were Jews, Muslims, and even a few Catholic monks and friars among their number. Several other groups he didn't recognize at all. They were beyond his youthful experience.

The Oddities' skin tones varied as greatly as their apparel. Willie noticed that those who'd come up from the ravine or rappelled down from the trees wore garbs of colour and pattern that helped them blend into the forest.

The men, women, and children kept coming until the clearing was full and they were backing up the mountainside. Many carried baskets of food and drink, and they were setting up picnic areas where they could meet their neighbours and enjoy a meal together.

While Willie's attention had been focused on the diverse multitude, he'd lost track of their escort party. Except for Freddy, they'd disappeared, or perhaps simply blended into the growing crowd.

Woodrow and the wolf, Brutus, stood patiently waiting beside him. The Pack leader waved and exchanged greetings with many of the people. Some of them came forward to thank him for the fresh meat he'd sent them. It was clear to Willie, however, that Woodrow was intent on meeting someone in particular. Brutus, too, seemed to know that there was someone yet to make an appearance. While he allowed himself to be patted by some of the children, his ears were raised and his eyes focused on the mountainside.

What started to bother Willie then was the interest seemingly focused in his direction. Many of the people gathered appeared to be having whispered discussions about him. It was if he were the different one, the freak in the crowd that people were pointing out.

A short time later, the crowd grew still. On the mountainside, two new figures had emerged from behind a jumble of boulders. They stood beside the albino called Marvin. The first was a small, stooped, elderly man. The gnarled wooden staff he held in one hand was taller than he was. His other arm was tucked into a plain brown robe that contrasted sharply with the wisps of white hair rimming his bare scalp. He wore a full beard, snow white and so long that it touched his knees. It looked as soft as lamb's wool and gave him an air of wisdom. He was also wearing a phylactery and a talith with blue fringes at the corners, in accordance with the Law of Moses. It was obvious from everyone's reaction that this was their leader.

The second figure was a female adolescent standing by his side. She was clad in a simple frock with a sash tied about her waist and wore her hair long, well down past her shoulders. It shone in the early-afternoon sun with the same pure whiteness as the elder's beard and their albino escort's hair. Unlike Marvin, her skin was a healthy nutmeg brown.

The leader used his staff to beckon Woodrow and Brutus to join them. Like the biblical Red Sea, the crowd parted to let them pass.

"You can come along if you care to, Willie," Woodrow said. He started to move through the crowd, not looking back to see if the youth chose to follow. Brutus dutifully fell in behind the Pack leader as he moved up the mountainside.

Willie promptly decided he didn't care to be left behind with all the unfamiliar Oddities, so he hobbled after them. It was awkward trying to climb the grade and he stumbled when his crutches slid on some loose shale. He might have fallen had Freddy not stepped in and promptly snatched him up, crutches and all.

Many in the crowd laughed as Willie tried, without success, to escape the giant's assistance. Reluctantly, he ceased struggling and resigned himself to the ride, cradled in two huge arms. Although Freddy's grasp was firm, it was evident from his grin that he intended no harm and was merely trying to be helpful.

"How are you, Old Man?" Woodrow called out, as they approached the leader of the Oddities.

"I'm not deaf, you know!" the elderly rabbi snorted. He waited until Woodrow bent down to embrace him, and then he whispered into his ear. "I'm just a little hard of hearing now and again, mostly when it suits my needs," he murmured.

The Pack leader smiled. "You're well, then?"

"I'm quite well, Woodrow," the wizened Oddity leader responded, "barring the usual assortment of aches and pains. And how's the world treating you these days? Besides the good soaking you took a while back?" The rabbi chuckled. Obviously, Marvin had related the earlier occurrence.

"Oh, before I forget," he added, "thanks for the meat you sent us. We had a wonderful feast. And yes, we made sure it was well cooked! I sent your people on with a cartload full of grain, some fruit, and some fresh vegetables. An excellent trade for everyone, I should say."

It didn't occur to Willie that it was the meat of the Smythe's livestock they were talking about. He simply looked on as they exchanged small pleasantries. He'd never seen such an ancient looking man, even at the monastery. He took note of the elderly leader's thick accent, which he learned later was Yiddish.

What did occur to Willie was that he couldn't see any place that fruits and vegetables could have come from—surely not from the bare subsistence farming in the small community here. *How do they feed all these people?* he wondered.

He found his attention drawn to the white-haired girl then. Freddy still wasn't setting him down, so he stared openly at her from his vantage point up in the young giant's arms.

The girl appeared to be about fourteen years of age. She was already considerably taller than her much older companion. Her tanned skin attested to a life spent out of doors. Her smile looked pure and innocent. She seemed to sparkle, just as her pure-white hair did in the mountain sunshine. It was her eyes, however, that Willie found himself fixed upon. They were pure white, too, and obviously sightless. Yet, there she was, looking straight up at him and smiling as if to welcome him in particular. He found it very disconcerting.

At length, the girl turned her attention to Woodrow and the Old Man.

"Pack leader," she said softly, interrupting their small talk. "Perhaps you and your young friend should come inside now. The rabbi is an old mountain goat, and he'll keep you out here all day talking. The people will finish their meals soon and they have chores to return to."

"Yes, yes, of course," the elderly leader stammered, but it was obvious that he took no offence from her remarks. "Do come in, come in. Where are my manners?"

"Right where they always are, my old friend, in your gentlest of hearts," Woodrow replied.

He turned then to the white-haired girl. "And hello to you, Melanie. How's my favourite young witch?" He reached down, gathered her up in his arms, and gave her a fond hug before setting her back down again.

"Woodrow, I'm getting much too big for that," she scolded him, but her smile was warm nevertheless.

"You'll never be too big for me to hug," Woodrow said, laughing. "That's what honorary uncles are for, after all. We give big hugs and a shoulder to lean on whenever it's needed."

Brutus gave a short yip, nuzzled her hand, and looked up at her with soulful eyes.

"And that goes for you, too. Am I right, Brutus?" She knelt down and stroked the wolf's head, and then she gave him a good scratching under his jaw and down his chest.

It appeared that everyone treated the Pack enforcer like he was some big, friendly dog, while Willie seemed to be the only one aware of the fact that the wolf was a murderous fiend. He considered expressing something to that effect, but the Old Man spoke up first.

"Come, come, Melanie. Now who's holding everyone up?" the rabbi admonished her, as if it was all her fault that everyone was still standing around idly. He started to walk away.

She shook her head in mock disbelief, but followed his lead. As she was about to pass behind the large boulders to the rear, Melanie turned back to Freddy.

"Be careful with our guest, Freddy. Please don't bang his head, and don't squeeze him too tightly. His leg hasn't fully healed yet."

When Woodrow saw the puzzled look that came over Willie's face, he held back briefly. "She's a witch, Willie. And yes, she's quite blind."

He moved on ahead before calling back. "Come on then, you two. Let's not keep the young lady and the Old Man waiting."

Woodrow and Brutus slipped around a grouping of large boulders and briefly disappeared from sight. Freddy followed along after them carrying Willie carefully, as he'd been instructed.

Hidden from view behind the screen of rock, a jagged slit opened into the mountainside itself. Freddy barely managed to manoeuvre his bulk through the narrow gap, a task made all the more difficult by the burden he carried. Despite Freddy's best efforts, Willie's shoulder was scraped in the process, but he refrained from comment.

Once the entrance was navigated, the way inside grew wider and more manageable. Willie expected to find that they were in a cavern of some sort, but the winding passageway continued deeper into the mountain through a series of interconnecting small caves and tunnels, some of which appeared to have been enlarged for the purpose. Their way was lit by a series of dimly glowing lanterns, whose light flickered and danced in the funnelled breeze.

Their pace was slow, no doubt set to accommodate the rabbi's age-weary gait. Several times, Willie had to duck down in the giant's arms to avoid getting brained by stalactites hanging overhead. The sounds of their passing echoed and reverberated through the caves and tunnels. Looking back, Willie could make out a long procession of Oddities following after them.

In time, they began traversing down a slight grade and Willie could make out a more natural light up ahead. It grew steadily brighter as they approached. A few minutes later, they reached the end of the passageway and made their way through a slightly larger opening to the outside world. More accurately, they came out into an inside world.

As his eyes adjusted to the sunlight, Willie looked down into a substantial, deep-sided valley. Mountain tops soared above him on all sides. The valley itself, lush with summer growth, was divided into tidy fields of barley and other crops. Several orchards and vineyards graced the upper slopes.

He could see sturdy stone-walled dwellings higher up on the mountainside, apparently built there so the bountiful valley land could be devoted to agriculture. He could even make out irrigation ditches that captured water from the mountain streams and delivered it to the farmlands. All in all, the valley was a surprising and spectacular sight to behold.

Freddy followed the others' lead and carefully carried Willie down one a path that led to a larger stone dwelling. This was the Sanctuary's communal meeting hall. It was here that the elders met to decide matters of importance to their collective, and where the Old Man sat at the head of their elected council. The doorway to the meeting hall displayed several markings, as well as a mezuzah. The Old Man touched the shining metal case and then kissed his fingers before he entered.

"We won't be long," Woodrow said. He followed several of the elders inside to confer in private. The door closed behind them and Willie and the others were left to fend for themselves.

With exaggerated care, Freddy set Willie down on the walkway next to Melanie and near the Pack enforcer, who also waited for Woodrow's return. Willie propped himself up with his crutches and kept a wary eye on the wolf, while Freddy waited to see if Melanie needed any more tasks done. His face showed that he was proud of his accomplishments so far.

"Would you get some bread and jam from the storage cellars for our guests, Freddy?" Melanie asked politely. "We'll wait for you in the gardens."

He beamed. "Freddy can do that," he proclaimed. "You'll see, Mel." He set off on his new mission with a determined stride that soon took him out of sight down the path leading into the valley.

"Come walk with me," Melanie invited Willie. "The garden is a little this way and it has a lovely view of the valley."

Willie wondered if he should comment on that.

"Or so I've been told," she added, with a light laugh, as if anticipating his reaction.

Perhaps sensing the youth's unease in the presence of Brutus, Melanie turned to the Pack enforcer and made a hand signal. The wolf yawned, and then ambled over to the shade by the doorway. He stretched out on the ground, rested his head on his forepaws, and closed his eyes as if to sleep.

Willie adjusted his crutches and followed the girl along the walkway past the meeting hall. He marvelled at the confidence of her light steps as they crossed the stepping stones, and he guessed that it came from years of familiarity with her surroundings. Nonetheless, a stumble on the uneven surface could easily pitch her into a nasty fall down the rocky slope. It reminded him to take care with his crutches, lest he do the same.

They soon reached the gardens, where a multitude of colourful plants and foliage spilled down the grade. Long trellises supported networks of healthy vines, intermingled with baskets of flowers. The ground cover was in full summer bloom and presented brilliant splashes of colour as it worked over and around purposefully arranged stones. A gentle mountain stream gurgled and splashed idyllically down one section of the slope.

They sat together on a handsomely carved wooden bench in a shaded spot with, as Melanie had promised, a striking view of the valley. From this vantage point, Willie could see the procession of Oddities winding their way down various paths to the valley, as they returned to their chores.

"As you heard, my name is Melanie. What is it they call you?" She turned to look at him, or at least seemed to. Once again, he found the sightless gaze disturbing. He looked away before he answered.

"The name's Willie. I'm from—"

"Medinia, I should think," she finished for him, "judging by your accent. Many of the people living here used to call that place their home." Willie thought he heard a touch of sadness in her voice. "Does your leg hurt much?" she asked quietly. She reached over and held her hand slightly above the wounded area for a moment, before she lightly touched his leg with her fingertips. "It's getting better, you know," she assured him. "I think it should be as good as new in another couple of weeks. You're a fast healer."

"How would you know that? I've got pants on. You couldn't see the wound even if you could see, could you?"

"No, you're right, I couldn't, at least not in the sense that you mean."

"Then Woodrow was right. You're some sort of witch, aren't you?" Willie's words sounded like an accusation.

"I suppose I am. Does that frighten you?"

"I'm not scared," he muttered, "least of all by a girl."

"Of course you are," she said. "I can see the spikes leaping out from your aura. I can't say I blame you, either. You're far from your farm. You've been wounded. And now you're surrounded by all these strangers, and you've been told one of them is a witch. Who wouldn't be a little frightened?"

His reply to that was a dismissive grunt.

"Well, if it's any consolation, everyone's likely a little nervous about you, too." She seemed aware of his sceptical look. "We don't get many outsiders here, except for Woodrow and a few other members of the Pack. Some of our people interact with the fortress garrison where they sell part of our produce, though. Other than that, we prefer to avoid the outside world. People like you … well, let's just say you remind us of other times and places—times and places that weren't so good for us."

"Your people are nervous about me? What have I ever done to any of you?" Willie asked incredulously. "It's the Pack leader and that damn wolf of his that you should all be afraid of; those two fiends and all those other creatures that came straight up from hell!"

"You're misjudging them, I think," Melanie replied with quiet assurance.

"I am not! They're killers and abominations!" He looked away, out over the valley, inwardly fuming that she didn't see what he found so obvious. *She's blind in more ways than one!* he thought.

Melanie shrugged her shoulders.

"They're the Pack. It's what they are. All I know is that they've been the best of friends to our people. They're the ones who brought most of us here to this haven. They've protected and watched over us. I'd hate to think what would have become of us without their help."

Willie sat and brooded for a time before he asked her another question, this time in a softer tone. "How did you know I come from a farm?"

She laughed lightly, but not mockingly. "I can smell it on you. Mostly, it's the hay and the animals. Oh, you're clean enough, all right," she assured him. "I'm sure Woodrow saw to that. He understands the importance of cleanliness, but farming gets ingrained in your pores, and it isn't easy to wash off."

Willie nodded. That much, at least, made some sense to him. "What about my leg? How do you know it's going to be okay?"

"Well, for one thing, I can smell the medicines that Woodrow applied to the wound. Despite what you may think of him, he's one of the most knowledgeable men in these parts. When it comes to matters of medicine and the like, I know of none better."

"Maybe it's too far gone for his medicines," Willie replied, still uneasy about his injury.

"Drop your pants," she said.

"What?"

"You heard me. Stand up and drop your pants." She laughed a little at his obvious discomfort. "I'm blind, remember? I just need a closer look, if you can call it that. You're pants are in the way and I'll get a better sense of things if they're not."

Reluctantly, Willie complied. "I don't know about this. It seems to me that maybe you see a little too well."

When his pants hit the ground around his ankles, Melanie reached out and passed her palms back and forth over the length of his calf and lower leg. She never quite touched the bandages, but her hand was close enough to feel the heat and better sense the aura emanating from his injured limb.

"You're healing very quickly. It smells fine, too. There's no gangrene or infection setting in." She seemed about to add another further comment but stopped herself.

"Well, I suppose that's good news, at least," Willie said. He still wasn't convinced that she really knew what she was talking about.

He snatched up his trousers. "I'm glad nobody was around to see this. I'd have a hard time explaining why my pants were down in the presence of a young girl. Witch or not, they might get the wrong idea."

Melanie laughed. "I guess it's a little too late for that. You've met my friend Yves, from the clearing?"

"You mean that mean-spirited little runt with the foreign-speaking tongue and all the knives?" he asked.

"That would be French that he speaks, and Yves isn't mean-spirited," she said. "Willie, you might try seeing things a little bit differently. I'm afraid it's your limited perspective on things that seems mean-spirited."

Melanie didn't wait for a reply. She turned around and appeared to focus on the shrubbery several yards away and slightly above them. "I think you'd better come out now, Yves, don't you?"

Nothing happened, so she repeated her demand. "Yves, come out, right now!"

Shamefaced, the dwarf came out from his hiding place. "I should never 'ave got so close," he muttered. "I knew you would sense me, for sure."

The young witch smiled gently. "Yves, if there were twelve men of your stature, and you were all standing on a hilltop a mile away, I'd know in an instant which one was you. You're my friend, and I keep you in my thoughts always."

He looked up at her and grinned.

"Just as I keep a thought on our friend Freddy," Melanie told him, "who happens to be bounding up the walkway, even as we speak. Now please come down here and tell me what the problem is."

The dwarf navigated the short distance with his awkward gait, all the while trying his best not to step on any plants. He hoisted himself up onto the bench, cheerfully taking Willie's place at her side.

Sure enough, a few moments later, Freddy made his way into the gardens. He had a basketful of small loaves of bread and cups of jam cradled in his arms.

"I got it, Mel!" he announced. "Hey, Yves! Didn't know you was coming, too. Don't you worry, though, I got lots extra."

Freddy made sure that they each took some bread and jam. Then, content that his mission was accomplished; he sat on the ground to eat his own share.

"Now, Yves," Melanie requested. "Tell me why you're spying on Willie. I'm assuming that it's Willie you're spying on and not me. It's not me you're spying on, is it?"

"Oh, it's dat one, all right. I would not spy on you, *ma cherie*." Instinctively, Yves' tiny hand went to the hilt of one of the knives sheathed on his belt. "Dat one cannot be trusted. He is from outside here. He probably tell where we be first chance he get."

Willie bristled. "How could I? You blindfolded me with that filthy handkerchief of yours, remember?"

"Well, you called me bad names!"

"And he hit me," Freddy said from where he sat. "And that wasn't nice. You can even ask Brutus."

"Now, Yves, I'm sure you and Freddy might have provoked him a bit. *Oui?*
Un peu?" Smiling, she added, "I'm also sure that Woodrow would never bring
anyone here who would cause harm to us."

"Maybe so, *ma cherie*, maybe so, but you don't always know what is in
men's hearts. Not even the Pack leader can know dat." It was the voice of
bitter experience.

                    *   *   *

The door to the meeting hall opened and the Old Man came out, steadying
himself on Woodrow's arm. The other elders followed. There was one other
Jewish elder among their group, but the rest were of other religions. They fairly
represented the three pillars of society: Jews, Muslims, and Christians, and
perhaps even a fourth, the deformed, abused, and displaced.

Brutus got to his feet slowly with a mighty yawn and then stretched
extravagantly as if to demonstrate to Woodrow that they had been here long
enough and it was time to be moving on.

Melanie heard the men talking in the distance and rose from the bench.
She helped Freddy gather the remaining supply of food and sent him to
distribute it to Woodrow and the others. She then escorted Willie up the
walkway at a leisurely pace, with the still sceptical Yves staying protectively
at her side.

"Rabbi, gentlemen," she said when they reached the hall, "I'd like to
introduce Willie to you. He's our guest."

Willie snorted at the same moment Yves did. Melanie laughed.

"Have these two been giving you a hard time, Melanie?" Woodrow
asked.

"Just boys being boys, Woodrow, and feeling their respective oats," she
replied sagely.

The Pack leader chuckled. "I'm sure you set them straight."

"I haven't gotten quite that far yet."

"Is there some problem?" the rabbi asked. His hearing really wasn't what
it once was.

"Have you got a problem young fellow? Maybe I—"

"Problem?" Willie finally exploded. "Problem? I've got nothing but
problems. My farm's been attacked and our livestock slaughtered. My best

friends are dead—never mind that they were only animals too. I've been chased and bitten by some wolf creature, like that cur over there supposedly becomes." The youth pointed at Brutus, sucked in some air, and continued his tirade. "I've been kidnapped from my home and kingdom. And I've been brought here against my will to this god-awful place that's filled with more freaks and geeks than you'd find in a hundred and one bloody sideshows!"

He looked around wild eyed. "Damn right I've got a problem. I've got loads of them. I've got a problem with you, and you, and you." Finally spent, the youth slumped over his crutches, refusing to look at any of them.

A look of genuine concern came over the face of the rabbi. He let go of Woodrow's arm.

"We know some of the same things that you're feeling, young man. Those of us living here know what it's like to lose friends and loved ones." He spoke gravely but showed no sign of taking any personal offence at the outburst.

Willie lifted his head. "Well, when our Medinian knights get here, you're going to lose a whole lot more of them!"

The youth's eyes frosted over with hatred as he spoke. A knife appeared in the foreign dwarf's hand behind him, but the rabbi waved it away with a sharp motion of his arm. Yves backed off instantly.

Willie didn't notice the dwarf's knife behind him, but for the first time, the youth saw that the arm that had been concealed inside the rabbi's robe lacked a hand at its end.

"I understand your hostility, Willie." The Old Man's voice was firm. "As for your knights, we've met—trust me. Some of us have met Skolish knights, too, and the knights of a half dozen other kingdoms. Most often it's been to our great detriment, lad, because life brings us all a certain amount of tragedy."

The rabbi paused long enough to be sure he had the youth's attention.

"The people living here have suffered more than their fair share," he said. "Some have been jailed; some flogged or branded. Others have been beaten and abused—or much worse—and mostly for just being a little different. Well, we may be Oddities, but we aren't any different! We bleed the same as you do, I can assure you. We need respect, and we need love, just like anyone else does. So, believe it or not, Willie, we Oddities are pretty much, just like you."

CHAPTER 10

The Great Forest

Walk a few miles in another man's shoes
See the world from another man's view
And, just maybe, you'll be a better you

August 1, 1461
The Euralene Mountains, Varakov

"Woodrow, why don't you take Brutus and go on ahead? I'd like to walk with this young fellow awhile, and then perhaps Melanie could escort him through the caves," the Old Man suggested.

"Melanie, would you and Frederick please go with them. Wait at the entrance for us. Frederick can give me a ride back."

"Yes, rabbi," the young witch replied with a nod of her head.

"You bet! I can do that!" the young giant enthused.

The elder Oddity waited patiently until the others had taken their leave, before he turned and addressed the young Medinian, again.

"That staff of mine is far, too heavy. If you would allow me lean on one of your crutches with you, I think I'd have enough strength to get to the entrance with you. I suppose I'll have to let Freddy give me a piggyback ride home again, though. The good fellow loves doing that, when I let him," the Old Man said with a wink, "even though it's not a terribly dignified way to travel."

Willie knew what he meant. It wasn't very dignified having someone carrying you. Although the youth didn't actually say it was all right, the old rabbi left his staff behind and slipped his only hand over the youth's forearm. Willie couldn't help but notice that it was gnarled and twisted with arthritis. Thus linked together, they began walking together at a slow-stepping, measured pace.

"Willie, I'd like to give you some advice, if I may be so bold. Will you humour me for a few minutes and hear what I have to say?" he asked.

There was a significant pause before the youth replied.

"I suppose so," Willie said sullenly. He kept his eyes fixed on the path ahead.

"I should begin with the Pack leader, then," the rabbi said. "My friend Woodrow, well he's a rather unique and complex individual. Most people rarely have the privilege to get to know someone like him. He's man of honour and compassion … despite what you may think at the moment. He's also blessed with a great intellect and an ever-questioning type of mind, as I'm sure you will discover for yourself, one day."

"Willie, you're going to find that Woodrow also has a wealth of experiences and teachings that come from his traveling many faraway lands. For the most part, he uses that knowledge for the benefit of other people. Just as he did in treating your wounds, despite, perhaps, also being their cause," the Old Man added, forestalling the youth's protest. "Woodrow's been the best friend we Oddities have ever had. He's helped many of us find asylum here in Sanctuary.

He then shook his head sadly and sighed deeply.

"But yes, the Pack leader and his kind suffer from a vile curse. Several of their members live with us here, in the times between when the moon-sickness has abated and before it sets in again. It's a more terrible affliction than perhaps any of us in Sanctuary has had to suffer and endure."

The Old Man struggled with what to say next, knowing that this lad was a victim of circumstances not of his doing. His heart went out to the youth.

"You've been caught up in this same human tragedy, Willie. And for that, I'm genuinely sorry for you." The rabbi slowed their progress to a stop for a moment. He faced the youth; wanting to be sure he had the young man's attention. "I have some knowledge of unwanted trials and tribulations," the rabbi told him gravely. "I've learned that from every hardship that we face, we can grow stronger. We can persevere, and we can overcome terrible ordeals and abuses! And," he added fervently, "we can become better people than we were, provided we allow ourselves to gain an understanding and empathy for other people's plights and sufferings. We can make a real difference for the better—if we don't allow ourselves to get lost in our own misery and hate."

They walked onwards in silence for a few minutes, while the Old Man caught his breath again. True to his word, the Medinian youth remained silent and attentive.

"What you see now as your worst nightmare could well turn out to be the best thing that's ever happened to you." His arthritic hand squeezed Willie's arm firmly. "Perhaps it's your destiny—I don't know for certain—but in Medinia, Woodrow tells me you were some sort of indentured serf on a farm. It would be safe to say that there was small likelihood of you ever becoming more than that."

No reaction was forthcoming from the youth.

"Would I be wrong in saying that like many young men your age, your dreams included one day becoming a knight ... a great knight out defending his kingdom's honour?" He saw that his question had hit close to the mark, when the youth shrugged his shoulders.

"It's a noble dream," the rabbi conceded. "Yet, if you were honest with yourself, you would admit that it's only just that—a dream. Knighthood is a very costly affair, as I'm sure you are aware. Only sons of nobles and rich barons need apply. Without meaning any disrespect, in all likelihood, back in Medinia, you would have lived and died as a farmer. If you did well and saved all your meagre wages, perhaps one day you may even have had your own small farm. And not that farming is such a terrible life," the Old Man added sincerely. "There's great honour in working the land. Many people do that here in our valley. But maybe you've been presented a completely different opportunity, a new path follow. This new path could lead you to places and experiences you've yet to even imagine."

He paused to let that thought sink in for a moment.

"Woodrow is the Pack leader. Yet, he's also the keeper of Lord Victor's castle. In some kingdoms they would call his position the chamberlain. Here, he's referred to as the castle keeper. That's about as high up as a person can rise in the pecking order, short of having royal blood, that is. Woodrow reports directly to Lord Victor, the king of Varakov. As the castle keeper, he's responsible for many aspects of the Varakovan court, and throughout the countryside," the rabbi added solemnly. "Woodrow owns a manor estate, where he resides with his stewards and staff. He's told me that Lord Victor paid a visit to his mountain retreat while you were mending. The king desires him to personally mentor and train you, to be part of Woodrow's personal staff."

The Old Man tugged on the youth's arm, causing him to turn his head and make eye contact again.

"Is this your worst nightmare? Or is it your greatest opportunity?" he queried. "My advice, if you'll take it, is to go and learn all that you possibly can. Let them teach you things that were never available to you before. Excel at your duties, and then make them give you more! Knowledge is power, Willie—power over your own life."

The elderly Oddity leader sighed.

"It won't be easy—I know that. I can only assure you that you won't be a prisoner. When you judge the time has come for you to go, Woodrow will not stand in your way. He'll even help you to leave. But there are important things you still do not know. Only the Pack leader and those of his kind can teach you those." He could see that the youth wanted to ask him what he meant by that, but he held up his handless arm. "I shall give you one last piece of advice from these old lips of mine: mind what Woodrow tells you. It will be intended for your own good, even if you have trouble believing that at times. And above all, I want you to be careful and to heed Lord Victor in all matters. His will is divine in this part of the world. Do not challenge him or be disrespectful. Lord Victor is the king of Varakov. When you live within the same confines of any king, you live by his pleasure. Be humble, and always control your temper."

The Old Man turned to face the youth once more.

"Walk a few miles in another man's shoes. See the world from another man's view, and just maybe, you'll end up being a better you. Yes, Willie, I am an Oddity. But I'm a rare commodity, and so, my boy, are you!"

"Am I permitted a few questions now?" the youth asked. They were nearing the end of the walkway to the cave's entrance. Melanie and Freddy were waiting for them.

The elderly rabbi smiled and nodded. He stopped their walking, to hear what the youth had on his mind.

"You're a Jew, aren't you? Willie asked. "I mean, I was raised for a time by a Catholic monastery back in Medinia. I've never actually met one before."

"I am Jewish," the Old Man confirmed. "But there's also a priest and several monks and friars living here, as I'm sure you've seen. There's even an imam. We have a small mosque, which is dedicated to the pursuit of studying the universe and of the writing of poetry. You might say when it comes to religious viewpoints; we're a rather eclectic bunch here."

"The Jews, you'd … never be allowed to live in Medinia," Willie stated bluntly.

"And that's why we live here in Sanctuary, Willie," the Old Man replied, with a quick laugh. "There's any number of places where we aren't welcome."

"But how do you all get along? Wouldn't you Jews be better off living with your own kind?" the youth asked.

"Which Jews?" the old rabbi asked. "Judaism has many types of followers. Our tribes have many divisions and there are many disputes between the sects. The Sicarius, the Pharisee, the Sadducee, the Essene, and let's not forget the Zealots. These various sects have been in opposition to each other for centuries, over matters big and small. I sometimes think we Jews can't live without adversity."

Not all so-called Christians get along either, Willie," he added. "Not everyone views the teachings of God in the same way."

The Medinian youth wasn't sure what to make of that.

"Did you know, Willie, our three religions all started from the same source? That we all share a common origin?" the Old Man asked.

He saw the puzzled look that came over Willie's face.

"His name was Abram, or Abraham, as he was later renamed," the old rabbi explained. "It was to the faithful Abraham and his heirs that God gave the land of Canaan for all time."

"Abram's first son, Ishmael, who was conceived with a female slave named Hagar, is the fount spring of Islam. He is called an apostle and a prophet in the Koran. All Arabs trace their heritage to Ishmael. Years later, Abraham would have another son, Isaac, by his wife, Sarah; though they'd thought she was barren. In turn, Isaac had a son, Jacob, who God renamed Israel and whose twelve sons begat the twelve tribes of the Israelites. Islam, Judaism, and Christianity," the Old Man said. "They all begin with Abraham. It's only their accounts of his life that differ … and whose religion it is they feel has divine claim to the holy lands. Is it the Arabs through Ishmael; or the Jews through Isaac; or the Christians through Christ? That is the great debate—the one that so many people have died for and killed for."

The rabbi let loose a long sigh. "You'd be surprised, Willie. If you truly listen to another man speaking about his beliefs—of his hopes and aspirations—you'd find we really aren't all that different. We're all God's children, you and I both, Willie."

The Medinian youth nodded his head at that. "I'm sorry for some of the things that I said earlier," he stated quietly. "I see now that you mean well. I want to thank you for your advice, and for your kindness. I'll keep what you've said in mind, Old Man."

"Old? Well, old I am," the rabbi confirmed, stroking his long white whiskers, "but not as old as some. I'm not nearly as old as Woodrow. Not even Brutus, for that matter." He barked out a knowing laugh. "And I'm not nearly as old as the Oracle who resides up there in the mountaintops."

"Who?" The youth was beginning to think that the old rabbi was rambling incoherently.

"The Oracle," the Old Man replied, pointing towards a distant peak. "He lives high up in the mountains, just below heaven's floor. You see, Willie," he added with a bright smile, "you can learn something new every day. Give it a chance, young man. You just never know what new knowledge will be revealed to you."

They met Melanie and Freddy at the cave entrance then. They were waiting patiently and impatiently, respectively. True to his word, the Oddity leader allowed the young giant to lift him up onto his broad shoulders.

In an effort to preserve at least some of his dignity, the rabbi tossed his beard over his left shoulder with an air of authority and then tapped Freddy on top of his head.

"Lead on my good man. And please try not to drop me, like before," he ordered, politely.

"Oh, Rabbi, that was only the one time. I've given you a hundred rides since then, and I ain't dropped you even once," the young giant protested.

"Well, let's try to make it a hundred and one, shall we?" the rabbi replied gravely.

"I can do that!" Freddy enthused.

"Good luck to you then, Willie," the elder added, looking down at the Medinian youth. "I hope we meet again one day soon. Shalom."

The Old Man waved good-bye while Freddy kept his hands firmly but gently locked on the rabbi's legs. They swayed and ambled their way precariously back down the path, looking very much like some ancient Indian Raja aboard his elephant.

Willie and Melanie made their way through the chain of caverns without speaking for a time. The Medinian youth was steadily improving with the use of his crutches, but he was content to follow behind the white-haired girl's lead, for she was a marvel to watch. She walked with a confidence and grace, despite her blindness. She seemed to flow like water around the obstacles they encountered. The numerous rock and crystal formations posed no concern for her.

The young witch seemed to treat the winding passage as if it were a game, or a test of her sightless skills. He didn't know if she was able to make out some images or had just memorized the various segments of the passageway. Whichever it was, he noted, she passed the test with flying colours.

When they came to the small cavern near the end of the passage, Melanie invited him to sit for a moment. She indicated a wide boulder, which appeared to have been chipped flat to serve as a bench.

"I often wait here if I know we have a visitor coming," she said when they were seated. "I like it because it's nice and quiet, and there's usually a cool breeze that blows in through the entrance. I seem to see things more clearly here. I suppose because there are fewer distractions."

They sat quietly for a moment. Willie decided it was his turn to say something. He didn't look at her, however.

"I apologized to the Old Man," he said. "I told him I shouldn't have said some of the things that I did. Your people have done me no harm at all. It's Woodrow, Brutus, and their kind that have caused all of this." He couldn't keep the bitterness out of his voice. "Anyway, I'm sorry," he finished lamely.

Melanie got up from the rock bench. "They're waiting for you. You had best go now," she said quietly.

"What's the matter?" he asked, grabbing her forearm. "I said that I was sorry, didn't I?"

"Yes, you did, Willie. I just don't accept it," she replied, pulling her arm free. "You're still looking down on us like we're some sort of inferior people. You're full of anger, and frankly, stupidity. You're full of hate and hurt pride. I can sense that you're almost choking on a need for vengeance."

With that said, she stepped outside the cave exit and into the brightness of the afternoon sun. Willie had little choice but to follow after her silently.

He found Woodrow and Brutus, waiting for him in the mountainside clearing below.

"It's not all your fault, granted. You've been raised in ignorance," Melanie said. "You think your biggest concern is this terrible ordeal you're going through. You're so certain that Woodrow and Brutus are the cause of all your woes. You look at the Oddities, and you look at me, as if we're freaks. You see everyone in terms of the problems you're facing, while actually, we're just players passing through a stage in your life, Willie, as you are through ours. If there are any real problems for you to deal with, you need to look for them in here, and in here," she said, tapping his forehead and then his chest. "That takes a different kind of seeing. It's called insight. And I'm afraid it only comes with time and a lot of hard work. So please, don't say you're sorry. At least, not until you know what it is that you're really sorry for."

He hung his head, not knowing what to say but still feeling angry. He didn't want to argue with her, but he didn't think she had any right to judge him, either. He was about to say so when she spoke up again.

"I have something for you. It's just a small gift, but hopefully you'll think more kindly of us. Call it a good luck charm."

The young witch reached for the leather cord that hung about her neck and pulled it up and over her head. Suspended on the end of the cord was a beautifully carved clear-crystal figurine. It was a shepherd holding a staff, the head of which was carved to resemble an eye.

"It's practical too," she told him. "If you ever need to start a fire to keep warm, or to cook with, you just need some sunlight. Let the sun's rays enter the crystal from above, and focus the beam that comes out the bottom onto some kindling and leaves until it comes to a fine pinpoint. It gets very hot on the spot where you focus the beam."

She demonstrated on some dry grass and twigs she gathered. The little pile of debris soon started smoking and then burst into flames. After she stamped it out, she slipped the leather cord over his head, which he lowered to accommodate her reach.

"I've always found the shepherd to be a comfort," Melanie said. "It's like he was there to help guide me home and watch over me. I hope he does the same for you."

"Thank you," he said, fingering the small crystal figure. He looked up, trying to think of what else to say, but she held up her hand.

"Good-bye, Willie. Good fortune to you," she added and then took her leave. She slipped back into the tunnel and disappeared from view.

Willie stood there for a few moments after she'd left, feeling confused and more alone than ever. He was sure that he was the injured party in this terrible misadventure, yet he knew that, somehow, he had hurt her too. He mulled over what had been said between them. When he didn't find the answer there, he sighed heavily and turned away.

He crutched his way down the slope to where Woodrow and Brutus waited beside the travois in the clearing.

None of this would have happened if it wasn't for them, he thought bitterly. Of that much, at least, he was certain.

*   *   *

It would be several hours of hard travel before they broke free of the forest's grasp. Once more, the giant trees denied the sky to them. It was only when they were fording one of the wider streambeds that the canopy above sometimes failed to block out the sky. At times, meagre snatches of sunlight filtered through. These broken beams resembled wisps of smoke more than anything else. They attracted dust motes, pollen, and insects, which danced in the air as if in some bizarre mating ritual.

During the second hour of their trek, a band of fine mist began rolling in, until it extinguished even that precious bit of light. From the young Medinian's perspective, it was as if the mighty forest had swallowed them up, and was then swallowed up in turn by the swirling fog.

He had no idea how they managed to continue traveling. As they pushed on, giant tree trunks would suddenly emerge from the shroud, and then, just as suddenly, disappear again. Where the forest had been oppressive and claustrophobic before, now it was as if they had entered some dream state, where their world was reduced to a few scant strides.

Willie considered the Oddities' choice to make this forbidding forest part of their home. He wondered if they kept lookouts in the dense woods. He thought it likely that they would, but even if there were an entire army of the deformed out there, he wouldn't see them in this soup.

The swirling mist tasted mildly salty, and heavy beads of moisture seemed to be suspended in the air. It was as if they were walking through the centre of a rain cloud.

In due course, all three of the travelers were drenched through. The mist weighted down their clothing and fur alike. It saturated everything it touched. By now, Woodrow and Brutus were navigating by pure instinct, but with the sure knowledge that Varakov proper lay at the bottom of the mountainside. They knew that eventually the forest would give way to the upper foothills.

The Pack leader shuddered as another giant wood behemoth made a ghostly pass a scant meter away. He was glad that he'd relented and allowed Brutus to accompany them until they were clear of the forest. Not that he had any real choice in the matter.

Indeed, the Pack enforcer would have just continued to watch over them from a parallel course. At least this way, Brutus had taken up the lead, and there was no better guide to be had in the mountains. Woodrow could just put his head down and concentrate on dragging the damn travois. He'd be more than glad to see the end of it.

Since the fog had rolled in, it had become a Herculean struggle just to walk and not get brained by a tree limb. His leg muscles throbbed, and his aching back was beginning to protest being hunched over for so long. He was soaked, miserable, *and far too old for this shit,* the Pack leader mused wearily.

When it came to the mountains and the forest, however, the Pack enforcer remained undeterred by any element. Whether it was a heavy fog or a winter storm, Brutus was the champion of his surroundings. The alpha male wolf wasn't as young as he once was, either, but he possessed an uncanny awareness of his surroundings.

The Pack enforcer led them around the giant trees and large, fallen trunks and limbs. He also avoided the sudden drop-offs into mountain crevices or fog-hidden ravines. Even by the Pack's standards, there was no better wolf at sensing the approach of danger, an enemy, or prey.

Well, Woodrow determined, *as Pack leader, I can cope with the conditions too.*

Despite his own undeniable abilities, he needed his four-legged comrade now. On two separate occasions, the Pack enforcer had given out warning whines to indicate that a change in direction was needed to avoid some unseen pitfall ahead. So well did Woodrow know his companion that he automatically turned in the direction that the wolf wanted him to. Indeed, it would be difficult to say exactly who had trained whom over their many years together. To say that the wolf's comprehension level and ability to learn was astounding would be to belittle his talents. The Pack enforcer was adept at communicating his feelings and intentions. He used body language and behaviour to make himself understood.

Brutus coupled that with a highly developed linguistic ability. While he couldn't talk, there was little worth saying that he couldn't convey. His vocal chords could climb all the way from a guttural bass, up and through the soprano scale. The Pack enforcer could speak volumes using sounds that ranged from yips, whines, and barks to snarls, growls, and, of course, howls.

For the moment, however, there wasn't much communicating going on. There was just a shared misery that came from Woodrow's strenuous labour under terrible conditions, and Willie's plain misery with his lot in life. So, it was a heartfelt relief for all that the forest came to an end when it did. The cloud of saturated mist still hung over them, but at least they no longer had to dodge the giant trees.

The trio made their way down the upper-foothill slopes, through grazing meadows and past the summer orchards, many of which were planted where the great forest had been denuded of its trees. In centuries past, the forests were far grander in scope than they were today. The trees had once covered most of the foothills and even vast sections of the plains, but timber had been needed for the building of homes, barns, and furnishings. More timber was needed to build ships, wharves, and the buildings that housed the tradesmen's wares. Logs were needed to heat homes, inns, and castles. There was an endless demand for wood and what could be done with it.

Axes had rung out over the centuries and still did. Mankind encroached on the mighty forest for its wood and for its land. Rows of sentinel pines; groves of birch trees, oak, and elm; and even stately chestnuts had been felled to fill the demand.

Farmland, orchards, and grazing fields had taken over the series of foothills, although there were strict regulations in place now. Woodrow and the Varakovan court had seen to that. Every new section that was cleared called for another to be planted in its place. Permits were now required, which limited the cutting of hard to replace, or long growing varieties of trees.

Pine trees were an acceptable crop that once seeded grew to sufficient heights every twenty years. The more valuable and much longer maturing oaks and chestnut trees were now strictly regulated. They couldn't be cut down without a permit. Their fruit provided important food for both man and the surrounding wildlife. They were a resource that needed protection from short-sighted men.

After the trio moved down through a shallow, fog-filled valley and began climbing up into the central foothills, the breeze quickened and freshened at last. The thick rolling mist finally gave up its claim on them. With a final flurry of its wispy tentacles, the moisture-laden band of cloud crept away, climbing the mountainside.

As the curtain of fog lifted, before them lay the farmlands of the lower foothills and the rolling plains of Varakov proper. From their vantage point, they could see the Varden River as it snaked its way through the countryside, until it finally turned towards the coast, emptying its waters into the endless expanse of ocean beyond.

Far out to sea, the late-day sun was being devoured by a steadily growing weather front. This newly forming storm seemed to have a considerable energy. They could see the dark clouds hanging over the equally dark ocean. An occasional distant bolt of lightning launched down at the whitecaps below, but the majority of the electrical output rumbled throughout the growing mass itself.

The storm was feeding. With a hungry mouth, it was sucking up the ocean's moisture below. When the storm came ashore and reached the coastal range, like a thousand storms before it, its mass would rise up in a vain attempt to scale the Euralene Mountains. When the heavily ladened clouds could no longer sustain the weight of themselves, the rain would fall in torrents, and the furies would be released.

It was too early to say how large a system it would become or how far it would back up over the plains when it finally came ashore and met the mountain range. That would determine the storm's duration and its intensity. There were occasions when the mighty sea bred some pretty violent storms.

Thankfully, as the trio of travelers traversed the central foothills, there was a roadway to follow, and the going was easier now. As night began to descend on the land, Woodrow picked up the pace somewhat. A short time later, they pulled up in front of an isolated outpost station. They would spend the night here, and complete their journey in the morning.

The outpost in the foothills was one of a half-dozen such stations as well as a number of hunting lodges in the mountains that the Castle maintained. There would be fresh horses in the stables, as well as ample supplies of anything else that they might need. This particular station was run by the McRaes, a middle-aged couple and their family, who the castle keeper had employed for that purpose.

As castle keeper, one of Woodrow's functions was to ensure that these outpost stations and the hunting lodges were operated efficiently. Often on short notice, the Varakovan king had Woodrow make arrangements for hunting or hawking expeditions. These outings could range in duration from a few days to several weeks. The size of the party would likewise vary from just the two of them, to upwards of a hundred in their party. The larger groups often included knights, nobles, barons, plus their entourages of servants and attendants. All their needs had to be met.

Woodrow's ability to anticipate and respond to Victor's wishes was one of the many qualities that endeared him to the king of Varakov. The castle keeper planned for these outings with a careful eye to detail. Over the years, he'd learned the value of preparation. The outposts and lodges had been constructed in locales where they each covered a specific region of the kingdom. At each of these key locations, the castle keeper had established a base of operations from which the hunting parties could be serviced.

Woodrow ensured each base was stockpiled with abundant supplies of food, clothing, medical preparations, and even additional weaponry. He recruited caretakers to maintain and care for each site. In this, he preferred to hire entire family groups to live in and maintain the stations, or to reside nearby.

With these operations already in place, Woodrow could then more easily arrange for additional supplies to be delivered or temporary shelters to be constructed, should a larger group require them. The caretakers on site were available to assist with food preparation, or in any number of other important tasks. It was far more sensible than carting half the castle's stewards and supplies with them every time Lord Victor wanted to venture out into the wilds.

Today, the Pack leader was simply glad to finally get someplace where he could rid himself of his burden. He freed himself from the travois with a deep sigh of relief. He stretched mightily and then bent down and stroked the neck of the wolf. It was time for them to part company. Brutus could return home now, and to Cleo, his mate. His Pack enforcer's duties were completed.

As if he was attempting to prolong the moment, Brutus bounded off to relieve himself, which he did in numerous spots, staking out his territory. Woodrow smiled and moved to help undo the straps restraining the youth.

"Stretch your legs out, son. All three of them, if you catch my drift," he said, as they both observed the antics of the wolf.

"There'll be warm water inside to wash up with, and dry clothing," the Pack leader advised. "I want to change those wet bandages, as well."

The youth made a face and once again declined the Pack leader's assistance in getting up.

"We'll get a hot meal and a good night's rest and then leave at first light," Woodrow said, disregarding the slight. "We've still got a long ride ahead of us tomorrow, and there's no saying when that storm brewing out there is going to make landfall. I'd like to be home before it does."

Willie got himself to his feet using the crutches with a more practiced confidence. He pegged himself over to a nearby bush, unbuttoned his fly, and answered his own call of nature. Looking back the way they'd come, he noted the grand scale of the terrain that they'd covered. He was impressed anew at the strength and stamina that the Pack leader had demonstrated, and without voicing a complaint. He still refused to say so, however.

The heavy band of mist that had enveloped them had continued to amble its way up the slope of the wooded mountainside. As the fog threaded its way through the trees it still gave them a ghostly appearance. Yet, above that, the peaks glistened with the dying rays of the sun, as they towered high overhead.

When the Medinian youth had finished watering the shrub, he buttoned his pants and turned his attention to the lay of the land ahead. He gazed out across the coastal plain, where he could see the winding river, hundreds of farms, and several small villages. He could see where the plain ended at the coastline and the vast ocean beyond.

Willie allowed his eyes to follow the coastal contour until they came to the uniquely shaped bay at the river's mouth. Something about the shape of it bothered him, but he couldn't decide what it was. His attention was then drawn out to the sea. He could see the distant storm that was building its mass out there. He'd seen storms before, but it was the immensity of the ocean that demanded his attention. It was the first time he'd ever seen the great sea.

The vastness of the ocean disturbed him more than the shape of the distant bay did. Its endless expanse made the land below them seem small. The water looked cold and stark and not the least bit hospitable. It was somehow ominous. Perhaps it was the way the storm crackled and tumbled out there, or the way it snuffed out the view of the setting sun, except for the final light still cast on the towering peaks.

"Welcome to Varakov proper, Willie," the Pack leader said. He came over to stand at the youth's side. "Those are castles and fortifications you can see along the coastline," he explained, pointing in that direction. "Most of them have small villages built up around them. Over there at the river's end, on the sheltered side of the bay, is Port Lupus," he added, pointing again. "The harbour is a regular stop on the shipping lanes. You can reach any port on the ocean, if you've a mind to … and the right ship is at anchor in the bay. The loading skiffs and the fishing fleets work out of the wharves, and—"

"Port Lupus," Willie repeated, dully. "It figures. I hate it already." The youth could now make out the unique shape of the bay for what it was.

Woodrow ignored the comment.

"The shipbuilding yards bring their timber down the Varden River from the mountains. Off the north-eastern end of the bay are marshes and salt pans and the dry docks for the fishing fleets. And, over there," he added, indicating a solitary tabletop mountain that stood out on the plains, "do you see that lone mesa?"

The youth nodded.

"We call that the Mesa-of-the-Moon. The castle located there is home to Lord Victor, the king of Varakov. My estate is nearby—and soon yours, too, for a time, at least. In any event," he shrugged, "that's where we're headed tomorrow morning."

"What am I supposed to do once when we get there?" the youth asked.

"When your leg's fully healed, maybe we'll put you to work at the castle," the Pack leader suggested.

"So, I'm to be slave labour, am I?" the youth sneered. "Do you work all your prisoners? Is that how we earn our bread and butter?"

The Pack leader didn't respond to that. He just shook his head and grimaced. He whistled sharply and Brutus ceased his meandering and ran up to him. Woodrow slapped a hand to his chest and the wolf responded by rising up on his hind legs and planting his forepaws there. That brought the two Pack members face to face.

Woodrow gripped Brutus firmly by the scruff of his neck and looked the Pack enforcer in the eyes. Slowly, he lowered his face, until their foreheads touched.

"Until the next moon, my friend," he whispered, softly.

Woodrow released his hold and the wolf dropped back down to all fours. The Pack enforcer turned his attention towards the youth. His eyes locked on Willie's and his teeth were bared briefly. The alpha wolf then walked over, lifted a hind leg, and pissed on the same bush that the youth had. Perhaps it was a simple show of dominance, or perhaps it was meant as a warning. In either case, Willie felt that the alpha wolf was imparting a personal message that it would be there, on the next cycle of the moon, and all had best be well with the Pack leader.

Brutus took one last look back towards Woodrow. The wolf raised his head skyward and let loose a howl from deep within his throat. The eerie howl reverberated off the mountainside. With that final salute, the noble animal loped off towards the forest from which they'd come.

"I think we're all prisoners, Willie, in one way or another," the Pack leader said a moment later. He stood watching the wolf until the animal had disappeared from view. "We can be prisoners of someone else's, or sometimes of our own." With that observation, Woodrow turned and started walking towards the station. He stopped partway there and then turned back a few steps. "I'll make it quite simple for you, Willie," he stated firmly. "There are no free rides here. You're going to work, for which you'll be paid a decent wage. You can spend it anyway you wish or save it up for a passage on one of those ships out there. That will be up to you when the time comes. Hopefully, you're going to learn a few things too," he added fervently. "To begin with—and just so we're really clear on this point—I don't abide slavery of any kind."

"Then why can't I just leave now, or as soon as my leg's gotten better?" Willie demanded.

"Because," Woodrow stated flatly, "there are things I have yet to teach you.

He turned away again before the youth could ask any more questions and hailed the station attendants, who had come to the door at the wolf's howl. The McRae family greeted Woodrow warmly and quickly ushered him inside. The couple waited at the door for his companion, while their young children lined up behind them to see who had arrived with the castle keeper.

Willie crutched his way over. He hopped up the steps awkwardly but made it inside without mishap. He was welcomed and was soon being fussed over because of his injury. It was a bit chaotic at first, but the youth found the family a nice distraction, and the home they maintained was wholesome and orderly.

The couple's three children were soon ushered off to bed, but like children everywhere, they were curious. They managed to sneak out of their beds and find nooks from where they could keep an eye on the newly arrived houseguests and stay out of their mother's eyesight.

The station couple insisted on assisting their guests in the task of getting cleaned up and dried off. The McRae woman brought towels, and despite his obvious embarrassment, she insisted on helping Willie out his wet clothes, clucking all the while that he didn't have anything that she hadn't seen before.

Her husband fetched dry clothing from the well-stocked station provisions. His family had already eaten supper, but his wife went back to the kitchen. In short order, she was reheating a wholesome stew to fill their empty bellies. She would never think to begrudge the castle keeper a hot meal. He was their benefactor, and besides, she was used to cooking on short notice for groups much larger than this.

While she prepared the meal, Woodrow dried himself and changed, and then saw to the task of changing the youth's bandages. He applied some fresh salve to several raw places before he redressed the wound, but overall, he was pleased with how quickly the lad was healing. He was well aware what that meant. He just wasn't looking forward to having to explain it to the already embittered youth.

That could wait, at least for now, Woodrow thought wearily. He was far too exhausted at the moment for another battle of wills.

It wasn't long after their meal that Woodrow was bedded down in the guest quarters. He was probably asleep even before the children were after they were chased back to their beds by their mother. The Pack leader was thoroughly spent and he slept a dreamless night away.

As for Willie, sleep eluded him for several restless hours. When he finally did drift off, his dreams were haunted with images of savage creatures chasing him through a dark, endless forest. It was a terrifying place, where even the trees reached down with their gnarly limbs and tried to grab him, too.

*   *   *

August 2, 1461
Varakov

When the morning came, the McRae woman had insisted that they eat a hearty breakfast. Her no-nonsense attitude brooked no argument, overruling Woodrow's protests that they really needed to be on their way.

"As far as I'm concerned," she'd told him, "it's more important that you have something warm in your bellies than it is for you to go gallivanting across the countryside."

Willie had no argument with that logic. After Woodrow attended to his leg again, and as they were leaving, the youth happily accepted the bundle of sharp cheese, fresh bread, and dried beef that she gave them for their journey. Woodrow kissed her cheek in way of thanks, and then he affectionately tousled the hair of the eldest of her children before stepping outside.

The Medinian youth added his sincere thanks to that of Woodrow's. These were simple, hard-working people. He could relate to their lives, even here in the foreign kingdom of Varakov. He bore them no ill will.

As they were about to go, Willie noticed the black sash that Woodrow was wearing this morning in lieu of a belt. The sash was tied off at his left side and its two ends hung down near that knee. When he commented on it, after Woodrow had stepped outside, the woman told him that the sash was the mark of the castle keeper's position in Varakov.

Willie met up with Woodrow outside by the barn, where they shook hands with the station attendant. He had horses saddled for them, with fresh water bags already packed. The travois had been stored away in the stable for some future day's use, but as far as Woodrow was concerned, it could be chopped up for kindling. He'd sworn that morning, as he rose out of bed stiff and sore, that he'd pulled his last load.

About an hour later, the two riders connected with the same roadway that

Simon, Barozzi and his mercenaries, and their Skolish captives had traveled. By then, Woodrow was already discovering that a full day in the saddle wasn't going to bring any relief to his aching bones.

Their next destination was Woodrow's estate, situated about a league outside the castle's formidable walls. It would likely be late afternoon before they arrived and their mounts were brushed down and stabled again. In due course, they or other steeds would then be rotated back out to the outpost, to return the station to its full complement.

As they rode, Woodrow's mind was on his duties as castle keeper and of the impatient king who awaited his return. As the hot summer sun beat down on them, he was reminded that not all the hunting outings were done in groups. There were those times when Lord Victor hunted alone. Times when he brooked no company, not even Woodrow's. When Victor returned, however, he expected to find the castle and the kingdom's business proceeding smoothly. Woodrow's function was to see that Lord Victor wasn't disappointed.

The castle keeper's extended leave of absence, long past the duration of the full-moon cycle, meant that his duties weren't being performed to Lord Victor's expectations. Despite having a capable staff in place to serve the king's needs, Woodrow knew that he was expected to be available on demand. In this regard, he had failed his liege of late. There would be consequences.

As they cleared the lower foothills and rode down the plains road, he saw that the storm brewing out over the ocean was beginning its roll towards the coast. The castle keeper dug his heels into the flanks of his mount to pick up the cantering pace. He wanted to be home before the bad weather arrived and they were given another soaking.

Willie was forced to respond in fashion, digging in his heels and urging his mount to keep up. Woodrow had double-wrapped his leg after their breakfast to protect it on the long ride, but the youth was thinking of matters other than his wounded limb. He was recalling with a great sadness how, not so long ago, the horse under his saddle had been his old loyal charge, Pegasus.

The youth stole a look back over his shoulder, half expecting to see his faithful herd dogs, Rigel and Sirius, there and running after them. The empty road he saw instead, matched the emptiness in his heart.

With a clattering of their horse's iron hooves, the two riders soon crossed over one of the many arched stone bridges that spanned the Varden River.

From there, they picked up the river road that followed along its western bank.

Up at its source in the mountains, the melting snow and turbulent streams spawned the river that cut down through the foothills. From there, the Varden snaked its way through the coastal plains, where the river widened and its waters slowed. The river then meandered its way northwest until it turned away just a few miles below the rising mesa, and headed west to empty itself into the sea.

The river and the river road were a bustle of activity. Skiffs, fishing boats, barges and log booms were common sights on the river. The Varden River and its adjacent road were both well-traveled routes for commerce. The two riders passed a steady stream of carts and wagons but few were hauling produce and other wares, today being Sunday. Most of the drivers seemed to be in a hurry to get to their homes following church services before the approaching storm arrived. Willie took note of the way people greeted Woodrow, though. They were respectful and courteous. Many of them called out friendly salutations. He wasn't sure if it was for the man or the sash of his office that he wore about his waist.

He ventured a question in his direction. "Do these gentle flocks of people know that they have a wolf-man living in their midst?"

Woodrow turned to look at him. "That was almost clever, Willie. There may be hope for you yet. A sense of humour might just get you through what lays ahead."

The Pack leader urged his mount onwards.

Willie followed along behind him. The more he thought about the implications of Woodrow's comment, the more he wished that he had just kept his mouth shut.

CHAPTER 11

THE MULTINATIONALS

When I'm out walking down these uptown streets
I'm the somebody that no-one greets
I'm the nobody they ain't anxious to meet

August 2, 1461
The Mesa-of-the-Moon, Varakov

LORD VICTOR'S YOUNG SKOLISH bride had passed away the day prior. Like others before her, a few days of periodic feedings and her weakened body had given up the ghost. She'd been mostly catatonic the last day.

Victor conceded that it was never intended to be a long-lasting union in any event. He considered the notion of perhaps one day taking a real queen to sit at his side and even having a real priest hear their wedding vows. That would be a first.

The thought amused him. There had been any number of mock weddings before—mock weddings, mock children, and mock heirs to the throne. He tried to recollect just who he was now. Was it Lord Victor the VIII? He'd have to ask Woodrow sometime. The castle keeper would know. He kept track of such matters.

The Varakovan king left the great hall to attend to the internment of his fallen bride. They were holding a brief ceremony in the private courtyard cemetery below the inner tower, where the mortal remains of Varakov's royalty were interred. The bones of his parents rested there.

Lord Victor joined the small gathering as leaves swirled about the courtyard dancing on the freshening breeze. He stood along side the mercenary, Barozzi, who he'd invited to join the funeral party. While the young Mary had not been a real queen or even a true princess, Victor wanted the affair to be treated with the dignity that he felt it warranted. He and the young woman had been intimate, more intimate than anyone could understand. Standing across the freshly dug gravesite from him were his bride's mother and sister. He felt that it was only right that they be allowed to attend the funeral to properly grieve, along with the other women prisoners. A small guard detail had escorted them up from their cell. The old Skolish knight had been left behind in his cell, lest he make a disturbance.

The old knight watched the sad affair through the small barred window of his cell, however. The last remaining male prisoner stood teetering on the wobbly, small bench he'd moved beneath the window. He remained silent as the shrouded form of the dead young woman was laid to rest, but Victor could see the tears of grief that ran down his face. The retired knight hadn't cried for the men when they had died, but the loss of the young farm lass was apparently more than he could abide.

The women, of course, were inconsolable. They wept and wailed in their anguish, even throwing themselves on the ground and tearing their clothing. Only the mother remained standing stoically and unmoved. Her tears would doubtlessly be shed in private. Both he and Barozzi much admired her for her stony reserve.

When the Sunday burial service was concluded, Victor personally escorted the female captives back to their cell in the company of the mercenary leader and the guard detail. It was there, in the castle dungeon, that Victor gave the women the gift of revenge.

After the women had been herded into their cell, they huddled about the mother, whose daughter would never again bring her joy. Victor went over and drew a handful of knives from the shelves of instruments of torture and persuasion. He came back to the women's cell then and tossed them onto the straw-covered floor.

At first, both the guards and the women stood transfixed, not comprehending his intentions. Only Barozzi seemed aware that something interesting was afoot. His eyes glinted with anticipation.

In a rapid blur, Victor pivoted and drove his fist deep into the solar plexus of the young guard who had abused both the mother and the daughter the night of the feast. The air expelled out of the fellow in a rush. He doubled over in pain and surprise. Clutching him by his collar, Victor hurled the man into the cell, where he crashed into the corner. The dazed young guard was slow in picking himself up. Blood trickled down his face from the gash incurred when his head made contact with the thick stone wall.

Victor slowly swung the cell door shut. He stared silently at the Skolish mother for a few moments. Perhaps a message passed between them. In any event, she was the first to stoop down and pick up one of the blades. Rising, her focus turned to where the young guard stood gathering his wits, as he tried to make sense of what had just happened.

The surviving sister and several of the other women followed the mother's lead then, until each of the knives was clutched in a hand. Those hands prepared to seek a measure of vengeance for the loss of an innocent young Skolish flower and vengeance for their dead men folk—vengeance for all that had transpired since they'd been so rudely snatched away from their homes. It mattered not that the object of their vengeance was a minor and insignificant player in their difficulties.

The brutish young guard had recovered enough to see what his predicament was. He staggered away in an attempt to put some distance between himself and the slowly advancing women. His retreat was hampered, however, when he reached the cold iron bars at the end of the cell.

The guard was trapped in the barred cage. Like any trapped animal, he saw that his only possibility for escape lay in attack. He prepared to launch himself off the bars at the nearest woman, probably hoping to wrestle a knife away. Perhaps he thought that all was not yet lost. After all, these were only women he faced, armed with knives or not.

Just as the young guard was about to spring forward, however, an arm reached into the cell, slid itself around his neck, and pulled him back into the bars. The old Skolish knight held on tightly. He used his free hand grip the arm that held the throat of his squirming enemy. At that point, the doomed guard's eyes literally bulged out, both in terror and from the loss of air to his lungs.

No one moved to help him. No one dared, lest they incur Lord Victor's wrath. Perhaps no one really cared either. Barozzi certainly didn't. The mercenary smiled when he saw the guard was helpless to defend himself. He watched intently as the man tried to kick out at the women with one foot, while his arms flapped about uselessly. He didn't even avert his eyes when the knives stabbed into the guard, over and over again.

The Varakovan king gave the mercenary due credit. Barozzi was no stranger to bloodshed. The guards all looked pale and stricken. They'd turned away and looked like they wished they were any place but there. Two of them were actually physically ill.

Even after the old Skolish knight relinquished his hold and allowed the guard's lifeless body to slide down the bars to the cell floor, several of the women continued taking their bloody revenge. The old knight took small solace in the death of the young guard. His eyes settled on the king and the mercenary. Although he didn't speak, his glare made it clear that he wished he was able to get his arms wrapped around their necks next.

Victor ignored him. He turned to the men of the guard detail. His expression clearly showed his disdain for their squeamishness.

"Be sure that you have them return the knives to you when they've finished," he commanded. "And clean up that vomit as well. It smells of your weakness."

The Varakovan king and Barozzi departed the vile scene at that point, leaving the guards clutching their sword hilts and wondering if they'd be adequate to their assigned task. The straw in the cell was already saturated in blood and gore. There wasn't going to be much left of the dead guard at the rate the women were going at his body.

Victor believed the guards would wisely decide to wait until the women captives had exhausted themselves before obeying his order. Regardless, he had other matters to attend to, and he left them behind to sort it out.

A short time later, after conferring further with Barozzi, he dispatched the mercenary to Port Lupus on an important errand. There was a special cargo that Lord Victor was expecting. He'd been informed that the awaited ship had made port that morning. Barozzi was given the task of finding the ship's captain and setting up a meeting for later that night.

*　　　*　　　*

August 2, 1461
Port Lupus, Varakov

The dark gathering storm clouds were still rumbling offshore, but already the trades people and merchants had begun closing up their shops and places of business. They worked at their businesses even on Sunday afternoons, after those who attended church did so, but now the onshore breezes were picking up and the smell of approaching rain was in the air.

Out in the protection of the sheltered bay, the last sails of several ships were being hauled down. The two Varakovan galleons among them were already battened down and riding at anchor. Their captains and crews alike were thankful to have a safe harbour to hunker down and ride out the encroaching storm.

There was no way of knowing at this stage if it would be a major blow, but this was a port town, and people here were knowledgeable enough to take precautions. They'd seen the weather mass brewing out at sea, and they knew that it would soon head their way. It was still early in the year for the big storms, which sometimes hammered the coast with gale-force winds, but one never knew for sure. Mother Nature could be unpredictable.

With that in mind, precautions were taken. Shopkeepers closed up a little earlier than usual. Windows were shuttered closed. Barrels and displays of wares were rolled up and stowed away, and store doors were barred and latched. There wouldn't likely be many customers out and about anyway.

From a distance, Vinnie noticed that another ship had left the coastal shipping lanes and was breaching the mouth of the wolf-head harbour. They too, were wisely seeking a sheltered harbour berth in which to ride out the weather. The gang leader could also see the signal flags flapping from the tower over the parapets of their three-story headquarters up on lookout hill. His lookouts had identified the ship. They were relaying their permission for the shore batteries to grant the ship safe entry to the harbour.

The gang's headquarters occupied a stone enclave that was an isolated, freestanding structure, straddling the hill between the docks and the better parts of town. In one sense this meant the Multinationals had a foot in both sections of the port town. In another, it meant that they belonged to neither.

The gang leader watched as the ship reached the much calmer harbour waters. The ship's crew would soon be reefing down their sails and closing up hatches. It was far better to pay the relatively small anchorage fee for a night in a welcoming port than to spend a nightlong battle in the inky black trying to stay afloat against the battering waves. This was a sea that could rise up to frightening heights, if she had a mind to.

It had been a number of years since Port Lupus and Varakov had been beset by a real killer tempest. None of the hurricanes or the deadly winter storms that had visited in the past had come calling recently. It was only a matter of time before one did, however.

People often died in those times, either during the storm itself or in the aftermath. A few years back, one such bitter January storm had welcomed the New Year with days of gale force winds and freezing rain. That was followed by more than a week of heavy snowfall that left drifts in places that were taller than a full-grown man. People had been cut off from town and isolated for months. Some froze to death, and even more starved. When the spring thaw came, the body count had been staggering.

Vinnie had taken to the streets with Lorenzo and a number of his men, as he did most late afternoons. It was usually when he began his day. He thought of it as the changing of the guard. The daytime activities in town were usually benign, which was why he preferred the later shift. The business sector of Port Lupus that operated during the daylight hours generally closed up as the sun was going down. With the fast approaching storm, they were doing that a little earlier than usual today, and were finding their way home to their families and their well-earned suppers.

The merchant classes generally lived in the better environs of the town. Up the hill above the harbour, their streets were made of cobblestones and had gas lamps along them that were lit each night. Their homes were solidly constructed and well maintained. There were parks and squares to walk through and pass the time in. There were churches of several persuasions, as well as numerous private halls and more dignified pubs for them to gather in with their own kind.

While the merchants certainly wouldn't be mistaken for nobility, they were definitely a cut above the common working class and some of the lowlife scum who frequented the dockyards at night. They didn't mix well with the less fortunate among them, nor did they have any desire to. The Varakovan knights and other fighting men were a different story, but they led their own lives and had their barracks to return to after a night on the town.

As Vinnie and Lorenzo and their men patrolled through the merchants' "better" part of town, the gang leader was reminded that regardless of his position of authority, these people didn't consider him to be one of them either. He saw the way they often crossed the street to avoid meeting him. Sometimes, that fact left a bitter taste in his mouth. This late afternoon was no different. Vinnie didn't much relish the idea of being out in this section of town when the weather hit. He didn't much relish being in this part of town at the best of times.

Back down the hill, the coming night would belong to the working-class blokes, the sailors, the downtrodden, and the hustlers. Over the years that he'd run the gang, he'd found that he was far more comfortable with their kind. Unless the threatening storm hit hard, they would fill the taverns later that night, as they would the bordellos and other dens of iniquity. To be sure, more than a few of these "respectable" merchants, and even knights of the realm, would be found cavorting with the riffraff or partaking in the pleasures of the flesh.

Depending on how long the storm lasted, the night might be a pretty quiet one, even down the hill. Then again, if the storm blew through quickly, it could mean a real busy night. The fact that is was a Sunday made little difference to anyone in the Port town. The local priests had resigned themselves to that fact long ago. They counted themselves fortunate to gather a flock during the morning services they held in the uptown churches.

Vinnie had observed the effects of foul weather in the past. People got juiced up in the aftermath of a good storm. They tended to drink more. They tended to fight more, and they liked to get laid more.

It must have something to do with all that energy charging the air, he mused. *Only time will tell what the night will bring.*

The gang leader put two fingers to his lips and whistled sharply to catch the attention of the Ohs flanking them out on the street. He made a quick circling motion with his hand and pointed back to their headquarters. He'd decided to wrap up the patrol early while they were still dry. He and Lorenzo could use the down time to get caught up on some of their bookkeeping chores. He told his second-in-command as much.

"Not that I fancy doing book work, but it beats getting soaked for no good reason," Lorenzo concurred. "Still, I'd rather cozy up with some female company and a tankard of ale."

"If you're a good lad and get the tallies right this time, maybe you can have the evening off to do just that," Vinnie said with a laugh. "If not, you can explain any discrepancies to the king."

Lorenzo shuddered at the prospect. If there was one thing that Lord Victor expected of them, besides keeping the order in Port Lupus, it was a good honest accounting of the ledgers. The king's coffers were always in need of replenishment. He had no desire to be the one to disappoint him. He'd seen what Lord Victor was capable of.

"Did I ever tell you how much I love doing ledgers?" Lorenzo asked with a wry grin. "They beat a night out with the ladies anytime."

*   *   *

August 2, 1461
Varakov

It was nearing dusk by the time that the two riders reached the last of the multi-arched stone bridges that spanned the Varden River before it reached Port Lupus and the ocean bay. They crossed over it with a clattering of their horse's hooves echoing out over the placid river.

Once the afternoon skies had begun clouding over, there'd been decidedly less people out on the road. They'd ridden for a considerable time and were feeling more than a little saddle weary by the time they crossed over the bridge and turned up the road that led towards the lone coastal mount.

As the sun was being swallowed by the sea, the winds picked up considerably and the sky darkened further. The two riders approached the table-topped mountain and saw the heavy drawbridge being raised up and closed for the night from where it spanned the deep dry moat that surrounded the ancient castle on three sides. From their vantage point they couldn't see the deadly iron spikes that lined the moat to receive any would be invaders who were repelled from the walls.

The immense stone walls of the castle loomed overhead, however, as they rode on. Silent carved stone gargoyles with fierce features stared down on them impassively from their recessed perches. Willie looked up in awe at the massive inner tower which climbed up the face of the mesa and disappeared from view in the growing darkness. In that moment, the young Medinian felt a sense of inexplicable dread, as if the massive castle were a living thing that could reach out and squash him like he was an insignificant insect. He wondered if the feeling was a harbinger of what fate had in store for him.

They were approaching Woodrow's estate as the main weather front pushed ashore across the length of the coastline. As they reached the manor and its collection of outbuildings, a steward rushed out to meet them from the stables and relieve them of their mounts.

The steward and Woodrow embraced for a moment after he climbed down wearily from his horse's back. The two men spoke a few words in private before Woodrow turned and introduced him to the Medinian youth.

"This is Micale, Willie," Woodrow said, "he and his wife are pretty well in charge of things around here.

"Bully for them," the youth replied. "Do you think I care? Why don't we just get inside before we get soaked?"

The steward just smiled at the young man's insolence and then led the horses into the stables.

As if in response to the youth's cold remark, sheets of rain began falling over the plains. Lightning bolts lit the skies over the Mesa-of-the-Moon, and the ancient and ominous castle in which the Lord of Varakov made his home.

The storm had arrived.

*　　　　*　　　　*

The Mesa-of-the-Moon, Varakov

A jagged lightning bolt forked down from the rolling mass of black cloud and lit the sky once more. A clap of thunder followed a scant few seconds later with an ear-deafening rumble.

Standing barefoot in one of the castle's upper parapets, Lord Victor gazed out across the plains towards the coast. Rain lashed down, driven by the brisk winds that brought the storm in from the sea. The king sought no shelter. Like the fortified castle, he seemed impervious to the storm. He was actually savouring the primal elements, which were being unleashed upon the land.

By the illumination of the lightning, Victor could see the tail end of the front already approaching the coast. He stood in the downpour for a while longer. The storm was intense, but he saw that it wouldn't likely last overly long.

The Varakovan king had made arrangements to meet someone in Port Lupus later that night if the weather permitted. It had been some time since his last walk through the streets of the harbour town. The storm would abate eventually, he determined, so he decided that he would keep the rendezvous. He would, in fact, arrive early and use the time to drop in on some others in his employ. He wouldn't want his men to think him lax in his attentions.

Lord Victor's hands clutched the edges of his shimmering cape as it billowed out behind him in the gusting wind. He climbed up onto the battlement wall and looked down at the rough cobble stones far below in the courtyards. The heady rush he felt was only heightened by the raging storm. He stepped out into the night air.

The winged Beast rode the air currents, fighting for updrafts against the onslaught of the winds that threatened to batter him inland. Finally, he reached an altitude where the wind slackened slightly and he could make better headway. Lightning continued to pierce the night sky as he fought the ever-changing currents of wind and rain lashed his reptilian body. He felt alive and totally invigorated. It was like rushing headlong into a battle with the Gods themselves, and let those Gods beware.

Victor needed this diversion. The castle keeper had only just now returned to his estate with a second rider in tow. Victor's castle watch had reported their passing by the walls near dusk. He assumed that the second rider had been the stricken youth from the mountain retreat. Thanks, no doubt, to Woodrow's superior medicinal skills.

It was an annoyance that the castle keeper had chosen to save the life of some simple Medinian farm serf over performing his duties to his king. Victor had no patience for the supplicants who came before him daily. The Varakovan king preferred Woodrow to screen the petitioners and weed out those issues that could be dealt with without wasting his time.

*   *   *

Port Lupus, Varakov

Port Lupus weathered the passing thunderstorm as it had so many before it over the centuries. As storms went, this one had passed through quickly. The harbour town had received a good long soaking, but other than for some windswept debris, no real damage had been done. The sky remained dark with cloud cover, but by the time that Lord Victor arrived the rain had settled into a steady drizzle. In another hour or two, even that would end.

Out in the harbour, the ships rode out the storm's passing with no great difficulties. Several of their crews were already being given permission to lower boats to take them into the docks for a night in town. Other ships, which had finished up their business in Port Lupus, would raise their sails on the morning tide. Fresh ships would arrive in due course to take up the empty berthing moors. It was always a busy port, and the nearby warehouses handled goods both coming and going.

In the Ohs' headquarters overlooking the harbour, Vinnie scanned the detailed ledgers on the table in front of him. The ships that came and went were all recorded there, as were hundreds of manifests and transactions.

"It looks like July was another good month, Lorenzo," he commented. His trusted lieutenant sat beside him at the table in his office. The two young men sipped at well-earned cups of wine while reviewing the carefully maintained records.

"I think the castle keeper will be pleased. Especially when I show him the revenue that the new bordello is bringing in," he added. "He'll be happy to see that venture's paying off so well."

"Then doubtlessly, so shall I."

The two gang members bolted up out of their seats. Drawing long daggers from their waistband scabbards, they spun to face the intruder, whom neither had heard enter the room. They automatically assumed crouched positions standing shoulder to shoulder should it prove necessary to defend against an attack.

"Victor! Lord Victor," Vinnie said, correcting himself when he saw who it was that had snuck up on them. "Ah, welcome, milord. Needless to say, you caught us a bit off guard."

The Multinational leader straightened back up. He quickly sheathed his weapon, and Lorenzo followed suit. The young men wore sheepish looks, which bespoke of their embarrassment at having been taken by such surprise. They'd even had the audacity to draw their weapons on the king himself! That action could be construed as treasonous, possibly with fatal repercussions.

Vinnie's next thought was one of sheer puzzlement. In order to get to this office, well inside their headquarters, their unannounced visitor would have had to pass at least a dozen of his men, his very best men. He had no idea how Lord Victor could have managed that.

"Vinnie, it's so very nice to see you again. And you—it's Lorenzo, if I'm not mistaken? I remember you from the feast." Lord Victor smiled. He was obviously amused to see that the two young men were so clearly flustered.

Even so, Victor was pleased with the two men's quick reflexes and their subsequent contrite manner. It didn't hurt their case that they'd been honestly at work on his kingdom's behalf before he had made his presence known.

"Yes, milord, Lorenzo, it is," the Ohs' lieutenant managed to reply. He'd taken a few deep breaths in an attempt to slow his racing heartbeat.

Lord Victor's ability to move about unnoticed, and to make his approach unseen, had served him well in the past. There had been times when he'd dropped in on some underling who had foolishly been enriching himself at Victor's expense. That seldom ended well. Such transgressions were rarely tolerated and never allowed to be repeated.

"So, we've had a good month, you'd say?" Victor asked, repeating what he had heard them discussing. "What's this about the new bordello?"

"I was just saying how well it's been doing, milord," Vinnie replied. "Woodrow was certainly right. He said that we should establish a place where the more affluent gentlemen could … ah, acquaint themselves with the Vamps in a classier setting. Now that they've got a more exclusive place to go to, they've been spending more freely. The overhead is running about twenty percent higher, but we're taking in a bundle! Our revenue's up more than fifty percent, and that's on top of the annual fee they pay for their private membership. In the first two and a half months, we've more than made back the extra initial outlay on the premises."

"There's even a bonus, milord," Lorenzo spoke up. "The Vamps are a lot happier, too! There's been a whole lot less fuss with them."

If there was one thing Lorenzo didn't relish, it was breaking up brawls between scrapping Vamps. Give him a couple of drunken sailors any day, over that.

"It sounds like we have a winning proposition all the way around," Lord Victor observed. "I've always said that it pays to keep our customers happy. As word gets around that Port Lupus treats its first-class guests in an appropriate fashion, the more ships we can expect to make port here—and that sea trade, gentlemen, is what we're after."

The king sat down at the table with his shimmering cape draped behind him. His silken garments were wet and his feet were bare, neither of which seemed of concern to him. He gestured for a cup of wine, which Lorenzo quickly poured for him. He motioned for them to retake their seats and lift their cups with him.

"Here's to new ships from new horizons and the wonders they'll bring to us in the future," Victor stated, raising his cup in salute.

He wasn't sure if his thoughts were really registering with the Ohs' lieutenant, Lorenzo, but he could definitely see the light of understanding in Vinnie's eyes. That was why he liked dealing with the young gang leader. He was glad that Woodrow had decided to take him under his wing when he was just a lad fighting to survive on the streets in Port Lupus.

Victor knew that Woodrow had put a lot of time and effort into mentoring him, with his blessings. The castle keeper had been instrumental in not only getting him recruited into the Multinationals, but also in educating and refining him. Combined with his own street smarts and his natural leadership qualities, the youth had advanced rapidly within the gang's ranks.

Three years back, Vinnie had used those leadership qualities to quietly form a group within the Multinational's organization that became known as the Ohs. They were young men from diverse backgrounds, but they were loyal to him. In a bold surgical strike, the Ohs had wrested control of the gang away from a brutish leader nicknamed Thomas the Terrible. He'd been a seasoned thug, twice the young man's age.

The proof of Vinnie's intelligence lay in the fact that he'd come to Woodrow first to get his permission to act. The proof of his capabilities lay in the fact that he had not come for any help to accomplish it.

Instead, Vinnie had delivered a blueprint for an improved organization. He would put an end to the senseless violence and ensure that better profits were had. Woodrow had listened to his proposal and was duly impressed. Enough so, that the castle keeper had then arranged for a private audience with the king. Victor had been impressed by the young gang member's plan, as well. He had given his blessing to proceed.

The leadership of the Multinationals had passed to Vinnie virtually overnight. It had been a bloodless coup, or nearly so. Thomas the Terrible had ruled the gang through intimidation and ruthlessness. That night, Thomas had simply disappeared from the face of the earth.

In his continued absence in the days following, the Ohs had rallied their support around Vinnie. No one disputed his bid for the leadership of the gang, when Vinnie laid claim to it. Most were just content to see his predecessor gone.

Under Vinnie's leadership, the improved operations had enriched the kingdom's coffers, far exceeding anything they'd anticipated. The young gang leader had wisely sought council from Woodrow, especially in the early stages of his leadership. As time passed, however, he'd brought more and more of his own innovations forward for approval, and then had successfully implemented them.

Vinnie had proven to be a charismatic leader. He inspired loyalty, and just enough fear in his fellow gang-members. He seemed to have an inherent understanding of when to use the carrot, and when to use the stick. That was something you couldn't teach. A leader either had it, or he didn't. Victor could appreciate that fact of life.

The Varakovan king finished off his cup of wine and got up from his chair to look out the window. "The rain seems to have come to an end," he observed.

He turned from the view overlooking the port and regarded the two gang members who had correctly risen from their chairs when he had. He was pleased that they showed the proper deference for their king.

"Why don't I accompany you gentlemen on your rounds this evening?" Lord Victor suggested.

It was, of course, anything but a suggestion. Although it was the first time that their liege had done so, it was certainly his prerogative if he chose to step out on a patrol with the Ohs. Victor was the king, and the Varakovan king went where and when he wished to.

"Certainly, milord," Vinnie responded, with a consensual dip of his head. "It's time we were out on patrol anyway. Is there any place in particular you'd care to visit?"

"None to speak of," Victor replied, indifferently, "although there's a meeting I wish to attend to at the Hangman's tavern in a few hours. Why don't we just walk the streets until then? We'll go wherever it is that your normal patrolling would take you, if you could round me up a decent pair of boots, that is. I seem to have stepped out into the night air without mine."

Lorenzo sped off to rifle through the closets of the sleeping quarters, returning with several pair of leather boots for the king to try on. Vinnie watched as Lord Victor selected a pair that looked like they would fit him, and then declaring them quite satisfactory as he stood up. The Ohs' second-in-command looked towards the gang leader when he recognized them as being an extra pair of Vinnie's boots.

The leader of the Ohs didn't seem to notice or even to care. His mind was elsewhere. The king's mention of a meeting later at the Hangman's tavern had piqued Vinnie's curiosity, but his place was not to question his liege. Lord Victor would apprise him of what he felt he needed to know. That, again, was a king's prerogative.

They made their way down the stairs and into the headquarters reception area. The other Ohs on duty were stunned when they saw Lord Victor accompanying Vinnie and Lorenzo. Certainly none of them had seen the Varakovan king come inside. Filippo's mouth hung agape in disbelief and Sergio could only shrug his heavy set shoulders in response to Vinnie's glare.

The Varakovan king wasn't exactly someone they wouldn't have noticed, had he entered in a conventional manner, like through one of the damn doors! Even if he'd pried open a window, surely someone would have seen him. Nevertheless, here he was, wearing his trademark shimmering black cape. It took several long seconds before they remembered their place and hastened to their bended knees. Lord Victor simply graced them an indulgent smile.

How the Varakovan king had come to be there was a mystery the gang members would likely never solve, but judging from Vinnie's expression, they would be discussing that very thing with him in the not-so-distant future. None of the Ohs was particularly looking forward to that.

At the gang leader's signal, a half-dozen of the puzzled Ohs fell in behind the trio as they took to the wet streets. Vinnie intended to see to it that the king was kept safe and amply protected. He motioned for his men to spread out and watch the perimeters as they moved through town.

*   *   *

The king of Varakov felt free to travel about any part of his domain. He would do so whenever the mood struck him. More often than not, it was without the trappings of an entourage or a regiment of knights or a detail of castle guards. This was more than a rarity for any other king; it was virtually unheard of in any other kingdom. It spoke a lot about the Varakovan king.

Between the mountains and the great sea, Lord Victor's rule was as absolute, as it was absolutely unique. Perhaps the greatest testament of this was that no one could remember it being any other way. There had always been a Lord Victor. It was said that his family line had ruled Varakov for over three centuries now.

Yet, precious little was really known of their king. The more elderly of the populace had known what they thought was his father's rule. He had been referred to simply as Lord Victor, as well. The queen mother had died birthing their son, it was said, and the prince was raised an only child before being sent abroad to study. When his father, the king, had grown somewhat aged, his only heir had returned. The ship bringing the prince home had arrived with great fanfare. A celebratory feast and three days of tournaments had marked the special occasion. A huge purse was contended for by knights from across the kingdom and from beyond.

Not long afterwards, it was said, the king had taken ill with a pox of some kind. After a time spent secluded in his sickbed, he had passed away. His son had then inherited the throne and had ruled Varakov ever since. The current Lord Victor had yet to marry and produce an heir, however.

It wasn't the place of commoners to question such things, however. What went on behind the castle walls was far beyond their station. What they did know was that the king's powers were legendary. His feats were whispered about. Bedtime stories often featured his bloodier deeds, and tales were told of young maidens who had caught his fancy and were never to be seen again.

There were even those, who claimed that the Varakovan king was in league with the dark powers! Such stories made for good entertainment, especially for people whose lives were spent in the mundane drudgery of scratching out a living, working a trade, or in service to one of the barons or landowners.

While he didn't really feel the need for them, it didn't bother Lord Victor to have a security detail of the Ohs tagging along. That was Vinnie's call, after all. The news that their liege was in town would likely spread like wildfire. Despite the fact that he did travel around the kingdom, it still wasn't everyday that the common people got to see their king. They were likely to be curious. A little crowd control was probably a wise precaution.

To tell the truth, Vinnie wasn't overly concerned about Lord Victor's safety. He'd seen the Varakovan king in action. He knew that Victor was more than capable of handling himself. The night of the feast in the castle's great hall was proof enough of that.

However, there were two new ships in port, and with them, crewmen who were strangers to Port Lupus. So, at his own discretion, Vinnie decided to take their walking patrol up through the streets and housing of the trades people and merchants. It would be safer there.

As it would turn out, it wasn't the best of decisions.

CHAPTER 12

Port Lupus

Are you scared? Are you shaking with fright?
Do you worry about things that go bump in the night?

August 2, 1461
Port Lupus, Varakov

VINNIE AND LORD VICTOR discussed a few aspects of their mutual business concerns as they made their way through the better sections of Port Lupus. The homes and cobblestone streets were well constructed. The community had an air of respectability, and perhaps an air of subtle superiority. The merchants, trades people, and the artisans who plied their crafts in present day Varakov couldn't be compared with the nobility class, but they could afford decent homes and many of the amenities in life.

The one real concern that these people had was the Multinational gang that demanded protection money from all their businesses. The cut that they took for their services was always a bone of contention. Granted, crime was kept to a minimum. Some would say, although not too loudly, that this was because all the real criminals were in the gang that supposedly kept the criminal element at bay.

Most would agree, however, that things were much better since Vinnie had taken over the Multinationals. His predecessor had been a vicious thug who had taken whatever he could from them with impunity. Vinnie, at least, seemed to understand that the merchants had to make a living. Since Vinnie and the Ohs had taken control, they'd put into place a structured system of tithe that was assessed equitably on all business activities. Most merchants would admit, albeit begrudgingly, that the tithe they paid was manageable, and that the business environment was much improved.

The Multinationals also worked hard at attracting new trade off the shipping lanes and making Port Lupus a desirable port of call. In the past, ships had often been targets for plundering. Now the captains of these vessels were finding that not only was there a thriving market for their cargoes here, but a relatively safe haven where they and their crews could find a variety of diversions after a hard haul at sea.

Port Lupus was a vastly improved town over what it used to be. Years before, the harbour had been a sad collection of decrepit, rat-infested warehouses and hovels. The plague of 1445 had been instrumental in changing that. Much to his credit, Lord Victor had seen to it that the entire area was burned to the ground in an effort to combat the disease. The death toll from the plague had still been severe, but in the ensuing years, they'd completed an entirely new and well planned reconstruction of the port.

Despite these improvements in living and working conditions, from which the merchant class mutually benefited, there was still a measure of discontent. They had to tolerate the Multinationals, but they didn't have to like them. The fact that the gang's collections went directly into king's coffers didn't matter either. It just meant that there was even less that they could do about it. If there was one thing that the merchants feared more than the power of the gang, it was the power of the castle. The edicts of the castle were those of the Lord Victor, himself. To disobey those, in any way, was to invite severe repercussions.

Tonight, as their walkabout progressed through the winding streets, word did indeed get around that Lord Victor was in Port Lupus. When the king's entourage came upon a picturesque square at one of the cross streets, they took the opportunity to sit on the benches and rest for a time by the fountain in the centre of one of the larger squares. Vinnie took advantage of the break and the privacy afforded them to dispatch one of the Ohs to a local pub to fetch them some refreshments.

Many of the citizens, who had thoughts of moving out of doors after the rains, quickly removed themselves and sought the relative safety of their homes. The cloud cover prevented the stars and the moon from shining through. The only light was provided by the whickered street lamps that lined the streets and flickered in the breezes in an attempt at holding back the dark of the night. Here and there, the entourage could make out candles and lanterns in the windows of the homes, as well as several anxious faces peering out at them.

Lord Victor and Vinnie lounged on one of the benches, conversing about the increased shipping trade that was finding its way into Port Lupus and the ship crews who sought liberty time in the taverns and in the brothels along the harbour front. They presented a constant challenge to the Ohs and their Multinational underlings. Months at sea could make a man thirsty for just about anything that wasn't salt water. It was a difficult task to ensure that they had a good time, without causing a civil disturbance while doing it.

"But give me those horny, drunken blokes to deal with anytime over this bunch," Vinnie remarked. With a wave of his arm, he indicated the merchant class that lived in the houses that surrounded the square. "At least the sailors are straightforward about what they want. Provide them with a good keg of ale and some lively lasses and they're as happy as pigs in shit. It seems like this crowd is never really content."

The Ohs gang member, who Vinnie had sent off, returned then from one of the local pubs that blended quietly into the neighbourhood. He'd brought back a large pint each for Vinnie and Lord Victor. The others would wait until after their anointed rounds before partaking in any libations, especially since the Varakovan king was under their protection tonight.

The Ohs were diligent in their duties and cautious when it came to their patrol assignments. It was becoming apparent that their presence was attracting more and more attention, and they were a little uneasy. An increasing number of the locals could be seen peering out their windows to see who was gathered out in the dark shadows of their square. There were several small groups gathered in darkened doorways, where they whispered their mutual concerns.

Whether it was because there were gang members out there or the ominously dark and caped figure, reputedly of their king, there was obviously a state of growing concern. Their fears brought about a degree of hysteria. Wives and children were rushed off to bed. Lights were doused. Blinds and shutters were closed in an attempt not to be noticed.

By now, Victor had noticed the reactions of these citizens as they cowered in darkened doorways or hid in their houses and peered out their shuttered windows. He could hear latches dropping into place as doors and windows were barred. He could feel their stares. He could sense their fears, and it was beginning to piss him off.

A hidden voice called out for them to be gone from the area, and Vinnie flinched. A second and then a third person took up the call, and the gang leader knew there was going to be trouble. As his eyes scanned the darkness, he sensed the king's growing rage.

Lord Victor was indeed outraged. The nerve of these merchants! He was their king, not some pock-ridden scum they could demand to be off. The Varakovan king rose up off the bench by the fountain and cursed angrily.

One newly darkened house then caught Lord Victor's attention. He stood staring at it, seeming to sense that the head of the household was now peering out between the cracks of the shutters. He uttered a deep-throated snarl. Before Vinnie or any of the Ohs could react, he tossed his ale aside. A few dozen running strides brought him onto the front stoop of the house, where, unaided, the door flew open before him.

By an eerie light with a greenish glow, the Ohs outside in the square could make out the form of Lord Victor and that of the soon lifeless merchant, who he held suspended in midair by the throat.

*　　　　*　　　　*

The gang left behind a neighbourhood that wouldn't be getting much sleep that night. The light of day would find them one less in number. The family in question would mourn the loss of their loved one. Their friends would commiserate with them at the unfairness of it all, but the crime would go unpunished. Indeed, the perpetrator had already dismissed it as of being of no consequence. Only the young gang leader remained troubled after witnessing yet another excessively violent action by his lord and master.

While it was true that Vinnie was not accepted by the merchant class as an equal, he had never intentionally punished one of them for such a minor slight. He had never slain one of them regardless of the circumstances. Yet, here was Lord Victor, snuffing the life out of a man for no reason other than he was offended. He had killed the tradesman as casually as he might have swatted a buzzing insect that was annoying him.

The gang leader had trouble concentrating on whatever Lord Victor was espousing as they returned to their patrol. To the king, it was as if nothing out of the ordinary had just occurred. Judging from the familiar looks of awe that adorned the faces of his men, the others did not share his troubled mind. Instead, it was apparent that Lorenzo and the other Ohs found Lord Victor's display of power an intoxicating experience. They were in the presence of a king with almost godlike attributes, and one with the ability to decide a man's fate in a blink of the eye. His was the ability to opt between life and death and then execute his decision with a will of cold steel.

It was the night of the feast, all over again, Vinnie thought with dismay. *Why was it necessary to kill the man? It was understandable that the presence of the gang members made these people nervous. We caused them due concern. Why was it necessary for one of them to be punished? And if punishment was some sort of object lesson, couldn't something less than someone's death have sufficed?*

Vinnie's mind was going into overload. The questions were coming fast and furious, but unfortunately, the answers were not. He was in a functioning state of shock. Somehow, he managed to keep up with the pace set by Lord Victor and to nod his head as if he was listening to his liege. Yet he'd have no recollection later of what was said or where their walk had taken them once they'd left the square behind them.

It wasn't until they stopped outside the newly renovated bordello that Vinnie was at last able to focus on where they actually were and what it was that Lord Victor was saying.

"Let us stop in for a few moments. You can show me what you and Woodrow have put together for our wealthier, travel weary guests?" the king suggested.

"Uh, as milord wishes," Vinnie managed to reply. He hoped Lord Victor hadn't noticed his lack of attention as he tried to regain his focus.

The upscale bordello was set back from the street, with a small cobblestone courtyard in front, bordered by a short, neatly trimmed hedge. Potted plants decorated the courtyard and baskets with colourful flowers cascading down from them hung from the eaves. There were several cushioned loveseats on the outside veranda, where the ladies, known far and wide as the Vamps, could sit out and take in some fresh air. They could also entice the better-heeled customers passing by to drop in for a visit.

Lorenzo quickly stepped forward and held the gate open for them to pass through. Vinnie led the king through the courtyard and up onto the veranda to the front door. Without Lord Victor's assistance this time, the door was opened in response to the gang leader's light rapping on it.

"Vinnie, my precious love, get those lovely cheeks of yours in here! We've—"

The middle-aged but still quite attractive madam stopped in mid-sentence when she saw who was following the young gang leader inside.

"Well, I'll be a monkey's harlot! It's bloody-well-the-king-his-very-self! I … that is … welcome, your grace. Do come in. Oh, where are my manners?" she stammered.

"This is such an unexpected but welcome surprise", she added, as she effected a short curtsy while she reflexively touched a hand to her hair to check that it was in place. Rising up quickly, the madam cuffed Vinnie smartly across the back of his head. "A lady needs proper notice when important guests are coming to call. How's a girl to know to look her best?" she stated, smiling sweetly at the king but then giving the young gang leader a look that showed her displeasure with him.

Lord Victor laughed. "Now, now my dear lady—?"

"Victoria, milord," Vinnie said.

"Ah, Victoria. That's an elegant and perfect name for such a becoming woman—and close to my own heart. Did your mother name you after me, by chance?" Victor asked, as he took her hand and brought it to his lips.

"No, milord," the flustered madam answered. A seldom felt blush came to her cheeks. "I'm a touch too old for that. Perhaps it was after your late father."

"Nonsense," Victor replied, gallantly. "At most, you're an early summer flower. And if you look this dazzling without any special effort, then I don't know if my poor heart could take seeing you at your finest."

The king smiled warmly and then indicated the young gang leader with a nod of his head in Vinnie's direction. "And in all fairness to the lad here," he added, "Vinnie wasn't properly advised of my intentions to visit, either. I trust we're not intruding."

"Of course not, milord, you're most welcome. And, I seriously doubt that this old girl could pose a threat to your heart's health, though there was a time … when I was a tad younger," she said, with a smile at the king's obvious blandishment. "Still, it's always nice to hear a little flattery."

Victor smiled graciously and placed her hand in the crook of his elbow, and then escorted her through the foyer.

"Now, why don't you show me around your premises? I'm told you run an excellent establishment here. We were just discussing how important it is that we show visitors to Port Lupus a memorable time."

Vinnie let them walk on ahead briefly, wondering how the king could be so gracious and courteous after having killed a man only a short time ago. It was like he'd already forgotten the event. The gang leader shook his head to rid himself of the image and then indicated that the Ohs should fan out and take up appropriate positions to cover all parts of the bordello. He elected to remain downstairs, while the house madam escorted Lord Victor up the stairs to view the upper level. He would check out the main lounge personally. He hoped the break would give him a chance to recover his senses.

Entering the lounge, he could see that business was good after all. Perhaps, in the aftermath of the short-lived storm, there was an increased need for companionship. Of course, having a few new ships in port, with their respective crews of female-deprived seamen, was never bad for business either.

Vinnie evaluated the room. He looked for both the potential for profit and the potential for trouble. When men took to spending their hard-earned money in the company of easy women and hard spirits, it could be a volatile mix.

Like tonight, he sensed. *There's electricity in the air. Maybe it's left over from the storm, or maybe I'm still in a daze from the events of the evening.*

In either case, Vinnie became more alert as he took in the crowded room.

As he had discussed with Lord Victor, this newly improved bordello had been mostly Woodrow's idea. The castle keeper had been right in all regards. The place was a goldmine. At the end of the main room, there was a stage and a sunken pit area where the musicians played. The ladies of the house would take turns singing and dancing seductively, or the Vamps would take to the stage as a group and put on entertaining and usually provocative skits.

The stage was the focal point of the lounge. The tables in the centre of the room faced the stage. Scantily clad barmaids circulated the room continuously, making sure that the guests were well served with food, wine, ale, or their sweet company. There were several more secluded and dimly lit nooks around two of the outside walls, where customers and the ladies of their choice could get better acquainted. A man could pay for a more intimate, private dance, or if he'd found the Vamp of his dreams, he could make the financial arrangements for a room upstairs.

Vinnie knew the upper chambers featured well-filled feather mattress beds and clean sheets. There was no straw with fleas and bedbugs in this establishment. The rooms were kept this way by a full support staff. These tasks were overseen by the diligent madam, who saw to it that the guests were cleaned up too, if need be. On occasion, there were guests who needed a little encouragement in this regard. Madam Victoria was never shy about giving it.

Keeping things running according to the house rules was where both the bordello madam and the Multinational organization came in. It was Victoria's function as the madam to see to the girls who worked there. Having worked the profession herself, she knew when they had it good, and she made sure that the working girls appreciated their improved lifestyle.

The madam could kick proper ass if she felt one of the house Vamps wasn't living up to the expectations that her higher fees commanded. On the other hand, if a customer got out of line with one of them, she was apt to personally give them an attitude adjustment, often a well-placed kick to their most precious piece of male anatomy. Vinnie had hired her for both those exact qualities.

It was the Multinationals who provided any real muscle that was required to run such an establishment. Members from the various echelons of the gang performed the services of bartenders and bouncers. At the first sign of any trouble, there were at least six men in Vinnie's employ on hand and ready to step in to resolve matters.

Should it prove necessary, they could be quickly armed with short, fire-hardened truncheons, and there weren't very many obnoxious drunks that posed any serious threat to them. In the very rare instance that more enforcement than this was required, someone could be readily dispatched to the Ohs' headquarters. In short order, enough help would arrive to put down a full-scale riot, if need be.

It was up to the other support staff to see to all the more mundane kitchen, laundry, and cleanup functions. It was Woodrow's theory that if you kept a clean, friendly working environment, then the vamps would be happier in their occupation, and their customers more relaxed and at their ease. They would have a good time, and they'd spend their money accordingly.

And satisfied customers were repeat customers, Vinnie could almost hear Woodrow saying.

Well, he'd certainly proven to be right. The bordello was bringing in more revenue for everyone. The Vamps benefited more substantially than they ever could have dreamed of out on the street, or in one of the lesser establishments. It was also certainly a lot safer for them, as well as being a much more lively a place in which to ply their trade.

At Vinnie's encouragement, the castle keeper made periodic visits to the bordello, where he did the best he could to keep the ladies healthy and clean. *Judging from the way the Vamps treat him, he must be doing right by them,* Vinnie allowed.

Woodrow was a popular visitor, he knew. That was partly due to the fact that he came during the daylight hours with his medical kit and did not seek any of their services in return. Quite to the contrary, he often spent time just talking to them, listening to their problems, or sharing a laugh over some customer's sexual proclivities.

What impressed Vinnie most was that for a man of his position, the castle keeper always seemed to have time for anyone who needed it. He never treated the Vamps as if they were beneath his station. His interest was genuine, and not the least bit feigned. Vinnie knew that from personal experience. In his mind that made Woodrow a rare individual. It also made for a friendship that he valued beyond words.

It had been a while since Woodrow's last visit to Port Lupus. Vinnie knew the castle keeper left for the mountains every month, during the phase of the full moon. He also knew why, but it was something he kept to himself. He just wished that Woodrow would get back. He needed to talk to someone he could trust. Woodrow would understand his concerns about Lord Victor and his recent actions.

In the meantime, he had duties to perform, and his liege's needs to be seen to. Lord Victor's tour of the establishment had concluded and he and Victoria were coming into the lounge. The gang leader could see that his services were required, even now.

"Vinnie, darling," the madam called out. She waved him over to a table, from which she was already having the current occupants cleared away. She soothed their feelings with a drink on the house as she had them seated elsewhere.

The madam ordered glasses and a bottle of the best wine brought over as she perched herself beside Lord Victor. The barmaids practically fought for the privilege of delivering it. When the lucky winner rushed it to the table, she was just as quickly dismissed. Victoria personally poured for the three of them and then proffered a toast to the king's health.

Vinnie drank deeply, thinking it was perhaps time to start getting drunk. He decided he'd finish the job properly, after Victor's departure. He already felt a little better as the wine coursed its way down to heat his belly.

"Vinnie, would you be a dear and introduce the next show for me?" the madam asked sweetly. "I've got a rather important guest to attend to."

The gang leader smiled politely. "Of course, mademoiselle, it would be my pleasure. The show must go on, and we wouldn't want the natives to get restless, would we?"

It really wasn't an imposition. Lord Victor was in good company and being well entertained. The Ohs were in position and keeping a close lookout. It was probably a good idea to keep the crowd occupied. They'd all noticed the arrival of the imposing figure of the Varakovan king. In his flowing, shimmering black cape and surrounded by a protective entourage, he was a hard man to miss.

While the crowd were mostly visitors to the port town, and not likely to know exactly who he was, it wasn't difficult to see from the special treatment he received that he was someone important. They were several hushed conversations being carried on, and the gang leader had already seen where that had led to earlier tonight. He didn't need a repeat performance.

So, Vinnie gulped down the rest of his glass and left their company for the stage area. He ducked behind the curtains to see if everyone was in place and ready to commence the show. At his signal, a few moments later, the oil-lit lamps in the lounge were brought down a notch, and he stepped back out to greet the audience. He cued the band as he did so.

*   *   *

Vinnie
Gentlemen, sit back. Relax. Enjoy your whiskey and beer.
But I suggest that your attention should be directed up here.
Because tonight you're in for a special treat.
So sit back and relax while we turn up the heat!

I'm talking about … women! Not your sisters, or your mommies, or
even your sweet aunts.
I'm talking about beautiful young ladies.
The kind that you dream of … getting into their pants.
These are the tartiest of trollops, vixen, and tramps.
Gentlemen, let me introduce you to
The vivacious, the voluptuous … Victoria's Vamps!

The ladies of the bordello entered then and were received with a great deal of enthusiasm by the male audience. The lead Vamp came to a stop beside Vinnie.

Vinnie

Meet Vivian; she hails from the Valley of Veils.
At six foot two, she gives new meaning to a sailor's tall "tail."

Vivian

Hey there, sailor boy. It's just ten cents a dance.
But two pieces of silver, buys a whole night of romance!
If the price is right, I can be yours for the night.
And I'll ooh and I'll ooh la la.

Vamps

Yes, we'll ooh and we'll ooh la la.

Crowd

Ooh la la.

Vinnie

Here's sweet Veronica, she was the musical tutor for a king.
When she played his flute, you should've heard him sing!

Veronica

I'll spank your bottom, if that's your fantasy.
I can dress up, be anyone you want me to be.
I can tickle you with feathers or whip you with leather.

And, I'll ooh and I'll ooh la la.

Vamps
Yes, we'll ooh and we'll ooh la la

Crowd
Ooh la la.

Vinnie
And who can forget Valerie? She's such a charming lass.
In all of the kingdom, there's no finer piece of ass!

Valerie
Ahoy there, matey. I hear you've been sailing the seven seas.
How long's it been, since you've been with the likes of me?
I can bring you a whole lot of joy.
More than any ol' cabin boy!
And, I'll ooh and I'll ooh la la.

Vamps
Yes, we'll ooh and we'll ooh la la.

Crowd
Ooh la la.

Vinnie
Well, vi va Violetta! She's wearing a fortune in silk, lace, and bows.
She's got a head, for figuring out ways, to make your assets grow!

Violetta
Come and see me, if you'd like to get some rest.
You can nestle your head between these love-ly breasts.
Cause, money, without honey, just a waste!
Would you care for a taste?
And, I'll ooh and I'll ooh la la.

Vamps

Yes, we'll ooh and we'll ooh la la.

Crowd

Ooh la la.

Vinnie

And last, but certainly not least, there's the heavenly Venus.
And her twin sister Venus too.
Why settle for one? Imagine what these two can do for you!

Venus 1

If you're willing to part with a little more of your treasure ...

Venus 2

We'll be sure that you get at least double the pleasure.

Both

How's your heart?
How's your dart?
Are they both up ... for the part?
And, we'll ooh and we'll ooh la la.

Vamps

Yes, we'll ooh and we'll ooh la la.

Crowd

Ooh la la.

Vinnie

So gents ... what more can I say?
Two pieces of silver, it's such a small price to pay.
It's a small price to be paid, for the way you'll get laid.
It's a small price to be paid for the best in the trade.
Guaranteed to make you, ooh and ooh la la, you horny scamps!

Gentlemen! What more can I say? Except, give it up for
The vivacious, the voluptuous ... Victoria's Vamps!

The Vamps on stage performed a provocative bump-and-grind dance around Vinnie, while the musicians struck up another raunchy number. The crowd responded with hoots and hollers, and shouts of "ooh la la" while the barmaids went back to working the room of appreciative patrons.

His task completed, Vinnie extricated himself from the working ladies and left the stage to rejoin the madam and her escort.

"Honey, anytime you want to join us full time, we'd love to have you on board. You really know how to sell an introduction," Madam Victoria exclaimed, happily. "And, judging from the way the girls were draped all over you, I'd have to say they'd probably second the motion," she added, with a licentious and knowing smile.

Despite himself, Vinnie blushed but then laughed.

"As attractive an offer that is, I think I'll stick with my present duties, if it's all the same to you Victoria. There's far less chance of me getting into trouble that way. I'm afraid that there's more temptation here than even a saint could handle, let alone a rascal the likes of me."

"Honey, that's just nature's way of telling you to come around for a visit. Some of the new girls have been asking about you. You should come by for a visit—when you're not on the job, that is," the bordello madam said, winking.

Victor laughed appreciatively.

"Now there's an offer any young man would kill for. Every job should have such fringe benefits!"

"You could bring your friend along, too," the madam said saucily, nodding her head in Victor's direction. "Even a hard working king needs a little recreation now and then."

Vinnie's mind involuntarily flashed back to the night of the feast and to the king's idea of recreation. Victor, however, roared out loudly.

"Now, that's the most insightful—and delightful—observation that I've heard in quite some time. I do believe that I'll keep that invitation open for another occasion, my dear," he said charmingly.

The king rose from his chair, as he brought the matron's hand to his lips in a parting gesture.

"Now good lady, regretfully, we must be taking our leave. Other duties call us away. Alas, a king's work is never really done, is it?"

Victoria rose with the intention of accompanying her guest to the door. Unfortunately, as her chair was pushed back, it accidentally caused one of the barmaids passing by to catch her foot on one of the legs. The poor girl was unable to recover her balance in time to prevent her tray, and its full round of refreshments, from flying off her outstretched hand.

The drinks had been destined for the next table over. They arrived somewhat ahead of schedule, and somewhat unexpectedly, for the patrons who had placed the order. The tankards of ale landed almost perfectly in the centre of the table. Sadly, from there their momentum caused them to bounce rather spectacularly, showering their contents on the men of both that table and the one next to it.

In the dimly lit room, it was difficult to ascertain exactly what had occurred. Most of the men, now sodden with beer, had been sitting with their backs to the incident and their seats facing the stage. Having almost a dozen partially inebriated men all jump to their feet at the same time only added to the confusion. Curses flew, pushes became shoves, and shoves became punches thrown. In a matter of a few seconds, an accident had escalated into several fights.

One ship's first mate chose that moment to lash out at the barmaid who had inadvertently tripped. He sensed that she was the one to blame when he saw her picking herself up, and he roundly cursed her out. If that wasn't bad enough, the ship's officer then cuffed her hard across the back of the head, propelling her forward where she collided with the house madam.

Vinnie was the closest to the action and the first one to react. He exploded with rage. Seeing the first mate strike the helpless barmaid, released the pent-up emotions that he'd been bottling up since their walk with Lord Victor had turned sour. The gang leader roared loudly and then promptly drove a fist into the man's face.

The first mate tumbled backwards, upsetting the table behind him in the process. This fresh disturbance caused the men who were already skirmishing there to spread their quarrel outward, like the ripples in a pond when a rock is thrown into it.

Seeing Vinnie wading into the ranks of the patrons with his fists flying brought a small smile of satisfaction to Lord Victor's face. It was actually a relief to see the young gang leader leap into action. The king had been starting to get concerned about him. He'd noticed that Vinnie wasn't acting quite like himself lately, but didn't know what to attribute it to.

Well, he thought, *there's nothing like going into battle to heat up the blood.*

Lord Victor decided to sit this one out. He deemed it unseemly for a king to get involved in a mere whorehouse brawl, even if it was a first-class establishment. Besides, it would give him the opportunity to see how his underlings performed in an unexpected situation. He would not be disappointed. While the Varakovan king assisted the two women from the impromptu battlefield, the Ohs moved in quickly from their respective positions around the lounge.

As Vinnie's second-in-command, Lorenzo immediately took charge. He signalled for two of the muscular, multinational bouncers to take up guard positions where Lord Victor, Victoria and the barmaid stood watching the action from the foyer. The king's protection was still their primary responsibility, after all.

While the other Vamps and barmaids fled the chaos for the relative safety of the stage, Lorenzo directed Sergio, Filippo, Eduardo, and the other Ohs into the fray. The gang members wasted no time in clearing a path to the side of their leader, where Vinnie stood trading blows with two more of the senior crewmen at the same time.

The Ohs' lieutenant was forced to stay at the fringes of the fight to assess developments, despite his personal preference to join in the fracas and lend a helping fist. He was better trained than that, however. Since Vinnie was caught up in the events of the moment, it fell to him to see that their men either got the situation under control or received further assistance.

Lorenzo assessed the situation with a cool head, opting to keep the other bouncers and the bartenders in reserve to give Vinnie and the Ohs room to manoeuvre. This also gave him more options as to where to disperse them if things got worse.

As it turned out, this wouldn't prove necessary. The ship's first mate still hadn't moved from where he'd dropped. His bloody face was pressed into the floorboards. When he finally came to, he'd be spitting out a few of his teeth.

Meanwhile, the other ship's officers in the centre of the ruckus had banded together in their struggle with the Ohs' leader but found their hands were full trying to defend against his attack. The young man's blows were lightning fast and delivered with punishing force.

By the time the Ohs reached his side, Vinnie had dropped another of his opponents with a hard left cross. At that point, Sergio grabbed up two of the officers by the back of the collars and slammed their heads together. Hearing that sickening thud and watching as their shipmates drop to the floor unconscious was enough to take the fight out of the others still standing.

The other Ohs then simply worked their way outwards to the perimeter of the lounge, subduing the combatants in the smaller skirmishes as they went. Almost as quickly as it had flared up, the mini-riot was brought to an end, leaving a large number of men standing there and looking sheepishly about the room. Most of them were still unaware of what had actually set off the disturbance.

That was when Victoria decided it was time to take charge of matters. The house madam strode back into the lounge and started barking out orders.

"All right you bunch of scurvy-ridden, lowlife ship rats, enough is enough! This isn't some flea-infested flophouse," she proclaimed as she glared about the room. "Pick up your friends, get these tables and chairs straightened away, grab some mops from behind the bar, and let's get this place cleaned up. Don't make me ask twice, people!"

Vamps, bartenders, barmaids, and patrons alike moved on her command. Although the senior ship officers were paying customers, they were also lifetime sailors who were used to taking orders. They willing complied, partly from not wanting to be singled out by the angry mistress of the house and partly because they didn't want to get kicked out. A few of their shipmates might be a little worse off, but they'd come here to drink heartily, dance with a pretty lady, and get laid. That mission hadn't been fully accomplished yet.

Lord Victor stepped into the lounge as Vinnie made his way back.

"God, but I love a strong woman!" the king roared, with a hearty laugh. "Gentlemen! Do a good job putting Victoria's house back in order, and if she approves of your work, the next round of drinks is on me. Let it be my personal welcome to Port Lupus and Varakov, and to this fine establishment. Enjoy the hospitality, and enjoy the many delights that are provided by the lovely ladies of the house."

Victor clutched his shimmering black cape in one hand and then bowed to the madam, with the other. His offer of a free drink was just the proper tonic to put everyone's mood back on the right track. The patrons cheered their acceptance of his offer and in their mutual agreement as to attributes that the Vamps possessed.

"I trust that you'll stand me credit for the drinks until Woodrow comes to settle our accounts?" Lord Victor asked with a smile. "I'm afraid that I've come by without any currency on my person."

"I think that the king's treasury can stand good for it," Madam Victoria remarked jovially.

She accompanied them to the door. Once there, she took Vinnie's scuffed up face in one hand and turned it from side to side. She clucked her tongue disapprovingly.

"Lad, you'll have to take better care. Such a pretty face! I'd hate to see you get it all busted up. You should leave the fighting to the bouncers. That's why we let them grow such big muscles," she said, laughing lightly. "But, thank you just the same. That was very gallant of you," she added, as she raised herself to her toes and kissed his cheek.

"Did you hear that Vinnie?" Lord Victor stated, and then laughed again. "Now you're gallant. If I'm not careful, she's going to steal you away from me, yet. We had best take our leave now, before she makes you an offer that I couldn't possibly begin to match—if you catch my drift."

Vinnie returned the laugh. "I agree wholeheartedly, milord. There are far too many distractions here, lovely as they may be."

"And, you sire," the madam said, turning to the king. "It was a privilege making your acquaintance." Her curtsy perhaps lacked the trained perfection of a lady at court, but it was all the nicer for its sincerity. "We'd be pleased to have you return when other commitments aren't going to make you rush off so early," she said, with a bold wink.

"Madam, rest assured, I'll be consulting my appointments calendar first thing in the morning," Lord Victor replied, as he took her hand to his lips. "Until then, my Vic-tor-ia."

Her knees actually felt weak. The king's eyes were mesmerizing, and the way her name rolled of his lips was so warmly seductive. It stirred something in her that hadn't been stirred in many years. The madam barely managed to step aside to allow her guests to take their leave.

*   *   *

August 3, 1461
Port Lupus, Varakov

It was just past midnight as Lord Victor, Vinnie, Lorenzo, and the rest of the Ohs' entourage took to the streets again and then to the lanes that wound through the dockyards towards their next destination for the evening. They walked in silence, content to just breathe in the late night air and clear their heads.

The night air around the seaport wharves wasn't exactly fresh. The salt breeze was filled with a jumble of conflicting odours, each with their particular pungent essence. The smell of gutted fish and the thick stench of hops from one of the breweries were the most prominent.

The king took notice of a few of the seedier lanes they passed by, and some of the less "classy" trades of the night that were carried out there. The whores at work were far less attractive, or perhaps just long past their primes. Women didn't particularly age well in that line of business. Nonetheless, there was a steady demand for these less expensive services, as well.

In due course, they approached the waterfront saloon, whose weathered sign proclaimed it to be the Hangman's Tavern. They could see Barozzi and several of his men loitering outside, obviously waiting for them. This didn't particularly sit well with Vinnie. He could feel the hair on the back of his neck bristle, and his stomach tightened into a fiery knot. The gang leader couldn't help but wonder what else Lord Victor was up to tonight.

If it involved Barozzi, it didn't bode well, he thought.

Nor, did he like the fact that there was something going on in his town and he had no inkling of what it was.

Stepping up onto the planks of the boardwalk that kept the tavern's entrance dry in times of inclement weather, Vinnie brushed aside one of the raiders, who deliberately stood in his path. He wasn't about to tolerate any insolence from these men-for-hire. This town belonged to the Ohs, not the foreign mercenaries.

His men obviously felt the same way. In a few heartbeats, they'd stepped forward, placing two of their number close by each one of Barozzi's raiders. Reluctantly, the mercenaries backed off. They weren't about to take a chance of starting a fight here. This wasn't their turf, and the odds were not in their favour. They were content to merely establish their presence there, on Barozzi's behalf.

"Gentlemen! Put away your dicks," Victor said, in a tone that brooked no argument. He stepped up onto the boardwalk with his shimmering cape flaring out behind him. No one offered an argument.

"You're all comrades here!" the king added sternly. "You're all on the same side—*my* side, in case any of you have lost sight of that fact."

"Of course, milord," Vinnie said agreeably, but he gave the offending raider a stare that spoke volumes, and it wasn't about camaraderie.

Barozzi gave his obeisance, as well. He waved his raiders off, signaling for them to wait for him across the street, while they went inside. Vinnie's men took up their vacated positions on the boardwalk, and both groups kept a wary eye on each other. Lord Victor and Barozzi entered the establishment, with Vinnie, Lorenzo and Sergio following behind them.

Inside the Hangman's Tavern, it was almost as dark as it was outside on the night street. Only a few dimly lit lanterns hung about the place. The mood of the room could be as dark too. Barozzi led them to the bar owner's private booth in the back, where the captain of one the ships in port waited with drink in hand.

The captain got clumsily to his feet at their approach and gave them a stiff bow. Barozzi had obviously warned the man beforehand to show some respect when the king arrived. Strangely enough, it was Lord Victor who made the introductions.

"Captain Galick, I presume. May I introduce Vinnie and some of his men? They usually tend to all matters in Port Lupus on my behest." This last part seemed to be said more for Barozzi's benefit, than the ship's captain.

The mercenary must have caught the implication, for he dipped his head as if conceding the point. He had the good sense to know that this wasn't the time or place for a pissing contest with the young gang leader.

"My name is Lord Victor. You could say that I'm your host here in Varakov," the king said. "Barozzi tells me you have the cargo on board that your employers wrote me about. If that's the case, I thought that we should meet personally."

"As milord wishes. I'm at yer disposal, good sire of Varakov," Captain Galick intoned. "If the price be right, that is."

He added this with a toast of his mug and then calmly retook his seat.

His point was made. King or no king, it was money that talked when you had precious cargo.

Victor nodded his understanding. He was slightly bemused, even. He then turned to the gang leader and his men.

"I think that concludes our time together for tonight, Vinnie. Thank you for a refreshing tour of the town," he said, "and for the use of the boots. I'll see to it that they're cleaned and returned."

Now it was the gang leader's turn to be reminded that he and his men had their limitations also. This was indeed their home turf, but they served there at Lord Victor's discretion.

"Goodnight then, milord," Vinnie responded. "I've no doubt that I'm leaving you in Barozzi's responsible hands." His nod towards the mercenary conveyed his meaning rather well.

The gang leader made for the door, followed in turn by the Ohs. On the way out, he gave the "eyes-open" sign to several of the working staff, who nodded in return. The gang's leadership regrouped with their men stationed outside. They then departed for their headquarters, but not before wagging a few fingers in the direction of the raiders hanging out across the street.

The gang leader and the other Ohs might be leaving now, but back inside the tavern, the Multinationals were well represented, just as they were in every saloon, flophouse, and bordello in town. His men would keep an eye on things for Vinnie and that was the best that he could do for the moment. He knew what Lord Victor and mercenaries the like of Barozzi were capable of. It was only common sense for him to have vigilant eyes kept on them.

That cautionary approach might one day make all the difference between life and death.

*   *   *

"'Tis a valuable cargo, my friends," the ship's captain remarked gruffly as he scarfed down his meal. Even the cheap fare of the seedy tavern was a welcome repast after weeks of ship's biscuits and salted beef. The captain was enjoying the bartering as well. Bartering came naturally to him. He'd been at it long enough. "There's short supply and I know plenty of other's who'd pay a pretty piece in silver for this cargo. Throw in a special bonus too, they likely would," he added, looking for every edge he could gain.

"Our offer is a good one, captain. You know it, and so do I," Lord Victor informed him icily. "I won't sit here and bargain with you like some three-penny whore."

He stood to take his leave, his shimmering cape draped behind his back. He looked down on the ship's captain. "I will, however, throw in a bonus for you," the Varakovan king offered. "I trust that it will serve to bring this business arrangement to a conclusion."

Without even having heard what the bonus was to be, the ship's captain knew that he was going to accept it. He knew it when, beneath Lord Victor's icy glare, he'd felt his genitalia shrink. The Varakovan king doubtlessly had many men like this Barozzi in his employ, and he wouldn't hesitate to use them.

Even if he somehow managed to weigh anchor and sail, the reprieve would be short lived. Sooner or later, this Barozzi, or someone of his ilk, would surely come looking for him. Assassins weren't the kind of enemies you wanted to make if you wanted to keep on breathing.

"We have some women visiting from outside of my realm. There are about a dozen of them. Perhaps it's time that they moved on," Lord Victor suggested. "Perhaps they should go on a nice long ocean voyage. I would think that they'd fetch a rather handsome price if they were to sadly wind up on some auction block. I'm sure that some wealthy prince in one of your more exotic ports of call would treasure such a cargo," the king added.

The captain blinked his eyelids. This was even better than he'd hoped for. In about a month's sailing time, he'd be in just the right port for such a commodity. He'd seen the demand for foreign women there. It was conceivable that he could get half again what he'd been offered for his cargo. He wouldn't have to share that take with his employers either.

"Done," he agreed quickly.

Victor smiled. It was a cold smile just the same. "Not quite so fast, Captain Galick. If your cargo performs as well as claimed, then I'm going to be in need of more than what you presently have aboard your ship. I want you to obtain them for me. You'll be properly compensated for your efforts."

"There's a quite the waiting list, milord. I told you, the supply is limited," the ship's captain warned again.

"I'm sure. But then, so are good customers, especially ones who value your company as much as we do. Perhaps you could use your bonus to improve our position on that list. You secure more such cargo for me, and I will, in turn, obtain more bonuses for you," Victor proposed. "So, do we have an understanding?" he asked, with a hard glint in his icy blue eyes.

"Aye, milord," the weathered sea captain responded. He offered his hand on it. "I believe we do."

Victor ignored the proffered hand. He was the king, after all.

CHAPTER 13

DUTIES TO THE KINGDOM

August 3, 1461
Woodrow's estate, Varakov

UPON THEIR RETURN THE prior evening, the castle keeper had been attended to by his aide, Simon, and by Micale and Nessa, his two manor stewards. They'd prepared a wholesome evening repast. The Medinian youth had declined joining them, claiming that he was worn out from their trip and just wanted to get some much needed sleep.

Woodrow had suspected that the youth wasn't in the mood to meet new people or to share a meal and conversation. He'd insisted on checking Willie's leg first and redressing the healing wound, however. Then he'd shown him to his sleeping quarters, taking along with a mug of his herbal brew that he'd had prepared.

The meal had been an uncommonly quiet one. Perhaps his staff had sensed his own weariness. Nevertheless, for a period of time afterwards, he'd then sat up talking with Simon and Micale, getting caught up on affairs in Varakov. Simon had reported on the events at the castle, which had transpired in his absence. This had entailed events from the time of Simon's reporting to Lord Victor, through the king's feast, and of the subsequent slaughter of the Skolish male prisoners.

The reports Woodrow received had been as concisely detailed, as they'd been gruesome to hear. When Simon had finally finished, Woodrow had gladly gone to find his bed. His mind had started reeling from the impact of Simon's report, and he'd been exhausted from their long trip. His body had protested the past week's exertions that he'd subjected it to.

A good night's sleep and a hot morning bath had helped ease the aches somewhat. He was looking forward to filling his belly again with a hearty breakfast. He could smell the aromas emanating from the kitchen as he made his way into the dining area. It was a welcoming blend of delicious scents.

"Good morning, Woodrow," Simon said, greeting him as he entered the dining alcove. Except for their new guest, the castle keeper was the last to rise, although it was still dark outside the window. "We've got a pretty full schedule," his aide added. "I don't think I'll get back up to Sanctuary until the month's end. If I'm not more caring, I think my wife might soon decide that she can live without me being underfoot, period."

"It's a wonder all women don't come to realize that," Woodrow said with an easy laugh. "If we can get caught up, maybe you can get away a week earlier and try to make it up to her. In the meantime, though, I'd like your help getting the lad squared away."

"Of course. If you'll excuse me for a moment, I'll see if they're ready with the meal," his lieutenant said and then withdrew to the kitchen.

This humble man was his most trusted confidant and valued aide. Only Brutus had been Woodrow's loyal comrade for a longer period. The castle keeper had great respect for Simon. Over the years he had come to rely on him to handle a great many of the demands of both Varakov and Sanctuary.

As Simon took his leave, the Medinian youth entered the dining hall on his crutches, coming from his sleeping quarters. Doubtlessly, he was following his nose there, too. Woodrow greeted him, but received only a nonchalant grunt in return for his efforts.

"If I know my staff, you can be assured that the food will stick to your ribs and see you through the day," he remarked. "Might I suggest that after you've eaten, you take advantage of a hot bath? I just did myself. You'll find it does wonders. Just be careful with your leg."

"A hot bath? Why? I got cleaned up already when we were at the outpost station," Willie protested.

"You're a still a bit ripe," Woodrow observed. "You smell like the horses we've been riding."

"I like the smell! I worked on a farm, or at least I did until you and your kind came along," the youth responded smartly.

"Touché," the castle keeper acknowledged. "However, regardless of the circumstances, you are here now, and you're a guest in my home. I will expect you to act accordingly."

He held his hand up to curtail the youth from responding.

"Whether you're a guest of your own choice or not," he added, anticipating his objection. "There are standards of behaviour to be upheld, both here and certainly within the castle confines. Lord Victor has decreed that you will be my ward during your stay with us. So, while you are here, you will be expected to live up to those standards."

Woodrow paused for a moment. He decided that it was time for them to come to an understanding.

"Willie, we need to call a truce," he proposed. "If you co-operate and learn what we have to teach you over the next two lunar months, then I will see to it that you are free to go any place of your own choosing. You have my word on that."

"Even if that's back to Medinia?" the youth challenged him.

"You'll come to realize that there's no going back home, Willie," the castle keeper said. "But, yes. If that's what you still want, I'll see that you get there as soon as it's possible."

"What's that supposed to mean? I'm free to go in two months, but not back to my home, if you decide it's not possible?" Willie pressed him, sarcastically.

The castle keeper kept his temper in check, but he informed the youth that there were constraints beyond his control.

"We live in Varakov under the good graces of Lord Victor, Willie. Only our liege decides who gets passage through the gap fortress. Only if the king deems it permissible, can you be allowed through the gates. If that remains your choice, I will appeal to him to allow you to make that journey. I can do no better than that," Woodrow vowed.

Willie's only response was a nonverbal one. His gesture was clear enough in its meaning.

Woodrow smiled grimly at the youth's stubborn impertinence. That strength of will could stand him in good stead through his life ... or, it could get him killed one day.

"As I have said, Willie, when the time comes, you won't want to go back home. You may still want to leave here, but you have to trust me when I say that you won't want to return to the farm in Medinia. It can't ever be ... the way that it was," he added, somewhat sadly.

Before the youth could question that further, Simon returned in the company of the manor's two attendants. Willie had seen them only briefly the night before, just prior to going to bed, where he had remained awake for most of the night tossing and turning. As he had understood from Woodrow, the married couple had ties to the group that everyone called the Oddities. Perhaps, they had some family member there. In any event, they were in Woodrow's employ, and he'd told him that they helped see to the needs of that community. Sanctuary, it seemed, was the common bond that linked them all together.

The two stewards came in carrying several platters of warm porridge, a rasher of bacon, bread and jams, and assorted fruits in a bowl. Willie watched as they set them on the headboard and then stacked plates and cutlery on the oaken table. Everyone could serve themselves, according to their individual appetites.

"So, am I in the company of more members of the Pack, here? Do all you folks run around howling at the moon too?" Willie queried, more than a little impudently.

Woodrow sighed.

"Lesson number-one, lad. Wolves don't howl at the moon. That's an old wives' tale," the castle keeper informed him.

He turned to the others.

"My friends, this insolent and ignorant young man is straight off a farm in Medinia," Woodrow said. "His name is Willie. For the next couple of months he's going to become our group project, as it were. We're going to bathe him outside, and inside, and see if we can't get some of the dirt out of his ears—and his brain-pan."

He saw the look the youth sent his way but chose to ignore it.

"Willie, this is Simon," he said, continuing the introductions. "And, yes, Simon is a valued member of the Pack. He is in fact, its beta human male, which is both an achievement and a responsibility that you will one day come to appreciate better. He is also my trusted and good friend," Woodrow added. "When you address him, you will address him with respect in your tone of voice. When he tells you something, you would be wise to listen to him with the same due respect. You'll find that his council comes from years of acquired wisdom that is far beyond your own. You might actually learn something of value—if you allow yourself to."

The castle keeper went on with the introductions without waiting for the youth to comment.

"Micale and Nessa are also my very good friends. They serve as my stewards, and they're in charge of keeping both the manor, and Sanctuary, in good working order. But, no, they're not members of the Pack," he added, in answer to the youth's prior comment. "I must say, however, if you give them any further grief and disrespect, I shall personally put my boot so far up your ass you'll be tasting leather."

"Woodrow! You're just scaring the young man," Nessa admonished him. "I declare, sometimes you men have all the compassion of stones and mortar. Can't you see what a turmoil he's been put through? Well, you can just talk to him after he's had something to eat, gotten bathed, and I've seen to that wounded leg myself."

"Thanks for the support, but I'm not hungry," Willie declared with an insolent stubbornness. "And I can take care of myself, pumpkin."

Nessa stood there for a moment, as if not quite believing her ears. Her temper flared up then.

"If you ever call me pumpkin again, it'll be my boot that'll be buried up your arse, sonny boy. Now, let's you and I fix a couple of plates of this lovely food that I got up so early to prepare. Then we'll take it up to your room and have a look at that leg. And then you can take that bath. And your reply would be, 'Yes, ma'am,'" she instructed him.

"Yes, ma'am," the youth conceded, if begrudgingly. He was reminded that it was Mrs. Smythe who had run their Medinian household, and he'd never dared to contradict her, either.

"Oh, oh, you're in for it now," Woodrow said with a chuckle.

"And, don't you even get me started with you, Mister Castle Keeper," she added with a quick glare.

"Yes, ma'am," Woodrow acknowledged meekly, much to the amusement of the other two men in his employ.

"Now you see what I have to put up with every day," Micale observed wryly.

"What *you* have to put up with?" Nessa retorted sharply. "Don't forget whose bed you like to share, my sweet."

"Yes, ma'am!" Micale said, smartly. He leaned over and gave her a quick kiss. "And I would have it no other way, my love."

With a disbelieving cluck of her tongue, Nessa went about filling two plates of food for her and Willie. When she was satisfied that the youth wouldn't go hungry, she hustled him out of the room and back to his quarters. She followed along with the food as the youth pegged along ahead of her.

While she removed the bandages from his leg, Willie attacked the plate of food that Nessa had insisted he eat. He ate with gusto and then thanked her sincerely. He'd decided to forgo offending the lady of the manor any further. Despite her feigned gruff manner, he found her touch was gentle and caring as she handled his leg. He was reminded, that like the Oddities up in Sanctuary, this woman wasn't responsible for any of the ills that had befallen him.

Willie was starting to realize that there wasn't anything to be gained by being nasty to people not responsible for his predicament. Besides, it really wasn't in his nature to be like that. *Except that I'm hurting, and I'm angry too! I've got every right to be put off with Woodrow, Simon and their kind!*

If he was honest with himself, he was scared and far from home. Here in Varakov, he found himself in an elegant manor, the likes of which he'd never even been close to before let alone stayed inside. A little over a week ago, a remote Medinian freeman's farm had been his whole world. The way it was looking now, he was soon going to see the inside of a castle and the court of a real king. He was slowly realizing that he could use some friends in this foreign land. It wouldn't hurt to have someone that he could talk to, and who'd perhaps understand what he was going through.

"How's the leg feeling?" Nessa asked. She was happy to see that he'd changed his mind about eating the meal she'd prepared.

"Not bad, really," he replied. "It gets a little stiff and sore as the day goes on, but Woodrow's been changing the bandages and putting on that salve concoction of his. I think it's healing pretty quickly for such a bad bite."

The youth paused, staring down at the raw wound.

"That's a big part of all this, isn't it?" he surmised. "My being bitten, that is. They think I've got … whatever it is they have … don't they? That's why my leg's healing so fast. Woodrow said my blood is poisoned, the same as his is."

"I'd have to say that's about the size of it, Willie," Nessa replied. "In the Pack, the wolves and the humans, they all have the same moon-sickness. I'm not sure exactly why that is or how they each came to contract it. Woodrow and Simon know a lot more about it than I do. I'm sure they'll be explaining it to you when the time is right."

"I think Woodrow's wanted to, but I haven't given him much of a chance. You could say I've been a little hostile towards him," Willie admitted with a grim smile. "Or you might say that it's been a really bad week, and I just can't help but blame him for causing it."

"Well, lad, I'm not about to defend actions, which I don't know the causes of," Nessa stated. "I will tell you this, though, for a man who carries so much responsibility on his shoulders, I've never met a more decent person than the castle keeper."

She saw the look of scepticism that came to his face.

"I know you might not want to hear things like that just now, but they need saying, nonetheless. I think you'll discover that for yourself one day," she asserted.

"You're not the first one to tell me that. I met the Old Man of the Oddities, as well as a young blind girl. They both told me I should be patient and to try to make the most of this change in my fate."

"Simon told us that Woodrow would likely stop in at the Oddities' village on the way here. So, you've met Melanie, have you?" Nessa asked.

"Yes, that's her. She's quite amazing, isn't she?" he remarked.

"Indeed she is," Nessa confirmed. "Indeed she is."

"I think she knew … that I might have the sickness," he stated. "She told me that she was a witch. I don't know the truth about any of that, but she's very sensitive to these types of things, isn't she?" There was still that touch of disbelief in his voice, an underlying hope that this would all turn out to be a mistake of some sort.

"Yes she is, Willie," Nessa said. "She has a natural affinity for seeing what people with eyesight can't."

He could have done without that. It certainly wasn't the answer he'd been hoping for.

"Now it's time for you to take that bath," the lady of the manor stated.

He could have done without that, as well.

*   *   *

The morning sun would soon show itself from over the Euralene Mountains. The castle keeper was impatient to be on his way, but he needed to discuss the day's agenda with his staff. He also wanted another word with the youth before he departed.

"I have to be returning to my castle duties, Willie," Woodrow said, greeting the youth as he pegged his way back into the room following his bath. "There are still a few things we need to go over before I leave. Please sit for a moment," the castle keeper added, indicating the chair next to him. "I take it from Nessa that you've eaten? Good. Beginning tomorrow, you'll be welcome to join the kitchen detail. You can pitch in your culinary talents. Everyone does. It makes for a more interesting fare that way."

"Does that include you, sire?" the youth asked rudely. "Or is the 'master of the manor' above all that? Does the castle keeper get his breakfast buns served to him each morning?" The youth obviously hadn't lost his sarcastic wit, or his attitude.

"Yes, for your information, I do pitch in on occasion," Woodrow replied. "I like to cook, actually. You were doubtlessly able to tell from this morning's fare that my many talents in the kitchen were sorely missed."

"Perhaps if you had gotten up with the rest of us, we could have been blessed with your expertise," Nessa remarked, coming in from the hallway with a fresh platter of biscuits and jams.

"I can see where our young guest needed his rest," she added, "but perhaps if you hadn't stayed up half the night yakking with Simon and my Micale, we all would have gotten a little more sleep."

"Yakking? Is that what Micale told you? I think that you'd better check on his whereabouts last night, Nessa, my dear. I myself was in bed fast asleep," Woodrow suggested innocently.

"Are you trying to get me into trouble, Woodrow? I declare, you know very well that only the most important of matters could ever keep me away from this angel of mine!" Micale asserted.

He manoeuvred his way around the table to his wife's side.

"My angel, I already told you that I was sorry," he added contritely.

"An angel, am I? Well, if you expect to be visiting heaven anytime soon, you had best be getting that sorry butt of yours to bed while I'm still in the mood," Nessa said suggestively. She then planted a kiss on her husband's lips.

Even the freshly scrubbed Medinian youth joined in the laughter that followed. That was how Simon found them as he re-entered the dining room.

"It's good to see everyone playing nice," he remarked. "Since you're all in such good spirits, perhaps we should just forget about the work that's been backing up in your absence."

He ducked the roll, which the castle keeper threw at him.

"Unfortunately, you're right. Duty calls and I have to get to the castle. Before I go, however, we should take a minute and try to straighten out whatever mess you people have made of things while Willie and I were busy trekking across the countryside," Woodrow declared lightly.

The biscuit that Nessa threw bounced off the back of his head with a thud. The castle keeper shook his head in mock disgust and then moaned about the lack of proper respect he was being shown.

They finally settled down to discuss the day's agenda. Woodrow was quickly and efficiently brought up to date. Simon gave him a succinct recap of which petitioners and supplicants were appearing to have their cases heard by the royal court. Micale then apprised him of the manor and estate's needs.

For his part, Willie kept quiet and ate another of the warm biscuits. He could relate to most of the issues that Micale spoke of, but as he listened to Simon and Woodrow talk over the details of the castle's agenda, he could barely make sense of what they discussed. The youth only grasped the fact that life in the king's court was a complex array of affairs. He was too intimidated, however, to ask questions, which would have only further demonstrated his ignorance.

With the schedule update now finished, it was time for Woodrow to be leaving for the castle. He knew that Lord Victor would be demanding much of his attention in the week ahead, so other matters were delegated to his aide and stewards. Micale and Nessa would see to the duties of the manor. They would also manage the sending of supplies and horses to the outpost. The more remote hunting lodges needed to be stocked up, as well. These lodges would be seeing more activity when the fall hunting season began. Lord Victor was known to close court for about a month at that time of year. While the crops of the countryside were being gathered, the king often liked to hunt and to roam about his kingdom.

Simon accepted the task of seeing that Willie's education began. The youth wasn't consulted on the matter. The two of them would start with a tour of the walled town that supported the castle. The Mesa-of-the-Moon was home to a variety of businesses, trades, and military activities. These were activities that needed to be understood if the youth was going to live and work in their employ.

They would then pay a visit to the castle grounds, where Simon would relate some of its history and its workings and protocols. When the youth had a clearer appreciation of them, they would enter the castle itself for a brief visit.

Woodrow then turned his attention to the Medinian youth.

"You, young man, are about to start on a grand new adventure. Simon will give you the benefit of his position and years of experience. He will take you places and show you things that would normally be beyond your station. As I told you earlier, this is a privilege that is being extended to you—and an imposition on him. I'd like your word that you'll mind your tongue and show him the proper respect."

The youth put down the biscuit that he'd been spreading jam on and looked the castle keeper in the eye.

"I'll give you my word. I'll perform whatever menial duties you ask of me, and I'll learn whatever it is you wish to teach me," he replied, solemnly, "but I'll expect you to honour your pledge too. You said in two cycles of the full moon, I'd be free to go. I intend on returning home then, despite what you say. Medinia is my home, and that's where I intend to go."

Woodrow sighed at the youth's stubborn will.

"So be it," he agreed. He accepted Willie's hand and they sealed the pact with a firm handshake.

*   *   *

August 3, 1461
Dumas, Medinia

"Good morning, Father," Lady Hillary Michelle said, greeting the king. "I trust you slept well."

"Indeed I did, daughter!" the Medinian king replied. The king was in his early fifties and his hair and cropped beard were more grey than black now. His eyes showed a more youthful zest, though, as he smiled up at his eldest child when she entered the dining hall.

"I'm glad you could join me, dear. That sister of yours is already out on a morning ride. I swear she spends more time in the saddle than most of my knights."

"She's a better rider than most of them too," Hillary Michelle declared. She was proud of her younger sister. Sarah Elizabeth's love of the outdoors was well known. She took to horses and swordplay and to the other rough and tumble activities that the son of a king might more be expected to pursue.

"Well, let her enjoy it while she can," her father said casually. "She'll reach womanhood soon enough, I suppose."

"Father, really!" Hillary Michelle scolded him. "Just because she'll soon be a woman does not mean she must abandon the things she loves."

"Well, what worthy baron or knight is going to want a wife that can outride him—and most likely outfight him, as well? She should be spending more time learning about court etiquette and dressing in silks and velvets like a proper young woman."

"Well, it hasn't been for lack of trying," his daughter replied. "Since Mother passed on, she's had every lady at court try to take her under their wing. We think they do it so that they can endear themselves to you. She just doesn't want her mother replaced—and quite frankly, neither do I."

"We'd rather you simply carry on with whichever court harlot avails herself to you. Just don't marry the strumpet," the princess added with a mischievous smile.

"Daughter! Sometimes I can't believe the things that come out of that mouth," her father said sternly. "What would your mother have said?"

The king couldn't maintain his outraged facade for long, however. His face broke out in a grin at the look of innocence that his daughter conjured up for him.

"But you may have a point," he conceded. "Have you seen the Lady Dauphine? She's up here visiting from the southern plateau. She's positively a country bumpkin. But what a body she has! A man could die happy ploughing that field!"

"Father, *really*!" Hillary Michelle exclaimed. Now it was her turn to feign shock. "Do you eat with that mouth? What would mother have said?"

It was a game that they'd played regularly on her mother when she was a little girl. Over breakfast, Hillary Michelle and her father would see who could slip the most outrageous comment into the conversation. After all, the lives of those who attended the king's court made for lively discussions that were often rampant with gossip about various indiscretions.

Her mother would always feign shock at the very idea of such talk at the breakfast table. Until the moment when she pointed a scolding finger at one of them, and on cue they'd laugh, knowing that a winner had just been declared.

"Ah, my child, you look more like her every day," King Renaud said. "You'll soon be the same age that she was when I won her over for my own. She'd be so proud of you and of the way you've taken over for her at court these many years now."

The king's wife had died giving birth to a male royal heir. Sadly, the infant boy had succumbed, as well. Hillary Michele had been eleven, her younger sister, Sarah Elizabeth, only six. The loss of their mother had been a hard blow to the two young siblings. Their father's sense of loss was perhaps even more. He'd shown no interest in remarriage, despite the pressure to provide a male heir for the future succession of the throne, and for the well-being of Medinia.

"The court is in our home, father. Mother taught me the importance of making it a place our people could be proud of. My dilemma," Hillary Michelle said sadly, "is the possibility of having to move away from here. I don't want to leave everyone and everything that's important to me," she added, obviously troubled. "And I don't know that I want to move to a strange new place and wed some man whom I haven't so much as laid eyes on. Sometimes I wish that I could just get onto a horse and go riding off too."

"If it comes to a marriage with the Skolish prince, I'd ask that you try your best to accept your duty to our people, and the importance of peace to them," her father declared solemnly. "It's the only reason that would force me to let you go. I would then pray each day thereafter that you and he could grow to be in love as much as your mother and I were."

"Only peace for the kingdom could compel me to go," Hillary Michelle vowed in return. She came around the table and hugged her father. "How will you people get along without me, though?" she teased. "Who'll put up with your saucy tongue?"

King Renaud laughed in his rumbling manner as the princess pulled out a chair and sat down to join him.

"Perhaps, I'll have to start looking for a new queen after all," he quipped.

"Well, if that's your plan, you had best get started before there are no more little kings left in you. That's all I have to say about that," she stated bluntly and then laughed at her own quip. "I just might end up having a child before you."

The king roared with fresh gusto and then scolded her half-heartedly once again. He truly loved his two daughters. Peace or not, he knew that the time was coming when they would marry and leave his castle to start families of their own. That was the natural way of things, except in the case of those with royal blood flowing through their veins, there came even greater obligations that had to be considered. Sometimes, in matters of the heart, duty to the kingdom had to outweigh the consideration of true love.

Father and daughter sat together enjoying a breakfast of hot bread with combs of honey, boiled eggs, and fresh fruit. They discussed matters that were before the king's court as they ate. In time that discussion came back to their meeting with Sir Reginald Toutant. The knight commander had presented them with a clearer version of the strife on the western frontier, although the matter was as yet unresolved.

During their discourse, the Medinian king had asked for Sir Reginald's appraisal of the Skolish contingent that he'd been in contact with. King Renaud had taken note of the fact that his eldest daughter had been more interested in Toutant's impressions of Prince Paulo. He considered that only natural. She knew so precious little about the man she might soon be betrothed to.

At the conclusion of their meeting, King Renaud had declared that they would continue the peace talks. Acting as their ambassador, Toutant was even now en route to Skoland to make the necessary arrangements for a meeting between the two royal families. The court advisors on both sides were advocating for a wedding. The consensus was that only through a union of marriage could a truly lasting peace come to fruition.

The Medinian king had agreed to the proposal of a late September festival. It would be an appropriate time for the two kings and their advisors to finalize the terms. The fall harvest gathering was an annual time of celebration for the people of both kingdoms. If a site could be agreed upon, the festive atmosphere might prove to be an inducement to talks of a lasting peace.

*   *   *

August 3, 1461
Kragonus, Skoland

The crimson red cloaked senior members of the Royal Order of knights and other court advisors attended to King Verdonk, and his son, Prince Paulo. There were conflicting thoughts regarding the raids into their homeland. There remained an unresolved anger at having a number their countrymen and women slain or carried off to some unknown fate. The debate grew heated as differing viewpoints were aired and challenged.

Sir Geoffrey Gaullé rose from his chair to state his thoughts on the matter. He waited until the men in the Kragonus hall stilled their bickering voices and he had their undivided attention.

"It appals me that an enemy would strike at us in this manner. To have them cross our borders and raid our frontier. To kill and kidnap our people! I agree, it's a bloody outrage!" Sir Geoffrey declared emphatically. "That doesn't, however, call for us to lash out blindly at the nearest enemy in sight. The evidence tells the story. I don't believe that the Medinians are the responsible party here."

"Then tell us. Who is responsible?" one of the knights in attendance challenged him.

"That I do not know," the knight commander conceded, with a shrug of his shoulders. "But not knowing who is responsible doesn't justify taking the wrong action."

"It's quite possible that we face a new threat from the west. Whether that threat originates in the mountains or from Varakov, I cannot say with any certainty. I do know, sir, that whoever is responsible, they went to a great deal of trouble to make it look like the Medinians attacked us," the veteran knight stated gravely.

He paused briefly and then added one further observation on the matter.

"Whoever is responsible, it suggests to me that they're taking an active interest in the continuing hostilities between Skoland and Medinia. If indeed, we face a new enemy, then it would be prudent to have the Medinians as our allies, not as our enemies."

"Perhaps, this raid was the act of a renegade band of Medinian knights who are in opposition to a peace between us," one of the king's many advisors speculated.

"It's possible, but I think not," Prince Paulo spoke out. "Their commander, Sir Reginald Toutant, struck us as being a man of his word. He was adamant that no Medinian troops were responsible for the raids on the Skolish frontier farms. He insisted that he would know if a force the size necessary for this action were unaccounted for. In addition, their frontier farms were raided at the same time that ours were. That could mean that we face a common foe."

"There's also the added evidence that some manner of creatures were involved in all this," Gaullé added.

"I heard about that," another knight remarked with a dismissive snort. "There's talk of giant wolves! Are we supposed to believe such nonsense? There may indeed have been a pack of wolves that came down from the mountains, but I hardly think that they would be working in concert with whoever raided Skoland and carried off our people. I still say you can't trust the Medinians."

There were more than few knights who showed their agreement with this statement. Several others made derisive comments of their own.

"You didn't see the tracks in the mountains," Gaullé retorted emphatically, as he stood up. "I did." His fierce look was enough to silence any further comments.

King Verdonk decided that the discussions had gone on long enough and that they weren't getting anywhere. He rose from his throne and signalled for their attention.

"This war has gone on far too long! Let's not lose sight of the real issue here. The war is draining our treasury, and worse, it's draining the kingdom of its able bodied men," the king declared. "I cannot say who, or what, was the cause of the disturbances in the frontier. I do know that Sir Geoffrey and my son were on the scene. They both concur that the Medinians were not the ones who attacked us. For our purposes here, that's the end of it. This is my decree," he added forcefully, "and you will abide by it. We will proceed with the peace initiatives. We have invited King Renaud and his people to meet with us. Perhaps, together, we can address this frontier issue further. It could well be a first step in an alliance between us."

The Skolish king paused and glanced around at each of the men gathered, looking for any further dissension. Seeing none, he then turned to his son and smiled.

"That action could well be a second step, actually," he stated. "To seal the peace, a royal marriage should come first. What say you to that, Paulo? I'm told King Renaud's eldest daughter is a most beautiful young woman. I think that it's time I had some grandchildren."

"Personally, Father, I'd rather be meeting the Medinians on the battlefield. But if duty to the kingdom calls, and a marriage serves Skoland's best interests, then certainly I'll at least look the royal Medinian wench over," the prince replied jokingly.

The laughter that ensued helped ease the tension, although Paulo noticed that Sir Geoffrey cast him a disapproving glance over his response.

*   *   *

August 3, 1461
The Mesa-of-the-Moon, Varakov

Woodrow reined his horse to a halt outside the castle stairway and dismounted. The warming rays of the morning sun had just begun to bathe the city streets as he'd ridden through them. It promised to be another hot summer day on the coastal plains. He'd kept his mount at a steady trot as he passed through the streets. His eyes had taken in every detail, from the merchants preparing for the day's business, to the guards who were stationed at each pair of the gates and who saluted him sharply as he passed through.

Woodrow gave over the reins to one of the stable hands. The groom would see to it that his steed was brushed, watered, and fed. He noted that the fellow was about the same age as Willie. He further noted that even a castle position as lowly as this required a well-kept and clean uniform. There were standards that a king's court demanded. He knew that well. In his position as castle keeper, he'd implemented a great many of those standards.

As he passed through the inner security checks, he cordially greeted the king's personal guards who were on station and was accorded the proper deference in return. Everyone on staff knew the castle keeper on sight. His will was instrumental in deciding who had access to the king and it was Woodrow who decided whose petition was heard and how it was dealt with.

The castle keeper spoke with Lord Victor's blessing. He wasn't there to win a popularity contest. He valued his impartiality and he tried to dispense justice even-handedly, regardless of who stood before him. Naturally, it did not always endear him to the men who came before the court with their own idea of what was justice.

When Woodrow entered the castle's outer receiving chamber, he could see that his absence had caused a considerable backlog. Although it was only early morning, there were already a dozen knights and minor barons dressed in their best finery in attendance. They were waiting to present their petitions on whatever matter drew them to seek a ruling or the king's blessing upon.

The castle keeper walked through their midst without slowing. His practiced gaze was focused straight ahead. His determined stride brooked no interference. He acknowledged no one at this point. Their time for his ear would come soon enough.

Leaving the outer chamber, Woodrow entered the rooms that served as his staff's headquarters. They were empty at the moment. He passed through them and into his private office, where he shut and latched the door behind him. Only after doing so did he open the wood-grained panel secreted in the end wall. He then lit a small candle, which sat in an ornate holder on top of his desk. Passing through the narrow entrance, he closed the panel again from the other side.

The candle's glow provided sufficient light to traverse the short hallway. At the far end, he extinguished the flame and set the candleholder down on a small shelf. He opened another panel door situated next to it, feeling with a practiced hand for the hidden clasp. He then stepped out from behind a richly woven silk tapestry, which depicted Hannibal's scaling of a mountain pass, riding on the back of one of his war elephants.

The castle keeper's privileged entrance led into Lord Victor's inner sanctum. Few people knew of its existence, or of the other hidden passageways that riddled the castle. There were several of these secret corridors that even Woodrow was not privy to.

The immense hall was still and dimly lit. Only a few tall beeswax candles provided any light. As he moved across the hall towards the king's private chambers, Woodrow could smell the lye that had been used to scrub the tiles clean. Despite the semi-darkness, he sensed that he was not alone in the hall.

Indeed, a moment later, Lord Victor addressed him from where he sat reclined on the steps at the foot of his throne.

"The prodigal son returns," the king intoned. "I understand that you paid a visit to our friends in the mountains on your way home, Woodrow."

There was little that escaped Victor's attention. Among the population calling Sanctuary home, there were some who were placed there by the king. The Oddity ranks consisted of grateful refugees who had been given a new chance in life, but these men were kept on the kingdom's payroll to keep an eye on any matters that held significance for the crown. They were spies in a sense, but that was to be understood.

The reporting by such men meant that information flowed back to the king from a wide variety of sources. Pooling that information gave him a clearer understanding of what was happening and who was making their presence felt in the kingdom. Lord Victor didn't like surprises. They were the signs of a loss of control and kings couldn't afford to lose control, or they didn't remain kings for long. They were usurped. Lord Victor understood this innately, and he had been the only king in Varakov for a very long time now.

His agents were entrenched in every conceivable area and group throughout the kingdom. If someone were to think to vie for his crown, he would learn of it in the earliest of stages and could take pre-emptive action before they could consolidate a power base. By keeping an ear to the ground, Victor had ruthlessly squashed a number of potential troublemakers over the years before they had garnered any real support.

This was one of the reasons Woodrow knew that, despite their being the only the two present in the hall, they were not necessarily the only two who were privy to their conversation. The castle had other ears listening. So he answered in the best way possible, with honesty.

"My Lord Victor, please forgive my prolonged absence. We did indeed pay a brief visit with the Oddities," the castle keeper replied, as he approached.

There was a decided deference in his tone, but Woodrow was not required in private audiences to bow before his liege. His was the only position in the kingdom that allowed such familiarity. Still, he knew better than to overstep this privilege.

"I trust that all is well with them?" Victor queried, without moving from where he reclined on the steps of the dais.

"Yes, it is milord. The Old Man sends you his greetings and his appreciation for your generous supply of meat taken on our raid," Woodrow related.

"Your generosity, you mean. On my behalf, of course," Lord Victor corrected him.

"This was questionable kill, sire. It was not fit for your table, or to serve to the guests ... at your feast," Woodrow stated bluntly. He was letting it be known that he'd been made aware of events that took place during his absence. The statement drew a brief laugh from the king. He looked pleased that the castle keeper had made sure to keep himself informed. That was a large part of his job description, after all.

"Rather than letting that portion of meat go to waste, I thought that you would prefer it went to good use. I had the Old Man instructed, upon delivery, to make sure it was well cooked before allowing his people to consume it."

"A wise precaution," Victor observed dryly. "They have enough afflictions to deal with as it is. Besides, you know I prefer my meat ... rather rare." The king smiled at his own remark as he directed Woodrow to sit on the stairs beside him.

"It was a precaution, though I've never seen a case where someone has contracted the Pack's curse, other than from being born to it, or from being bitten. Despite all my years of study, I still cannot say for certain why that is," the castle keeper admitted.

He sighed heavily as he sat down on the steps beside Victor.

"To be honest, I've more questions now than I had when I first started trying to make sense of it. Why do some of the offspring born to the Pack contract it, while others don't? Why are there three nights of transformation, and always during the full phase period of the moon? What is it about that time of the lunar month that triggers these changes in us? It's certainly not like any other plague I've ever encountered. But I've bored you with these questions before, haven't I?" Woodrow said with grim smile.

"You never bore me, Woodrow," Lord Victor stated. "That's why I want you here. I don't much like it when you're not available to me. I concede the need for you to leave each month, but the duration must be kept to a minimum. There are duties here that I've come to rely upon you to handle."

"Yes, milord," the castle keeper said, acknowledging the rebuke.

"I value your council, Woodrow. You are an excellent keeper of my castle—and of me," Victor added. "You've always performed your duties to the kingdom to my satisfaction."

"Thank you, milord."

The king sat up from his prone position, signalling an end to any further reprimand. The morning sun was penetrating the hall through the many stained-glass windows. The light cast shadows across the room as it struck the life-sized marble statues. Victor seemed to be looking them over from across the distance as he formulated his thoughts.

"What do you think of our actions to the east?" the king asked his advisor.

"They continue to trouble me, milord. My opinion hasn't changed," the castle keeper replied with conviction.

Victor nodded his head slowly. He was aware that Woodrow had not been in favour of his plan when the king had first broached the subject.

"Our defences face the west, Woodrow, towards the sea. Historically, any invader has had to approach us from the sea. Our fortifications line the coast, and the harbour at Port Lupus offers the only real hope of a safe landing. Our ships and our bombards give ample defence there," Victor noted.

The Varakovan king was referring to the strategic locations of their coastal fortifications, each manned by well-trained troops of knights. Their capable commander, Sir Curtis Grottolio, saw to that. No enemy fleet, or even a lone vessel, could approach the coast without being spotted. Any sighting sent the appropriate signal fires running along the coast.

In conjunction with the Multinational gang's signal tower, the commander's disciplined Varakovan forces helped control all access to the sheltered bay at Port Lupus. Their armed galleons, shore bombards, and strategic archer-stations equipped with fire arrows gave the wolf-head bay plenty of bite of its own. They could decimate any fleet that dared to run the course through the harbour mouth.

Unfortunately, the devastating shore bombards were large, unwieldy contraptions and could not be mobilized for an effective field battle. This was one of the many concerns that Lord Victor had of late. He foresaw a different enemy approach that needed to be faced.

"To the east, we've always had the mountains providing us protection. They're a natural barrier with very few reachable passes. Thankfully, the only significant one has been in Varakov's control for several centuries now. The mountains have kept us out of the endless Christian crusades, and now the Muslim encroachment on the rest of Europe. Even Ivan has no choice but to kowtow to Russia's Tatar overlords."

"Then, why do you concern yourself to the east? Why intervene in Skolish and Medinian affairs?" the castle keeper asked, as he had when Lord Victor first discussed the raids he was planning. He hadn't gotten an answer then. Would this time be any different?

Victor continued staring into the distance, his shimmering cape draped behind him as always. Moments passed before he replied.

"Because, Woodrow, I've seen them coming. I've had a vision of their armies coming down from the Euralenes and emerging from the forest tree line to invade the foothills. I've heard their battle cries. I've seen great armies in combat, slaughtering each other. I've seen it, sometime in the future. But not the distant future, I suspect. That's why I sent the raiding parties," Victor added. "I needed to assess them and to create an element of fear and uncertainty at the very least. At best, I hoped to have them renew their hostilities. The two kingdoms united, I'm convinced, would in due course begin looking elsewhere for their expansionist goals. Varakov would make an ideal conquest. It would give them a gateway to the sea, and to its bounty and trade."

Woodrow did not dispute the fact that Lord Victor had seen what he claimed to have. If Victor said he'd had a vision of a future invasion, then he had. In recent years, the king had ventured deeply into the black arts. It had begun shortly after he'd made a solo venture into the mountain peaks in search of the one they called the Oracle. He'd returned a changed man, even more distant than before, perhaps. Yet, somehow, he had come back more energized too.

Victor had brought some object back with him from that trek. He had carried it in a plain burlap sack and taken it straight away up into his private tower chamber. Several months after this, the king had presented him with the emerald-green gem amulet. It had been chiselled into the likeness of a wolf. About a month after that, the first dark warlock had arrived, and stayed. Others had followed.

Woodrow decided to express a thought.

"Perhaps all that you actually accomplished was to give them further reason to unite, to face a common foe. Perhaps our actions ... will only serve to make them take notice of us. You've told me in the past that fear is a double-edged sword. Men who fear an enemy will sometimes strike out at that enemy. They may attack us first for fear that further attacks are being planned on them."

"You're suggesting that my actions might be a self-fulfilling prophecy, Woodrow?"

"It's possible that your vision has led you to a course of action that would result in its coming to pass, yes," the castle keeper conjectured. "Perhaps we should see what develops and bide our time before acting again."

"Now you see, Woodrow? That's why I value your company! You think in broader terms than most men. You're a predator, like me. You're always on your guard, and you sleep with one eye open. You know to keep an eye on the enemy as well as the prey and to expect the unexpected if you wish to prevail."

The Varakovan king considered his options before he spoke again. He seemed to capitulate then to the castle keeper's line of thinking.

"Very well, we shall bide our time," Victor agreed, "and then see what transpires with our neighbours before acting again. But make no mistake about it. We will act if it's called for."

Something in Victor's tone made Woodrow feel sure that he had already decided that such a need would arise, and in the not-too-distant future.

"Let's take a walk in the courtyard and enjoy a bit of the morning before the sun is too strong and the day's dreary business begins, shall we?" the king suggested then.

"Certainly, milord," the castle keeper responded. If Victor wanted to ensure their privacy, they were better off outside.

Passing through a heavy oaken door, Victor led Woodrow into the inner courtyard and then up several flights of stone stairways to the battlements. This lofty vantage point gave them an unobstructed view out over the coastal plains towards the sea and Port Lupus. As his liege stood staring out over the kingdom, the castle keeper was struck by the similarity of the moment to one of the portraits that hung over the fireplace mantle in the great hall. In the portrait, Lord Victor stood in this very battlement. He was pictured with his long black hair, slightly touched by silver at the temples and blowing back in the breeze. His ever-present shimmering cape billowed out behind him. His ice-blue eyes lay brooding in the recesses of his pale complexion.

His features were regal and striking yet held an aura of some inner conflict. He had the appearance of a man destined to rule, but also one who stood very much alone.

"Times of great uncertainty lay ahead, Woodrow," Victor said after a time. "I've looked into the future, but I cannot see it with any real clarity. Our enemies are coming, however, and they're coming from up there."

The king pointed towards the mighty forest that scaled the midsection of the towering mountain range, and in the general direction of the Euralene gap.

"We will bide our time with our neighbours, Woodrow, but I'm going to have commander Grottolio commence the construction of a series of new fortifications in the foothills," he said. "Should my vision come to pass, at the very least, they'll slow down the advance of the invaders."

The Varakovan king went on in some detail as he described where he saw these defensive constructions being erected. He then talked of a forced conscription of labourers for that task, as well as of men to be recruited for training in the army. His comments left Woodrow with many concerns, but as yet, he wasn't prepared to make any further comment regarding Lord Victor's plans.

When the king was ready to leave the battlements, he took hold of the castle keeper's shoulder and they descended the stone steps together.

"You don't much care for the coven-council I've retained, do you, Woodrow?" Victor asked, although he already knew the answer.

"There's not much for me to like, milord. Their practicing in the black arts doesn't sit well with me, as you know," the castle keeper replied truthfully.

"They've been a great help to me, nonetheless," Victor asserted. "I've begun harnessing powers which could greatly assist us, if in fact Varakov is invaded. With each passing week, I'm getting stronger and more adept. There are already things that I can do that no ordinary man could. If I continue to learn at this rate, I could soon grow beyond any threat, even an invasion."

Woodrow was uncertain as to the king's meaning. Lord Victor was already powerful. He was not like other men, already. *What did he mean that he was still learning? Learning what?*

It was to be only a few short minutes later that the castle keeper was given his first inkling as to what the Varakovan king meant.

Victor came to a stop as they were walking through the courtyard. He stooped down and picked up the lifeless body of a sparrow, which lay on the ground beside a small shrub. There was nothing to indicate how the bird had died. Perhaps it was simply from old age. In any event, judging from the stiffness of its tiny body, the bird had been dead for some time now.

Victor laid the sparrow in the palm of one hand. He looked upwards, towards the large chamber of the inner tower that soared high above them. His gaze was fixed there for a time as if he was demanding to be felt by whoever was up there.

When the Varakovan king judged the connection made, he looked down at the sparrow in his hand. His eyes grew inflamed then with the same emerald-green glow that Woodrow's amulet had given off that night back in his cabin retreat. It was the same eerie glow that the stewards reported to Simon had occurred when Lord Victor slew the young Skolish farmer.

The castle keeper looked down to where the sparrow lay in Victor's palm. The same eerie greenish glow seemed to infuse the small body now. Slowly, the bird became reanimated with life. The stiffened legs relaxed and took a more natural position. Yet this was anything but natural.

Woodrow was startled when the small creature's eyes popped open. They too were glowing. The bird righted itself and then flapped its tiny wings and lifted off Victor's hand. It propelled itself into the air, flitting ever upwards, until it passed out over the castle wall and disappeared from his sight.

As he watched the sparrow fly off, the castle keeper was uncertain whether the sparrow really lived anew or if it was some unexplainable extension of Lord Victor's willpower.

CHAPTER 14

COURTS AND CARGOES

But, is true love my destiny?
Will I feel it when I'm in his arms?
And what will he feel for me?

August 3, 1461
The Mesa-of-the-Moon, Varakov

WILLIE AND SIMON KEPT their mounts at a slow trot as they traveled the roadway to the double-walled castle. The youth balanced his crutches across the saddle in front of him. The thought had occurred to him that he might use one of them to strike Simon unconscious and attempt an escape. The thought of riding back up to the heavily wooded mountains didn't hold much appeal to him however.

Even if he was successful in dispatching Simon and making it to the forest, he doubted that his leg was yet strong enough to carry him far. He had no idea how he'd go about crossing over the mountains and the pass would surely be heavily guarded, if he could even find his way through the dense forest.

He would wait, he decided. He tried to convince himself that this was simply the most prudent thing to do and that it wasn't because of the constant knot in his belly when he thought of the possibility of his future as a wolf-creature. He told himself that he just wasn't healthy enough to leave yet. He'd also given them his word that he would remain for two lunar months and learn what they had to teach him.

While the youth struggled with these thoughts, Simon rode quietly alongside him. He could see the youth was apprehensive. It was only natural. The youth was out of his natural element. He was far from his home, and far from the life that he was comfortable with.

"Give it time, Willie," the castle keeper's aide said, as if reading his mind. "Use these next months to learn what you can. You'll be amazed at the number of things you've never experienced before, or even been made aware of. If Woodrow has pledged to let you go free after that time, then you can hold it as true. He's a man of honour. He'll keep his word to you … and you should keep yours to him."

"I will keep my vow, Simon," the Medinian youth replied guardedly. "Time will tell if he'll keep his."

Despite his sarcasm, Willie recognized the sincerity in Simon's voice. The youth seemed to know instinctively that he wasn't being lied to. That helped a bit in loosening the knot in the pit of his stomach. He glanced over at the Pack's beta male. Simon wore a waist sash similar to the one the castle keeper had worn again this morning, but smaller. It obviously marked him as being part of Woodrow's staff.

"Can I ask you a question Simon?" Willie asked hesitantly. "About something else, that is?"

"Ask away," Simon replied.

"Do you know how the Old Man lost his hand?"

The Pack lieutenant looked over at him with a raised eyebrow. "He didn't lose it, Willie. That would imply he misplaced it, or perhaps, that he suffered an accident. His hand was chopped off."

"Why?" the youth asked.

"It was called a pogrom. It's a long story, but the short version is that the rabbi's people had their property confiscated and were ordered out of their homeland by those in power. In some districts, many of his faith were slaughtered. He and the other luckier ones were expelled. The rabbi's people were herding their flocks towards the border when a troop of soldiers rode them down and charged them with stealing their own animals. They decided to make an example of the rabbi because he was their spiritual leader. They cut off his hand, seized the herds, and sent them on their way to starve. That's one of the reasons Woodrow offered them a new home in Sanctuary."

Willie felt a little ill after learning that. He wished he hadn't asked.

They rode on in silence along the tree-lined road after that, until the last bend in the road, which brought them into view of the outer walls of the castled city. In the clear morning light, the youth was afforded a much better view of the castle than when he and Woodrow had passed by ahead of the prior evening's storm. It was more overwhelming now that he could see its enormity more clearly.

The Mesa-of-the-Moon seemed to rise up further as they approached, despite the fact that weather and time had worn down the table-topped coastal mount. The lone mesa came from an age prior to the upheaval that gave birth to its sister mountains in the Euralene Range to the east. Even still, it bespoke of power and strength as it stood its vigil overlooking the coastal plains and the sea beyond.

Willie could smell the faint odour of salt in the air that the onshore breezes carried inland. Higher up in the castle's tower, the view of the endless ocean on the horizon was spectacular, but from down on the road, there was only the scent of the distant sea. Simon told him they were still about two hours ride from the coast and the town of Port Lupus.

The youth's attention came back to the immense castle walls as they approached. The road they were riding led uphill to the drawbridge and the outer gates. Behind and above that, Willie could see the inner walls that surrounded the forbidding castle. The immense castle with its stone battlements soared even higher than the walls. The great inner tower seemed to climb to the upper reaches of the mesa itself.

There were dozens of battlements at various heights that faced every conceivable approach to the castle's outer walls. Any enemy that assaulted the castle walls would find themselves facing the alternating merlons and crenels, from which archers could rain death down upon them. Overhanging turrets and bartizans allowed the defenders to launch a wicked crossfire from which there would be no escaping. With only the front facing of the castle exposed, the Varakovans could concentrate all their forces in the defence of that side of the mesa. To the rear was only the mount itself, and it offered no approach.

As they crossed the lowered drawbridge spanning the deep dry moat, the Medinian youth took note of the sharp iron spikes that lined the moat. He correctly surmised that they were set there to impale any invader who was repelled back while attempting to scale the walls above. The two riders dismounted in front of the outer gates. Simon handed Willie the reins of his horse to hold, while he passed under the large portcullis, with its own array of heavy iron-spiked bars and cleared their entry with the guard station.

Woodrow's aide was well known to the guards on duty, and he wore the familiar sash of the castle keeper's office. The youth with him had to be accounted for, however. Simon dutifully signed the registry. In effect, he was vouching for Willie, lest the lad was the cause of any disturbance that needed to be accounted for.

Once inside the gated walls, they stabled their horses with the livery and then set out on foot through the now busy streets. Willie managed his crutches quite well, and Simon kept a moderate pace to accommodate his gait. As they walked, he pointed out the local businesses and trades that he felt were of interest. Some of these were related to those enterprises found in Port Lupus and were acting as agents for the selling of their wares in the market and to the castle.

Willie was amazed by both the variety and by the sheer quantity of the goods and services that were proffered. The local village that held their fall market in Medinia could easily have been held on any one of these streets and still would not have had the same wonders to behold. He'd never been to the castled city of Dumas, where the Medinian king held court, but he couldn't imagine the market there competing with this place either. Only the visiting caravans brought a largess that came anywhere close to the richness of the goods that were readily available here.

They took their time negotiating the upward winding streets, stopping several times for Willie to look through a shop or to watch a transaction taking place. They listened to haggling carried on between customers and clerks, watched the comings and goings of a widely diverse people, and took in the aromas of the baked goods and fresh fish from the seaport, mixing with that of the different livestock that was for sale. It was as enticing as it was intoxicating.

The youth knew that he could spend an entire week here and still not likely take it all in. There was a virtual labyrinth of crookback streets with sights to behold. Wains and ox-carts hauled their produce and wares to and fro in every direction. Today, he had to satisfy himself with a cursory inspection, made all the more difficult when so many different things caught his eye at any given moment.

Simon smiled at the antics of the fidgety youth.

"We'll be back again, Willie. In the meantime, why don't you buy us a couple of pastries to enjoy along the way?"

He gave the Medinian youth a few coins and watched as he went up to a clerk and began bargaining for the pastries like a seasoned crone. He laughed when the lad came back, all the while complaining that despite beating the fellow down, he'd still been robbed. He returned Simon's change and then handed him the still warm baked delicacy before biting into his own.

They continued their stroll up through the city streets as they ate the sweet confections. Simon watched with amusement at the way Willie would peg a few steps and then pause to take a fresh bite from his pastry. The morning was progressing well. The youth was much more relaxed, and Simon could tell that he was already seeing fresh possibilities in this new adventure of his.

The castle keeper's aide's position in the kingdom was adequate to the task of gaining them entrance through the second gate, as well. The only part of the castled city that Simon wasn't ordinarily given access to was Victor's inner sanctum. That one time following the raids was his first and only venture into that part of the king's private domain.

There were still many areas of the castle that Simon hadn't seen. Yet, after having viewed the great hall and having had a private audience with Lord Victor, he didn't envy Woodrow's handling of the weightier matters with their liege. He was quite content to work in the castle keeper's service and simply help out with the requirements of his office and those of the manor.

Willie's eyes followed the contours of the stone walls of the castle as it rose overhead. While the city dwellings had a Romanesque design to them, the soaring castle was distinctively gothic in structure. The immense inner tower appeared to be a second facing of the mesa. It was nearly impossible from where they stood below to distinguish one from the other.

Willie took note of the stone masonry work. The castle walls were chiselled flush for at least the first thirty feet and offered not so much as a handhold that he could see. Higher above that there were more bartizans with varying size loopholes in the walls that served for launching arrows, the youth assumed, judging from the number of sentries armed with crossbows that were on duty.

The Medinian youth also took note of the rather gruesome looking collection of gargoyles that stood out in stony-eyed watch on those below. The stone sentinels hung out from their recessed perches and appeared ready to come to life and swoop down to attack any foe that had the temerity to lay siege to the castled city.

An involuntary shudder swept through Willie. He felt small and vulnerable beneath their stony gaze. He found himself wondering if he would ever really be free to leave this kingdom, despite the assurances of Woodrow and the others that he would be in time.

The young Medinian tried to shake off these morbid feelings as he followed Simon up the stone stairway to the entry into the immense and foreboding castle. Inside, they proceeded from one checkpoint to the next. While Simon was quickly passed through, Willie found that he was eyed suspiciously and then searched carefully. Inside the castle proper, it did not matter that he was with Simon, who was known to the guards. It only mattered that he was not.

Despite Willie's youth, he was potential trouble, and the guards took that very seriously. If they hadn't, then they wouldn't last long on the job. Lord Victor would soon see to that. Security was an imperative in any king's court, but here in Varakov, it was as if they were expecting an assassin to arrive at any moment. There was no going through the motions by these muscular and suspicious guards, for that might encourage just such an attempt.

Willie was manhandled more than he cared to be, but he was finally granted access to the outer chambers, with the proviso that he remain in Simon's company at all times. One of the guards had even attempted to confiscate the lad's crutches, but the castle keeper's aide had stepped in and put a stop to that.

"What do you think he's going to do, hobble up to the king and hit him with them? He needs them for support until his injured leg heals," Simon instructed the guard.

The guard looked as if he really didn't care if the youth had to crawl along the corridors. He purposefully bent down and passed his hands roughly over the bandaged leg, which sent an angry flash of pain streaking to Willie's brain.

The youth grimaced and let out a moan from the unexpected handling of his wound. That only seemed to satisfy the guard, however. He stood back up with a smirk on his face and issued a warning that the youth was free to proceed, but that he would be keeping his eye on him.

"One step out of line, boy, and you won't have need of these to help you walk out of here, because I'll personally bounce you down the stairs outside," he threatened as he handed the crutches back.

Willie was much too intimidated by his surroundings to protest. He simply slid the crutches under his armpits and fell silently in behind the castle keeper's aide. Simon gave the indifferent guard a long wilting glare before turning away. He didn't have the authority to do much more than that, however. Castle policy was clearly on the guard's side.

Once they entered the outer receiving chambers, however, the incident was soon forgotten. Willie was content just to soak in the atmosphere of the grand chamber. The room was richly adorned, as one would expect of a king's reception hall. He and Simon stood along an ornately appointed sidewall, where they could get a good view of the proceedings without drawing undue attention to themselves.

The king's court was a beehive of activity by now. There were clusters of knights, richly apparelled landowners, and at least a dozen members of the merchant class. They were gathered in their own separate groups, discussing their various private and commercial matters. The youth had never seen so many people of such obvious importance gathered in one place before. His eyes darted about the room as he tried to imagine what grave issues had brought them here to seek the court's ear.

The castle keeper arrived a short time later. He spotted Willie where he was standing alongside Simon, but as with the others, he gave no sign of recognition. He went directly to his offices, where he sat with his aides and reviewed the order of business for the day.

His staff had sifted through the various petitions, recommending which matters held the most urgency and estimating the time they would require of the day's agenda. They also flagged out any of those issues that Woodrow might deem needed to be heard by the king.

With a working schedule established, the castle keeper came back out into the ornate reception chamber. Two of his aides followed behind him, carrying the scrolls stacked in the order in which they would be dealt with. Woodrow proceeded to the head of the room, where he took a seat at the royal council table that was situated on a raised dais.

Woodrow sat to the right of the bejewelled throne. The throne in the reception chamber was a far more elaborate affair than the one in Lord Victor's inner hall. This position was reserved at all times for the king, whether he was in attendance or not. Two large stained-glass windows rose up from either side of the throne. The afternoon sunlight would often stream into the reception chamber through these windows. By design, the dazzling reflections of coloured light would shine directly in the supplicant's face. It was intended to be unsettling.

For today's hearings, the castle keeper's primary aide remained at Willie's side, where he could explain what was occurring should the youth have any questions. The youth was grateful for Simon's company, for he was feeling out of place in such august company. These people may be Varakovans and not Medinians, but they were unmistakably of a station far outranking his lowly position in life.

Yet, as the aides read out each petition and the applicants approached the council table to be heard by the castle keeper, the youth began to have second thoughts. Several of the issues that were presented struck him as being of minor consequence or even trivial in nature. A number of the men who spoke did so rather poorly, he thought. Others seemed to drone on ponderously and at great length. Sometimes, it seemed that they would never get to the point. The youth wondered how Woodrow had the patience to listen to them.

A dispute over grazing rights took one landowner a good fifteen minutes to detail what could have been simply stated in a few short sentences. When the Medinian youth mentioned this, Simon just smiled and shrugged his shoulders.

"If there's one thing that I've learned about the aristocracy," he whispered back, "it's that they figure if they're long winded enough, people will think they've got something worthwhile to say."

Willie failed to stifle the laugh that escaped his lips. Several heads turned in his direction, and for a moment he became the centre of their unwanted attention. The castle keeper had noticed also. He was about to call for a return of order when he felt the familiar, warm vibration emulating from the amulet that hung from his neck.

"The king, Lord Victor of Varakov," he announced formally as he rose from the council table just moments before Victor made his entrance.

The petitioning nobles, landowners, and knights alike immediately dropped to one knee, waiting until the king bid them rise. Simon tugged on Willie's sleeve, pulling him awkwardly down off his crutches to join him on bended knee. Only the castle keeper remained standing, although he bowed deeply before his king, as Lord Victor approached.

Most everyone's eyes were cast steadfastly at the floor. Willie's were the exception. The youth couldn't help sneaking a look at the Varakovan monarch. It was odd, really. In his years of living in Medinia, he'd never seen any member of the royal family, let alone King Renaud himself. Now, here he was newly arrived in a foreign land, and already he was kneeling before their liege—and in the royal castle, no less.

The youth could see that Lord Victor was a striking individual. He observed that the Varakovan king seemed to flow across the room more than actually walk. He was dressed in baggy black silk pants and a loose-fitting white silk shirting. A shimmering black cape was draped over his shoulders and back.

The cape shines in the strangest manner, the youth thought. *It seems to absorb the light and then cast it out again. The material ripples like it's some sort of a liquid, rather than a silk fabric.*

As for the king himself, the youth noted that he was tall and well proportioned, looking as physically fit as any of the knights in the room. His long black hair was streaked with a slight touch of silver at the temples. His eyes were an icy blue, and it appeared that they missed very little as they gazed about the grand reception chamber. When he commanded his subjects to rise, it seemed to Willie that those eyes settled directly upon him.

"Your highness, we were just hearing from Baron Straub as to his concerns for the grazing pastures in the foothills near his estate," Woodrow said.

The landowner's chest quickly swelled at the mention of his name.

"Hearing him endlessly, I'm sure," Lord Victor mused aloud, as he settled back into his throne chair.

It was enough of a rebuke to deflate the landowner's ego just as quickly.

"I'm sure the good baron won't mind if you render our judgment at a later time," Lord Victor stated, making it quite clear that he didn't really care if the good baron did mind. "Right now, I'd like to meet your new protégé. Step up here lad," the Varakovan king commanded.

Only after Simon gave him a hard nudge with his elbow did Willie realize that the Lord of Varakov was speaking about him. His knees promptly turned to jelly, and a fearful knot cramped his stomach yet again. Somehow, the youth willed his arms to move, and his legs to follow as he propelled himself forward on his crutches. They carried him through the crowd, which parted before him as if he was a leper. With his eyes cast towards the floor immediately before him, he approached Lord Victor of Varakov.

"What's his name?" the king demanded.

"Willie, milord. William of Medinia," Woodrow replied, knowing to whom Victor was speaking.

"Crutch your way forward then, wee Willie of Medinia, so that I can see who it is that comes into my kingdom uninvited," Lord Victor intoned.

Willie did as he was commanded, although he heard the order through ears that were muffled by the roar of racing blood sent by his pounding heart. He came to a stumbling halt at the foot of the dais. He knelt awkwardly again, thrusting his crutches out to the sides. With his eyes still cast down at the floor, he waited to be spoken to.

"Well, he looks like a simple enough farm boy," Victor stated as he looked down appraisingly at the youth.

"You may rise, boy," Lord Victor granted, addressing himself to the young Medinian for the first time. "How's your leg? It appears to be bleeding at the moment. Has your wound not being attended to?"

Willie's eyes were automatically drawn down to his injured leg. He was surprised to see that he was, indeed, bleeding. It didn't appear to be serious, but the side of his pant leg was stained red in a number of places. The guard's rough handling of his leg had undoubtedly caused part of the wound to reopen. He wondered briefly if he should say so. Wisely, his instincts told him that it would probably be best not to make a complaint.

"Yes, it has milord. The castle keeper has given it his personal attention. The leg's healing fine. I must've chafed it on the ride here this morning, your grace … sire … your highness," the youth stammered.

"I see. I'm glad it's healing fine. I'd hate to have to be put down like some lame horse," Victor joked, to the chuckles of some of the court petitioners.

"So tell me, Woodrow, have you found honest work for our young Medinian guest?" Victor queried, in a tone of amused indifference. "You know what they say about idle hands being the devil's workshop. Perhaps, for the safety of the kingdom, I should have him thrown into a dungeon cell with what's left of our other foreign guests?"

"I don't think that will be necessary, milord," the castle keeper replied easily. Unlike the inexperienced youth standing nervously before the king, he had a sense of when Victor was being deadly serious and when he was merely toying with people. He realized that the current situation was beneath Victor's concern. Therefore, the point of this exercise was more than likely directed at him and not the youth.

"Perhaps, his majesty might suggest a suitable position that will ensure the lad stays out of mischief," Woodrow suggested, knowing that he was playing directly into Victor's hands.

"Well, from what I can see, he doesn't impress me as being of castle material as yet, does he?" Victor observed aloud.

"Not at this time, no, milord," Woodrow conceded. "It is my intention to see that he is taught, however."

Victor turned towards his castle keeper. His left eyebrow arched inquisitively.

"As milord directed me to, earlier," Woodrow added, hoping to remind Lord Victor of their conversation regarding the youth's fate.

This was the exact point that the Varakovan king had wanted to make clear, but to have the castle keeper make it for him was all the more preferable.

"Very well, then. I'll leave his education—and his *grooming*—in your capable hands. In the meantime, let's find something suitable for him to do," Victor suggested. "Are you good with animals, Willie of Medinia?"

"Yes, milord. I … I've been around them all my life," Willie asserted, more confidently now.

"Of course you have," Victor replied in a demeaning tone. "But working in the king's stable is not the same as mucking out some pig sty on the farm back home," the Lord of Varakov informed him. "You'll start by helping the squires with their duties. If your work proves to be satisfactory to the stable master, and you make progress under the castle keeper's tutelage, then we'll see to it that you are moved on to other things."

The king paused to see that his message was registering with the youth.

"Should you fail in your duties. Well, let's say that we don't waste dungeon space on farm boys from Medinia. Is my meaning clear enough for you, young Willie of Medinia?" Lord Victor asked.

"Perfectly clear, milord," Woodrow spoke up.

The Medinian youth was grateful for that, for he'd lost the ability to respond.

The ice-cold look in Lord Victor's eyes mesmerized the Medinian youth. Those eyes told him that there would be no more hesitation in disposing of him than there would be in squashing an annoying gnat.

"Very well," Lord Victor accepted. He stood up from his throne and took his leave from the chamber, as the petitioners once again went down to their knees.

The Varakovan king had allowed the castle keeper to speak up for the youth, thereby committing him further still in taking responsibility for the lad.

*　　　　*　　　　*

Willie was relieved to put some distance between himself and the Mesa-of-the-Moon, and the Lord of Varakov. After they'd collected their mounts at the outer gates, he rode alongside Simon as they made their way back to the manor. He hadn't spoken much to the castle keeper after the court session concluded, even as Woodrow had personally seen to the suturing of his aggravated wound. The magnitude of the visit to the Varakovan court had overloaded his fragile senses.

Simon sensed the impact that the city, the castle, and especially Lord Victor had taken on Willie. He chose not to burden the youth further with his own thoughts. He would allow him some time to mull it over and digest it. He would be there when and if the youth decided that he needed his council.

*　　　　*　　　　*

August 3, 1461
Dumas, Medinia

"Milady, why are you sitting in your room?" the young handmaiden asked her mistress, as she came into her bedchamber. "It's such a beautiful summer day. Why aren't you outside enjoying it like your sister?"

The princess had returned to her room shortly after breakfast with her father. She was lost in thought about what the future held for her and she hadn't wanted to be disturbed.

"Charlene, for someone that I have to practically drag out of bed every morning, you have a lot to say about what I should be doing," Lady Hillary Michelle retorted. "Shouldn't you be doing your chores or something else useful?"

"My chore is making sure milady is properly attended to," Charlene answered smartly. Her familiar tone of voice suggested there was closeness between the young women that went beyond their disparate positions.

The Medinian princess didn't often scold her long-time attendant and companion, despite the young woman's propensity for gossip and her clever ways of avoiding any work that required actual exertion. They'd practically grown up together, after all. Over the years, they'd become close and caring friends who shared the feelings and dreams that girls have in those years as they mature into ladies of the court.

Instead, the princess just sighed and continued staring out at nothing in particular from her perch on the window box sill.

In mock exasperation, Charlene sighed back at her, more loudly still.

"Lady Hillary Michelle, for the life of me, I can't understand what you're moping on about. It's every girl's dream to marry a prince! He'll ride you off to his castle. There'll finally be peace in the land, and you'll live happily ever after. It's so romantic!"

"It's so romantic? It's so … such a crock!"

This opinion was voiced from the other side of the room, where the king's youngest daughter came striding across the threshold, fresh but dusty from her morning ride.

Unlike her older sibling, the younger princess kept her raven black hair closely cropped to her head. Like her sister, she was slim and attractive, but she was also stronger and more adept at riding and handling an assortment of weaponry. She loved nothing better than to train with Toutant's young knights and demonstrating that she could match them in both skill and endurance.

As always, she had enjoyed her morning gallop across the fields, but her mood wasn't cheerful, and with good reason. She was worried about her sister.

"Do you want to trade your cow there for a dozen of my best egg-laying hens," the young princess cackled, like an old crone. "Or perhaps, trade your war for the hand of the beautiful princess?"

"What's so romantic about being bartered off like some livestock at the market?" the Lady Sarah Elizabeth declared, with adolescent indignity. "Why should any woman be forced to marry a man she's never even met just to put an end to a stupid war that the men started in the first place? They didn't need her to start it, so let them put an end to it without her!"

"I know what we should do!" the young princess stated vehemently, as she flopped down on her older sister's bed. "Let the Skolish prince marry Charlene here. We'll switch the two of you around, and since they've never met Michelle, no one will ever be the wiser. That way you're saved to marry whomever you wish, and Charlene gets her fairy tale Prince Charming. It's the perfect solution!"

Only her sister called her by her middle name, and then only in private. Michelle had been their mother's name, and her sister had taken to shortening her name after the death of their mother. In many ways, she'd become a surrogate mother and protector of her younger sibling as much as she was an older sister.

Hillary Michelle got down off the window box sill and crossed the room to where her sister sat on the bed, hugging her knees and plotting her strategies. She sat down beside her, held out her hands, and then her sister fell into her arms. She held her as Sarah Elizabeth began to sob.

"I don't want you to go."

"I know you don't," Hillary Michelle said, comforting her. "I don't want to leave you either, but there comes a time when we must start lives of our own. One day, it will be your turn. Who knows, maybe if she learns to behave herself, one far, far distant day it'll even be Charlene's turn to wed some ogre!"

That quip brought a brief smile to her sister's face and a loud groan of protest from the saucy handmaiden.

"I declare, the two of you are always making fun at my expense. If King Renaud himself didn't need me to take care of you both, I'd be out of here in a flash," Charlene admonished them with a show of hurt pride.

"Come here, Charlene," Hillary Michelle said, holding out an arm. "We still love you, too!"

The handmaiden bounced down on the bed. "I still don't see what you're so concerned about. Would you rather marry some ordinary man? A lady was meant to be chaste and charming and to be swept away by a handsome prince upon a white stallion. Like I said before, it's utterly romantic!"

"It's utter nonsense!" Sarah Elizabeth declared. "That's just a foolish fairytale. All men want is someone to lord over and to breed sons with to follow in their footsteps, and to cook and clean up after them. Princes are no different, except they're probably even more insufferable. Women are nothing but chattel when it comes to marriage!"

"The union of men and women is neither so black, nor so rosy," Hillary Michelle stated, looking first at her sister and then her handmaiden in turn. "Men and women were meant to be partners, sharing in hopes and dreams, and sharing in sorrow and grief. And yes, sharing each other's bed and producing children. Without the other, neither of them is truly complete. And it takes true love to forge a lasting bond."

She ushered the two young women out the door, with a kiss and a hug for each. Charlene was sent off to her chores and her sister to bathe after her morning ride.

Alone with her thoughts once more, she stood staring out the window again, but she took little comfort from the view.

But is true love my destiny? she wondered. *Will I feel it when I'm in his arms? And what will he feel for me, this prince of Skoland, whom I've never even met?*

*   *   *

August 4, 1461
Port Lupus, Varakov

It was well after midnight when two figures came into the darkness of the loft of one of the Multinational-controlled warehouses. They didn't light a lamp; instead, they moved quietly through the dark loft to stand by the open, but partially shuttered windows overlooking the docks. They didn't speak. Their attention was focused on the piers below, which faded in and out of view in the swirling mist that drifted in on the sea breeze.

Thankfully, the misty tentacles dissipated as they rose into the night air. The glow of the street lamps was just strong enough to cut through the haze and afford them a view of the ship's captain and his men where they stood waiting below.

A few minutes later, the distinctive clip-clopping of hooves came echoing down the harbour lanes. They were made by the team of horses that drew the prisoner wagon towards its rendezvous. In short order, the wagon that they pulled came into view. So did the four well-armed outriders who escorted it.

Even in the semidarkness and mist, it was easy enough to recognize Barozzi's raiders.

The ship's captain peered up the gloomy street trying to see the approaching wagon. It wasn't until they were almost upon him, however, that the lead horses broke out of the mist that obscured his view.

"Bloody spooky," the captain muttered.

He signalled for his men to be on the alert in case there were any underhanded moves on the part of the Varakovan mercenaries. The sailors spread out across the dock, their hands resting lightly on cutlasses and daggers. They'd been in their share of close-quarter fighting. The life of these seasoned tars was not without its share of booty and adventure, nor the troubles and dangers that usually came with it.

If the ship's weathered captain thought the night was eerie, he could only imagine how the Skolish females felt, if he cared. The women lay huddled together in silent terror, locked inside the barred prison wagon as it bumped its way over the cobblestones. They'd been dragged out of their cell in the middle of the night to the violent protests of the elderly former Skolish knight. Locked inside his own cell, however, there'd been nothing he could do to prevent it.

Barozzi sat next to the driver. He and his men were heavily armed, but not because they expected any trouble from the women. It was more important that they make a serious statement to the seafaring captain and his crew. In due course, they would hand over the required payment in silver, along with the bonus Skolish wenches, as promised. First, they would get the message across to Captain Galick that all business transactions were expected to be honoured, or a severe penalty clause would be invoked.

Once that was accomplished, they would then supervise the loading of the cargo that was bound for Lord Victor's castle.

"Good evening to you, Captain," Barozzi called out as the wagon was reined to a stop. He stepped down from his perch, but his hands never left the hilt of his sword or the handle of the wickedly curved long knife that he had sheathed in his waistband. "I trust that all is—as it should be."

"As agreed," Captain Galick replied curtly.

The captain intended to deliver on his end of the bargain, as well. It didn't mean that he trusted the hired mercenary assassin, however. He walked over to the prisoner wagon and made a show of inspecting the live cargo it held. All he could really see in the haze and mist was that there were, indeed, women huddled behind the bars.

"Excellent," Barozzi exclaimed, slapping the captain on the shoulder. The mercenary's action caused him to jump to the side like some startled peeping Tom caught at the window.

Captain Galick felt foolish and intimidated at the same time. He hadn't even heard the assassin's approach. It was just a little more reinforcement that these were not men to be taken lightly, or doubled-crossed.

"Shall we get to it, then?" the raider leader asked.

The ship's crew was called forward. One by one, the women were assisted down from the wagon. Each had her hands quickly tied before they were led off and lowered into one of the ship's longboats moored at the pier. None of the terrified women offered any resistance, save for one, who broke loose for a brief moment, only to hug her remaining daughter and to tell her to be brave. Barozzi slapped her hard. She was then bound up and taken away like the rest.

When they were put on board the ship, the women would be taken down into the hold and celled again.

Once they put to sea, there'd be no place for the women to escape to, Captain Galick mused. *I might even allow them some freedom of movement about the ship. Maybe, I'll even allow them to provide some carnal entertainment for my men. After all, considering where they were going, they might as well get used to it.*

*   *   *

Woodrow sensed the tensing of muscles in Vinnie's body as they stood side by side watching the events unfold below them. He reached out and put his hand firmly on the gang leader's shoulder, not so much to restrain him, but to remind him that restraint was called for. If he hadn't, the headstrong gang leader might well have gone out and challenged Barozzi right there and then on the docks.

Woodrow knew that it was one thing to spy on the proceedings below and quite another to interfere. Barozzi was acting under Lord Victor's expressed authority. While it was true that the castle keeper carried great clout in Varakov, as did Vinnie in his position here in Port Lupus, neither had the authority to intercede. They couldn't prevent the ship's captain from putting his mark to the parchment that Barozzi gave him. That document carried the king's seal.

The armed raiders did nothing to assist the ship's crew in making the transfer. They remained on their mounts and watched the sailors with an air of superiority. It was as if the mundane detail was beneath them. They sat with deadly crossbows slung across their backs and their hands on their sword hilts. None of the sailors thought it wise to suggest to them that they should pitch in and help.

"I don't like this, Woodrow," Vinnie stated flatly. "Not one little bit."

The gang leader's voice was devoid of emotion. It was a dangerous sign. The young man was close to losing it.

"I don't much care for it, either," Woodrow responded evenly. "As despicable as their trading of these helpless women into slavery, it's what Victor is getting in exchange that worries me all the more."

As if to emphasis the point, the sailors began the next part of the exchange. They rolled at least fifteen stubby barrels from the pier to the back of the prison wagon and then hoisted them aboard. The wooden kegs were followed by four rectangular-shaped crates about five feet in length. If anything, they resembled shortened coffins.

Despite making several discreet inquires, neither Woodrow's nor Vinnie's contacts had been able to ascertain what the ship captain's side of the transaction was. That troubled them both.

"It's a god-awful ugly price to pay for it … whatever that damn cargo is. I have a sinking feeling that it doesn't bode well for any of us," Vinnie said bitterly. He didn't even notice that the palms of his clenched hands bled from where his nails had dug into them.

*   *   *

Captain Galick lifted the lid on the chest of coinage and then hefted one of the sacks of coins, as the prison wagon's doors closed shut behind him. The weight felt right. The gold and silver sacks were clearly marked. He decided it was wiser not to inspect the contents further, lest he give the mercenary any measure of offence. Suffice it to say, it was a large sum of money, but then it was a valuable cargo too.

As if he had read the captain's thoughts, Barozzi addressed him.

"It's all there, just as we agreed."

The raider leader ignored the ship captain's protests that he had never doubted it for a moment.

"We keep our bargains, captain," Barozzi said. "Now you be sure to keep yours and come back to visit us real soon. The king's expecting you to bring a lot more of the same. And we wouldn't want to disappoint Lord Victor, would we?"

"I … I'll do the best that I can," Galick stammered.

"Relax, Captain. You come through as we've all agreed, and you'll be a rich man. Lord Victor's very generous with his friends," Barozzi promised. "You'll be well paid and there'll be another bonus in it for you, maybe even better than this batch."

He nodded towards the female prisoners with a knowing leer. That look made up the captain's mind.

"I'll be back," Galick declared. "But like I told your Lord Victor, the quantities you're wanting will cost a premium. The demand's high, so the cost will be too. It can't be helped. These things take time and considerable skill to make properly. They tell me that they're still perfecting the process."

"I'm sure that they are. I never underestimate man's ingenuity," Barozzi affirmed. "And neither does Lord Victor. That's why we have so much faith in you, my good Captain. You're an ingenious fellow yourself. That's why we're depending on you."

The mercenary leader gave the captain a lingering look. It was enough to convey that they were holding him personally responsible. They expected him to succeed.

"You just bring that cargo. We'll have your money ready, and we'll get to work on your next bonus," he added.

The two men shook hands and their exchange was completed. The sailors climbed down into their longboats and manned the oars. Captain Galick stuffed the one sack of coins inside his shirt, closed the lid on the rest, and then passed the chest down to waiting hands before getting aboard. The way he figured it, the sack was the first instalment on his share of the proceeds. He would count it later, at his leisure.

Barozzi stood on the dock until the mist swallowed up the longboats as they were rowed across the bay to the seafaring ship. The raider leader wondered briefly what a life at sea would be like. The thought sent a shudder coursing through him. The idea of being confined on a ship during a battle, or even worse, in one of those raging ocean storms, didn't sit well with him. The very notion filled him with dread. If things went badly on board a ship and it began to sink, there would be no escape.

To be trapped like a rat and drown in the great sea would be a horrible fate, the mercenary decided emphatically. *Give me the desert of my homeland. It too can be a merciless sea, a sea of endless sand. Still, a man could survive there, even in the worst of conditions. I have.*

$*$ $\qquad$ $*$ $\qquad$ $*$

When Barozzi and his men departed with their mysterious cargo, the docks remained quiet for a time. The mist continued its swirling dance as it rolled ashore before rising and dissipating in the night air. Then, stealthily, a lone figure crawled his way up onto the same pier where the exchange had just taken place.

Lorenzo's back ached from the strain of the precarious perch that he'd wedged himself into. Underneath the pier, above the waterline, was a crawlspace barely big enough for a man to remain unseen in. It was bad enough that it stank of dead fish, as he now did, but worse, he had to chase a nest of rats out of there with his truncheon. It was a disgusting and filthy duty he'd performed.

"I hate rats," the Ohs' second-in-command muttered, "the four-legged ones, as well as the two." To make matters worse, he'd failed to discover what the cargo contained. He did manage, however, to overhear most of the conversation between the ship's captain and the raider leader, Barozzi. He was sure that Vinnie and the castle keeper would find that of some use, but since the mercenary had been acting under Lord Victor's authority, he didn't think that it would come to anything.

It was one thing to spy on Barozzi and his men, the Ohs' lieutenant thought. No one in his right mind would trust the mercenaries. It was always a good idea to keep an eye on those bastards, but what of Lord Victor? You just didn't go around spying on the king's business. Lord Victor could strangle a man like he was a rat. He'd seen him do it.

$*$ $\qquad$ $*$ $\qquad$ $*$

Lorenzo left the warehouse loft shortly after delivering his report to the Ohs'
leader and Woodrow. He felt somewhat better about it once Vinnie assured
him that they weren't spying on the king. The gang leader told him they were
merely watching out for Lord Victor's interests. This was their town, after all.
If the likes of Barozzi and his raiders were out doing business in it, then they
had better have their eyes open. The king counted on them to make sure that
Port Lupus was under control.

"Under control, indeed!" the gang leader snorted, after his lieutenant
departed. "I've never felt so less in control of anything before. We've got some
serious problems, and I think it's only going to get worse."

"I'd have to agree," Woodrow stated thoughtfully. "If the captain is
bringing a second and larger shipment in, then it poses a number of questions
that I don't have answers for. Lord Victor hasn't made me aware of his plans
once again."

The castle keeper paced about the loft as he considered what the
implications were.

"The type of money Barozzi was talking about would seriously drain
Varakov's treasury. That's not something Victor would normally do, not
without at least discussing it with me. Then there's his talk of trading more
captives."

"That bothers me too," Woodrow added. "Victor could be planning more
raids across the border, or else he has something else in mind. I'm growing
more and more concerned about what his hidden agenda might be."

"Not to mention the way the king's been acting, lately," Vinnie spoke up.
"Victor's growing more … I don't know … aggressive. And his powers are
incredible. I've seen him do things no ordinary man can do. We all have, but
lately … lately it's getting downright scary."

"His powers are growing," Woodrow confirmed. "And so are his hungers.
I fear that the Beast within him is demanding more the deeper that he delves
into the black arts with that foul coven of his."

"What do you mean, the 'Beast' within him?" the gang leader asked. "You
mean his dark nature?"

"Not exactly, Vinnie. I'm afraid there's a great deal more to it than that."
Woodrow sighed deeply. It was time the gang leader knew the truth. "Victor
suffers from an affliction more in the nature of that which plagues those of us

in the Pack," the castle keeper explained wearily. "That's not something we've revealed to anyone else before, not even you."

There was a disquieting despair reflected in his tone.

"With what's happening now, I think it's time that you were told the truth," Woodrow stated bluntly. "I've known the king for a great many years now, Vinnie. I know him better, I think, than anyone else. There are times when Victor is forced to hunt for prey too. It just has nothing to do with the lunar cycle that affects us."

"It has something to do with the young Skolish woman from the night of the feast, doesn't it?" Vinnie surmised. "The one they say is dead now?"

Woodrow slowly nodded. Simon had told him of her passing away a few days after Lord Victor's feast.

"Victor needed her lifeblood to feed on. How he became that way, I don't honestly know. It was before my time here in Varakov. But unlike the Pack, the times he needed to feed were rare. At least they were in the past. Since those coven bastards and their hags got here, the Beast inside him seems to have grown stronger and more demanding. Victor must satisfy his cravings more often now."

Woodrow took the amulet on the chain from around his neck and handed it to the Ohs' young leader.

"It might also have something to do with this."

Vinnie looked over the exquisite jewelled carving of a wolf's head carefully, noting the dull green glow it emitted.

"Victor can cause it to glow much brighter when he commands it to," Woodrow explained.

"I've seen something like that. The same glow came from his eyes when he destroyed that Skolish farmer. Even though Victor wasn't armed, and the farmer had a sword, the poor bastard never had a chance. Victor was just playing with him, like a cat would with a mouse."

"Therein, perhaps, lies our true problem," Woodrow mused aloud. "I see a cruelty in Lord Victor that wasn't there before. He's changing, and I don't think even he knows what into."

"What are we to do then?" Vinnie asked.

"I wish I knew," Woodrow said, sighing. "Victor has chosen not to confide in me yet. I don't know if he doesn't trust me, or if he simply hasn't yet reached the point where he chooses to enlighten me. He's always sought my council in the past even when we were in disagreement."

"Maybe he already knows what you would say," Vinnie speculated. "And maybe he just doesn't want to hear it."

Woodrow smiled grimly.

"Now you see, Vinnie, that's why I knew you were the right person to groom into the leadership role of the Ohs. You're insightful."

The gang leader snorted.

"Well, I think for the time being we must be on our utmost guard," the castle keeper warned. "From the little bit that Lord Victor has confided in me, I think there's a very good chance that there's a war coming."

"Victor talked about that at the feast. He got everyone worked up about Medinia and Skoland invading us," Vinnie stated uneasily.

"Yes, he believes there'll be a war with the kingdoms to the east," Woodrow confirmed. "I think the cargo brought in tonight, and the next shipment to come, are both tied in with that."

The castle keeper went on to explain the vision that Victor had revealed to him when they stood on the castle battlement. He concluded with the recent episode with the dead sparrow.

"He brought it back to life?" Vinnie asked in disbelief.

"In a manner of speaking, I suppose. It's more likely that Victor imposed his own willpower to somehow reanimate the bird. It was like it was a test. He kept his attention focused on the inner tower at first," Woodrow recalled. "My guess is that he was in touch with the members of his coven. Somehow he was drawing some sort of power from them." Woodrow looked down at Vinnie's hands. "The king wears an amulet quite similar to the one you're holding."

"I know. I've seen it in action," the gang leader said bitterly. "Only on his, the carving is of a winged creature. I've never seen anything like it before. Maybe it represents the Beast that you say is inside him. If that's the case, and its demands on him are growing stronger, then I'm more afraid than ever that there are ugly times ahead of us."

"Once again, that's quite insightful, my young friend."

Woodrow accepted the amulet back from Vinnie. He recalled Victor's warning, as they stood over the feverish farm youth that night in the mountain cabin, about the consequences of his not wearing it. *If it's a question of loyalty, as Victor indicated, just where does mine really lie?*

"It's time that I headed for home," the castle keeper said. He slipped the amulet chain back over his head. "I've got a new and rather unruly house guest to attend to. His name's Willie. And he's quite a handful, just like you used to be."

Woodrow smiled with genuine affection and then tousled the gang leader's hair.

"If he turns out, half as well, we'll be doing all right. I'll bring him into town someday soon to meet you," he promised.

They climbed down the ladder from the loft. Vinnie opened the doors to the warehouse, while Woodrow gathered up the reins of his horse. They'd brought the animal inside when the castle keeper first arrived and kept it out of sight and contented with a bag of oats.

"Keep your eyes and ears open, Vinnie," Woodrow advised as he mounted.

"And your back to the wall," the gang leader finished for him.

CHAPTER 15

DISCUSSIONS

It's my life to gamble, my dice to throw
It's my horse to ride, win, place, or show
And I'll bloody well learn what I need to know
And I'll bloody well reap what I choose to sow

"The New Moon"

August 6, 1461
Woodrow's Manor, Varakov

WILLIE WAS HELPING WITH the cleanup of the kitchen. The late dinner had been enjoyed by all, with everyone pitching in to help in the preparations. The youth had been responsible for making the fruit and vegetable salad and for baking the bread rolls that Nessa had him knead and roll into sections.

The salad turned out all right. *What could you do to a salad?* He'd washed the lettuce, cut up the vegetables and fruit, and then mixed them together in a bowl. Nessa had supplied him with her homemade oil and vinegar dressing for it.

The bread rolls, however, had been overlooked while he was cavorting with Simon and Micale. They'd been teasing Nessa about how bossy some women could be in the kitchen. For her part, Nessa claimed men were only a hair above a donkey when it came to the skills required for cooking. They needed a woman's guidance for their own well-being. Needless to say, the rolls had started to burn before anyone noticed.

No one seemed to much care, however. They just scraped off the charred edges and dunked the rest in the gravy from the roast. All that seemed to really matter was that they were enjoying a wonderful meal and their time together.

Willie especially liked the conversation between the four of them. At first, he'd just listened, but gradually, the others drew him in by seeking his opinion on the subject at hand. They didn't belittle his notions, but nor did they condescend to him as if he was some idiot. They asked him what he thought, and then someone would agree or disagree. It resulted in a lively debate between peers.

The castle keeper was returning after dark, as was his custom. They'd prepared an extra plate for him. Nessa had wrapped it in a damp cloth and left it in the slowly cooling oven to keep warm. They were just finishing with the cleanup of the meal's aftermath when Woodrow could be heard riding up to the stables.

"Well, I think we're off to bed now," Nessa said, stretching out her arms and yawning. "It's been a long day."

"It has?" Micale queried.

"Yes, it has," she said, giving him a fierce look.

"She wants me! You can tell by the fire in her eyes," Micale said, laughing loudly.

"Oh, I want you all right," Nessa quipped, "about as much as—"

Her husband chased her out of the kitchen before she could finish the thought. Judging from her laughter as he pursued her, they wouldn't be going to sleep quite yet.

"Well, I guess that just leaves us," Willie observed, smiling at the couple's antics.

"Sorry, lad, but I'm ready to call it a night too. Would you do me a favour and help Woodrow with his dinner?" Simon asked.

The Pack lieutenant was up and out into the hallway before Willie could come up with a response. The youth didn't really want to be alone with the castle keeper. He was still debating whether he should leave for his room when the issue was resolved for him.

"Hello there," Woodrow said, greeting the youth as he came into the kitchen. "Mmm, something sure smells good."

"It's your dinner," Willie replied somewhat nervously. He removed the castle keeper's meal from the oven. "Nessa asked me to stay up and get it out for you. They've all gone off to bed. I was just thinking about … doing the same …" he added, his voice trailing off.

"It's not that late. Would you mind keeping me company for a while?" Woodrow asked. "I hate to eat alone. Besides, it'll give us a chance to chat."

The castle keeper took the tray of food from the youth and carried it out to the dining table. Somewhat reluctantly, Willie followed along. When Woodrow indicated the chair opposite him, the youth joined him at the table, again reluctantly.

"There's some fresh cider in the cold room," the youth said, jumping back up. "I'll get you some."

"Pour yourself a glass, as well," Woodrow called out after him, laughing. "And try to relax, Willie. I only bite when the moon is full."

"That's not all that much of a comfort is it?" the youth said as he came back with a couple of mugs of the strong cider.

"No, I suppose it isn't," Woodrow conceded. He nodded towards the youth's injured limb. "How's the leg holding up?"

"Fine, I guess. There hasn't been any more blood. Nessa keeps a close eye on it. She makes sure I use your salve and put a fresh bandage on it every morning and night. It feels pretty good, and it's been getting stronger every day. I've been walking on it most of the afternoon without the crutches. It just looks real ugly, is all."

"A lot of that should clear up as the muscle mass rebuilds," the Pack leader said, trying to reassure him. "You'll always have some wicked-looking scars, though," he warned him, honestly. "There's not much I can do about that."

"Well, as long as I can walk and run again. My pants will just have to cover the rest, I suppose," Willie reasoned, trying not to sound as bitter as he still felt.

They sat in silence for a while as Woodrow ate. The food was probably delicious, but he had no real taste for it. They both mulled over the events that had brought them to this point. Neither of them was happy about it, but neither could change it. They each would just have to live with it.

Woodrow pushed the plate away after a few more bites. He took a deep drink from the mug of cider and then grimaced as he set it back down. The Medinian youth smiled at that.

"That's the same look we all had. Micale says it's because his wife didn't let him put enough sugar in it. Nessa said it was because he can't follow a simple recipe. You know, for two people so obviously in love, they sure don't agree on much. It doesn't seem to matter, though, if you know what I mean," he added. He gave a sideways nod of his head towards the hall leading to their bedchamber, where even now, sounds of the couple's mutual enjoyment were drifting their way.

"You're right about that," Woodrow concurred, laughing. "I don't think that I know of any other couple who still act like honeymooners after being married half as long as they've been. True love and devotion between a man and a woman can be a wondrous thing."

For an awkward moment, it almost looked like the two of them were agreeing on something. Willie quickly put an end to that.

"So tell me Pack leader, can a young man filled with this vile disease of yours, ever hope to find the love of a good woman like Nessa?" the youth asked. "Or am I destined to be alone like you and Simon?"

A pained expression passed over Woodrow's face. It told the youth that he had struck a nerve. A deeper one, perhaps, than he had intended.

"Simon has a wife. Her name is Tiffany. She lives up in Sanctuary and I'm sure you'll meet her soon enough. As for me, I … lost my wife. She was killed many years ago," the Pack leader replied quietly.

"I didn't know," Willie quickly apologized. "I'm sorry."

"There was a time," Woodrow added, almost as if he hadn't heard the youth, "when I was that much in love too. I sometimes let myself forget that. I guess if you keep yourself busy enough, you can forget almost anything for a time. Then, out of nowhere, it all comes flooding back on you like a torrent, until you think that you'll drown in it."

The Medinian youth didn't know how to respond to that. He sat silently, remembering his own fallen comrades, and how their deaths still haunted his dreams.

As if he was reading his mind, the castle keeper spoke up.

"I think that I can appreciate the losses you feel, Willie, for your home … for your dogs and your horse. I know they were your friends. I'm truly sorry that you got caught up in all this. And now it's beginning to look like there may be further conflict," Woodrow added. "I think there's going to be more acts of aggression that will invariably take a toll on the lives of more innocents. If it leads to an all-out war, I fear that we may see a lot more suffering by the people of Medinia, Skoland … and Varakov."

The castle keeper felt compelled to relate some of the details of the transaction earlier that week between Barozzi and the ship's captain. He tried to explain what it intimated. He was a little surprised by the lack of reaction on the youth's part when he told him of the plight of the Skolish women.

"I shan't waste my concerns on them. I've got my own reasons to hate the Skolish. They're the enemies of Medinia, after all," Willie said coldly.

"It doesn't bother you that they've been sold into slavery? That their husbands and sons were killed?" Woodrow asked with concern.

"The Skolish aren't innocent! They've done more than their share of raiding and killing too," Willie declared vehemently.

"Plenty of Medinians have suffered at the hands of the heathen Skolish," he assured the castle keeper. "Their armies have crossed the river and attacked our kingdom countless times. They've laid waste to our farms all along the river valley, claiming that the land belongs to them. If it weren't for our brave knights, they would've taken everything we have."

"So you admire these knights of Medinia?" Woodrow asked.

"Of course I do. What's not to admire? You'll see for yourself, if you Varakovans ever go up against them," Willie declared proudly. "If I were a man of means with my own estate to support me, then I'd join them in a heartbeat. I'd have the bravest charger, and I'd ride into battle willingly to defend and avenge my people."

"Do you know that even now as we speak, your king and the Skolish king are trying to negotiate a peace?" Woodrow asked.

"I doubt that very much. If they are, it's probably just a ruse. Part of some strategy that the Medinian knights have worked up to catch the Skolish butchers off guard," Willie surmised.

"Has it ever occurred to you that Skoland can probably claim the same grievances against Medinia?" Woodrow asked, in an attempt to draw the youth out further. "Haven't your armies invaded their lands and laid waste to their farms? Haven't they suffered death and injury, as well?"

"Not near enough, the way I see it," the youth vowed fervently. "What do you know about it, anyway? I know about it firsthand. My father died fighting those Skolish bastards."

The young man was obviously distraught. His hands were clenched into fists and he quivered from the tensions the emotions wrought.

"I'm sorry to hear that," the castle keeper said softly. "How did it happen?"

At first, it didn't appear that the Medinian youth was going to answer him. He got up from his chair and mechanically went about clearing the dishes from the table. When he finally spoke up, his voice was laced with fresh hurt and bitterness.

"My father was a skilled mason working on a large estate at the western end of the Kolenko River valley. He and my mother lived there. There was a call-to-arms to do battle with the Skolish, who'd been making bold forays across the river again. Anyway, the noble who owned the estate decided to join up with the knights and he took along his men to serve in the infantry. My father saw it as his duty to enlist with them," the youth declared proudly. "He marched off with the others to teach the enemy a lesson they'd not soon forget. What he didn't know at the time was that my mother was pregnant with me. He never came home."

The Medinian youth glared at Woodrow almost as if this was somehow his fault too.

"Do you understand? I never even met him! His battalion was caught in some Skolish trap and they were massacred. My mother was left to raise me alone. She worked herself to death when I was only a young boy and I was left at the monastery. Satisfied?" Willie raged. "The Skolish were responsible for all of that. I told you they weren't a bunch of angels, didn't I?"

"Weren't the Skolish just defending their homes and families? Didn't—"

The Medinian youth wouldn't let the castle keeper finish.

"I told you, I don't care what you have to say. We fight them because they're the enemy, and they're not to be trusted, damn it!" he swore. "What do you know about it anyway?"

The youth turned and was going to leave the room for his quarters, but Woodrow reached out and grabbed his arm, holding him back.

"That's twice now that you've asked me what I know about it. I happen to know a great deal about it, Willie, up close and personal. Lad, I've held dying men in my arms as their guts spilled out on the ground. I've seen great armies kill in the name of their gods, and I've heard every manner of justification for their causes—and trust me, the one thing that they all have in common is a good and noble cause. There's always a 'cause' that's worth killing for—or dying for."

The youth pulled his arm away. He didn't want to hear it. His body seemed to slump as if the tensions held trapped in there were too much to bear. He turned and walked away towards his sleeping quarters.

Woodrow watched him go.

*   *   *

"First Quarter–Half Moon"

August 13, 1461
Varakov

There was nothing wrong with Willie's work ethic. He dove into his assignments in the castle's stables with vigour. Actually, he found the work quite therapeutic, even if he couldn't have put that name to it. The past week toiling in the royal livery had enabled him to work up a good, honest sweat, and it felt good. Even his leg seemed better for the demands he put on it.

His years on the Smythe farm had easily prepared him for the tasks that the stable master assigned him. Indeed, except for the livery uniform that he had to wear, the work was pretty much the same as he'd always done. One difference was in the type of animals he helped care for. There was no livestock here to tend to. There were no herds to round up and move in or out of the grazing pastures. That type of work was done on the farms of the coastal plain, which the youth could see as he rode past on his way to and from his castle duties.

Not that you could see much in the early morning here. He was used to getting up well before the dawn, but here the sun didn't make much of an impression until its rays finally crested the mountain peaks. On the other hand, it stayed light considerably longer on this side of the Euralenes. He still found it a little bit eerie the way the dark ocean seemed to swallow the sun at the end of each day.

While there were no cattle and sheep to care for in his new work regime, there were certainly horses, and lots of them. Giant war steeds came and went, bearing Varakovan knights as they went about their duties. The huge destriers reminded him of the Medinian knight's chargers. They were bred, trained, and geared up for battle. They were spirited animals and their size was more than a little intimidating at first encounter.

Except for that one visit by the Medinian knights to the Smythe farm, he had only admired them at a distance. On the Varakov's castle grounds, he was involved with their daily care. Once he got used to their size, he found that they responded well to his firm, but gentle administrations.

The stable master noted this, as well. He was a good hearted master and he was pleased by the diligent way that his new apprentice went about his work. Whether the youth was mucking out the stalls, spreading bales of hay, or toting pails of oats, he did so without complaint or laziness. He also seemed to get along well enough with the other squires who shared in these tasks. The master of the king's stables dutifully reported these facts when he filled out the work logs.

The only real difficulties that Willie was encountering had to do with his studies each night back at the manor. He wasn't a dull student, just a neglected one. Each evening, following a good washing up and the passing of Nessa's inspection, the manor's inhabitants would gather for the preparing and eating of dinner together. The youth grew more and more comfortable in this routine and he was always encouraged to participate in the discussions that took place. It was after the dinner's cleanup that the inadequacies of his education were addressed.

Simon had taken to working with him on his reading and writing skills. His early years with the priests had exposed him to some of the basics of each, but he'd been apprenticed to the Smythe farm before he'd fully mastered the written word. The castle keeper's aide seemed bound and determined to correct that.

While the lessons were progressing each night, Woodrow would return home from his duties at the castle. He would quietly eat whatever Nessa kept warming in the oven and he seemed content to just listen in on whatever lesson that Simon was conducting. He never interrupted, but when he'd finished his meal, Simon would invariably withdraw and the head of the manor would take over.

With the castle keeper, it was never the same thing twice. Woodrow would bring up a new subject each night. He would make several comments or observations upon it. His purpose was to present new ideas for Willie to consider, but then he expected the youth to go and research the volumes housed in the manor's library.

With Willie's leg largely mended, Woodrow had also started taking him for walks beneath the night sky. He would point out the different constellations, stars, and planets that various scholars had come to identify so well. Some of these the youth knew from the priest who had tutored him, but Woodrow's knowledge was far more extensive.

Later, back inside the manor on the trestle table by the open hearth used to heat the manor in the winter, Woodrow would then show him the same star systems on the charts that he kept in his library. The charts mapped out the movements of the heavens in great detail. In this manner, the youth quickly related what his eyes had seen to that of the recorded documents.

On one occasion, Woodrow told him of a distant prince named Ulugh Beg, who had been a noted astronomer, and of the observatory he'd built at Samarkand in central Asia in 1420. It was a three-story building in the province of Transoxiana, from which the prince had used his precise instruments to produce exact astronomical tables. The man had successfully catalogued well over a thousand stars. Unfortunately for the prince, Woodrow told him, his father had died and the prince then had to take over the throne in 1447. A short two years later, his own son, Abdal Latif, assassinated him in order to seize power for himself. It had been a great loss of a scholarly man and an inquiring mind.

On another such walk, they'd discussed the nature of the living things around them. They talked about the flora and the fauna that was indigenous to the area and the mysteries that they represented. Woodrow would then take him into his laboratory and they would talk about the properties of the plants and herbs that went into his medicines and salves. A great deal of this knowledge, it seemed, also had ties to the Islamic world.

Tonight was no different, except for the topic of discussion. Woodrow talked and Willie listened as they walked beneath the stars.

"The Moors expanded their empire from China, across Egypt and North Africa, and then finally they arrived in Europe," he explained to the youth. "The Germanic tribes, better known as the Visigoths, had ruled Spain up until the Moor's arrival in the seventh century. But the Visigoth Empire was already in a state of collapse, and the Moors quickly conquered and assimilated the population. They've flourished in Spain for the past seven hundred years, although there are growing signs that the forces of Christendom are about to try to change that yet again.

"Regardless of your religious leanings or beliefs," Woodrow lectured, "it's important to appreciate that the Moors brought with them a far more advanced culture than anything that was known in Europe at that time. They brought order and structure and prosperity. At all social levels, their own people were far more educated than the Europeans. Unlike Christianity, Islam encourages literacy and the teachings of the Koran to all its followers. They value knowledge and creativity, and the majority of their people are able to express themselves with verses of poetry and the making of music."

"The Moors are also masters when it comes to the movements of the stars and planets in the heavens," he explained. "Astronomy and mathematics play a major role in their everyday lives and educational pursuits. When they came to Spain, they created stunning architecture and buildings, with fountains and running watercourses. Those advances then filtered out through the rest of the western continent. The Moors even introduced oranges to Spain, which thrived there. The harvesting and marketing of oranges brought great wealth to the region for centuries."

Willie listened patiently, but he wasn't entirely convinced that the followers of Islam were so much more advanced than Christians. He would wait, however, until he had time to study more on the matter. It was just one more indication that he was learning, whether he realized it or not.

"The Moors were also responsible for bringing the use of paper that began with the Chinese," Woodrow said then. "This was a major advancement over the vermilion or parchment that was used in Europe at the time. The Moors are great believers in the written word. They're known for having public libraries with thousand of volumes about every aspect of life and thought. Back then, they'd already translated the libraries of Alexandria when they took over Greece. They'd even translated the Bible into Arabic."

"The priests say that the Moors are godless heathens," Willie challenged in return, despite what the Old Man of the Oddities had told him about all religions stemming from the same Abraham. Like the rabbi, Woodrow calmly told him that this simply wasn't true.

"To call yourself a truly knowledgeable man, you must first learn about the world that we live in and judge it with an unbiased eye," he said. "Christianity is our faith, but it's merely one piece of the puzzle. When you look at the belief structure of mankind's religious sects—whether it be the Jews, Christians, Muslims, or any of the others—you can't help but see them all for what they really are."

The youth couldn't resist asking him exactly what that was.

"You'll see them all, as people looking for the same answers," Woodrow had replied evenly. "They've all seen the intricacies of the world we live in. They've all looked up into the night sky, at the sheer enormity and complexity of it all. They've all felt small and insignificant, and they've all wondered who could have created all of this? All religions," he stressed, "share a belief in a creator. And, generally speaking, they believe in a beneficial and caring one, as evident in his giving us life and the means to sustain it."

"There is a God," Woodrow said. "I believe that there has to be, just like all the different religions do. They just can't agree on the details."

Their subsequent discussion touched on the ongoing conflicts between the three pillars of society in Europe and beyond. They talked about religious history and conflict—from before the time of the crusades, through each of the many crusades, and then up to the present day when these same unresolved issues threatened to flare up again across Europe and Asia.

"Consider the ant for a moment," the castle keeper asked then. "If the ant were capable of thought, he would likely believe that the universe was that part of the forest in which his colony had their shelter and food. It would be all that he knew and all he could understand. What notion of God would come of that limited perspective? Look around you," he'd added. "Look up into the night sky. Doesn't it make you feel a bit like that ant? How can we ants really expect to understand who, or what, God really is? How preposterous! How arrogant! Yet the religions of mankind all declare that they know, and they're willing to persecute others, go to war, and kill in the name of their particular definition of God. The very same God, whom they all agree, is the giver of life and the creator of all that we see. Does that make any sense to you?"

Willie didn't reply. It was a lot to consider. These notions stimulated the youth's imagination, however. When they returned to the manor, he retired to the library and began reading on his own from the many volumes housed there. In time, he would come to talk over what he was able to decipher from these with Woodrow, Simon, and the others. In time, he would find himself doing exactly what the Old Man had advised him, when he and the rabbi had parted ways. He would absorb the knowledge that was offered to him, like a sponge.

August 15, 1461
Varakov

It was a warm night, but the sky was overcast with grey clouds and it was raining steadily, so Willie, Woodrow, and Simon settled before the unlit hearth with mugs of mulled wine. Tonight, the three of them were talking about the history of the kingdom of Varakov. Woodrow had begun by giving the Medinian youth a brief recap of the recorded history of the region.

The kingdom lay on the coastal plain of a well-traveled sea lane, and there were many colourful stories of upheaval and strife that the castle keeper related. There had been many an invading force over the centuries that had sought control of the natural harbour and the surrounding coastal lands that lay west of the Euralenes.

Woodrow told Willie accounts of the first known tribes and clans that had settled the region. He talked of the migration of the warrior nations, which followed. He explained how each of these new invaders had its time under the sun, leaving behind their own lasting imprints in the way of culture and development.

Invariably, with time, the conquerors were themselves conquered. Some new and stronger nation's forces would arrive, one that couldn't be beaten back into the sea. The current citizenry were either killed or driven off. On occasion, the losing side was simply absorbed by their new master's one, or the men and male children were put to the sword and the women taken as slaves or wives to bear them children. This interbreeding of cultures accounted for much of the diversity in the people of the region.

Simon told Willie about the Roman influences that could be found here. When the youth returned to the castle city the next day, he was instructed to look for the Romanesque influences on the buildings and churches. He described the method of construction they used in those days and the building features Willie should look for.

"When you examine the lower and older portions of the castle itself, you'll see those same structural features," the Pack lieutenant explained. "Then as the castle rose higher in more modern centuries, you'll see where the builders of those later times turned to a more Gothic design."

"Varakov is an ancient land, Willie," Woodrow added. "Different cultures ruled for varying times. Some were builders; some were content to simply occupy what was already there."

"The Romans were builders then?" Willie observed.

"Perhaps more than any other nation," Simon replied. "The Romans ruled a vast empire, lad. They built roads where none existed and that then connected every part of their empire. They built fortresses and coliseums, aqueducts, temples and churches, and much, much more."

"The Romans were also the ones who built the series of arched bridges that span the Varden River," Woodrow added.

Their talk this night ended with the last two centuries of history, as yet unrelated. This was the time of present day Varakov, as it were. The castle keeper knew it better as the time of Lord Victor. That would have to wait for a later discussion. Woodrow wouldn't avoid it, but he knew the youth wasn't ready to hear about that yet, or to understand it.

Maybe he will be, he thought, *after the next transformation.*

*   *   *

August 16, 1461
Varakov

Willie and Nessa entered the church by the side doors and quietly moved down the outer aisle to the rear where they found a partially empty pew. They genuflected and then joined the Varakovan congregation in prayer. In a similar manner as found in his church in Medinia, the front pews were reserved for the wealthier citizenry who made substantial donations. Unlike his church back home, the Medinian youth felt ill-at-ease here. It wasn't because of the class distinction, however. He cautiously looked around the church half-expecting that at any moment someone would shout out that he was a wolf-creature and the son of Satan and didn't belong there.

Before retiring the night before, Willie had quietly approached the manor steward and his wife and asked if they ever attended church services. Micale had laughed bitterly and said he hadn't set foot in a church since he was a lad and one of the priests had belittled his father for not making a donation for the building expansion they were planning. His father had barely been able to afford to put food on the table for his family and told the priest as much. Their family had been ostracised by the church and their community after that. The incident still struck a raw nerve with the manor steward after all these years.

When Micale had left for bed, however, Nessa had said she'd be happy to accompany him to church that Sunday, if that was what Willie was asking. So it was that the two of them had taken a horse and buggy ride together in the morning to join the congregation of the nearby country church.

Much to Willie's relief, no one in the church congregation took particular note of them. The priests conducted the Mass services in Latin and though none of the congregation spoke or understood the language, they made the sign of the cross and mouthed the appropriate responses in turn. A few hymns were sung and then the visiting bishop of the diocese delivered a fiery sermon. He espoused the strict doctrine of the Catholic faith and warned of the wickedness of Jews and Muslims alike. He cautioned the faithful to remain steadfast and true to the mother church in these trying times. He told them to take solace in the fact that Spain and other nations were seeing the true light and dealing harshly with the Christ killers and the Islamic heathens. He foresaw a day when they would be persecuted and finally banished from all of Europe. By God's good grace, the same would hold true here in Varakov.

After they received the priest's final blessing and left for home in their buggy, the Medinian youth was subdued. He had wanted to attend church thinking to pray for his soul in the dark days ahead and to perhaps make his confession to one of the priests. Instead, he'd come away feeling worse. He was reminded of his talk with the Old Man. The kindness that the rabbi had shown him and the encouragement he'd given, stood in stark contrast to the harsh doctrine he'd heard today.

That night Willie dreamed the Old Man was trying to point him in the direction of salvation. Unfortunately, when the rabbi held his arm up, there was no hand at the end of it.

August 17, 1461
Varakov

"You'll feel pain, both physically and mentally," Woodrow explained. He deliberately kept his voice devoid of emotion, although what he was describing was a highly emotional event. "The pain will strive to overwhelm you. Your senses will be on fire, and your body will go through a tortuous transformation."

The castle keeper and Willie were out on another of their walks. The night sky was clear and the stars abound overhead. Tonight their talk wasn't about religion, or philosophy, or history. The time was at hand, Woodrow felt, to discuss the fast approaching Barley moon and the transformation that it would bring with it. The moon, which hung high in the sky tonight, was nearing its fullness. He could already feel its faint tugging and the prickling sensations that accompanied it. He observed that the Medinian youth did, as well.

"And then, you will come up for air. That's as good a way to describe it as any other, I suppose," the Pack leader told him. "It's like the sensation of almost drowning and then bursting up out of the water and sucking in huge gasps of air."

"And then what? Do I start craving for the taste of hot blood in my throat?" Willie asked, his words dripping with bitterness. "Do I want to run around looking for something to kill?

"Yes."

That one word response shocked the youth as nothing else had. The castle keeper's brutally honest and dispassionate answer cut deeply into his soul. It terrified him.

"You must concentrate on who you are inside. You must cling to your best memories. You must remember your humanity," Woodrow advised him.

"My humanity!" Willie replied, almost choking on the word. "What about your humanity? Ever since I got here, you've lectured me on everything from the stars in the heavens, to religion and politics, to the nature of man. You say that we're all God's creatures. You say we're all part of the whole scheme," the youth ranted, "and how it's in our nature to be hunters while maintaining a harmony with our prey."

"Yes."

"Then you say that I have this dark side, and to keep it under control, that I have to remember my humanity?"

"Yes."

"It's all just bullshit!" the youth swore angrily. "It's just you trying to justify your murderous instincts and behaviour!"

Their nightly talks had covered a wide range of subjects. Woodrow had sought to light a spark within the young man, a desire to learn. Tonight he'd hoped to give the youth an understanding of the Pack's world; the world that Willie was about to enter whether he liked it or not. Well, it was apparent the youth had been listening, for now he threw it all back in his mentor's face.

"It's important that you heed me, Willie," Woodrow said. "You need to prepare yourself for the coming nights ahead. You must build a foundation for yourself. You must have beliefs that will nurture you through it. You must learn."

Willie held up his hand and cut him off with an angry retort. "You're always talking like you know what's best. Why don't you just give it a rest for once?"

Woodrow remained silent, thinking it was perhaps best that he let the youth get it off his chest.

"You're just like me, Woodrow. You're full of, doubts," Willie stated. "Half the time, I don't even know what you're talking about. You delude yourself. You don't even recognize what you are or how evil you are! You're … we're creatures from hell—and likely damned for all eternity!"

The youth turned and ran back to the manor as fast as his leg would enable him. The Pack leader followed after him, but Nessa stopped him in the entryway.

"Let him be for now, Woodrow," she urged. The youth had flown past her when he came in and had disappeared down the hall to the solace of his bedchamber. She'd correctly surmised that the castle keeper would be coming in next.

"He has to know what to expect," Woodrow protested. "He has to be told how to prepare himself for what is coming.

"He will," she assured him.

"There's precious little time, Nessa. Brutus will be here in two night's time."

"I'll look in on him, later," she suggested, "and then tomorrow, after breakfast Simon can talk to Willie on their way to the castle."

"But he's my responsibility," Woodrow insisted. "I'm the—"

"Yes, he is, but perhaps it requires a new voice just now to get through to him," she interrupted. "He's scared, and he's got every right to be. And right now I'm afraid you scare him too. Woodrow, you represent all that has gone wrong in his life. Simon doesn't, at least not as much. Let him give it a try." Nessa spoke her mind calmly, but in that tone she used when she wasn't about to be dissuaded.

At the mention of his name, Simon came into the entry hall. He'd witnessed the youth rush by as well. He placed his arm on his long time friend's shoulder and gently but firmly drew him back outside.

The two men walked down the lane to the edge of the roadway in silence. Simon took in a deep breath when the moon came into view from behind the clouds as they sailed past across the night sky.

"I don't know whether I love or hate the sight of that rock out there," Simon remarked as he stared up at the moon's pitted features. "I can feel it tugging at my soul and heating my blood."

"The lad will have a hard time of it," the Pack leader stated, flatly.

"We all have a hard time of it," his lieutenant observed with a tight smile. "It goes with the territory, as they say, but at least we'll be there for him. He won't be alone."

"I know that, Simon, but this full moon cycle will be his first. It will be a very difficult time for him," Woodrow said wearily. "And I can't help but feel that I'm to blame."

"You saved his life," Simon stated simply. "We were in Medinia on the king's mission, and events transpired that were beyond our control. Unfortunately, the lad got caught up in it all. You did what you had to do, Woodrow. There's no point in blaming yourself. Willie is going to be part of the Pack now, for better or for worse."

*   *   *

"May I come in?" Nessa asked, knocking lightly on the door to the youth's room. Not getting a response, she opened it anyway and entered. She quietly shut the door behind her.

Willie lay on his bed, staring up at the ceiling. He did not acknowledge her or look her way when she spoke to him.

"I was feeling a lot like you do when I first came to live here, Willie," Nessa said, as she crossed the room and sat down on the end of the bed. "I was scared and lost too."

"I'm not scared," he muttered, but his voice betrayed him.

"Of course, you are," she said. "Only a fool wouldn't be scared, and you're no fool, Willie. In any event, you'll be leaving for the mountains soon. You're in for an experience of a type, which you can't yet possibly understand—any better than I could, not being one of them. I just want you to know Willie that I care for you. I care what happens to you. Micale and Simon care, and, yes, Woodrow does also, perhaps him most of all. We all care about you. We want to be your friends, if you choose to let us be."

She stood to take her leave.

"I'm going to become some kind of deranged, filthy creature! I'll probably kill someone that I don't even know!" the youth said, bitterly. "How am I supposed to live with that? I'll be damned for all time!"

"You won't kill anyone," Nessa replied forcefully, "because you won't let that happen, Willie. You're going to see your dark side run wild in these nights ahead. Maybe that's not such a bad thing. You'll get it out in the open, and maybe you'll see it for what it is. We all have our dark sides, Willie. Even we ladies do. We all struggle with the darkness that we keep bottled up within us. We all face times of dilemma, when we have to choose which side of our nature we will listen to."

"What if the darkness is stronger than I am? What if I can't control it?" Willie lamented.

"I believe that you're a good spirit, young Willie of Medinia. You'll see this through, and you'll be all the stronger for it. Try talking to Simon tomorrow, and if you can, talk to Woodrow too. They can help you, and they'll be there for you. You can count on that," Nessa advised him, with a gentle assurance.

*   *   *

August 18, 1461
The Mesa-of-the-Moon, Varakov

The sun had not yet crested the mountains to the east as Woodrow made his way through the dark and quiet city streets. The clopping of his horse's hooves echoed down the well-worn cobblestones and between the buildings that housed the population who lived within the protection of the castle's immense double walls.

The castle keeper had a full day planned, and he wanted to try to spend some time with Lord Victor, if he could arrange it. His mind was filled with thoughts of what needed to get done before he was called away to join the Pack. Engrossed in his own thoughts, he almost didn't heed the approach of the horse and rider coming up at a quick trot from behind. He was just turning to see who it was when the rider called out.

"Ho there, Woodrow," Vinnie hailed him.

The castle keeper reined his mount in and waited for the Port Lupus gang leader to catch up. Vinnie brought his horse to a prancing halt when he reached the side of his old mentor and friend.

"Are you trying to wake up the neighbourhood?" Woodrow said with a smile.

"Not exactly," Vinnie replied with a laugh. "The guards at the gate told me that you'd just passed through, and since we're both going to the same place, I thought I'd better keep you company."

"You have business at the castle?" Woodrow asked. "I don't recall seeing your name on the day's agenda."

"I don't recall putting it there, either," the gang leader replied, a little apprehensively. "Apparently, Lord Victor did. One of the castle stewards came by and rousted me out of a sound sleep to tell me that the king requested my presence at my earliest convenience. I took that to mean that I should get here as quickly as possible."

"Most prudent," the castle keeper said with a chuckle.

"Let's hope I'll not rue my punctuality afterwards," Vinnie responded in a mirthless tone.

The two men rode on together to the inner gate security checkpoint. After they were cleared by the second guard station, they rode to the stables and turned their mounts over to the squires on duty. They proceeded up the castle stairway, under the watchful eyes of the stone gargoyles protruding from their sentinel perches in the formidable battlements overhead.

At the castle entry, the guards passed them through with little formality. They were well known figures, but more importantly, according to the logs the king was expecting them. Flickering torch lamps lighted their way through the stone corridors, casting ominous shadows as they went.

Outside the reception chambers, at the guard station, Vinnie handed over his sword and the long-bladed knife that he always carried. His bow and quiver remained with his saddle and horse. The guards still gave him the mandatory and thorough frisking.

The young gang leader stood still, patiently allowing them to do their job without any interference or resentment. Vinnie understood the workings of the castle. If nothing else, it served to remind him of where he was and in whose presence he would soon be.

The castle keeper waited while the guards performed their dutiful search, and then he led Vinnie inside. His plan was to see the revised agenda and then advise Vinnie as to when Lord Victor would see him. As it turned out, that wouldn't be necessary. One of his staff was awaiting Woodrow's arrival. It seemed that the Varakovan king wished that both he and Vinnie report to him immediately upon their arrivals. The castle keeper gave the steward some brief instructions as to what needed preparing for the morning session that would follow and then dismissed him.

He and Vinnie then passed through the outer chamber hall and approached Victor's inner sanctum. They stopped at the last guard station, where the gang leader went through one final inspection before they entered through the ornately carved doors. Woodrow's more direct private passageway was never intended to be a shared with others, not even the sanctioned gang leader.

The two men entered the great hall and approached the dais, where Lord Victor sat stretched out in his throne. The king was eating grapes from a golden bowl with carved ivory figurines around the outside. Although it was difficult to make out his features in the predawn darkness, Lord Victor appeared at ease.

The castle keeper bowed deeply, and Vinnie knelt, until bid to rise. It was important to show the proper respect. Woodrow never failed to do so when others were present. It was only when he and the king were alone that he allowed for some informality, and even then it was only at Victor's insistence.

"You may rise, Vinnie," the king intoned, as he slid another flavourful grape from the cluster into his mouth. He then set the bowl aside on the four-legged serving tray that a steward had placed beside the throne.

The great hall was shrouded in darkness. A few dancing shadows and silhouettes were cast by the odd beeswax candle that flickered in its sconce recess. The dimness could have been further beaten back. That could have been accomplished simply by lighting any of the dozens of lanterns situated about the great hall. Lord Victor preferred these conditions, however, when he wanted to relax, or to sort things out in his analytical way. He found that the darkness took away the distractions.

Victor's pale face stood out against this dimly lit background. His icy blue eyes shone clearly and were well adjusted to the absence of light. When the king came down from the dais, he seemed almost to float over the stairs rather than step. His ever present shimmering cape rippled with a liquid-like texture.

"Gentlemen, it's so good of you to join me," he said. He took each man's shoulder in hand and led them to the fireside, where ornately carved wooden chairs and a low trestle table faced the glowing embers in the giant hearth. "Refreshments, if you please."

In answer to his summons, two stewards stepped out from the shadows and eased a pitcher and several steins onto the table. They poured the drinks while Victor and his guests settled into their seats. The stewards served their king first, then Woodrow, and finally the young gang leader. Without speaking, they then bowed, turned, and disappeared behind the hanging tapestry that led to the service corridor and out of hearing range. They knew their tasks and their place. They'd been well trained by the castle keeper.

Woodrow's senses were finely tuned, perhaps even more so by the approaching period of the full moon. They told him that they were still not alone. These were feelings that he often had here, so the castle keeper was not overly concerned. One presence that he felt came from out in the darkest recess of the corner of the great hall. As a matter of precaution, he would keep that part of the room in his peripheral vision during his audience.

"I find that we need an early morning fire, even in the summer months, to chase off the dampness in here," Victor stated. "It won't be long until the fall season is upon us. The trees will be turning colours all too soon, and the last of the crops will be harvested. In a few short months, the birds will fly south, and then we'll feel winter's bite once more."

"Perhaps we're due for one of those long, hard winters. We haven't had one for a number of years now," Woodrow observed aloud, wondering where this conversation was leading.

"Mother nature has a habit of reaching out from time to time," Victor agreed. "Winters can bring harsh times."

There had been occasions when severe winters had devastated the kingdom during Lord Victor's reign. Several of those winters had brought frigid storms that paralyzed the countryside and left behind terrible death tolls in their wake. A few had even caused more death than the times of the plague. Yet, Woodrow suspected the king had other reasons for bringing up the winter, which still lay several months distant.

The king took a sip of mead wine, which signalled to his guests that they could now drink, if they chose. One took their cues from the king in such matters if they valued being in his company. If the king drank, it was best to follow suit.

They made small talk and drank their refreshments by the glowing embers. Outside, the dawn was breaking. Throughout the rest of the castle, the daytime staffs were coming on duty, replacing the more skeletal night shifts. Guard duties were changed, and fresh details of stewards went about their assignments.

Inside their protected city walls, people were commencing their day's activities and beginning to perform their work chores. Willie, and the other day-shift grooms and squires arrived at the stables and set about their tasks, tending to the horses' feed and the livery equipment. For the most part, it was like any other day in the lives of the citizenry in the Varakovan castled city. Inside the great hall, it was another matter.

"I asked you both here to discuss the kingdom's revenues," Lord Victor said. "I'm thinking the time has come to raise the level of the levies we charge for the various services that we provide."

"My lord?" Vinnie questioned. "Our revenues are already up considerably. As we were discussing in Port Lupus, sire, there's been an influx of new shipping business and commercial trade. Plus, there's the new bordello—they're all doing well."

"That's the point, gentlemen. The revenue gain has come mostly from our new enterprises. It's the pre-existing business that has stagnated. I think we need to substantially increase our efforts in that area," Victor instructed them.

"You want to raise the taxation rates for the tradesmen, milord?" Vinnie asked.

"Yes. With them, the shop owners, the riffraff, and every other subject who lives and prospers under our benevolent protection and my secure reign," Victor decreed. "I think they've forgotten that it costs a great deal to keep the kingdom that way. You will re-educate them."

"They protest the tariffs we impose as it is, my Lord Victor," the castle keeper reminded him.

"Precisely right, they do protest, and much too often. Now we'll give them something to protest about," Victor replied. "The royal treasury must be built up for the winter ahead, and they will be required to contribute their fair share. As will the landowners, and the good knights, and the barons. Woodrow, I want you and Vinnie to make the appropriate rounds of the realm—after your return from your monthly odyssey, of course."

Lord Victor was well aware of the approaching full moon. He knew that it signalled the time for Woodrow to assume his role as Pack leader and to leave the castle's affairs to others.

"Gentlemen, I want to see a healthy increase in the revenues we are collecting," the king said. "I suspect that you are both aware of certain purchases I have recently made, if not all the particulars. In all likelihood, I will be making further expenditures in the near future, for the good of the kingdom."

Lord Victor saw the look exchanged between them. He saw that they were aware of at least some of the details concerning his transaction with Captain Galick. The king knew that Vinnie would have seen to that following his meeting at the Hangman's Tavern with Barozzi and the ship's captain.

"You gentlemen occupy the positions that you do, because you are smart enough to stay aware of what goes on around you. I have always valued that good sense," the king said amiably.

Victor took a long drink from his stein before continuing. When he did, his instructions left no room for argument.

"Whether it's wood from the forests to heat their homes, or venison to fill their bellies, or wine to cloud their heads, I want you to collect ten percent more for it than we have in the past, Vinnie. When they groan about it, and they will, you can tell them that it's a temporary measure, if you feel the need to explain yourself at all, that is. You might be better off making examples of a few of them. The others will fall in line quickly enough."

With that final directive, Vinnie understood that the issue wasn't being put up for debate. Despite some serious reservations, he would have to comply with the king's wishes.

"As you command, milord," he said obediently. He sensed that his presence was no longer required. The gang leader rose from his seat and set down his half-empty stein. He knelt on one knee again, before taking his leave. He would have new assignments and dozens of instructions to convey when he gathered the Ohs and they put the Multinationals organization to work. He knew he had best get started on it.

Victor dismissed Vinnie with a wave of his hand, but he bade the castle keeper to remain behind as he got to his feet. Woodrow retook his seat and drank lightly from the diluted honey and wine mixture that the king preferred to be served during the day. Victor waited until the gang leader had crossed the great hall and departed before addressing him further.

"Well, my friend, your constraint has been appreciated," the king said lightly. "However, I'm sure you have some questions before you commence your own workday."

"It has occurred to me that I'm being left out of your confidence, milord," Woodrow said evenly. "As the keeper of your castle for these many long years, I've always been privy to your considerations. Once again, it would seem that I'm being left out of the loop. Naturally, that concerns me, milord, and it makes me wonder if you doubt my loyalty."

Lord Victor took his time formulating his response. This, if nothing else, raised warning bells in Woodrow's subconscious. He strove to keep his features as devoid of expression as Victor's were. In all negotiations and dealings with the king, it was imperative to keep one's wits sharp and to be prepared for anything.

The castle keeper had learned from his years of service that Victor rarely revealed all of his plans and thoughts. The Varakovan king tended to release information as it was needed, and only in as much detail as was necessary to carry out his bidding.

"It is not so much your loyalty that is in doubt," the king remarked, choosing his words carefully. "I think it is more a question of your divided loyalties. It is most difficult to serve two masters."

"My only service is to you my grace," Woodrow vowed.

"Nonsense, my friend," Victor responded with an abrupt laugh. "You know as well as I that your heart is with the Pack, and with those who dwell under your protection in Sanctuary."

"We dwell in Sanctuary under 'your' protection, sire," Woodrow replied. "I would never presume to think differently."

"Well said, Woodrow, but that's all they are, mere words. They have no real substance. The Pack, and the Oddities for that matter, they all look to you. You are their guiding light. I may be the grantor of a Varakovan haven, but it is you that they see as their saviour, and it's to you that their primary loyalty is given."

"It is to you, Lord Victor, that we have *all* sworn our loyalty," the castle keeper pledged. He dropped to one knee before his liege, as if to empathize that point.

"Rise Woodrow, and sit," Victor commanded quietly. He waited until the castle keeper had done so before speaking again.

"Woodrow, you remain my closest confidant," Victor stated emphatically. The king sounded sincere.

"What was in the crates and kegs then, milord? What is it that commands such a heavy price to be paid?" Woodrow asked.

"We will have that discussion upon your return," Lord Victor promised. "I assure you, we will. For now, let it stand that the cargo we received is an integral part of our future defence."

"Then your vision of a pending war remains unchanged?" the castle keeper asked.

"Essentially, it has not," Victor replied slowly. "Although it's not a clear image that I've seen, I've seen the same vision several times now. There's always snow ... lots of snow. There's a raging blizzard that obscures the foothills, but I can see armies fighting, and men dying everywhere."

The Varakovan king stared into the glowing coals as if searching his mind for a clearer recollection of that last vision. It was too murky, however, and still beyond his grasp.

"I can't help but think that time will soon be here," he said then. "I'm convinced that it will be this coming winter. We will need to be prepared for that eventuality. We'll need more fighting men."

"Are you sending Barozzi out to recruit more mercenaries then?"

"No," Victor replied. "Barozzi will be leading the caravans across the gap in the fall, as he's done before. I have reports that the Medinians and Skolish are planning a joint harvest festival. The same reports suggest that an alliance through a royal marriage is being planned. At the very least, that would lead their two kingdoms to a permanent truce in their fighting. At the worst, it could mean a merging of their two armies and an invasion of Varakov. I want Barozzi there to be my eyes and ears and to assess the situation."

By 'reports', Woodrow knew that the king meant his network of spies had informed him of what was transpiring on the far side of the Euralenes. This didn't bode well if Lord Victor was planning to take some sort of pre-emptive action.

The Varakovan king saw the look of concern that came to the castle keeper's face. He held his hand up.

"I know, I promised you that I wouldn't provoke them or take any action to bring them to our doorstep. Barozzi will be given his orders. Besides, the Medinians and Skolish are used to him by now," Victor added. "He's established an excellent cover over the past few years. He brings them caravans of exotic wares that they can't get from anywhere else. They fail to look beyond the obvious, so they invite the adder to dine with them, so to speak."

The castle keeper received reports too. He was well aware that the preparations for the caravan's supply had already begun. Several warehouses in Port Lupus were stocked with goods purchased from incoming ships. The resale of the rich selection of wares that the caravans would carry to Skoland and Medinia would bring a generous profit in silver and gold back into the Varakovan treasury.

Wouldn't it be ironic if that the same coinage was then used to fund a war against them, he thought.

"Go now, Woodrow," the king commanded. "Go and tend to the supplicants and their petitions with your usual grace and efficiency. Then be off to hunt with the Pack under the damnable full moon. I promise that we'll sit down again upon your return. There will be much that we will discuss and decide together at that time."

The castle keeper rose, bowed to the king, and then took his leave. His mind was already evaluating Lord Victor's last remarks, and those words that had gone unsaid but were equally important. He departed through the passage entrance hidden behind the tapestry that led directly to his office.

"Send in Barozzi," Victor called out after he was gone. He spoke to the seemingly empty hall. A few minutes later, however, Barozzi was escorted to the fireplace by one of the hooded coven warlocks.

"Greetings milord," the raider leader addressed his liege. He dropped to one knee, rising only when the king gestured for him to do so. He then stood in awkward silence, unsure if he should presume to sit or remain standing. He opted to stand, unless he was invited otherwise by the king.

Barozzi was never completely at ease in the Varakovan king's presence, but he felt especially uncomfortable being in the company of one of these dark sorcerers. When the foul-smelling warlock had come to fetch him, he had uttered only two words, "Lord Victor." Then, with an arthritic motion of his parchment thin, gnarled hand, he had indicated that the mercenary should follow him. If Barozzi hadn't been specifically summoned to the castle to meet with Lord Victor, it was doubtful that he'd willing follow this foul practitioner of the black arts anywhere.

"You and I must discuss this year's caravans," Lord Victor said, motioning at last for the mercenary to sit. "I have a few new instructions that I want you attend to."

*   *   *

August 19, 1461
Woodrow's manor, Varakov

He had been informed that it would be coming, so he shouldn't have been so surprised when it finally did. Nevertheless, Willie almost jumped out of his skin at the wolf's piercing howl that broke the stillness of the night.

Brutus stood atop a rock outcropping that protruded out over the foothill grasslands. With his head raised up, he let out a long, plaintive wail into the night sky. He was announcing his presence to the world below. He was proclaiming his very existence. He then stood waiting and listening as the sound reverberated off the wooded mountainside.

Below him, farm dogs barked in both fear and defiance. Sheep bleated as their flocks stirred restlessly, despite the relative safety of their pens. Cattle lowed nervously and horses fidgeted in their stable stalls.

Far behind Brutus, back up on the mountainside, came two, then three, and then four distant howls, in acknowledgement to his call to the night. His song proclaimed that he was of the Pack, as did theirs. He knew the sound of their voices intimately. One of them was his mate, Cleo.

Down there, miles below, were others of the Pack. The others that he had come to retrieve and to protect, just as he had done with each cycle of the full moon for all these many years now. Tomorrow, when they left the low lands, there would be one more than usual. The young two-legged one, who they called Willie, would be joining them as they traveled back up into the mountains.

The alpha male wolf's sensitive ears twitched slightly, as from the manor far below, he heard the Pack leader and Simon answer his primal call. Their human vocal chords lacked the power that emanated from the wolf's own throat, but it sufficed. Their distant calls told him that everything was, as it should be.

Brutus waited until things quieted down again across the landscape below. The wolf howls had a discernable effect on every living creature within earshot, and that covered a goodly number of square miles. Unlike the vocal responses of the farm dogs and the restless activity of the domesticated livestock, the nocturnal animals that roamed freely in the forests and across the foothill meadows had frozen in place and gone silent.

The creatures of the wild assessed the situation for every possible peril. They called on their senses of smell with quivering nostrils. Their ears stood on end, preening to hear even the faintest rustle of grass or breaking of a twig. They knew instinctively that the predators were out hunting for food under the moonlit sky, just as they were. The difference was in their position on the food chain.

When no imminent danger presented itself, the grazers cautiously resumed their foraging for food and water. They would stay ever alert, however, stopping every few minutes to lift their heads and to assess the sounds and the smells that were carried on the night air.

Brutus took one last look up into the sky. He noted the near fullness of the moon, just a last sliver away from reaching the zenith, which would trigger the Pack's next transformation. Even now, he could feel its insistent tugging at his very core.

The Pack enforcer shook his powerful head as if to clear these thoughts. He then bounded down from his perch on the outcropping and entered the foothills. Only the gentle swaying of the waist high grasses betrayed the route he took as he wound his way down through the foothills towards the distant estate.

CHAPTER 16

THE GATHERING OF THE PACK

August 20, 1461
Varakov

IN THE DEWY, PREDAWN morning, six fellow travelers left the manor property traveling together. Five of them were on horseback. The sixth loped along on four legs. Woodrow and Simon led the way initially, with Nessa, Micale, and Willie, riding three abreast behind them. Brutus, the ever free spirit that he was, roamed at will, choosing to investigate the surrounding territory.

The alpha wolf had taken up residence at the edge of the estate orchard after arriving sometime after midnight. He preferred to remain outdoors. He wasn't a house pet, after all. He did, however, accept a bowl of water and some meat when Nessa came out in the still darkened morn. He wasn't a dog, but he wasn't above a free meal. He'd watched quietly from the edge of the trees as she and Micale loaded the supply bags and saddled the horses.

Although they weren't members of the Pack, the wolf had known the couple for several years now. They caused him no concern. The new one was another matter. That one had the blood of the Pack flowing in his veins, but he was not, as yet, one of them. If anything, he was still a possible enemy. There were members of the Pack that hadn't returned from the last hunt because of him and his two brave dogs.

The wolf harboured neither hatred nor animosity towards the Medinian youth for that. Those were human traits. The youth and his dogs had only tried to defend themselves and their herd. Some prey fought back, after all. The fierce bull had also acquitted himself quite well. Only time would tell if the youth was now a friend or still an adversary.

In the meantime, Brutus was content to run a course that was roughly parallel to the riders and wouldn't disturb their horses. He loped along, steering a path around the farms they passed so their dogs and livestock didn't detect him either.

For his part, Willie was wary of Brutus as well. He'd gone to bed shortly after hearing the alpha wolf's distant howl last night. He hadn't slept much, however. The problem wasn't just the thought of the fierce predator out there in the dark; it was more the fact that he would soon be a similar creature himself. He'd lain in bed, feeling the intense prickling sensations that coursed through his body and sensing what they meant. That was what really scared him.

As they rode along, Nessa and Micale managed to exchange glances, which the youth, lost in his thoughts, didn't pick up on. They were concerned for Willie, but they realized it would be better to allow him to reach out to them first. If they started in on him with advice, it would just seem as if it were another unwanted lecture. They would bide their time instead.

The sun finally peaked over the Euralene range as they entered the foothills. The warmth of its rays soon took the edge off the cool morning air. Perhaps it was the fast approaching forest, or perhaps it was the sheer magnitude of the snow-capped peaks that soared high above them. They each had their affect on a person. In any event, the two stewards' patience finally paid off. Willie was ready to talk to someone, and he ventured a question in their direction.

"Do you often visit the Oddities' village and take them things?" the youth asked quietly, still looking ahead at the backs of Woodrow and Simon as they rode ahead. Although his question wasn't directed at either one of them in particular, it was Micale who answered first.

"We go as often as we're needed," he replied. "We try to let them live their own lives without interference. It's what they prefer. They're mostly self-sufficient, anyway. They prefer to avoid contact with the world of the *normals* as much as possible. We sometimes help them arrange to sell their excess farm produce and some of the crafts they manufacture. Other times we help them to buy supplies or some of the things they can't make for themselves," he added.

"What are they in need of now?"

"Woodrow has prepared fresh medicines that will help see them through the fall and winter," Nessa explained. "He's always been generous with his time and efforts on their behalf. He's never asked for anything in return, save that for the three nights of the full moon cycle, the people of Sanctuary remain in their valley. That's when they leave the forest and mountainsides to the Pack and their monthly lunar hunt."

"What about you and Micale? You won't be able to get back to the manor before nightfall," the youth asked, making eye contact for the first time. Also, perhaps for the first time, he was expressing concern for someone else's plight, not just his personal well being. It made Nessa smile.

"You needn't worry about us," Micale assured him. "The Oddities will tolerate us in their Sanctuary for a night—or three, on occasion."

"We'll spend the time with our daughter, Willie," Nessa added quietly, almost as if she was reluctant to disclose this piece of information.

"Your daughter? You have a daughter living with the Oddities?" the youth asked, in a stunned tone of amazement.

"Yes," Nessa replied evenly. "She's lived there for some time now."

"She's not actually our birth child," Micale explained. "We found her one day when she was about two years old. Nessa and I were with a troupe of performers back then. We were passing by a burnt out house at the edge of the forest, many miles to the north of here. We almost didn't hear her cries. She was locked in a hidden cellar, and it took us nearly a half hour just to locate it, and another hour to clear the fallen debris."

"We don't know how long she'd been in there, but the ashes of the home were cold," Micale added. "The poor thing was starving. We fed her, then we looked all over the neighbouring countryside, but we couldn't find anyone who would acknowledge knowing of her."

"We think they knew full well who she was after we told them where we found her. You could tell from the way they recoiled away," Nessa harped with uncharacteristic bitterness.

"One of them even yelled at us to take the 'devil child' away from there," Micale added scornfully. "We realized that her parents had either been killed or driven off, so we decided to keep her and raise her ourselves."

"We couldn't just abandon her," Nessa explained. "Unfortunately, wherever we went, we had problems. Whenever people saw that she was different from the other children, they became abusive or fearful."

"After years of constantly moving about with the troupe, we happened upon Varakov. We heard rumours about a place called Sanctuary," Micale said. "I was able to meet with the castle keeper after one of our performances, and he arranged for us to sit down with the Old Man and the Oddity council. They accepted our daughter into their community. We've been working for Woodrow ever since, and we do whatever we can to help them."

"You must miss her terribly," Willie observed.

"We do, and she misses us, but it's the best solution for everyone. This way she's accepted and protected. And she's become an important part of her community," Nessa added with obvious parental pride.

"Thanks to Woodrow, Nessa and I have a decent place to work and live," Micale stated with conviction. "We've made good friends here, and we have the opportunity to make a real difference for our daughter and all the others who've suffered just because they're different."

"I'd like to meet her … if that would be all right. Maybe I could help—you know, with bringing the supplies or something …" Willie's voice trailed off for a moment. He then added another thought, more decisively this time. "Or maybe I could just tell her what good parents she has and how they've gone out of their way to help me even though I haven't made it easy for them."

Nessa reached across and gave his arm a squeeze.

"You're a good young man, Willie, and you've got a whole lifetime ahead of you to help, and probably a very long one too. That's one of the things you've got to learn about, and the men who can tell you about that are right up there," she added with a smile and a gesture of her head.

"You can meet our daughter and her friends when we get to the forest clearing," Micale informed him. "For that matter, you'll likely be meeting Simon's wife too. She'll be going with you to the Pack gathering."

"Simon's wife, Woodrow mentioned her. Her name's Tiffany, isn't it?"

Nessa smiled again. "The answers are up there with those two, Willie. Go on."

"Trust me, lad, if she tells you that's what you should be doing, then that's what you should be doing," Micale said with an abrupt laugh.

"Why is it then, that *you* don't pay more attention to me? Why is it …" Nessa started to say.

"Ride lad, ride for your very life," Micale interrupted, still laughing.

Willie joined in his laughter, and then dug his heels into his horse's flanks and galloped on ahead, out of the field of friendly fire.

*   *   *

It was just past midday when they reached the tree line and dismounted. Brutus disappeared into the woods for several minutes and then came back into view on the narrow snaking trail that led to the hunting lodge. The alpha wolf finally took up a position off the beaten path, taking care to stay downwind of the horses so he would not spook them.

When the others had passed by leading their mounts, the wolf followed behind them to the small but amply provisioned hunter's retreat. They would not be using any of those supplies; the foodstuffs and other provisions stored there were intended for royal hunting parties, not that the castle keeper wouldn't have been entitled to anything he wished. Lord Victor would have been the first to say so, but on these monthly excursions, Woodrow thought of himself as the Pack leader. His role as the keeper of the castle had to be left behind.

Their horses would be left with the attendant and his family and picked up again on their return trip. The dense woods were no place for horses, or for the general population for that matter. That was one of the reasons that the lodge had been built near the outer edge of the great forest. The other was a matter of safety. The hunters of the Pack ranged far and wide through the forest for three nights each lunar month.

The lodge was meant to serve as a base to set out from and to return to following a royal hunt. The members of the Pack were based much deeper in the mountain forests, and at a higher elevation. That was their Sanctuary. The Pack members were content to share their haven with the Oddities, and the reverse was also true. They shared a common need for seclusion, and they managed to stay out of each other's way.

This was one of the many subjects that the Pack leader and Simon had been discussing with Willie during the past few hours. The youth was mulling these things over in his mind while Woodrow approached the lodge. The Pack leader knocked on the entryway and was soon ushered inside. He returned a few minutes later with a small entourage. They went by the surname of Stusyk.

The caretaker and his family quickly and efficiently had the horses corralled. The animals would be watered, fed, and brushed down before they were secured in the stable. Willie watched with amusement as the children scurried about, competing for different chores and generally acting up for the benefit of their guests.

Willie assumed that the Stusyk family must have been expecting them when he smelled the food cooking and saw the bountiful spread in store for them. Indeed, they had been. The attendant and his family knew the monthly routine. Woodrow and Simon almost always arrived in the day preceding the full moon, sometimes accompanied by Nessa and Micale, sometimes not. The family always had a meal prepared for the travelers that could well feed a group twice their size. Willie found them to be as cordial as the McRae family he'd met on his first journey into Varakov proper.

The Stusyks were also familiar with Brutus, who remained outside at the edge of the trail. Not that he was forgotten or ignored. After the horses were secured, the youngest daughter claimed the duty of taking a bowl of water and a soup bone out to him. She'd been doing this for a number of years now, and her parents knew that it was safe for her to do so.

They'd had great concern and anxiety when they'd initially taken over the lodge and met Brutus for the first time. It was only natural. Wolves were not exactly a welcome species. If anything, they were hated and feared. Most people considered them a predatory species that needed to be hunted down and destroyed.

Their trepidation had been clearly evident when Woodrow had first introduced them to the alpha wolf. Before any of them had been able to react, their then toddler daughter had stumbled over to Brutus and started bashing him on the head with her little hand. The wolf had responded by licking her face with his rough tongue and grinning.

After reviving the mother from her faint, Woodrow had made sure that he and Brutus spent time with the family so that they had a chance to get know one another. It was important for the new attendants to understand their role here, at the outer edge of Sanctuary. The Stusyk family lived in isolation for much of the time. They'd been here for four years now and seemed quite content to work their small farm in the foothills and maintain the lodge in the forest edge.

Willie quietly observed how Woodrow treated these people. He didn't order them about or look down his nose on them. Granted, there was something to be said about the position of authority that Woodrow held over these people. Yet, Willie was slowly becoming aware that it was more than just the office that the man held; it was more the man in the office.

The group didn't remain with their hosts for long on this trip. They went inside and sat at the long dining table in the large central room of the lodge. There were bowls of fresh spinach and mushroom salads, and freshly baked black bread. The aroma of the venison and barley stew that simmered in the blackened fireplace kettle competed with the trout that steamed in butter and herbs. It gave the travelers hunger pangs after their long ride. The meal proved to be just as delicious as it smelled.

After saying their thanks and good-byes to the Stusyks, the travelers left the lodge and set off into the trees. The supplies they toted for the Oddities were in the backpacks that everyone now shared in the carrying of. Only Brutus remained unburdened, which left the Pack enforcer free to roam ahead, alert to any danger that might arise. Their loads weren't large enough to warrant pulling a travois, and it made for easier traveling without one. Of that, the Pack leader was the most certain.

Willie found the going hard enough as it was. The farther east they traveled, the higher they climbed. The trees were as large and overwhelming as he remembered them being. They were forced to dodge and weave around the wood giants that soared skyward and turned the afternoon sun away. Ever upward they traversed the slope. The youth had long since abandoned his crutches, but it wasn't long before his leg began to throb from the exertion.

Woodrow led them into a small creek-cut gorge, which flowed down from the same general direction they were heading. For a while, at least, it made for an easier climb. Regardless, the youth felt more and more uncomfortable as the afternoon progressed. Yet it wasn't just the throbbing in his leg that made him strike up another conversation with the Pack leader and Simon. It was another feeling entirely.

"Will I get these same itches every time the moon gets near its fullness?" the youth asked as he scratched at his arms and then his legs.

"I'm afraid so," Simon replied with a rueful chuckle. "We call them the 'moon-prickles.' Regular as a woman's monthly flow, they are."

Woodrow laughed. "That's crudely put, but accurate. There's a cycle to the moon's phases, as you well know, Willie. The moon reaches its peak fullness every twenty-nine and a half nights, to be precise. The prickles that you're feeling—that we're feeling—they're the early signs of the onset of the transformation."

"We go through three nights of transformation," Simon explained. "For one cycle of the moon, it's the twenty-eighth, twenty-ninth, and thirtieth nights following the last full moon. For the next cycle, it will be the twenty-ninth, thirtieth, and thirty-first following nights. You could say that we live by the lunar calendar."

"The full-moon cycle that's beginning tonight is called the 'Barley' moon, in these parts," Woodrow told him, as he paused to consider the terrain ahead.

The creek bed they'd been following was meandering off in another direction now. Woodrow used the root of a tree to propel himself up out of the swale, where he managed to catch hold of another root to stop from falling backwards. When the Pack leader was clear, he reached back and helped each of the travelers in turn to climb out. He assisted Willie last and then picked up their conversation where they'd left off.

"The Barley full moon is followed by the Harvest full moon. That one occurs each year about the latter part of September, when the moon is closest to the autumnal equinox. Which means," he added, "that the moon rises on the eastern horizon, exactly opposite to the setting sun—in this part of the world, that is. I've been to places where it's different, though. Places where the star formations are different, too."

The youth absorbed this information, and it then occurred to him that not all moons might have the same power over him.

"Will different moons make us react differently? Are some of them more powerful than others?"

"No," Woodrow replied with a certainty that came from years of experience. "Whether it's one full moon cycle or another, the transformation is the transformation. They all cause the same change in us."

"I think the Harvest moon is the most beautiful, however," Simon spoke up. "It's usually the brightest full moon of them all, and it makes for an awesome sight when it hangs on the horizon before taking to the sky. As you would well know, farmers find its light strong enough to finish harvesting their crops by."

The youth nodded his head. He and the Smythes had done their share of working under the moon light back in Medinia to get the last of the harvest in.

"Regardless of which moon cycle it is, however, the Pack gathers together to celebrate it, and give our thanks to Diana," Woodrow explained.

"The moon goddess?" the youth asked.

"That's her," the Pack leader confirmed. "The Romans named her Luna. The ancient Greeks called her Artemis or Selene. She's been known by many different names. We've come to know her as Diana. She's the goddess of the hunter and the protectress of his mate. We honour her and give thanks for the blessings she brings."

"It's pretty hard for me to think of any of this as a blessing," Willie muttered doubtfully. "And worshipping a moon goddess called Diana seems rather paganish to me. We're Christians, aren't we?"

"Some of us, but we're pagans too. Perhaps pagans first and foremost," the Pack leader stated. "It would be foolish and false to deny it. Every full moon we are reminded of what we are. We're primal creatures—and savage ones, at that. I want to be perfectly clear, Willie. We hunt our prey, and we provide kill for the benefit of the Pack. We are cursed, yes, yet we are blessed too. Diana brings about this transformation, which we each must suffer through and endure, but she also brings us together as the Pack. And we are all the stronger for that unity."

They were picking their way around the trees, moving ever upward on the mountain slope, when Brutus came bounding back. The alpha wolf interrupted any reply the youth was going to make about this dark statement.

"We're almost to the clearing," Simon told him.

"Now you'll meet our daughter," Micale said, as he and Nessa caught up with them.

In another few minutes, the travelers stepped out of the forest and into an open mountain glade. The mid-afternoon sun lit up the meadow, providing a dazzling contrast to the dark and gloom of the forest. At first, it was actually painful to their eyes as they adjusted to the new conditions. There was a momentary, stinging blindness. Tears formed and pupils shrank. When he could see again, Willie looked over the expanse of the lea but didn't catch sight of anyone. He then noticed the direction that Brutus was looking. He followed his gaze. A moment later, he saw the group from Sanctuary step out from the far tree line. They were just to the south of their own position. He recognized them at once, especially the girl with the long, snow-white hair. He looked over to Nessa.

"That's right, Willie," she said with a smile. "That's our Melanie and her friends. Now you know why we have to let our daughter live up here. The outside world would never accept her."

Willie nodded his head briefly in agreement. He well knew from their previous encounter that Melanie was different. Different, indeed! He could only imagine the stir that someone like her would have on the people back home in Medinia. She'd be lucky not to be stoned to death.

It then occurred to him that after this Barley moon, maybe he would no longer be welcome there, either. That's what Woodrow had meant when he made his promise that Willie would be free to leave, but that there was no going home, not to the way it used to be. That realization caused a moment of profound sadness to come over him.

The two groups parted the tall meadow grasses and bright summer flowers as they approached each other. Brutus and Freddy were the first to meet as they ran on ahead of the others with their usual exuberance. The others seemed content to just walk and enjoy the breathtaking scenery that the mountain clearing offered.

"It's beautiful out here, isn't it, Willie?" Melanie called out to him.

"Mother Nature in all her glory," he called back.

It was easy to forget that she was sightless, at least in the conventional sense. Yet, there was no denying the truth of her statement; it was indeed beautiful. The brightly flowered mountain lea provided them an entirely different perspective. Instead of the dark canopy they had been traveling under, they were now still surrounded on all sides by tall trees but also by the majestic snow-capped peaks and the open sky.

The mountainside they'd been climbing continued to rise well above the tree line, as did those in the Euralene Range farther to the north and south. The mountains were starkly set against a crisp blue sky. The perpetually snow-covered peaks reached and in some cases disappeared into the solitary clouds that drifted by. All in all, it was a glorious late-summer afternoon, witnessed from a most spectacular mountain meadow setting.

While Brutus and Freddy chased each other about the lea in another rough and tumble game of tag, the two groups came together in the swaying grasses. Willie immediately recognized Chakula, the dark-skinned jungle man with his ritual scarring and tattoos. He also remembered his companion, Marvin, the pale albino who now stood under a bright parasol, which he'd opened upon entering the sunlit clearing.

These two were content to take up station at the perimeters and provide any security that might be required. They were each armed with a hardened staff, and they carried bows and quivers of arrows strung over their backs. Willie wasn't sure that there was anything for them to be guarded from. Still, he somehow felt better knowing that her cautious friends provided protection for Melanie when she traveled.

There was someone in their group, however, whom the youth didn't recognize. The female figure was wearing a shawl with a cowling hood, which covered her head and hid her features. She removed it slowly as she walked up to Simon. The two of them embraced with an obvious passion.

From Willie's vantage point to the side, she appeared to be quite lovely and thus a little out of place, considering the peculiarities of her traveling companions. That was his opinion, at least, until she and Simon parted and they turned to greet the others. He was then confronted by her startling disfigurement.

The hand of the devil marked her face.

*   *   *

"Willie, this is my wife, Tiffany," Simon said, introducing her to him.

The youth started to respond and then stammered something unintelligible, as he found himself flustered by the appearance of her face.

"That's all right, Willie," she said, graciously. "I'm used to people staring. I've been shunned most of my life. People can't help themselves. They've had superstitions ingrained in them all their lives. I'm really not a child of the devil, I assure you."

She was referring to the large wine-stain birthmark that covered almost the entire right side of her face and neck. It stood out in sharp contrast to the quite lovely features of her left side. It was as if her nose separated two entirely different faces. These visible birthmarks were commonly said to have been caused by the hand of Satan. Willie knew that like Melanie, Tiffany could well find herself being stoned in many communities.

The Medinian youth felt his face turning red with embarrassment. To his credit, he shook his head from side to side.

"No, no, it's not all right," he replied. "It was rude of me, and I apologize. It's very nice to meet you, ma'am. Your husband, Simon, has been most quite kind and patient with me, and I've been looking forward to meeting you."

Simon's wife smiled at him, and he knew that he was forgiven. She and Simon then sat cross-legged in the lea with Woodrow, Melanie, and her adoptive parents, Micale and Nessa. The Pack leader wanted to go over the applications of the medicinal supplies they'd brought. It would become Melanie and Tiffany's responsibility to administer them to the people of Sanctuary should the need arise.

As they were talking, Willie finally noticed that there was another member of the Oddities' party whose approach he hadn't noticed. That was partly because he'd been focusing on Melanie and then on Simon's wife, and partly because the fellow had been trailing behind the others, and his head didn't clear the tall grasses of the meadow.

He saw the diminutive Yves approaching now. As before, he could see that the little man was armed with multiple sheathed knives. Willie hesitated in acknowledging him, not sure of the greeting that he would receive in return. The last time that they'd met, it hadn't exactly been on friendly terms. As it turned out, the little man proved to be more amiable on this occasion.

"*Oui*, it is *un bon jour*," Yves agreed, picking up on Willie's greeting with Melanie. "Beautiful." The dwarf's heavy accent made the word sound like 'bew-tee-ful.'

He plunked himself down beside Willie and nodded his head in a friendly greeting. The two of them actually conversed for a time. Willie learned that Yves knew Micale and Nessa quite well. He had, in fact, traveled in the same performing troupe with them for a number of years. Yves had been both a jester and a skilled knife-thrower in their act back in those days, and he'd been with them when they'd discovered Melanie as an abandoned babe. He'd entered Sanctuary, partly due to his own desire to be with those who wouldn't make sport of him, and partly to keep a close eye on the small child they'd all cared for.

As they talked, it became apparent that the wee man was prepared to leave the hostility of their past encounter behind them. Indeed, when they parted company a short while later, Yves even carefully shook his hand.

"Best of, how you say, the luck, with your change over, and I have the hope you will not go, how is it? Insane in the head," he said, as he twirled his finger by his temple.

Willie laughed, possibly because he'd been entertaining the same notion himself, but hadn't been able to express it quite so quaintly.

When they parted company, the others gave him the same encouragement in their own more subtle ways. It was Melanie, however, who reached up to kiss his cheek and wish him well.

"You take care of yourself, Willie of Medinia. Listen to Woodrow, and to Simon and Tiffany. They'll look out for you," she whispered in his ear.

"I'll try," he promised. He reached inside his shirt and withdrew the clear crystal shepherd that hung on the cord around his neck.

"It's your gift," he said, "I wear it for good luck."

She smiled and then turned away to rejoin her friends. Willie stood watching for a time as she walked away with her arms locked in with those of Micale and Nessa. He wished that he could have gone with them instead of taking the journey that still lay ahead.

The manor couple and their blind but gifted stepdaughter were trailed by Yves and flanked by their two contrasting guards from Sanctuary. Freddy was now bounding across the meadow from his play with Brutus in an effort to catch up to them, all the while clamouring for them to "wait up."

Willie and his companions returned their last wave good-bye, just before the trees to the south swallowed them up.

*   *   *

It was now their turn to step back into the forest. The only difference was in the direction they took. Their course was to the northeast and to a still higher elevation. Their final destination was near the upper tree line on the mountain. That was where the caves were found, Willie was told, which served as the dens and meeting places for the Pack.

The last time that they were near here, Willie had been unconscious and strapped into a travois. The Pack leader had bypassed the caves to take the youth to his cabin. This time, they would be spending their nights with the Pack, although Woodrow intended to visit his mountain retreat during the daylight hours, after each reversion had subsided.

Willie walked beside the Pack leader as they followed the lead of Brutus beneath the canopy of the remaining forest giants. Simon and Tiffany were content to follow a ways behind and to get caught up after their prolonged separation.

The Pack's lieutenant did his best to bring his wife up to date on everything that had occurred since last they'd been together. He included as few details as possible of his visit with Lord Victor. He didn't want to worry her. Nevertheless, like any good wife, Tiffany knew when something was wrong. She could sense when there were things troubling her husband.

Up ahead, Woodrow was doing some sensing of his own. He correctly concluded that the youth needed to talk some more before they reached the caves.

"Earlier, when I said that we were pagans, Willie, I meant that we have a dark nature, one which we should not, and can not deny. We're primal hunters. We're part of the natural—or perhaps the unnatural—order of things. Nevertheless, there exists a symbiotic relationship, or a mutual dependency, if you prefer, between the hunter and his prey. They exist together within a food chain that ebbs and flows between feast and famine."

"There you go again," Willie groused. "Can't you ever just speak in plain terms? I could do with a little less philosophy and a little more basic reality."

The Pack leader laughed heartily. "Perhaps you're right. I do have a habit of over-thinking a subject at times. It comes from having lived so long, I suppose. I've had an extraordinary long time to think about things. What I meant to say was there are times when the growing conditions are good and the grass-feeders population grows with it. In those same good times, the hunter's numbers grow, as well. Since there are more prey animals to be found, wolf packs start to have larger litters. Even secondary members of their packs will be allowed to have a litter. Primarily, the hunters weed out the old and weaker members of the herd and some of its young. In either event, the herd gets culled, and this helps them to stay strong and to survive during the hard times."

"It still sounds to me like you're justifying your actions," the youth said, "but I'll grant you that it doesn't seem any worse than when man raises livestock and poultry for slaughter. At least the deer and the elk have a chance to get away."

The Pack leader laughed. "You'd be surprised how often that very thing happens. I think you'll find that prey animals are very cautious, very fast, and very agile. It takes skill and patience if you hope to get up close and personal."

"What do you mean, up close and personal?"

"We're not talking about a hunter hiding in a blind or up in a tree and shooting an arrow at some unsuspecting animal, Willie. We're talking about an organized hunt. A proper hunt requires cunning, strategy, and luck. They all play a role, because when you make a kill, it's always up close, and it's always personal."

*   *   *

Like the Oddities Sanctuary village, when they arrived at their destination, Willie found it rather unremarkable at first sight. One minute they'd been skirting the trees of the thinning forest, and the next, the Pack leader had said that they were there. *There* wasn't anywhere as far as Willie could discern.

At least the heavy forest is behind us now, the youth thought with relief.

They could actually see the sky again. The late-day sun had broken through the tree tops and the fresh breeze had swept away the clammy claustrophobia that Willie had endured beneath the thicker canopy below. He was far less concerned that the sun didn't provide nearly as much warmth at this altitude.

A little ways ahead, the youth could see where the forest ended completely. After that, only the bare mountain rock face remained, until you reached the snow-capped peak—as if you ever could, that is.

To Willie's eyes, nothing about where they were seemed to indicate the caves that they were said to be seeking. He looked over the surrounding terrain and then over at the yellow-eyed Pack enforcer. Brutus sat on his haunches with his tongue lolling out and stared right back at him. Willie thought, and not for the first time, that it looked as if the alpha wolf was laughing at his expense.

"Okay, smart ass. If we're here, where's everybody else?" he asked the wolf though not expecting any answer.

The youth put his foot up on a tree stump and began rubbing his leg. The limb was definitely getting better, but the exertion of the day's strenuous hike had caused a steady dull ache to set in.

As if in a belated reply to the youth's question, the Pack enforcer yipped once and then bolted towards a thick but stumpy evergreen. The tree grew out at right angles to the slope before it turned back skywards. Brutus slipped around its branched trunk and promptly vanished.

"So, where did he go ..."

The youth's voice trailed off as he realized that he was talking to himself. They'd all vanished. Woodrow, Simon, Tiffany—and now Brutus!

"Cute," he muttered, and then again, somewhat louder this time. "That's real cute people!"

"Are you coming?"

Willie jumped at the sound of Simon's voice. He turned in that direction and could see the Pack lieutenant's head sticking out from the underside of a rock face.

"Real cute," the lad muttered once more.

Willie walked over to where the slope dropped off at the base of the rock facing. Bending down, he peered into the hole that Simon had slid back into.

"Come in feet first," he heard Tiffany call up.

"Lovely. Just when we finally get the sun back, you want me to crawl into some dark hole in the ground," he complained.

With that stated emphatically, he then made his way down the slope then boosted his self up and over the rock rim. He turned around carefully and, as instructed, backed into the opening feet first. He slid some eight feet down a relatively smooth slope and then fell to the cave floor on his ass. Two of his traveling companions were there waiting for him. Simon reached out and helped him back to his feet. It took several seconds for his eyes to re-adjust to the dimness. It was then that he realized that the Pack's leader and its enforcer were no longer with them.

"What happened to Woodrow and Brutus?"

"The Pack leader has gone on ahead. He must prepare the Pack to meet you. As for Brutus, he came in by a different entrance. Since he got us all here safe and sound, he's probably gone on ahead to join his family," Simon conjectured.

"He has a family?" Willie asked, with surprise.

"Maybe we should sit down for a minute and we'll explain a few things about the Pack—and about these caves," Simon suggested.

"That'd be nice," Willie replied with a hint of sarcasm. "I think I've had ample surprises for one day. In fact, I think maybe I should just wait right here until you all come back. At least there's still enough light coming in the hole to see by."

While Willie cast an appraising look around the grotto that they'd slid into, Tiffany sat down on what appeared to be a crystallized bench. Above her head was a cone-shaped growth that hung down from the cave ceiling and ended in a slow dripping, circular point.

The youth decided to look for somewhat safer seating and finally opted to just sit down in the open space where he was currently standing. His body was prickling like crazy now. He didn't even know where to begin to scratch. He willed himself to refrain from scratching at all, but it was difficult not to succumb to the urge.

Simon leaned himself up against a column that rose from its base on the cave floor to the ceiling overhead. He observed the youth's fidgeting. He knew without being told that Willie was in a state of discomfort. He knew because he was feeling the same way.

"Do you know what it is that I'm leaning against?" he asked.

"It looks a little like a tree," the youth replied. "You can see the way that it widens at the base for the roots, and then branches out up at the ceiling. Except maybe, it's made out of some sort of crystal."

"A good observation," Simon acknowledged. "Where Tiffany is sitting, that's called a stalagmite. It's been formed over several centuries from the mineral water that seeps down from up above. That formation over her head is called a stalactite. Can you see the little straw-like hole in the end? That's formed as the water drips down through the centre and deposits ring after ring of what's called calcite. If the hole becomes plugged, the mineral water will seek out a new route," he explained. "Usually, it's down the outside of the straw, which creates layers as they crystallize. That, in turn, forms the larger stalactite structure. If the drip is strong enough, it falls all the way to the floor and forms the stalagmite."

"So that column you're leaning on is where the two of them have grown together?" Willie surmised.

"Most likely," Simon replied. "You'll see lots of different formations as we move on through the cave system."

"How many caves are there?"

"Dozens," Simon answered. "Where we are now is the northern entrance to a whole series of caves, or grottoes. The Pack has made these our home. There are plenty of others that are simply freestanding caves. Then there are the caverns that lead into the Oddities' valley to the south. You saw those with Woodrow."

"Some of those caves have been enlarged, though, or they've had new passages dug out to gain access to one chamber to another," Simon explained. "The caverns here are more naturally formed. They're interconnected by a combination of passageways and shafts that were carved out centuries ago."

"Carved out by the water?" Willie surmised.

"Indeed," Simon affirmed. "The ridges and gullies throughout the mountain chain have a lot of sink holes, depressions, and crevices. They trap the water from all the rains and melting snow. The water works its way down into the mountains and erodes away the softer, more soluble rock, like limestone. You'll see some underground steams that flow through some of the sections. In a few of the caves, you'll even find small ponds and spring-fed pools."

Simon paused, as he took a moment to look about the grotto. "There are a lot of places like this, where the moisture seeps through more slowly. I suppose that it picks up minerals from the rock as it passes through. These are some of the formations that result."

"There are other types of formations too," Tiffany added. "You'll see lots of clusters and knobs of crystals on the walls, and even much larger deposits where the drippings have flowed over a cave floor. Some of them have the appearance of a gentle ocean wave that's been frozen in time. They're really quite spectacular."

"Why does the Pack live here?" Willie asked them.

"Mostly because it's isolated," Tiffany answered, "and because the grottoes make for good dens where the young can be kept safe."

"Plus, the hunting is good all around us," Simon added. "The Pack's territory is extensive. We can roam throughout the mountains from this home base to find our prey. Different cave exits give us access to ridges and valleys over much of the Euralenes. That's one of the ways we make sure that no one area ever gets over-hunted and depleted."

"There are a few larger caverns, where we can gather each month," Tiffany told him then. "We call them rendezvous sites. On the full-moon cycle, all the Pack comes together in one designated place."

"Speaking of which," Simon said, "why don't we carry on this conversation while we walk? We've still got a ways to go yet."

"Like I said earlier," Willie replied uneasily, "maybe I should just wait for you here." "I'm not overly fond of dark, closed-in places."

"Willie, my lad, the moon will soon be on the rise. You don't want to be alone when it arrives," Simon said.

"There'll be enough light filtering in for us to see by, so don't worry about that," Tiffany assured him, "and there'll be some lamps lit that some of the Pack maintain where they're needed."

"The cavern where we're meeting the Pack is large and a lot roomier than this opening," Simon informed him. He extended his hand again. "You'll feel better when we get there."

Somehow, Willie doubted that, but he reluctantly accepted the assistance and pulled himself up. He then did the same in assisting Tiffany to her feet.

"Everything will be okay, Willie," she quietly assured him, giving his hand a squeeze.

*   *   *

Tiffany hadn't exaggerated when she spoke of the spectacular cave formations they would encounter. As they moved through the labyrinth of scenic chambers, any phobia Willie had concerning closed in spaces had all but vanished. There was a diffuse sunlight that filtered in through cracks, crevices, and other entrances of varying size. In some of the darker confines, there were a few weakly-lit lamps set into the walls. The dim light they cast was kept just sufficient enough to see by.

Willie marvelled at the diversity of it all. Their walk took them along rough, curving passageways, where they often had to side step or duck under the myriad of crystalline growths. They made several climbs and descents through shafts that were smooth and rounded by the passage of water, and time.

Each of the caves was a wonder in its own right. Each was different in size, shape, and in the textures of its formations. As Simon had said, there were pools of spring water in some. In others, slow flowing streams bubbled to the surface at one point, only to disappear into a chute at another. Willie even saw a frozen waterfall that on closer inspection proved to be a flowstone of calcium carbonate, which resembled sheets of ice.

The youth made his self a promise that if he survived this ordeal, he would come back and spend more time just exploring. There were dozens of passageways that they didn't take. Several of the corridors led off in different directions from the one they now traveled to their rendezvous with the Pack.

The Pack's beta male took care climbing down the ledge leading to the next section of their trek, and then he reached up and assisted his wife down. He then turned back and did the same for the Medinian youth.

"How is it that the Pack has both wolves and humans in it?" Willie asked as he accepted Simon's assistance. "Doesn't that defy the nature of things?"

"It's true. It does seem to defy logic," Tiffany agreed. "It's because we share the same affliction that we've been drawn together. You can pick up the same scent from us all. It sets us apart. I really don't know what causes that."

"Do you?" he asked, Simon.

"Not entirely, no. The common Pack scent that we share is at least part of it, but it's a long story, Willie," Simon replied. "Suffice it to say, the Pack is unique in that it's an ancient bonding between similarly moon-afflicted humans and wolves. It began long before my and Tiffany's time, and long before the time of Woodrow and Brutus. And before the two who led the Pack before them."

"There have always been two inseparable companions, if you will, who lead the Pack," Tiffany added. "One comes from each of the two species. They are the alpha males of each. And when the time comes for those alpha males to step aside, when they're too old to lead the hunt, then two new companions will take their place. But the two of them must be prepared to face any and all challengers for the right to be the alpha leaders."

"You're starting to make them sound like royalty," Willie said.

"I suppose, in a sense, they are. You'll be able to see for yourself," Simon told him. "We're here now."

*　　　　*　　　　*

The last passageway brought them to the cavern of the gathering. It opened up onto a winding ledge that wound down to the cavern floor below. Willie looked down into the largest cave he'd seen yet. He could see quite clearly as the ample cave entrance faced west, overlooking Varakov. The setting sun was casting its rays directly inside.

For the moment, however, Willie's attention was riveted on the cavern below. For there below him, was the Pack. The Pack had occupied his mind with loathing, hatred, and dread. He'd thought about this moment a great deal, ever since he'd become aware of his condition in Woodrow's cabin. It was hard to believe that was only a month ago. It seemed like a different lifetime.

Here he was now, coming to meet this band of strangers in their torn rags, who would soon become creatures of the moonlit night. If that wasn't bad enough, there were always the twenty or more adult wolves and a number of their young in attendance.

"What are they doing with Brutus?" he asked quietly. Willie nodded with his chin down towards the group immediately below them.

"Those wolves are paying their respects to the alpha male and the alpha female. That would be Brutus and his mate, Cleo. She's the beautiful silver and grey one standing at his side," Simon pointed out. "Over there, the humans are doing much the same with the Pack leader," he added.

"Why do they do that?" Willie asked him.

"Because these three lead the Pack," Simon explained patiently. "If the Pack leader's wife were alive, or if he'd taken a new mate, then she'd be standing there as well."

"Sit here quietly and just observe them while we get changed, Willie," Tiffany said quietly but firmly. "We have to wait until they're ready to summon you."

Simon and his wife slipped into a short tunnel off the passageway, where they took ragged clothes from their backpacks and got changed into them. Despite the circumstances, they took a few moments to reach out and caress each other. They'd been apart for quite some time, and it was obvious they missed each other's touch.

When they returned, Willie looked over their way, but he quickly averted his eyes. Tiffany's body was now as much exposed, as it was covered, just like the bodies were of the people below them. This caused him a moment of embarrassment, yet no one else seemed to care that everyone was so scantily clad.

"I'll go down and let the Pack leader know that we await his command for your introduction to the Pack," Simon said.

"My ... introduction?" the youth asked, with obvious nervousness.

"Stay with Tiffany until you're called for," he replied. "She'll explain the way of things." Then he was gone, following the curving ledge as it descended to the cavern floor.

Tiffany sat down beside him, but he kept his eyes turned away. She could tell from his shortened breathing pattern that the youth was clearly getting distressed.

"Try to relax, Willie," she advised. "I want you to observe their behaviour. Watch the way the other wolves approach Brutus and Cleo. Watch their body language."

The youth could see the subservient manner in which each wolf presented itself to the alpha wolves. Generally, they kept their fur flattened and their ears lowered. They approached with their posture low, their fangs sheathed and their tails curled under their rumps. Some wolves would literally crawl forward.

These traits did not show up in either of the alpha wolves. The fur on Brutus and his mate was fluffed up and shone luxuriantly. They held their heads and tails high. Their ears stood erect and proud. At the approach of certain wolves, their hackles fairly bristled. They bared their fangs almost ritually, as if they felt the need to assert their authority. Inevitably, the particular wolf would cringe even further.

Understandably so, Willie thought. *So would I.*

With other wolves, especially the younger ones, Brutus and Cleo would accept the fawning nuzzles and licks accorded their ranking in the Pack. All in all, it was certainly apparent that Brutus and his mate were the acknowledged leaders of the wolves.

A moment later, a lone black and grey wolf about the same size as Brutus approached the alpha male. This one didn't cower or crawl, as the others had. Instead, he gazed at the Pack enforcer through his single eye, almost as if challenging Brutus. Willie assumed that he'd lost the other eye in a brutal fight of some sort, for there was considerable damage to that side of the animal's head.

Both male wolves unsheathed their savage-looking fangs and uttered deep-throated snarls. It appeared that they were about to attack each other. Brutus advanced and took the other wolf's muzzle in his jaws. Yet, it wasn't an attack; it was more an assertion of his higher ranking. At that point, the one-eyed wolf submitted by lying down, rolling over, and exposing its side and belly to the Pack enforcer.

"That's One-Eye. He's the Pack's beta male. He's Simon's counterpart and he's the head of one of the smaller family groups that make up the larger Pack."

She explained further when she saw the confused expression that crossed his face.

"You see, Willie, every wolf pack is really an extended family. "There are aunts and uncles, brothers and sisters, and younger siblings from any new litters. Usually in wolf packs, it's only the alpha male and female that mate and produce a litter. The whole pack will then take up active roles in the raising of the young. That way, the pups learn to demonstrate the same respectful behaviour to the other higher-ranking wolves."

"Do they fight a lot to prove who is dominant?" Willie asked.

"Actually, not that often," Tiffany answered. "Wolves rarely find the need to fight to exert their dominance. If there's any actual infighting, it's usually during the mating season, and then it's Cleo who does the brawling. Sometimes she needs to remind the other females who's in charge of breeding. Generally speaking, pretty well every wolf knows and accepts its place in the pecking order."

"Although, I must say," she added with a chuckle, "the senior wolves are very tolerant when it comes to the young ones. Sometimes, they can get pretty rambunctious, you know. Wolf pups love to wrestle and pounce on each other and pretty much anything else they come across. It's part of their hunting instinct."

"Like that one over there."

Tiffany pointed out a juvenile wolf, which even now was trying to creep up on one of its unsuspecting sibling sisters as she sat quietly grooming herself.

Creep was perhaps a misnomer, for the young male wolf was at that awkward stage. He seemed to be all legs, large paws, and counter-productive motions. There was precious little of the grace of movement and co-ordination that would develop as he grew into adulthood. Still, he had managed to get into position undetected and was about to launch his assault.

His sister remained blissfully unaware. The young male's tongue rolled happily over his gums as he prepared to take his sister by surprise. He crouched low and was coiled to spring to the attack, just as he'd been taught to do.

That was just before a small silver-grey blur flashed across the cavern floor and bowled him over instead.

The third juvenile on the scene, Tiffany explained as she laughed quietly, had been born the runt of the six-pup litter that Cleo had produced in early March. He'd proven to be a determined little fellow, however. The runt of the litter had not only survived; he'd grown strong over the spring and summer months. He still lacked the height and overall length of his brother, but he was solidly built and chunkier than the others were.

"Hey, look at that! Now that's gratitude for you," Willie observed. He couldn't help but chuckle as they watched the antics of the young wolves.

Down below them, the sibling sister had awakened to the fact that two of her brothers were wrestling behind her. She'd turned and jumped into the fray, nipping her little heavy-set rescuer for good measure. For his part, the chunky runt seemed just as willing to wrestle with her as he was with his bigger brother.

"Have you noticed how all the juveniles' eyes are blue, but not any of the adults?" Tiffany asked. "Pups are born that way, but the colour usually changes to a yellow-gold as they get older."

"When Brutus looks at me with those eyes of his, they look like two miniature suns. I think he can see right through me with them," Willie whispered. "That's one of the reasons I don't feel very comfortable around him."

"Brutus is a pretty clever animal, Willie," Tiffany stated. "He has to be, or he wouldn't be the alpha male. His primary concern is for the welfare of the Pack. As the Pack's enforcer, he must safeguard the Pack leader, as well as the Pack's territory. He'd die fighting in the defence of either one rather than submit to an enemy."

Down below them, a drum was pounded three times. All the activity below them came to a slow halt.

"It's time," Tiffany said, quietly.

CHAPTER 17

The Transformation

The moonlight beckons like a moth to the flame
I can hear the wind calling out my name
I can hear it whispering through the trees
I think that I'm losing my sanity
What the hell is happening to me?

"The Barley Moon"
One night before the apex of the full moon

August 20, 1461
The Euralene Mountains, Varakov

WILLIE FELT A RANGE of sensations as Tiffany led him down the winding ledge. His initial response to the summons was a feeling of dread, and now it was all he could do to will his legs to move. He sensed the eyes of the Pack following their progress from below.

At the same time, his brain was afire and his eyes burned. The moon-prickles continued to intensify as they coursed through his body. The gathering on the cavern floor had quieted at his approach, yet his ears were assaulted by sounds. It was as if he could hear their breathing and even their heartbeats.

The contingent of wolves formed into a long row, facing inward from his left. The ragged, scantily clad human contingent did the same in a row to his right. When they reached the cavern floor, Tiffany gave his hand a firm squeeze.

"Keep your eyes down and kneel when I do," she whispered. "There's nothing to be afraid of here. We are the Pack. These are our brethren."

Her reassurance helped him to focus on the task at hand. He drew in a deep breath and exhaled slowly. Tiffany led him through the gauntlet between the two rows of the Pack. She set the pace, which resembled a bridal procession moving stately down a church aisle. Each pronounced step was punctuated by a brief pause. At each step, the Pack members at that spot moved slightly inward. They took in Willie's scent, as if to register his odour for future reference. It bore the same taint as did their own—the distinctive scent that marked the Pack.

At times, teeth were bared or a low growl issued from a husky throat. These sounds came as often from the human side, as it did from the wolves. Willie kept Tiffany's counsel; he lowered his eyes and kept his manner submissive. Finally, they neared the end of the gauntlet. On a stone pedestal in front of them stood the Pack leader, with the Pack enforcer and his alpha mate— Woodrow, Brutus, and Cleo. That was the moment when the newcomer was challenged.

When they came to the last pairings in the gauntlet, Willie recognized Simon in his torn, filthy rags. Across from him, One-Eye, the beta-male wolf, stepped forward and bared his deadly fangs. The animal's hackles rose and he growled deeply but did not lunge. Instead, the wolf turned his head and looked up to Brutus and Cleo, standing above. As if having made his displeasure known; the second most-dominant male wolf then backed away to retake his place in the line.

To Willie's relief, their next step brought them to the base of the pedestal. He likely wouldn't have made it any farther. Following Tiffany's lead, he knelt respectfully and bowed his head.

First, Brutus stepped forward and placed his substantial right paw on the youth's shoulder, and then his mate, Cleo, placed hers on the other shoulder.

Last was Woodrow. The Pack leader placed his foot lightly upon the back of the youth's head. He looked out over the assembly and declared, both vocally and with gestures that the youth was now one of them. Willie was part of their collective Pack, from this night forth.

"Rise, Willie of the Pack," he instructed. The three Pack leaders stepped back and waited while Tiffany and Willie stood.

His voice stern, Woodrow declared, "In the years ahead, it will be your choice whether you walk a solitary road or run with the Pack. In either case, you are always one of us. You will always have a home to return to."

Simon stepped forward with a wicked looking knife in his hand. He smiled at Willie and then went about rending the youth's clothing with the blade, until his body was as exposed as the other humans.

Brutus gave a yipping howl, and then Cleo joined in, followed by Woodrow. One by one, each Pack member followed suit. Their howling songs overlapped each other and as one faded away, another rose, each an individual signature. It was the attestation of their existence and of their identity.

While the cavern walls reverberated with wave upon wave of vocal harmony, Willie heard and felt the sound of the Pack throughout his being. It was the undeniable song of his Pack.

Willie's blood was boiling up inside. The surface of his skin, from his scalp down to his toes, pulsated in waves of pins and needles. He found it more and more difficult to concentrate. His senses were bombarded with too many stimuli for his brain to process. The sounds, the smells, the sights—his every sensory input was in overload.

Willie staggered to the cave entrance and sucked in the night air in a vain attempt to clear his head and slow his racing heartbeat.

The Pack leader came to stand by his side. "It will soon be time," he said. "Try not to fight it. You must find your centre and ride out the coming storm."

Woodrow had experienced this moment countless times. He was doing so even now. There was little that the Pack leader could do for the youth at this stage. Still, he would be there. Over countless lunar months, he had endured firsthand the intensity of the transformation. It mattered not if the skies were overcast and blocked the moon from view; the cycle came when it came. The three-night cycle of the full moon triggered the change in them all. The Pack members were all creatures of the moon goddess, and it mattered not if they were in the darkest of caves or down in the bowels of the earth—the tide arrived when the tide arrived.

"Try to focus your mind on your friends," Woodrow said. "Think of Pegasus, Rigel, and Sirius, and what they meant to you. Think about the warmth of the farm on a summer day as you and your friends went about your chores. Let that be your haven to ride out the storm."

*　　　　*　　　　*

Initially, it was all centred on the acute pain that drove Willie to the ground and took his breath away. His body contorted in agony as wave after wave of pain pulsated throughout his being. It overwhelmed him and swept him away.

Every cell of his body started to mutate, altering itself into new patterns of shape and function. Bone thickened in places. Skin rippled and reformed over new muscle mass in his legs, arms, and shoulders. The capacity of his lungs, even the size of his heart, expanded to fill the cavity of his enlarged chest.

His fingers and toes crackled as they elongated and broadened. Nails extended, growing stronger and more like claws. His hair grew and thickened until it resembled a mane. His teeth enlarged into savage fangs that grew into the new spaces in his extending jawbones. His eyes blazed blood red, as if they were outlets of a soul burning in hell.

Then, from deep within the pain, a fount of new strength arose. He could feel it growing. As Woodrow had foretold, it was a feeling he welcomed. He no longer fought the pain; it was outside him now. He gave into the insanity of the transformation, thereby saving his sanity. He took refuge in his haven. He kept his focus on Sirius, Rigel, Pegasus, the friends he had long cherished. A last, tortured gasp escaped his misshapen mouth and the final stages of the transformation swept over him.

*   *   *

The three nights of the full-moon cycle had arrived, marking the passage of another lunar month. The Barley Moon in late August of 1461 commanded the clear horizon where it glowed with a burnt-orange, set ablaze by the departing sun. The near full moon, of the night before the apex, rose and broke free of the mountains. Her outer rim paled, and then gradually the rest of her surface. She became a pristine white save for those vast, grey crater markings on her surface that stood out so clearly.

Diana climbed above the mountain peaks and took up her station in the night skies. She was the goddess that the Pack knew as the protectress of the hunter and his mate. Tonight, the moon goddess had come forth in all her splendour as if she were welcoming a new initiate to her fold.

Diana called out to her children, both old and new. As always, they answered her undeniable call.

*　　　　　*　　　　　*

When at last the metamorphosis was complete, a deep-throated snarl rumbled forth from the moon-child who had been Willie of Medinia. Weakly at first, he raised himself to one knee. He inhaled the night air deeply and then slowly released it. Over and over again he filled and then emptied his newly expanded lungs.

The oxygen coursing through his bloodstream awakened him to a new reality. He gradually became aware of himself and tried to reclaim what was left of his wits. He sensed a raw power deep in his core, the likes of which he'd never felt before. He slowly rose to stand erect on his enlarged clawed feet. He was a creature of the Pack now, fully transformed. His brain was clouded and his thinking unclear. He felt a primal rage simmering within him that threatened to boil over although, as yet, he had no clear focus to vent it upon.

The other Pack members came staggering out of the cavern to stand together on the mountainside and acknowledge the arrival of Diana, Goddess of the Moon, and the reason for their existence. Whether two-legged or four-legged, they were undeniably her creatures and, as always, they were united by her irresistible call.

The young wolf-man remained to the side of the cave entrance, watching the others through blazing red eyes. Low growls emanated from deep down in his chest now, but he was not even conscious of his making them. He was tense and angry but incapable of saying exactly why that was. He looked away from the Pack and up into the sky, focussing for a time on the nearly full moon hanging overhead.

His growls ceased when he sensed the approach of others. Turning his attention away from the moon, he then faced Woodrow, Simon, and Tiffany. He knew instinctively who they were, even though their appearance was as radically altered as his own.

The transformation had been less dramatic in its impact on Tiffany's features. Her wine-stain blemish was no longer visible within its new facial structure and hair, but her jaws and snout were less distended than those of her male counterparts. He could still see her in there. This was not true of the males; they were redefined entirely. Yet he knew instinctively who they were.

Willie's eyes moved away from the two wolf-men and returned to the figure of the beta male's wife. He found himself looking at Tiffany's body lasciviously. It felt strangely erotic to see her pure animal form, clad only in ripped rags that barely covered her. His young male eyes were tracing the flow of her legs. As his eyes rose up over her thighs, he heard Simon's menacing snarl.

Having been caught in the act, red eyed if not red handed, Willie dropped his gaze and backed away. He felt a hot flush of guilt and shame. Those strong emotions triggered a flood of others, the primary one being a deep sense of isolation. He didn't belong here. He didn't fit in. He didn't fit in anywhere.

The rage within him flared up like a stoked fire sending crackling flames from his belly to his brain. These creatures were the reason his entire life had gone to this hell. He hated them.

Why should I feel guilt about anything? None of this is of my doing!

The Pack's beta male stepped forward. He sought to forgive the youth his unintended urges and to lessen the tension. The Pack leader tried to indicate that he wished him to join the Pack circle as they gathered to pay tribute to Diana.

The young wolf-man who had once been Willie of Medinia allowed his eyes to follow the Pack leader's gesture up towards the full moon's surface, yet all he was aware of was his anger and self-pity. He let loose a long howl, but it was not a howl of celebration to honour the moon goddess, or a call to hunt; it was a howl of despair and loneliness.

The newest Pack member broke away then and ran, even as the others reached out to comfort him. He scrambled down the rocky slope with reckless abandon and then disappeared into the great forest.

*   *   *

The Euralene Mountains, Varakov

A young female elk stepped cautiously out into the forest clearing. She raised her trembling nose into the twilight air and tested for the scent of danger.

Behind her, still hidden in the foliage, was the last of the two calves from her first pregnancy. They'd been born to her that spring. Her other calf had been lost to nature's predators two months earlier.

She had experienced a difficult first birthing with two calves and was left weak and exhausted. In the end, she and her calves had become separated from the rest of the herd. Luckily, the spring and summer months had provided a bountiful food supply. She and her remaining calf had survived. She had honed her survival instincts, as a mother must do when protecting her young. That was why she'd lingered so long at the forest edge, waiting and watching for the slightest movement or sound. It was why she now tested the air yet again for any scent of a predator carried on the breeze.

Her goal was a quiet pool of water in the little meadow where the grasses were lush and tender. When the sun cast its last rays on the mountainside, she decided that it was safe to venture forth. Every few steps, she paused to re-evaluate the situation by sight, sound, and smell. Her every sense was on edge and her body quivered.

Her calf stumbled after her. Its awkward legs were still not fully under control, but they were getting stronger. They would need to be, for soon enough it would be winter. Before then, they would have to keep on the move in hopes of finding the herd. If not, the predators would surely get them when the snows came. The herd was their only hope of protection.

They drank at the pool's edge and ate freely of the grass, until the young mother sensed it was time to find the shelter of a thicket and bed down for the night. She called softly to the calf to follow her. With a last mouthful of sweet meadow grass, the calf turned to obey its mother's summons.

At that same moment, a gigantic, bellowing mass of destructive power charged out of the forest cover. The grizzled brown bear's roaring savagery was directed at the prey animals a few scant yards ahead of him.

As intended, the bear's deafening roars and the suddenness of its attack froze the calf in its tracks. It was virtually beheaded by one savage slash, delivered by four-inch curved claws and the strength of the massive paw behind them. The calf was dead before it hit the ground.

Not that the elk calf would have escaped had it tried to run. The giant brown bear had planned and executed the kill with the precision of the veteran hunter that it was. Its silver-tipped fur attested its many years' experience.

Despite the bear's advanced years, it was still quick and agile enough to run down almost any prey over a short distance.

There had been a time, however, when the bear would have got both the calf and the mother, who even now was bolting across the meadow. The young mother elk came to a stop at the farthest forest edge, to stand for a time, bleating out her sorrow. Her last calf lost, she would have to wait to the next spring to bear a new one, provided she could manage to survive until she found the herd.

The huge male brown bear rose up on its hind legs and roared its defiance in the female elk's direction. The sight and sound of the great beast, which stood nearly eight feet tall and weighed thirteen hundred pounds, was fearsome indeed. Terror stricken, the young mother elk turned and fled into the woods.

Satisfied that its hunting prowess had been properly acknowledged, the bear dropped down on all four legs. Even then, he remained over four feet high at his shoulder hump. In his two-hundred-square-mile home range, there was no single predator more ferocious, and the brown bear feared no other creature.

There were a few of the other mountain predators that the bear preferred to avoid, however. Wolves were among those. In his lifetime, he'd had several confrontations with wolf packs. On one occasion, he'd come across a den of young pups with only their mother there to try to protect them. Without a pack to harass him, she'd been no match for his hungry fury. She and her pups had been a welcome addition to his diet.

There were other times when the veteran bear had come across wolf packs with their recent kill. If there weren't too many, he was sometimes able to drive them off and steal their prey. If he was able to kill a few of the wolves in the process, that was all the better. They were competition for the prey animals, after all. To the mightiest predator went the spoils. That was nature's way.

The only other creatures that the bear was slightly wary of walked on two legs. Only a month ago, they'd come with their dogs and their flying pain-sticks. He had fled from those at first and from the clamouring canines they unleashed, until, finally cornered, he'd turned on the dogs and in a snarling rage had hurled himself into their midst. It had been a bloody battle, but the bear had emerged victorious. Their torn and shredded carcasses affirmed that.

The bear had then doubled back on his trail and waited patiently for darkness. The three creatures that walked upright on two legs had built a large fire to huddle around for safety during the night, but little good that did them. For an animal of his tremendous size and girth, the bear was capable of great stealth, and the fire only served to blind the prey.

Much as he'd stalked the elk tonight, the bear had worked himself into a close perimeter, downwind of the hunters, and crouched at the edge of the underbrush. He'd waited for the right moment and then had launched a roaring charge into their midst.

One man had died instantly. A sweeping slash across his neck, and the man's head had rolled free of his body. The bear had been on top of the second man an instant later. His powerful jaws had crushed that one's skull with ease, but the third man had then sent a flying pain-stick into one of its shoulders.

The brown bear had risen, hurt and bellowing with anger, as the man let loose a second pain-stick. That one had sunk deeply into the bear's thigh. Killing that final enemy had been a satisfactory revenge, and the man's remains were then scattered all over the mountainside.

The pain-stick in his shoulder had worked itself out quickly. Rejected by the powerful muscles there, it hadn't penetrated deeply. The arrow that had found his thigh was another matter, however. The bear had easily snapped off the exposed shaft; it had been no more than a stick, yet the pain did not abate. Not understanding that the arrowhead and part of the shaft remained in his leg, the grizzled bear knew only that he still felt the pain, and it infuriated him.

*　　　　*　　　　*

Willie ran with an ease that he'd never experienced before. Each drive of his legs sent him bounding further through the night. After he entered the forest, he turned north, running just inside the tree line where the going was easiest. He was attempting to distance himself from the others of the Pack, and from his anger and shame.

Far behind, he could hear the howling calls of the Pack. They were in pursuit of him. He shuddered involuntarily. Deep within his clouded mind lurked memories of another time and place when the Pack had pursued him. At that time, he'd been terrified. Now he was confident that he could outrun them forever. His once-injured leg felt strong and sure beneath him. It was the one blessing of the lunar transformation.

The forest no longer seemed an alien place. Despite his initial rage, he soon found himself running in an exhilarating state of wild abandon. An exquisite new agility enhanced his gait. He rarely broke stride and he instinctively avoided obstacles in his path. His lungs filled to an expanded capacity that would carry him for miles. He panted lightly while he ran effortlessly through the woods. The moonlight that broke through at the edge of the forest provided ample light. His eyesight was keener and his senses more alive than ever before.

A short time later, he discovered a faint but well-traveled path that made the running even easier. He picked up the pace and ran faster still. Spotting a fallen tree in the path ahead, he bore down on it. At the last possible second, he leaped through the air. The thrill of clearing the obstacle in his path without even breaking stride was a heady rush. It wasn't until he landed that he saw the path bend sharply away from the edge of a cliff.

It was too late to halt his forward momentum, and he would surely have gone over the cliff edge if not for the big, shaggy bush that he crashed into. The impenetrable obstacle sent him bouncing backward across the rocky ground, instead of splattering on the rocks in the canyon far below. His life had been spared. Yet, what had appeared at first to have been a thick bush now rose up and roared defiantly at him.

Willie had been saved from plummeting to his death. Unfortunately, he'd been saved by running full tilt into the biggest bear he'd ever seen.

The grizzled bear had eaten his fill back in the meadow and was dragging the remains of the elk calf's carcass back to a small grotto he was considering for his next winter den. It was at the base of a large tree, a little farther down the cliff side path. He'd been almost back there when the newcomer crashed into his backside.

The bear rose up and turned to face the intruder. Its face, breast, and paws were stained with the blood of his prey. His fresh roar of defiance was delivered with a shake of his huge head that exposed his formidable teeth. The roar clearly signalled his intention to fight to defend the carcass.

Willie scrambled backwards along the ground but came to a stop against the mountainside rock wall. The bear dropped down to all fours and assessed the strange creature in front of him. He shook his head again, sniffing the air. His nostrils took in the scent of two mortal enemies, wolf and man.

The bear growled menacingly. He didn't know why this creature carried both these scents, but he knew that he didn't like it. He shuffled forward a few steps and then stopped to shake his head and roar anew. Twice more the bear did this, while the distance between them slowly closed. The display was meant to intimidate, and it was succeeding.

It wasn't terror that Willie felt, however, or even fear. Perhaps there wasn't time for those reactions. What he felt, if anything, was resignation. Instinctively, he knew that even with his new abilities and strength, he was still no match for this giant. It wasn't even close to a fair contest. One on one, the bear was easily a thousand pounds heavier, with the claws and teeth to match. The young wolf-man had no chance.

Perhaps, that was why the rage welled up in him once more. He wasn't a prey animal; he was a predator, and he'd die fighting like one.

Willie slowly got back to his feet, keeping his eyes on his adversary's movements. There was no place to retreat to. If he turned and tried to run for the woods, he knew the bear would be on him in a flash. Instead, he took one step forward. His eyes burned like fire as he stared at his giant foe. He bared his own savage fangs and growled right back at him.

The bear accepted the challenge. He didn't charge. He didn't have to; the enemy had nowhere to run. Instead, he rose up on his hind legs again, ready to step into battle and rend its smaller opponent apart.

Willie issued a second deep-throated growl. He prepared to hurl himself at the bear's legs while attempting at the same time to avoid those deadly forelimbs and claws. If he was lucky, perhaps he could do some damage there and gain some space in which to manoeuvre. He growled a third time and watched the bear's movements, looking for an opening to attack.

To Willie's astonishment, his enemy ceased his advance and actually took a ponderous step backwards, then another, before it dropped back down to all fours. Proud of his own fierceness, Willie took one more step forward and growled again. This third growl was echoed by a new voice, then a second one, and then a third. The voices grew to six, then fifteen, and then more.

The Pack had arrived.

Now it was the bear that had nowhere to turn. His back was to the edge of the cliff. Enraged, he roared at the new arrivals as they stepped around and over the fallen tree and advanced on him. They came on two legs, and they came on four. They came with blazing red eyes and with the savage fangs of deadly predators in their own right.

The giant bear found itself vastly outnumbered by creatures he'd never encountered in his travels. Their scents were strange and maddening. Wolf, yet not like any wolf he had ever come across. Man, yet not like the ones that he had killed. Whatever they were, the bear knew that there were far too many of them.

The Pack advanced, spreading out on either flank. The grizzled bear slowly retreated until it was at the edge of the cliff and there was no further ground to concede. Now there would be a battle. The bear would charge, for it had no other option. It had to break through the enemy ranks.

Once more, the bear rose up and shook its head furiously. Its silver-tipped fur swayed back and forth, as if free of his muscular frame. A thunderous roar issued from his awful maw. It was a fearsome display of the animal's savage fury, meant to paralyze the enemy with terror and intended as a prelude to his charge, a charge that was forestalled by a chunky silver-grey mutated bundle of juvenile warg-wolf.

The runt of Brutus and Cleo's litter dashed to the rescue. The juvenile was larger now, but he had just managed to catch up to the Pack and was not about to slow down to assess the situation or stop to follow the lead of the senior warg-wolves. He simply charged headlong through them.

Perhaps it was because, like Willie, he was going through his first full-moon transformation and its overwhelming effects. Or perhaps again, much like Willie, he was just headstrong and defiant. In either case, the young warg-wolf took everyone by surprise, including the giant brown bear. He darted past the startled Pack leader and Brutus. His teeth glistening in the moonlight, he ran right at the giant bear's exposed groin area.

The bear howled with newfound rage and from intense pain. A sharp set of teeth threatened to geld him. The bear swung a heavy foreleg and backhanded the compact young warg-wolf through the air. Luckily for the juvenile, it wasn't a forehanded slash. The bear's claws would have gutted him like a fish. Nonetheless, it was a powerful blow, and the young warg-wolf slammed into the rock face, fell to the ground, and lay still.

Willie's roar of renewed rage mixed in with those of the other Pack members. He started to advance on the bear's exposed flank, while both Brutus and

One-Eye leaped forward to support him. The two senior warg-wolves took up positions on either side and slightly behind the young wolf-man. The three of them advanced like a spearhead, preparing to hurl itself at the enemy.

At the cliff's edge, the infuriated bear half-turned to meet this latest challenge. It was all the opening that Woodrow needed. He took matters into his own mutated hands. He was the Pack's leader; if someone's life was about to be sacrificed, it would be his.

The Pack leader charged ahead in four running strides and then cartwheeled through the air and drove his clawed feet deep into the giant bear's flank.

The force of the Pack leader's driving attack rocked the bear sideways and off balance. It was enough to cause the bear to teeter precariously at the cliff's edge, where it tried but failed to regain its footing. With a final defiant roar issuing from his savage maw, the bear dropped over the edge.

A few moments later, the Pack leader followed suit.

*   *   *

Woodrow landed hard on the rocky ground at the edge of the cliff. His momentum carried him sliding feet first out over the edge. His fate would have been the same as the giant bear's had Willie not reacted as quickly as he did. He was the only one in a position to act in time.

The Pack leader's hands clawed futilely at the ground as he slid over the cliff edge. Willie lunged, diving face first across the rocks. The young wolf-man's outstretched hand managed to grab one of the Pack leader's wrists out of midair, and he struggled to hang on. His claw-like nails dug into Woodrow's flesh, but then he was being dragged over the precipice as well.

Far below them, the grizzled bear's body was dashed into a pulp on the jagged rocks. Woodrow and Willie would have followed him down, had not Simon leaped forward then. The beta male barely managed to secure Willie's dragging feet before he went over the ledge entirely.

The Pack leader swung in open space, staring up into strained features of Willie's distended face. He marvelled at the tenacity he saw there, the dogged determination to hang on regardless of the outcome.

Their two deaths had been averted by a few scant inches. Several other members of the Pack rushed forward to assist. They first helped to secure

Simon and then dragged Willie back up to the cliff ledge before reaching down to pull the Pack leader to safety as well.

A few precious moments later, the Pack's leader and its newest recruit lay sprawled a few yards apart on the rocky ground. The rage within Willie had subsided, at least so that it no longer ruled his actions. The two wolf-men stared at one another across the distance between them, yet it was a distance that separated them no longer. They each had willingly risked their life for the sake of the other. They were bonded as never before by their unselfish actions.

High in the night sky, the goddess Diana shone her blessings down on her fierce hunters. The Pack had stood together in the face of danger. An enemy of one was an enemy of all. They raised their voices in a chorus to the night to proclaim that fact.

Slowly, the two wolf-men got back to their feet. Side by side, they went to Brutus and Cleo. The Pack enforcer was licking the motionless form of his headstrong, unruly offspring. There was a chunk of meat and coarse fur wedged in the juvenile warg-wolf's teeth, part of the bear's genitalia.

The runt of Brutus and Cleo's litter had won his encounter with the giant bear but now showed no response to his sire's anxious coaxing.

*   *   *

August 21, 1461
The Euralene Mountains, Varakov

When the dawn broke upon the land, a fresh round of agony would ensue. In the meantime, the Pack had split into two groups, with the largest led by Simon, Tiffany, and One-Eye. They'd moved down the mountain trail to deal with the carcass. Bear, especially one of this age, wasn't the best of meat, but it had been bravely earned and wouldn't be allowed go to waste.

A much smaller band had departed for Woodrow's mountain retreat. Willie had growled out his insistence on being the one to carry the inert body of the juvenile warg-wolf. He had carefully picked him up and cradled him in his arms so he would not aggravate his injuries. Brutus, Cleo, and the Pack leader had then taken up positions in the lead and flanking Willie as they made the journey.

374 ■ Run with the Wolves

For the next few hours, Willie's stride never faltered, although the Pack leader knew that he must be exhausted despite his increased strength and stamina. On the long trek, the young wolf-man growled a restrained but firm no whenever Woodrow indicated that he would carry the juvenile for a while. He silently commended the youth's dogged determination.

As they finally neared their destination, the juvenile warg-wolf came to with a sudden gasp and then groaned aloud in discomfort before closing his eyes again. Brutus and Cleo visibly relaxed. The juvenile lived, at least for now.

For a reason that he couldn't yet fathom, Willie felt a tremendous sense of relief as well. While they walked along now, low growls issued from deep within in his throat. Strangely, they were almost soothing to the ear. At least they seemed to reassure the injured young warg-wolf and kept him still. It was as if the animal sensed that the young wolf-man was trying to help him.

Once they reached the remote cabin, there was precious little to do but wait for the dawn. After carefully laying his burden down, Willie sat close by. He kept up his deep, soothing growls to let the juvenile know that he was still there.

In their present condition, Woodrow could only function on a basic level. His reasoning capacity was primitive; it was that of a hunter, not a healer. The intricacies of medicine were well beyond his current capabilities, both physically and mentally.

The Pack leader entered the cabin, however, and dragged a blanket outside in which to wrap the young warg-wolf. Somewhere, in the deep recesses of his brain, he sensed this would aid in keeping the juvenile warm and help to prevent shock from setting in.

He then made a sign to the two alpha warg-wolves as he knocked over a barrel of rainwater. Brutus and Cleo came over and lapped at the pool it created. They carried the water in their mouths to their injured offspring and fed it sparingly to him.

The group spent the remaining predawn hours keeping vigil over the juvenile. The experienced alpha members of the Pack knew that it was questionable if he would survive the rigours of the reversion when the sun rose.

Willie felt only helplessness and responsibility. The young warg-wolf had come charging to his rescue with no regard for his own well-being. He'd taken a severe blow from the bear and hit the rock wall hard. Perhaps his actions had been rash and headstrong, but Willie felt a growing concern for him. He could only hope that the little fellow would survive the ordeal.

*   *   *

When the dawn broke at last, Simon, Tiffany, and the rest of the Pack members were sent sprawling to the ground in much the same manner as they had the evening before. Mercifully, the reversion process was somewhat briefer, but it was still an exhausting and agonizing time.

The same experience was endured with their brethren at Woodrow's mountain retreat. The Pack leader and his companions were driven to the ground in torment, as well. For the second time in his life, Willie felt what it was like to have every cell in his body mutate. Once more he sought deep within himself for a haven where he could ride out the storm.

After that storm had abated and he was able to function once more, Willie dragged himself over to the juvenile wolf. He noted with relief that the young wolf was still breathing, but barely. He slipped his arms under the runt's blanket, lifted him up, and got shakily to his own two feet. He followed Woodrow into the cabin, where he would soon learn about preparing healing concoctions.

When Willie felt the reverse transformation coming upon him, he'd taken shelter once again in thoughts of his friends Sirius, Rigel, and Pegasus. At some point during the storm, a star formation had occurred to his fragmented mind; the constellation known as Ursa Minor. In the light of day, he recalled hearing a priest use the Latin name Ursa Minoris, meaning Smaller Bear, to describe the formation. More commonly it was known simply as the Little Dipper, because its seven brightest stars seemed to form the shape of a water dipper in the northern skies, with Polaris, the North Star, at the end of the handle.

Willie didn't know if the juvenile wolf had already been given a name, but it seemed to him that Ursa would be appropriate for the fierce fellow he had carried here in his arms. If the brave young wolf lived, he would ask the Pack leader's opinion.

*   *   *

"The Barley Moon"
The apex of the full moon and the night following the apex

August 21–22, 1461
The Euralene Mountains, Varakov

The following two moonlit nights, and the ensuing dawns, would bring with them the same punishing ordeal of transformation and reversion. Each agonizing occurrence would be acutely felt, but Willie would gradually become more adept at building an internal defence to better endure its effects. He was learning that his mind could be focussed elsewhere and by taking refuge in these thoughts, the violent storm would eventually pass by. He would draw much needed strength from the memories of his old friends, as well as from the new friendships he was building even now.

The injured juvenile wolf spent the first day mostly in the care of Woodrow, who spoon-fed him. His doctoring was much the same as it had been for Willie not so very long before. He worked now under the watchful eye of that same youth who hung about the doorway.

Willie finally spoke up. "Is he going to make it?"

"I didn't think so, for a while," Woodrow answered, over his shoulder. "I could barely find a heartbeat at first."

The Pack leader bent over his patient, gently coaxing the young wolf to take the herbal broth and sedative he'd concocted after the dawn's reversion. Woodrow looked as ragged and exhausted as Willie felt.

"Why don't you give me a hand here?"

"Are you sure you want my help?" the youth asked. "This was all pretty much my fault."

"We all had a hand in the making of our present circumstances, wouldn't you say?" Woodrow replied. "So why don't we try to put that behind us and see if we can get some medicine and nourishment into our little bear-fighter."

Willie came inside and made his way to the table. His clothing was filthy, little more than rags now, and his hair had grown out wild and tangled. He'd refused to go and get cleaned up or groomed while the Pack leader worked to heal the juvenile.

"Yes, you two can come in too," Woodrow said. Willie turned to see Brutus and Cleo standing in the doorway.

Woodrow kept his attention on his patient, however. "Willie, I'll hold his head up, and you see if you can get some of this down his throat."

Willie talked mostly nonsense to the young wolf as spoon-fed him, but he found that the juvenile responded well to the soothing tones of his voice and managed to lap up the mixture. Afterwards, the four comrades went outdoors, leaving the young wolf on a blanket by the fireplace to sleep. Woodrow suspected there were several cracked or broken ribs, but thankfully they hadn't punctured a lung.

Willie was pleased to hear the Pack leader express the opinion that the transformation coming that night would actually assist the healing process, provided the juvenile wolf again survived its rigours.

He and Woodrow spent the better part of the next hour cleaning up and then cutting each other's hair. The body hair that had grown the night before had moulted away of its own accord, with the help of a good scrubbing.

While they groomed themselves, the Pack leader tried to ease Willie's concerns about the young wolf. He spoke of several examples where bones and wounds had healed far more rapidly in members of the Pack than they did with ordinary people.

"How's your leg?" Woodrow asked him, to illustrate his point.

It was true. Willie's leg was fully healed now. There was scarring, to be sure, but no more than he'd seen on most of the other human members of the Pack. He'd seen the faint outline of teeth marks on Woodrow's arm while they washed up, and he remembered that the Pack leader had shown those marks to him the last time they were at the cabin. It was when he'd also stated that he was proud to be part wolf. Willie thought that he understood that much better now.

"I think our determined young friend must take after his sire," Woodrow said. He made sure he'd caught the Pack enforcer's eye. "I remember one particular night when a curly-horned ram damn near knocked Brutus off a mountainside. It broke three of his ribs while it was at it."

Brutus cast his eyes down and dropped his ears. He knew full well from the Pack leader's sign of the ram's horns what was being discussed, and it actually seemed to embarrass him.

The Pack leader chuckled. "I'm going to suggest that in the future, it might be best if we leave the giant bears and the mountain rams alone. Let's stick to hunting deer and elk."

"Or maybe just rabbits," Willie replied with a laugh of his own.

*   *   *

Like Willie had before him, the young wolf responded well to his treatment, well enough that he survived the transformation on the second night, the apex of the full-moon cycle.

After that, the Pack leader assured the youth that the transformation process would do the rest. Just as Willie's leg injury had improved immensely that first night, the second night's mutation of the juvenile's cell structure strengthened and began mending his cracked bones and damaged tissue.

Relieved, Willie spent a frantic yet exhilarating night running in close proximity to the mountain retreat. He had good company, joined at various intervals by the Pack leader, or by Brutus and Cleo. They'd also taken turns watching over the recovering juvenile and countering his desire to get up and join in their wild runs.

At some point during the night, his eyes blazing and his mind afire, Willie came to appreciate the various companions on his mad dash. They were, as he was, and kindred to him in their wildness of spirit. They matched him stride for stride and leap for leap. There was a sense of harmony in the way the more experienced Pack members adapted to his pace and path.

For quite some time they allowed Willie to lead them. Then slowly they began communicating changes in direction and flow, by using subtle signs and low, deep-throated growls. While they didn't hunt for prey, they were soon running as a Pack should, in full support of each other. Before the dawn's light, Willie was well on his way to learning just what that meant; and back in the mountain cabin, the young wolf was well on his way to a full recovery.

Woodrow had agreed wholeheartedly with Willie's suggestion for naming the juvenile wolf. He thought the name Ursa, or Little Bear, was most appropriate, with one slight amendment, changing it to the masculine form, Ursis. The Pack leader was well aware of the way the young wolf responded whenever Willie was nearby. He'd also noted the deep concern the youth displayed for the young wolf. It occurred to him that these two might be destined to be a Pack team like he and Brutus were, if perhaps, a rather difficult and unruly one still in need of training. It was a good beginning, however.

Willie spent the next day tending to the young wolf. Woodrow let him take over that duty after he showed him how to mix and prepare the medicine, as well as the sedative. It was still vital to keep the rambunctious juvenile calm and rested while they waited for nightfall. The full moon would do the rest. For the present, Woodrow was just content to see that Ursis was going to recover from his encounter with the fierce bear.

The Pack leader was confident enough in that regard to rejoin the Pack for the third night's hunt and insisted that Willie do so as well, leaving Ursis in the care of Cleo and other four-legged Pack members skilled in tending to the needs of the injured and the young. This was a common and accepted role for relatives of the juvenile members of the Pack. The wolves were an extended family group, and they saw carefully to the well-being of their own.

The final night's hunt of the Barley moon had a comic and humbling aspect to it, in terms of Willie's first efforts as a working member of the Pack. Woodrow, Simon, and Tiffany had taken turns preparing him. They'd instructed him in the manner of the hunt, stressing the need for teamwork and of each member's position and role. The tactics that the Pack used were time honoured and everyone knew their place. That is, with the exception of their prey.

The young wolf-man took his place among the ambushers and hunkered down to wait in a concealed swale. A herd of deer had been scented where they rested among the trees of a copse in a nearby valley. The deer were forced to make a dash for freedom when several Pack members approached them from upwind and flushed them from their hidden shelter. They then chased the prey animals towards the ambush and the fresh legs of those waiting.

Willie waited by the others with growing impatience, but managed to keep himself under control, at least until the first buck came bounding towards them. He couldn't sit quietly any longer for the Pack enforcer's signal; he leaped past Brutus and plunged out of their downwind hiding place. The startled buck reared up at the sight of this latest apparition and then dropped its head and charged down the slope. Willie narrowly managed to fling himself aside, or he'd have been impaled on the stag's formidable antlers.

Precious time was lost before he was up and giving chase with the others, conscious only of the fact that he'd just ruined the ambush. The opportunity for a clean kill had been lost. The buck and its herd were moving swiftly into the denser forest, with the Pack in distant pursuit.

Willie's emotions took over once more. He sprinted ahead of his brethren and the long, loping pace they set as they followed the bounding and dodging herd through the trees. He slowly closed the gap until he was right behind the hindquarters of the deer at the rear of the quickly disappearing herd.

This elder doe was the slowest and least agile of the fleeing prey. The animal was about to prove itself still capable enough of eluding the young wolf-man, however. Willie got into position and leaped for the killing blow. He thought he had timed his strike perfectly, and the notion flashed through his mind of how proud the others would be of him when they saw his first kill.

Unfortunately, he never considered just how quickly even an elderly doe can plant her hooves and change direction. Willie's clawed feet had just left the ground when the doe suddenly swerved sharply to her left. It left him flying through empty air, until he then crashed into a very large tree.

The head-strong, newest member of the Pack learned another valuable life lesson that night, once he'd regained consciousness, that is. Willie learned that leaping through the air and crashing into a large tree, much like running full tilt into a giant grizzled bear, was generally a bad idea.

In either instance, a young wolf-man could do himself a serious injury.

*   *   *

August 23, 1461
The Euralene Mountains, Varakov

After the morning's ritual grooming, Willie sat alone at the edge of the gorge in front of Woodrow's mountain retreat. There was a sizable knot on his forehead from his encounter with the tree. The reversion had not erased that memento. In the light of day, and with the three nights of lunar transformations behind him, he realized that there would be many more lessons still to learn. Looking back on the past month, he reflected on how far he'd come from the simple life he'd known on the Smythe farm back in Medinia. He considered what unknowns might still lay ahead.

The youth knew there was still a great deal to be learned under Woodrow's tutelage regarding the Varakovan court of the dark and powerful Lord Victor. He would have to learn if he wanted to survive the experience. He understood that there was also the strong possibility of a war being waged between Varakov and his homeland of Medinia and their old enemy, Skoland.

Willie knew Woodrow was going to try his best to prevent that war. After his initial animosity towards the Pack leader, he now found himself actually looking up to the man. He'd even go so far as to say that he was coming to value Woodrow's guidance, and his friendship.

The Medinian youth fingered the carved crystal shepherd that hung from his neck. He pondered the friendship that had been extended to him by Melanie, the Old Man, and other Oddities of the haven they called Sanctuary. He realized now that being different wasn't the quality that defined a person; it was a person's actions, and their interactions with others, that truly defined them.

Finally, as a new member of the very Pack that he'd once so dreaded, he would be forced to learn more about his own dark nature. It would be unavoidable, for he knew that when the goddess Diana took to the night sky, he would forever be compelled to run with the wolves.

Author's Note

The journey into this saga began when I penned the lyrics to a few songs with a Halloween theme for a Toronto band. On the following pages, you can read the lyrics as they were originally written.

Those song lyrics inspired the writing of a tale about the plight of a group of characters who had to deal with life-changing afflictions not of their choosing. The telling of that story evolved into this epic trilogy.

I trust that you have enjoyed reading *The Pack*. Please look for volume two, *The Oracle*, and volume three, *The Beast*, in the continuing series of *Run with the Wolves*.

T. c. Tombs

Ya Just Gotta Howl
(The Wolf-Man's Lament)

Woodrow   There's just no light quite like moonlight
              When your heart starts pounding
              And the blood is sent singing through your veins

              There's no night quite like a full-moon night
              With your body transforming
              And your hair growing out into a mane

Sax (the howl)

The Pack   It begins somewhere deep down in your bowels
              Like something perverted and foul
              It starts as a rumbling growl that grows and grows
              Until ya just gotta howl!
              And the Pack is on the prowl

Woodrow   There's no bite, quite like, a wolf's bite
              When your prey lays bleeding
              But your hunger, overcomes your shame

Sax (the howl)

The Pack   It begins somewhere deep down in your bowels
              Like something perverted and foul
              It starts as a rumbling growl that grows and grows
              Until ya just gotta howl!
              And the Pack is on the prowl

Woodrow   There's no sight quite like inner sight
              When you hate what you're becoming
              But your hunger overcomes your shame
              And you're slowly, surely going insane

Sax (the howl)

The Wolf-man's Legacy

The Pack Leader
It's lunacy beneath the moon
The wolf-man's howling 'neath the moon

The wolf-man runs on the moor
The wolf-man is out on the moor
Memories of when and might-have-been and why
You've got to lock all the secrets inside

The wolf-man stands at the door
The wolf-man stands outside the door
The fates decreed that you're cursed for life
Left you dancing upon the sharp edge of the knife

And if the damned must live, without the touch of grace
And if your soul's condemned to eternal hell
And if your heart cries out in its shame
And you'd stop, but blood is all you can taste

The wolf-man has lost his love
The wolf-man has long lost his love
You've lost the right, in the full moon light
To hold a loved one through the night
You've closed them out. You've got no home
You run, but you stand alone

It's lunacy beneath the moon
The wolf-man's howling 'neath the moon
The wolf-man's just baying 'neath the moon
The wolf-man's out screaming 'neath the moon

Inspired by Pink Floyd's *Dark Side of the Moon*
Track 8 "Brain Damage"

Just Like You: The Oddities

Old Man   You see; we've been put down
We've been cursed at and accused
We've been mocked at and misused
We've been laughed at and abused

Melanie   We are the Oddities
Rare commodities, don't you think?

Males
Oddity 1   We've been called geeks and freaks

Oddity 2   Fools and ghouls

Oddity 3   We've been left scarred and marred

Oddity 4   And feathered and tarred!

Old Man   You see; we've been put down
And we've been pushed round

Females
Oddity 1   We've been called witches and bitches

Oddity 2   Despots and harlots

Oddity 3   We've been seized and diseased

Oddity 4   Whatever, whenever they pleased

Melanie   Just because we are the Oddities
Rare commodities, don't you think?

Old Man   You see; they've displayed us. Sentenced and jailed us
Dunked and stocked us. Branded and flogged us
And even hanged us

All   Just because we are the Oddities
Such rare commodities, don't you think?

Old Man   I know I am an Oddity
                     But should you think the less of me?
                     Granted, we don't look the same
                     But cut us, don't we bleed?
                     And like you, love is all I need

Melanie   I may be one of a kind
                     But through and through
                     I'm just like you

**Inspired by Pink Floyd's *Dark Side of the Moon*
Track 6, "Us and Them"**

Photo by Walter Corbett Productions

T c TOMBS earned degrees from Trent University and Wilfrid Laurier University in Canada. Like many Canadians, he loves hockey and golf, and he has a passion for medieval history, folk lore, literature, film, and music. Terry and his wife, Sandra, live in the Greater Toronto Area in Ontario, Canada, where they have raised five daughters.